SOME MEMORIES ARE BEST
NOT REMEMBERED

"I don't know anything about your missing files," Max said.

"Do you expect me to believe you?" Jolie asked.

"I don't expect you to do anything except cause trouble. That seems to be the one thing you're good at doing. Dredging up old memories, putting people through the misery of reliving a past better left forgotten."

Jolie took a tentative step toward Max, pausing when only a few inches separated their bodies. "Do you honestly think that anyone involved could ever forget about those brutal murders? If you'd been shot and left for dead beside your mother's lifeless body, would you ever be able to forget?"

"Probably not," Max admitted. "But you have no proof that the snooping you and Theron were doing is in any way connected to those men attacking Theron."

"I don't need proof. I know in here"—she slapped her clenched fist on her belly—"that somebody wanted Theron stopped before he unearthed any information that might force the D.A. to reopen the Belle Rose case. And so help me God, I'm going to find out who the son of a bitch is. Theron might not be able to continue searching, to keep digging for the truth, but I can. And I will."

Max uncrossed his arms and eased away from the wall. "If what you believe is true, then you could wind up getting yourself hurt, maybe even killed . . ."

Books by Beverly Barton

AFTER DARK

EVERY MOVE SHE MAKES

WHAT SHE DOESN'T KNOW

THE FIFTH VICTIM

THE LAST TO DIE

AS GOOD AS DEAD

KILLING HER SOFTLY

Published by Zebra Books

WHAT SHE DOESN'T KNOW

Beverly Barton

ZEBRA BOOKS
KENSINGTON PUBLISHING CORP.
http://www.kensingtonbooks.com

ZEBRA BOOKS are published by

Kensington Publishing Corp.
850 Third Avenue
New York, NY 10022

All Kensington titles, imprints, and distributed lines are available at special quantity discounts for bulk purchases for sales promotions, premiums, fund-raising, and educational or institutional use.

Special book excerpts or customized printings can also be created to fit specific needs. For details, write or phone the office of the Kensington Special Sales Manager: Kensington Publishing Corp., 850 Third Avenue, New York, NY 10022. Attn. Special Sales Department. Phone: 1-800-221-2647.

Zebra and the Z logo Reg. U.S. Pat. & TM Off.

First Printing: April 2002
10 9 8

Printed in the United States of America

To my husband, Billy,
my safe harbor in all of life's storms.
Thank you, my love,
for being at my side, day and night,
when I needed you the most.

Prologue

Ivy wound around the crumbling chimney, gluing itself to the ancient brick. The ramshackle house nestled in the grove of cedar trees, its weathered wood gray from age, remnants of white paint staining only a portion of the surface. Most of the sharecropper shacks had been torn down years ago, along with the old slave quarters that had been located closer to the main house. Now almost totally reclaimed by nature, this one bedraggled structure remained standing. Jolie had overheard family tales about how her great-grandfather Desmond had kept his mistress here, back in the Twenties, and that various men in the family had used the place for clandestine meetings with bad women. Past sexual peccadilloes didn't really interest her, but one present-day bad boy did. *Maximillian Devereaux.* Sandy had told Jolie that her older sister, Felicia, had given her virginity to Max in this very house. Jolie hadn't wanted to believe it, but Sandy would never lie to her. They had been best friends since they were in diapers. And Jolie had been in love with Max almost as long. Of course, Max didn't pay any attention to her. She was sure he thought of her as just a kid, which was probably good, considering he was, and always would be, forbidden to her. But she was fourteen now. Almost a woman. And only four years younger than Max.

Unrequited love hurt—hurt like hell.

She wasn't supposed to be here. Spying on people wasn't something she made a habit of doing. Nor was lying. She'd told her mama she was going to walk straight to Sandy's house, which was three-quarters of a mile up the road from Belle Rose. Mama approved of Sandy as a friend. The Wells family had been a part of Sumarville, Mississippi, as long as the Desmonds had. Jolie's maternal ancestors had been plantation owners prior to the War Between the States and afterward became part of a certain segment of Southern society Aunt Clarice referred to as the genteel impoverished. It had taken her years to understand what that meant. Her mother's family had possessed good breeding and a lineage back to Adam, but they had been as poor as churchmice, except for their land and a large decaying mansion.

But her mother had made a good marriage to a rich man. Daddy's ancestors had been sharecroppers years ago, but Great-Grandfather Royale had started his own business and invested wisely, so his son and grandson became very wealthy. Being rich wasn't something Jolie thought about much. She'd overheard others referring to her as a spoiled brat or that snobby little princess. But Mama had pointed out that others were jealous of her because she possessed both good breeding and wealth. And Aunt Clarice reminded her to *consider the source*. A Desmond, or in her case the offspring of a Desmond, never paid any attention to what riffraff and underlings said about them.

Jolie really couldn't explain what had prompted her to take the overgrown path through the woods that lay between the Desmond and Wells property instead of taking the gravel road. She'd been daydreaming, a habit Mama said was a foolish waste of time. But Aunt Clarice told her to dream all she could now, while she was young. She'd wondered if that meant when people got older, they couldn't dream anymore.

As she crept toward the cottage, she thought about what she would see when she peeped in through the dirty windows. Would Max be there with Felicia? Would they be making love? If she caught them together, she knew her heart would break and she'd want to scratch out Felicia's big brown eyes. That girl had eyes as big as saucers!

No one knew how she felt about Max. Not even Sandy. She didn't dare share her deepest, darkest secret with anyone. If Mama ever found out . . .

"That boy's just like his mother," Audrey Royale had said on more than one occasion. "And we all know that Georgette Devereaux was a New Orleans whore. How she duped poor old Philip into marrying her and passing off that bastard son of hers as his, I'll never know."

Jolie didn't care if Max really was a bastard or if his mother had been a whore. If Max would ever look at her—truly look at her—and see what was right before him, she would be the happiest girl in the world. If Max were to ever love her the way she did him, she'd defy her mother to be with him. She'd defy the whole damn world.

As she reached the rickety steps that led up to the front porch, Jolie heard laughter. Fluttery female giggles mingled with deeper male chuckles. The sound stopped her dead in her tracks. Someone *was* inside the house. Was it Max and Felicia? In all the years she'd known Max, she'd never heard him laugh. But if he was having sex, maybe he was enjoying himself enough to laugh.

Well, are you going to look or not? she asked herself. *Do you have the guts to see for yourself what's going on in there?*

Taking small tentative steps, she eased around to the side of the house, moving in the direction from which the laughter came. Small twigs and dried leaves crunched under her feet, the noise minuscule as it blended with the louder chorus of nature. Within the wooded area, birds chirped, squirrels scurried, and grasshoppers and other insects bounded hither and yon. As she neared the back window on the left side of the structure, her heartbeat drummed loudly inside her head. A sense of dread momentarily halted her, but youthful curiosity urged her forward until she reached the window. Standing on tiptoe, she pressed her face against the cracked pane and peered inside; then she blinked several times, trying to adjust her eyesight. Unable to make out more than two bodies writhing on a metal bed in the far side of the room, she lifted her hands, cupped them to either side of her face to block out the afternoon sun and took another look.

Jolie Royale gasped in disbelief; her shock and anger mixed with dismay. While a plethora of emotions bombarded her young mind and heart, she seemed unable to stop staring at the sickening sight. Her father, whom she adored, straddled the naked black-haired woman beneath him. His bare butt rose and fell as he hammered into the slut. Huge tears welled up in Jolie's eyes. How could her daddy betray her mother this way? And with *that* woman? With Georgette Devereaux!

Forcing herself away from the window, away from a sight that she would never forget—not to her dying day—Jolie hurried through the woods as tears streamed down her flushed cheeks. What was she going to do? She couldn't tell Mama. But she had to tell somebody, didn't she? Oh, God, did Max know? Did he have any idea what sort of woman his mother was? *A New Orleans whore!*

As her mind filled with frantic jumbled thoughts, Jolie ran and ran, until she reached the gravel road. Out of breath, her lungs aching, she stopped to consider her options. Where should she go? What should she do? Go tell Aunt Clarice. She'll know what's to be done about Daddy and that awful woman. Aunt Clarice understood matters of the heart. She'd heard more than one person say so. It was because her mother's older sister had loved and lost years ago and was still devoted to her dead fiancé.

When Jolie reached the iron gates that opened to the driveway that led to the 1846 mansion at the heart of the Belle Rose plantation, she doubled over and took several deep slow breaths. Using her fingertips, she swiped the tears from her face, then wiped her mouth with her hand. Just in case she ran into Mama or Aunt Lisette, she had to appear perfectly calm, as if nothing were wrong. Aunt Clarice wouldn't be home until later, since this was Saturday and she kept the dress shop in town open until six.

Jolie decided that she'd just have to go to her room and stay out of everyone's way. Mama and Aunt Lisette probably wouldn't even notice her. They'd been arguing all week, but Jolie had no idea about what. Every time they realized she was nearby, they both shut up immediately. And there was nobody else around the house today, except probably Lemar Fuqua, who would no doubt be busy in the yard. Her daddy had loaned Lemar the money to start his own lawn service, and part of the repayment was that he come out to Belle Rose on Saturdays to maintain the grounds. The only servant who lived on the plantation was Lemar's twin sister, Yvonne, who'd been the housekeeper for as long as Jolie could remember, as had Yvonne's mother, Sadie, before her. But she wouldn't have to worry about Yvonne today. Saturday afternoon was her time to do the shopping in town.

So, what are you going to tell Mama about not going to Sandy's? Tell her Sandy wasn't home. No, that lie could be checked too easily. Say you've got a headache and came back home to take some aspirin and to lie down for a while.

When she rounded the house and approached the expansive back veranda, Jolie saw Lemar's old blue pickup parked on the north side. The truck bed held those new lilac bushes her mama had ordered to replace the ones that had died last year. Jolie glanced around, searching for any sign of the tall lanky black man who always greeted her with a smile and a piece of peppermint candy. Maybe he was taking a break and drinking iced tea in the kitchen, as he often did. She liked Lemar. He was one of the nicest people she'd ever known. She considered both Yvonne and Lemar family, as did Aunt Clarice and Aunt Lisette. On the other hand, her mama considered them only as loyal family servants.

As she headed for the back door, she noticed several dark spots, reddish in color and partially dried, splattered on the grass and back steps. Odd, she thought. Maybe Lemar had spilled something, some chemical that he used in his gardening. Jolie entered the house through the back door. From the mudroom just off the porch, she walked down the long center hallway. Suddenly a peculiar sinking feeling hit her square in the stomach. *What's wrong?* She sensed something odd, then realized the house was eerily, unnaturally quiet. Aunt Lisette almost always kept music playing and when she didn't, she sang or hummed. And often as not, when left alone together, Aunt Lisette and Mama argued. Especially lately. But there was no music, no singing, and no quarreling.

"Mama?"

Silence.

"Aunt Lisette?"

Silence.

"Lemar, are you here? I saw your truck outside."

Silence.

"Mama, where are you?" Jolie called loudly.

Something was wrong.

"Aunt Lisette, please answer me."

No response.

Oh, God. Oh, God!

Jolie ran down the hallway calling for her mother.

She whirled around in the foyer and headed up the wide spiral staircase. When she'd taken only a couple of steps, she glanced up to the top of the stairs. Aunt Lisette! The name echoed inside her head.

Lisette Desmond's half-naked body lay sprawled on the stairway landing; her diaphanous silk robe hung open, revealing one round white breast and the expanse of a long pale leg. Jolie forced herself into motion. She climbed the stairs quickly, despite the fact that she felt as if heavy lead weights hung about her ankles. As she neared her aunt's still body, she looked down at Lisette's billowing platinum blond hair, now stained with red. *Blood!*

Her aunt was dead. In a purely reflex action, Jolie lifted her hand to cover her mouth as she gasped.

"Mama!" Jolie screamed.

No answer.

Jolie thought she must be asleep and having the worst nightmare of her life. This wasn't happening. It couldn't be real. Aunt Lisette wasn't dead.

Turn around and go back downstairs. Find Mama. She'll tell you that everything is all right. Once you see her face, you'll know you're safe. You'll be able to wake from this horrible dream.

As if in a trance, Jolie turned her back on the gruesome scene and fled down the stairs. She raced from room to room, searching for her mother, calling for her repeatedly. She found no one.

She swung open the door to the only remaining downstairs room, the recently remodeled kitchen, a large square room that overlooked the backyard. She scanned the area from the row of windows across the back wall to the pantry door at her right. As her gaze traveled down toward the glossy wood floor, she noticed first the feet and then the legs. Cold fear consumed her. After entering the kitchen, she made her way slowly toward the round wooden chopping block in the center of the room. Lying there, perfectly still, not a lock of golden blond hair out of place, Audrey Desmond Royale stared sightlessly up at the ceiling, a single bullet wound in the middle of her forehead.

Jolie dropped to her knees and grasped her mother's hand. A warm hand. Maybe she wasn't dead. Maybe Mama was still alive!

Call for an ambulance. Now!

When she rose to her feet, she heard movement behind her. *Footsteps?* Just as she started to turn to face the intruder, something sharp and stinging hit her hip. Despite the pain, she fell to the floor and rolled, seeking a place to hide or a means of escape. Within seconds she felt another sting as something hit her shoulder, and then a third burned into her back. She knew that this was no dream. Whoever had murdered Mama and Aunt Lisette was going to kill her, too. Only a split second before Jolie passed out, she fully comprehended the fact that she'd been shot. Three times . . .

Chapter 1

Max Devereaux tossed his jacket on the chair as he walked across the wide-plank wooden floor in his bedroom. Pausing momentarily outside the bathroom, he bent to untie his shoes. He removed them, then quickly ripped off his socks. Usually he didn't scatter clothing—he'd always picked up after himself, despite having servants—but tonight he just didn't give a damn. He was bone-tired and had the headache from hell. He hadn't gotten more than two or three hours sleep each night for the past week, ever since Louis's heart attack. His mother hadn't left her husband's side, so not only did he have to make time to continue to oversee all the Royale & Devereaux business interests, but he had to keep the household at Belle Rose running smoothly, too. Now it looked as though he'd be taking over both jobs on a permanent basis very soon. The doctors had told them this afternoon that there was little hope Louis would live another day.

Max loosened his tie as he shoved open the half-

closed bathroom door. He didn't have any time to waste.
A shave, a quick shower, and some clean clothes. Then
he'd rush back to Desmond County Hospital. The last
thing he wanted was for his mother and sister to be
alone when Louis died. He'd left Aunt Clarice with
them, but she was a bundle of nerves herself. And that
damn sycophant, Nowell Landers, who'd been sniffing
around Clarice for months now, was with her. The poor
woman didn't realize the man was playing her for a
fool, and she didn't seem inclined to listen to advice
from those who tried to warn her. Everybody in Sumarville knew that Clarice Desmond hadn't been quite right
in the head ever since she came home from her downtown dress shop on a warm Saturday evening twenty
years ago and found her sisters, her niece, and Lemar
Fuqua, lying in pools of their own blood. Only the low-
est, most vile scum would take advantage of a dear,
sweet, unbalanced soul like Clarice. But damn it all, he
didn't have time to deal with Nowell Landers, not right
now, not with Louis dying and his mother falling apart
before his very eyes.

Max stripped down to his black boxer shorts, turned
on the faucets, and filled the sink with hot water. As he
reached out to open the mirrored door of the medicine
cabinet, he caught a glimpse of himself and chuckled
mirthlessly. He was a sorry sight; that was for sure. He
looked more like a bum than a businessman. But what
could he expect—he'd stayed at the hospital last night
and gone straight to the office this morning, still wearing
his rumpled clothes. He had rushed back to the hospital
for each ICU visitation period today; and tonight he'd
said his final farewell to a man he loved and admired.

Hurriedly he lathered his face with shaving cream
and ran a new disposable razor over his two-day-old
beard. With small patches of lather still clinging to his
skin, he turned on the shower, removed his shorts, and

stepped beneath the tepid spray. As he washed himself, his penis grew hard. He hadn't been with a woman in weeks, and his body badly needed release. He'd been too damn busy to even stop by to see Eartha, let alone take the luscious redhead to bed.

The impending death of someone you knew, someone close, had an odd effect on a person, making him want to reassure himself that life went on, to celebrate the fact that he was alive in every way that mattered to a man.

Just as Max stepped out of the shower, the phone rang. Without giving a thought to his wet naked state, he tromped out of the tan-and-white-tiled bathroom. His feet left moist footprints as he trekked across the bedroom floor. His heart raced wildly when he lifted the receiver, as fear coursed through his body, instinctively knowing bad news awaited him.

"Devereaux here."

"Max."

God damn it! His instincts had been right. He could hear the barely constrained tears in his sister's voice.

"Mallory, honey, is everything—"

"Daddy's dead, Max." Mallory Royale choked on her tears.

"I'll be right there, baby. Stay strong . . . for Mama. Okay? Can you do that for me?"

"Mmm-hmm . . . yes . . . I—I can."

"Tell Mama that I'll handle everything when I get there."

"Max?"

"What, honey?"

"Aunt Clarice said that you should call Jolie."

"Yeah. Okay. Tell her I'll take care of that, too. Later."

Max gently returned the receiver to the base, took a deep steadying breath, then swallowed the emotion lodged in his throat. There had been a time years ago when he'd hated Louis Royale, but his feelings about

Louis changed drastically over the years, after his mother married the man whom he'd once blamed for his father's death.

Philip Devereaux had been a good, decent man who'd made an honest woman out of Georgette Clifton and had accepted the child she carried as his own. Max didn't know if Philip had been his biological father, and somehow it didn't really matter anymore. He could have a DNA test run, but unless he planned to print the results on the front page of the *Sumarville Chronicle*, no one in the county would ever believe he was a legitimate Devereaux. There had been no physical similarities between Max and the small timid Philip, who like his father before him had been a freckle-faced redhead. Years ago Max had convinced himself that sometimes sons looked like their mothers. He certainly did.

He'd spent his entire life pretending he didn't care that local society looked down their snobby noses at him, even after he became Louis Royale's heir apparent. And those old rumors lingered to this day, those whispered innuendoes that Maximillian Devereaux—the bad seed—had possibly been the one who'd slain the Desmond sisters and Lemar Fuqua. Some people had said, "That boy just wanted to clear the way for his mama to become the second Mrs. Royale."

The fact that Max's wife had been murdered less than three years into their marriage had only added fuel to the ancient gossip flames. It didn't matter, of course, that there had been no substantial evidence against him in either case. People simply enjoyed painting him as a villain.

As Max towel-dried his hair and then dressed hurriedly in jeans and a short-sleeved cotton shirt, he thought about the arrangements that would have to be made. The funeral would be a major event in Mississippi. The governor would attend the service. He and Louis were old friends; they'd been fraternity brothers.

Trendall Funeral Home would handle the arrangements. Here in Sumarville, there were only two funeral homes. Trendall for the whites; Jardien for the blacks. Burial was still a segregated event in Mississippi, even in the twenty-first century.

Max shoved his wallet into his back pocket, clipped his cellular phone onto his belt, then raced out of his room and down the stairs. He picked up his car keys off the intricately carved commode in the foyer as he headed for the front door. Hurriedly tapping in the security code, he wondered if he should stop by Yvonne's cottage to tell her about Louis's death. No, better just phone her on the way and have her come to the house and prepare things for the family's return. Yvonne had been a part of the household long before he and his mother moved into Belle Rose. Indeed Yvonne and her brother had grown up on the plantation along with the Desmond sisters, and Yvonne's mother had been the family's housekeeper.

Within five minutes of his sister's call, Max headed his Porsche toward town, his foot heavy on the gas pedal. He just hoped that Mallory would be able to handle things until he arrived. His half sister was only eighteen and quite immature for her age. She'd been spoiled rotten by their mother and Louis. Sometimes Max wondered if Louis had doted on Mallory and spoiled her so shamelessly because his only other child had cut him completely out of her life.

As the sleek black sports car sped along the back roads of Desmond County, Mississippi, Max made a mental list of what needed to be done as soon as possible. He wished that contacting Jolie Royale wasn't on that list. He hadn't seen Louis's elder daughter since she was fourteen; nor had he spoken to her once in all the years since Louis had sent her away from Belle Rose. No matter how many times Louis had issued her an invitation to come home, even if just for a visit, or how many times Aunt Clarice had pleaded with her to return to Sumarville, Jolie had adamantly refused. She had told her father and her aunt that she would never set foot on Belle Rose property as long as *that woman* lived there. That woman being Georgette Clifton Devereaux Royale.

Yvonne lifted a fresh-baked skillet of cornbread from the oven, then turned it out onto a plate. Since he'd moved back to Sumarville after living in Memphis for the past eight years, her son, Theron, came to her house for a late dinner every Thursday evening. She had wanted him to move in with her, but he'd laughed at her suggestion.

"Mama, I'm thirty-eight and have lived on my own since I left for college twenty years ago," Theron had told her. "Besides, you know I'd never live on the old plantation. Belle Rose may be home to you, but not to me."

She didn't necessarily believe her son was wrong to feel the way he did about her living in the cottage provided by Louis Royale, the same cottage her mother had occupied all the years she'd been the housekeeper for the Desmond family. Theron was a new breed of black man. A modern African-American who resented anything connected to the old ways, to anything that even hinted of subservience to whites. But there were things Theron didn't know, things he couldn't possibly understand. The Desmonds had been her family. As long as Clarice lived, Yvonne would never leave her. How could she ever explain to Theron the deep emotional bond that existed between Clarice and her? Even if she told him the complete truth, would he be able to accept her devotion to a white woman?

"Supper sure looks good." After she placed the cornbread on the table, Theron pulled out a chair for her. "You're the best cook in Desmond County."

Yvonne simply smiled modestly as she sat down and lifted a white linen napkin from atop the white linen tablecloth. She had always loved nice things: elegant linens and china and crystal. Although her home was modest compared to many, she took pride in the cottage and its contents. She had learned from the Desmond sisters how to conduct herself as a proper lady.

"Being a true lady has nothing to do with the color of one's skin," Clarice had once told her.

As they ate the cornbread, fried potatoes, chicken, and okra, Theron discussed his plans to eventually run for district attorney of Desmond County, and perhaps one day, even governor. Yvonne responded positively to all his ideas. She was very proud of her only child, who even as a boy had been brilliant beyond her wildest dreams. If her husband were alive, he'd be so proud of their son. But Ossie had died when Theron was only ten. To this day she missed Ossie, but she could see the man she had loved in his son. Tall, broad shouldered, and handsome, with a thousand-watt smile that warmed her heart.

Yvonne had scrimped and saved and accepted help from Clarice to send Theron to college, and he had worked diligently, too, attending school and holding down a full-time job. But in the end, it had been worth every sacrifice. Theron had graduated magna cum laude and later went to work straight out of law school for a prestigious firm in Atlanta. After working there for several years, he'd taken an even better offer with a firm in Memphis, so she'd been surprised when, three months ago, Theron had returned to Sumarville and opened his own practice.

"I realize I need to live here for a year or so before I put my plans into action." Theron lifted the jug of iced tea and refilled his empty glass. "But I have the backing to run for office whenever I say the word. And once I've established my practice here in Sumarville and folks get to know me again, the African-American vote alone would be nearly enough to elect me."

"You have some fine ambitions, son." Yvonne stretched her hand across the table and laid it on Theron's arm. "But if you reopen that old can of worms about the Desmond murders, you won't accomplish anything except to offend a lot of white people."

The muscles in Theron's arm tensed. He jerked away from his mother's touch. "Damn it, Mama, when are you going to get it through your head that I don't give a damn about offending any of the uppity white folks in these parts. If I can prove beyond a shadow of a doubt that Uncle Lemar didn't murder Audrey Royale and Lisette Desmond and then commit suicide, all of our people"—Theron thumped his fist on the center of his chest—"and the decent, fair-minded whites will respect me for having solved a twenty-year-old murder case."

When he'd first mentioned his intention to do everything within his power to reopen the case and clear his uncle's name, Yvonne had hoped and prayed he would change his mind. If he tried to get the case reopened, he was bound to rile the whole county—both blacks and whites. She'd never forget how tense race relations were twenty years ago when the local sheriff's office had come to the conclusion that Lemar Fuqua had murdered Audrey and Lisette and then shot himself. A double-murder and a suicide.

Everyone who'd known Lemar said he wasn't capable of murder and she agreed wholeheartedly. Her brother had been a kind, gentle man. And he'd been fond of the three Desmond sisters his entire life. They had played together as children and grown up together at Belle Rose. Twenty years ago when Lemar had been branded a murderer, she had tried her best to persuade the local authorities that they'd made a mistake, that they should look elsewhere for their killer. But an ugly rumor that had spread like wildfire convinced the townspeople of Lemar's guilt—the vicious rumor that Lemar had been deeply in love with Lisette and had gone mad when she became engaged to Parry Clifton. Even the whispered supposition of an interracial love affair had been enough to once again bring to the surface the fear, anger, suspicion, and hatred that had long existed between the two races.

"I know you don't want to listen to what I have to say, but I'm your mama and you owe me the courtesy of hearing me out," Yvonne said.

"You've already given me your arguments against my trying to get the case reopened. I understand your fears, but believe me, I know how to take care of myself." Theron grabbed his mother's hand and squeezed tenderly. "I realize there are remnants of the Klan still around these parts, but the days when they could get away with murdering a black man are long gone."

"It's not so much the Klan that I'm worried about." Yvonne looked deeply into her son's hazel eyes—eyes identical to her own. "Since we know that Lemar wasn't the murderer, that means the real murderer might still be alive and still living in Sumarville. Don't you think he's going to feel threatened? If he believes there's any way you can unearth the real truth, he's going to try to stop you."

"Good." Theron hit the table with his fist, rattling the dishes and silverware. "I'd like nothing better than for my investigation into the Desmond sisters' murders to smoke out the real killer."

"Son, why now?" Yvonne asked. "It's been twenty years and—"

"You know I've wanted to prove Uncle Lemar's innocence all these years, but I needed enough time so that I could reach a point in my life where I felt confident that I could do it without being stopped by the local authorities. I'm a wealthy respected lawyer, with a lot

of powerful connections. The time is finally right. That's
why I've come home. The time is now."

Jolie Royale locked the door of her condo, then tossed
her purse and keys on the table in the small foyer. As
she meandered slowly into the living room, she kicked
off her red three-inch heels and padded barefoot across
the beige carpet. Her date with Gene Naughton had
ended on a sour note. She'd been seeing the Atlanta
investment broker for over a month now and he
expected their relationship to move on to the next stage,
which for Gene meant sex. She liked Gene well enough
and enjoyed his company, but she thought of them
more as friends than lovers. He was attractive and virile
for a man of forty-five, but he didn't arouse any unbri-
dled passion in Jolie. Maybe she expected too much;
maybe she had always expected more from relationships
than she'd ever found. It wasn't that she was a simpering
virgin, but even at thirty-four she didn't have a long list
of former lovers. In fact the exact opposite was true.
Not counting any girlhood infatuations, she'd been in
love twice. Or thought she had. Both relationships had
ended years ago. The first affair had occurred when
she'd attended Instituto Marangoni in Milan, Italy.
She'd been twenty-one when she'd lost her virginity to
a gorgeous young Italian named Arturo. She'd been in
love the way only the young and foolish can be in love.
He'd broken her heart, of course, when she'd discovered him in bed with another woman. Five years later,
while still working in New York, she'd convinced herself
that she was in love with a brilliant, struggling actor who
swept her off her feet. Paul Judd had sprinkled stardust
in her eyes, and it had taken her nearly a year to realize
she wasn't in love with the man, but with the man she
thought he was.

After making her way into the kitchen, Jolie opened
the refrigerator to retrieve a can of diet cola. She

popped the lid and lifted the drink to her lips before returning to the living room. Sinking down into the overstuffed white damask sofa, she felt between the cushions for the remote control and punched the ON button. The nightly newscast appeared on the TV screen. Jolie hit the MUTE button, then lifted her feet to rest atop the glass and wrought-iron coffee table.

What was the matter with her? Why hadn't she just invited Gene home with her? What horrible sin would she have committed by sleeping with a perfectly charming man who wanted to advance their relationship to a more intimate level? *Remember what Cheryl says, "You're just going to have sex with the guy, not marry him."* But the trouble was that she wasn't Cheryl Randall. The woman who'd been her personal assistant since she'd moved to Atlanta and started her own fashion design business six years ago was a free spirit who went through men the way some women go through Kleenex. Jolie was a far cry from a free spirit. She took things seriously—her personal life as well as her professional life. Talent alone had not made her one of the premiere designers of children's wear in the United States. A lot of hard work, determination and a very serious, focused personality had made her a success.

But was a successful business all she wanted from life? Didn't she want more, need more? At thirty-four her biological clock had begun ticking a little faster, so if she wanted a husband and children . . . But did she want a husband? Did she want children? Maybe. If she could find the right man. Someone she could envision spending her life with, growing old with and loving with a mindless passion unlike anything she'd ever known. Was that asking too much? Probably. Most people simply settled for what they could get, for whatever came along that passed for that once-in-a-lifetime love.

As Jolie finished off the cola, she chuckled at her own romantic stupidity. Love never lasts.

Okay, so for a few really lucky people, it did last. But

for the majority, it didn't. Most of her friends were either divorced or had gone through a series of unsuccessful live-in relationships. At least she'd never made those mistakes; she'd never married and she'd never lived with a man. She had always liked her independence far too much.

More than one man had told her that she kept a protective shield around herself and sent out negative vibes, rejecting a guy before he ever made an advance. She wasn't consciously aware of being an ice queen bitch—something she'd overheard one acquaintance telling another about her at a party a couple of years ago—but maybe she was. Maybe, despite years of therapy, she had never truly recovered from the trauma she'd experienced twenty years ago. Even now there were times when she awoke in a cold sweat after dreaming of discovering Mama's and Aunt Lisette's bodies. In those horrid nightmares, she could feel the sting of the bullets that had entered her body. Thank God the killer had thought she was dead.

Stop this! Stop it right now! Just because Aunt Clarice called last week to tell you that Louis Royale had a massive heart attack is no reason for you to dredge up the past. The painful, better-off-forgotten past. What did it matter to her that a man she hadn't seen in twenty years might be dying? She had stopped thinking of Louis Royale as her father a long time ago. The day he married Georgette Devereaux, she had cut him out of her life forever. She could never forgive him for bringing that woman into her mother's home less than a year after her mother's murder.

Leaving the empty cola can on the coffee table, Jolie stood and made her way to the bedroom, pausing en route to lift her discarded high heels from the floor. In order to get a good night's sleep, she should probably take a sleeping pill. She seldom resorted to drugs to sleep, but in the past week, she'd taken something twice. Tonight would make three times. Lifting her arm, she reached behind her and clasped the zipper tab on her dress, but before she could yank it down, the phone rang. God, don't let it be Gene. She hadn't broken things off with him tonight and she should have. Ending an affair before it began had become her trademark. What the hell was she so afraid of?

Jolie sat on the edge of the bed as she picked up the telephone receiver. "Hello."

"Jolie Royale, please."

Her heart skipped a beat. After all these years, she recognized the voice. Deep baritone, thick Southern accent, and undeniably commanding.

"This is she."

"Jolie, this is Max Devereaux. I'm sorry to inform you that your father passed away tonight."

Her breath caught in her throat. What could she say? What should she say? No one, least of all Max, would understand if she told him that Louis Royale might have died tonight, but *her* father had died nineteen years ago, on the day he married Georgette.

"Did you hear me?" Max asked, his tone sharp with displeasure.

"Yes, I heard you. You said that Louis Royale passed away tonight."

"Visitation is planned for Saturday night and the funeral for Sunday afternoon, but I can change those plans if—"

"No. There's no need to change the plans for me."

"You will come home for the funeral, won't you?"

"I . . . I don't know."

"Damn it, woman, the man was your father. If you couldn't show him any love and respect while he was still alive, the least you can do is show up for his funeral."

"Go to hell, Max!"

Jolie slammed down the receiver, then fell across the

bed and curled into a fetal ball. Tremors racked her
body as she tried valiantly to control her emotions. But
suddenly, uncontrollably, she cried. Tears of regret.
Tears of loneliness and hopelessness. Tears for herself. Her mother. Aunt Lisette. And yes, tears for her father, too.

Chapter 2

There were days when Eartha Kilpatrick hated everything about Sumarville, and on those bad days, she
found herself being less than charitable toward others.
At thirty-nine, she felt trapped in a life that wasn't anything like the one she'd once dreamed of having. A
teenage pregnancy, then marriage to a real louse had
set her on the wrong path. Raising two kids after her
divorce hadn't been easy, nor had taking care of her
father, who'd died four years ago, after suffering from
Alzheimer's since he was fifty. She supposed she should
be thankful for her blessings. She'd inherited the
Sumarville Inn from her parents and had taken over
the management of the town's only hotel/motel after
her father's illness made it impossible for him to continue running the business. Both of her daughters were
away at college on scholarships. And she had an interesting man in her life, even if their relationship was pretty
much a backstreet affair.

As she passed the mirrored wall in the lobby area of

the hotel, she caught a glimpse of herself and smiled secretly. Unlike a lot of women approaching forty, she hadn't lost her figure. Men still found her attractive. Men like Max Devereaux. Of course she knew the limits of their relationship. Friendship and sex. He'd been totally honest with her from the very beginning. The guy had been burned badly by his one and only marriage. And it didn't help that the rumors about him having killed Felicia Wells Devereaux still surfaced from time to time. Although she knew Max was no saint and he possessed a dark, dangerous side, she had never believed him capable of murder.

Eartha entered the restaurant and walked straight to the bar. Glancing around, she inspected her employees as they swept the floor and set the tables for breakfast the following morning. Only two customers remained at the bar, which would close in thirty minutes. A couple of regulars, both middle-aged men who didn't want to go home to their wives.

"What'll it be, boss lady?" R. J. Sutton, her recently hired young bartender asked.

She smiled at him. The guy was damn good looking, and if her instincts were right, a bad boy to the core. If she were a few years younger, she'd be tempted to find out just how bad he was. Perhaps that was the reason she found Max so irresistible—she'd always had a weakness for hellions.

"Whiskey and water." Eartha watched R. J. as he lifted a bottle of Jack Daniels from the shelf. He was tall, lanky, and broad shouldered, with thick blond hair that hung almost to his shoulders.

After he filled her glass halfway and added the water, he turned and set it in front of her. Just as she started to say thanks, she noticed his gaze leave her face and settle at the restaurant's entrance.

"Trouble's back," he said.

She glanced over her shoulder, then groaned when she saw Parry Clifton, shirt halfway unbuttoned and dark hair rumpled, leading a woman half his age through the doorway. "Well, that didn't take long." She'd checked Max's uncle and his latest "lady friend" into the hotel less than an hour ago.

"That guy's been here a couple of times a week since you hired me," R. J. said. "Why do you put up with him? You've got to know that the women he brings here are hookers."

"Sumarville doesn't have hookers. Our little town has two-bit whores. Well, actually, probably twenty-dollar whores might be more accurate." As Parry approached, Eartha took a couple of sips from her glass, then turned to face him. "The bar's closing in a few minutes. Maybe you should take your friend over to the Firewater since they stay open until one o'clock."

"Trying to get rid of me?" Parry plopped down on a bar stool, then yanked his companion down onto the stool next to him. "Candy here will think we aren't welcome."

With an aggravated expression forming on her face, Eartha glanced at R. J. "Get Mr. Clifton and his guest a drink, then close the bar for tonight." With her glass in her hand, she rose from the stool, made her way around to inspect each table, then headed for the kitchen.

Sipping leisurely on her drink, she surveyed the entire room, checking to make sure everything was clean and sanitary. Here she was going through her nightly routine, bogged down in mundane chores, when what she wanted—what she'd always wanted—was to run away to Nashville. Silly woman! She was too old to start a singing career. All the new country singers were young, just kids. She'd lost her chance, thrown it away in the backseat of Trent Kilpatrick's daddy's old Mercury more than twenty years ago.

On Friday and Saturday nights when the restaurant provided live entertainment, she always sang a couple of songs to an appreciative audience. And every time she heard the applause, she pretended she was at the Grand Ole Opry.

"Miss Eartha?" R. J. cracked open the kitchen door and peeped inside. "Phone call for you."

"Who is it?"

"Mr. Devereaux."

"I'll be right there." Why would Max be calling her on a Thursday night at nearly eleven o'clock? Her heart caught in her throat. Lord, maybe old man Royale had died. Poor Max would take it hard when his stepfather passed away. He thought the world of his mama's husband.

Eartha entered the restaurant, slipped behind the bar, set down her glass, and lifted the receiver from the counter. "Hello."

"Is my uncle there?" Max asked.

"Yes, he's here."

"Do me a favor, will you? Get one of your guys to drive Uncle Parry out here to Belle Rose. Do whatever you have to do to get him here. He's needed at home. Mama needs him."

"Has Mr. Royale—?"

"Louis died a couple of hours ago."

"I'm so sorry. If there's anything I can do . . ."

"Just get Uncle Parry home as soon as possible." Max paused, sighed loudly, and said in a long quick rush, "Make sure that whoever he's got with him tonight doesn't come home with him."

"Don't worry. I'll see to it."

"Thanks, Eartha."

"Sure, Max. Anything for you." As she listened to the dial tone she realized just how true that last statement had been. *Anything for you.* She had warned herself not to fall in love with Max, warned herself that there was no love in the man. He was a passionate lover, but an unemotional one. He gave her physical pleasure and took his own but kept his heart—if he had one—hidden and well protected.

"We're closing up a little early tonight," Eartha said, glancing at the two male customers, who quickly finished off their drinks and left.

"You'll lose your loyal clientele doing stuff like this," Parry told her.

"Mr. Clifton, my bartender, R. J., is going to drive you home tonight." Eartha glanced at Candy. "Has he taken care of you?"

The twenty-something bimbo blushed and nodded. "Yeah. I get my money before . . ." She cleared her throat. "In advance."

"Fine." Eartha came out from behind the bar, laid her hand on Parry's shoulder and squeezed. "Max just called. Mr. Royale died a couple of hours ago. Max wants you home. Now."

"Louis died?" Parry stared at Eartha, his eyes bloodshot and glazed with tears. "Poor old bastard. I'm going to miss him."

"R. J., leave everything. I'll finish here and lock up." She delved into her pants pocket, retrieved her car keys and tossed them to R. J. "Drive Mr. Clifton to Belle Rose in my car. See him inside and take him straight to Max."

"I've got my own car," Parry said.

"Your car will be safe here overnight," she told him. "You've been drinking and don't need to drive. Max and Mrs. Royale and Mallory are going to need you in one piece. The last thing they could handle right now would be your having a wreck."

Parry heaved his thick broad shoulders, then sighed as he slumped over in defeat. He eyed R. J. "Boy, you know where Belle Rose is, don't you?"

"Yes, sir," R. J. replied. "I reckon everybody knows where Belle Rose is."

"I sure as hell hope Louis did right by my sister and her children in his will," Parry mumbled. "Guess we'll be seeing something of Miss High-and-Mighty Jolie Royale now. She'll be coming home to claim Belle Rose."

As R. J. led Parry out of the restaurant, Eartha busied herself with clearing away the dirty glasses, washing them and wiping the bar clean. Jolie Royale. She barely remembered the girl. Plump. Blonde. High-strung. And totally spoiled. The princess of Desmond County. Only months after his first wife's death, Mr. Royale had sent his daughter away. Folks had said how sad it was that the girl has survived the Belle Royale massacre only to lose her mind and have to be sent away to an asylum. Of course, later on, they'd learned that Jolie had never been in the nuthouse at all; she'd been sent to an expensive boarding school in Virginia.

Eartha had asked Max once about his stepsister, but she'd never asked again—not after the deadly glare he'd given her and the sharp response, "I don't discuss Jolie with anyone."

Parry Clifton snored like a freight train roaring down the tracks. The guy had talked nonstop for the first fifteen minutes, then he'd quieted and fallen asleep. The snoring was a great improvement over the jabbering. R. J. instinctively didn't like the man. His drinking and womanizing reminded R. J. too much of his own worthless father. After his mother's death when he was six, he'd been at his old man's mercy. He'd learned to steer clear of him as much as possible, to become invisible. That way, he didn't get knocked around as much. He had no idea if Jerry Sutton was alive or dead and didn't give a damn either way. He'd run away at fifteen and had stayed on the move ever since. For the past seven years, he'd drifted from one town to another, picking up whatever job he could. He'd lucked out when he arrived in Sumarville. Eartha Kilpatrick's bartender had up and quit on her that very day. Fate had dealt him a winning hand three weeks ago.

The huge white wrought-iron gates came into view, the entrance to Belle Rose. He could see the old plantation house from the road, although it set way back at the end of a long tree-lined drive. He'd learned pretty fast once he arrived in Sumarville that a couple of old families still ruled the roost in these parts. He hadn't learned all the players or their roles in this antiquated Mississippi town's drama, but he knew that Louis Royale was the richest and most respected man in the county and that his stepson, Max Devereaux, wielded the power of a prince.

When he drove up to the gate, he noticed the security cameras and realized he'd have to identify himself before he would be allowed inside. He rolled down the car window and said, "I'm delivering Mr. Clifton home."

Suddenly, without any response or any warning, the gates opened. He shifted gears on the five-speed sports car and zipped through the entrance and up the drive. As he drew closer to the house, he noted the grandeur of the mansion. Tall double columns flanked the two-story portico that divided the two wings of the house. A huge wraparound veranda spread out across the front and down the sides. The twin second story balconies, graced with intricate white wrought-iron latticework topped the veranda. He knew what kind of people lived in houses like this. Over the years he'd picked up odd jobs from the rich snobs who lived in luxury and were suffocating from breathing such rarified air. These people were wealthy, ancestor-worshiping snobs who considered themselves better than the rest of the world.

R. J. stopped the car in front of the house, right in the middle of the circular drive. He hopped out, rounded the hood, and opened the passenger door. Mr. Clifton sat there, his head thrown back, his mouth wide open. R. J. shook the guy. His eyelids fluttered several times before he forced open his bleary gray eyes and glared at R. J.

"You're home, Mr. Clifton."

"Home?"

"Belle Rose."

Parry Clifton struggled to get out of the car, bumping his head in the process. "Damn!"

R. J. slid his arm around the man's waist and lifted him to his feet. Where the hell was Max Devereaux? He sure could use some help with this guy. Clifton was six-feet tall and probably weighed a good two-sixty. R. J. headed Clifton toward the veranda. Thank God, there were only half a dozen steps up to the porch.

When he finally managed to half-carry half-lead the guy up on the veranda, the massive double front doors opened and Max Devereaux appeared. Devereaux sized up the situation and seeing his uncle's condition, scowled before he came forward.

"Well, you're a sorry sight," Max said, then turned to R. J. "Thanks for bringing him home."

"No problem. He slept most of the way."

Placing his arm around Clifton's waist, Max took his uncle from R. J. and all but dragged him into the house. Max paused in the doorway, glanced over his shoulder, and said, "Tell Eartha thanks."

"Sure thing."

The front door closed in R. J.'s face, effectively dismissing him. What had he expected? He was nothing more than a servant who'd done his job. Hell, at least Max Devereaux had said thank you, which was more than most of his kind ever did.

R. J. headed down the steps to Eartha's car, but before he reached the bottom step he thought he heard someone crying. Stopping abruptly, he listened. The sound came from the side of the house. A rather loud, mournful weeping. So what? he thought. The lord of the manor has just died. It was only natural that the family would be mourning. But what the hell was somebody—some woman from the sound of the crying—doing outside on such a hot, humid night?

Get in the damn car and go back to town. Whoever is crying has nothing to do with you. This is none of your business.

Instead of following his own good judgment, he walked back up the steps and around to the side veranda, searching for the source of the pitiful crying. Huddled against one of the one-story columns that supported the veranda, R. J. saw the shadow of a woman. Her black hair shimmered in the moonlight, which outlined her slender curves. He knew he was asking for trouble if he spoke to her, but damn if he could just walk away and leave her.

"Hey, there. Are you okay?"

She jumped and gasped simultaneously, jerking her hand to her mouth. "Who are you?"

"R. J. Sutton," he replied. "I work at the Sumarville Inn. Miss Eartha asked me to drive Mr. Clifton home."

"Is Uncle Parry all right?"

Uncle Parry? That meant this woman was Clifton's niece, sister to Max Devereaux no doubt. "He had a little too much to drink, but he's all right."

When she took a tentative step in his direction, he saw that she was young, just a teenager. But she was beautiful. Breathtakingly beautiful. "I heard you crying," he said.

"My father died tonight."

"Mr. Royale. Yeah, I heard. I'm sorry."

"Did you know my daddy?"

"Never had the pleasure."

"He was a very special man."

"I'm sure he was."

When she moved closer to him, only a couple of feet separating them, he caught a whiff of her perfume. Something subtle and probably very expensive. One good look at her told him that she was not only too young for him, but way out of his league. Miss Royale lived in this big fancy house and belonged to whatever upper-crust society that existed in Mississippi.

"Is there anything I can do for you?" he asked, all the while his common sense warning him to back away, to leave this damsel in distress to be taken care of by a real knight in shining armor.

"That's very kind of you, Mr.—?"

"R. J. Sutton."

"Oh, yes, you told me already. Well, hi there, R. J." She offered him a fragile smile. "I'm Mallory. Mallory Royale."

Heaven help him! He wanted to put his arms around this sweet thing and comfort her. *Big mistake*.

She looked up at him with a pair of dark blue eyes, so rich and deep a blue that they appeared almost black. Totally disregarding the warning bells going off inside his head, he reached out and wiped a tear from her cheek.

"Mallory!" A rough baritone voice called from behind them.

Every muscle in R. J.'s body tensed. Damn! Max Devereaux had just seen him touch his baby sister. R. J. swallowed hard. The last thing he wanted to do was to be forced to confront the big man himself.

"I'm here, Max," she replied, "talking to Mr. Sutton."

"You shouldn't be out here alone. Come back inside."

R. J. sensed rather than saw Max. Actually, he kept his back to the man, just the least bit uncertain what would happen if he turned to face him.

"I had to get out of there for a while," she told her brother. "I can't bear to look at Mama, to see her in such pain."

R. J. felt Max's powerful presence as he moved past him, then saw his long lean shadow hovering over Mallory. "It was nice meeting you, Miss Royale. Again, I'm sure sorry about your daddy." R. J. didn't make eye contact with Max as he backed away.

"Mr. Sutton?" Max called.

Damn! Another couple of minutes and he'd have

been in the car. He forced himself to turn and face the new master of Belle Rose. "Yes, sir?"

"Wait up a minute." Max turned to Mallory. "Go inside and force yourself, if you have to, to stay at Mother's side. She needs both of us now."

Groaning softly, Mallory nodded, then headed toward the back of the house. Max strolled leisurely toward R. J., his movements a slow, steady stalking.

"I don't want to see you anywhere near my sister again," Max said. "Is that clear?"

"Perfectly clear."

R. J. didn't wait for Max to say more. He wasn't a fool. He knew a warning when he heard one. Mallory Royale might be the prettiest thing he'd ever seen and she might bring out the male animal in him, but no woman was worth getting the hell beat out of him. And he was one-hundred-percent sure that Max Devereaux didn't make idle threats.

"I want to telephone Jolie." Clarice nervously twisted the lace handkerchief she held in her hand.

"Max has already called her," Yvonne said.

"But she didn't agree to come home and she must. She simply must."

"If you haven't heard from her by tomorrow, we'll phone her." Yvonne put her arm around Clarice's small shoulders in a comforting gesture. "Calm down and don't fret. You can't make that girl come home if she doesn't want to."

Yvonne worried continuously about Clarice's mental health. Her dear friend had been high-strung and emotional as a girl—a trait of all the Desmond females—then overly sentimental and a bit melancholy after her young fiancé's death in Vietnam years ago. But ever since discovering the bodies here at Belle Rose twenty years ago, Clarice had been slightly unbalanced. Everyone pitied the poor woman, believing her to be crazy.

But Clarice wasn't crazy. She had simply dealt with a horrific tragedy in her own way—by withdrawing from reality.

"Clarice, honey." Nowell Landers took Clarice's small hands into his large ones. "Yvonne is right. You're getting yourself all worked up. I can't bear to see you this way."

Clarice pulled away from Yvonne and went directly into Nowell's arms. That man had woven a spell over Clarice these past six months, and Yvonne wasn't sure she liked the power he held over her. He'd shown up in town on a Harley, rented a room at the Sumarville Inn, and came calling on Clarice. The man claimed to have known Jonathan Lenz, Clarice's long-dead fiancé.

"We were buddies in Nam," Nowell had told them. "I was with Jon when he died."

That was all he'd needed to say to entice Clarice, to have her open her heart to him. Yvonne wasn't as opposed to Nowell's devotion to Clarice as Max was, but like Max, she didn't quite trust Nowell. But the man seemed to make Clarice happy; happier than she'd been since her fiancé died thirty-six years ago. But what did a rugged, rough-around-the-edges, former military man see in a frail, mentally unstable, albeit lovely, sixty-year-old woman? Clarice had a little money of her own, but surely not enough that a man would marry her for it.

"Why don't you let me take you upstairs and put you to bed?" Yvonne suggested.

"But I'm needed down here." Clarice lifted her head from Nowell's shoulder and scanned the room, her gaze traveling from a weeping Georgette to a forlorn Mallory to a quiet, withdrawn Max.

"Everyone will be going to bed soon," Yvonne said. "There's nothing more that can be done tonight. Besides, Max will take care of everything."

"Yes, of course he will. Max is such a good man." Clarice patted Nowell's cheek. "I do wish you and Max liked each other."

"Don't worry about Max and me," Nowell said. "He'll eventually come around, once he realizes I'd never do anything to hurt you."

"Mr. Landers, I really think I should get Clarice to bed." Yvonne looked at him pleadingly.

"Certainly. You go on with Yvonne." Nowell turned Clarice around and placed her hand in Yvonne's. "I'll come by tomorrow morning. But if you were to need me, have Yvonne call the inn any time of the day or night."

"You're so dear and sweet, so much like . . ." Clarice's thoughts seemed to trail off into nothingness, as if she'd suddenly forgotten what she intended to say.

Nowell kissed her cheek, then turned and walked out of the front parlor and into the foyer. Clarice watched him leave, her gaze soft with tenderness. If that man broke Clarice's heart, Max would have to stand in line to beat Nowell Landers to an unidentifiable pulp. Yvonne wouldn't tolerate anyone hurting Clarice.

No one, least of all her own son, understood her devotion to Clarice Desmond. But then, no one knew the secrets they shared. Secrets that bound them together forever.

Chapter 3

While balancing the breakfast tray with one hand, Max eased open the door to his mother's bedroom. Yvonne had fixed only toast and coffee. Georgette was a picky eater. He supposed that was why at fifty-six, she maintained her youthful figure. The early-morning sunshine filtered through the sheer panels covering the windows that faced east. After entering the room, he set the tray on the seat of one of the two Louis XV–style chairs flanking the fireplace. The room had been redecorated three years ago by a Memphis interior designer, a project his mother had greatly enjoyed.

"Good morning," Georgette said, as she lifted herself into a sitting position in the middle of the massive iron bed, which was draped in red-and-gold-print toile and dressed in antique Desmond linens.

"Did you get any sleep?" Max asked.

Georgette pushed the long strands of her black hair away from her face. A face that had aged well and still retained the great beauty on which she prided herself.

And hair that a skillful beautician colored to subtle perfection. "On and off. Did you?"

"A couple of hours. Maybe."

She glanced at the tray resting in the velvet-upholstered chair. "Did you bring my coffee?"

"Yes." He lifted the tray and brought it to the bed. "And some toast, too. You should try to eat something."

He placed the tray on her lap, then removed the decoratively embroidered white cloth covering the meal. Four slices of lightly buttered cinnamon toast on a china plate. He lifted the small silver coffeepot and poured the hot black liquid into a china cup. The china and silver had been in the Desmond family for six generations.

"Do you mind if we talk while you eat?" he asked. "We have a great many decisions to make."

Georgette brought the cup to her lips and sipped the gourmet coffee that she had sent in from New Orleans every month. "I suppose there are things that can't wait. But I do so dread having to face the reality of Louis's death."

"Do you want to go with me to Trendall's this morning?"

Shaking her head, Georgette responded quite adamantly. "Mercy, no! I couldn't bear it. Please, darling, you handle all the details."

He had assumed this would be her reply. He loved his mother dearly but knew her shortcomings better than anyone. She was not an emotionally strong woman and depended on others to handle life's mundane chores. She had relied on her husbands, first Philip and then Louis, to make her decisions and take care of her. Now that Louis was gone, Max understood that it was his place to assume those responsibilities.

"Considering all the people who have to be contacted, I think it best to have visitation tomorrow night and the funeral Sunday afternoon," Max told her.

"Yes, of course, dear," Georgette replied as she tore a half slice of toast in two. "Whatever you think best." She nibbled on the toast, then suddenly looked directly at Max. "Will you call *her* again?"

Max didn't have to ask his mother who *her* was. "I think Aunt Clarice is going to call her today. I see no reason I should contact her again."

"Do you think she will come for the funeral?"

"I don't know."

"She broke his heart. Such a spiteful, unforgiving girl."

"She's not a girl any longer, Mother. She's thirty-four." Max would never defend Jolie to his mother or to anyone else, but he thought he understood Louis's elder daughter. She hated Georgette the way he had once hated Louis. But where he had lived in Louis's home and learned on a firsthand basis what sort of man his stepfather was, Jolie had never given his mother a chance. Louis had begged her numerous times to return to Belle Rose for a visit, but she had cruelly refused time and again.

"This house is hers, you know." Georgette's ring-adorned hand trembled ever so slightly. "I'm sure he bequeathed Belle Rose to her. She'll probably kick us all out the minute she learns that she can."

"What makes you think Louis left the house to Jolie?" Max pulled up one of the Louis XV–style chairs next to the bed and sat.

"He told me, years ago, that Belle Rose belonged to Jolie because it had been her mother's home, because it had been in the Desmond family since the day the land was purchased and the house was built."

"Louis could have changed his mind." Max didn't know the details of Louis's will, which Louis had kept private, but he couldn't—wouldn't—believe that Louis had left Belle Rose to Jolie. Surely he had at least divided it equally between his two daughters.

"You mustn't let her take everything away from us."

Georgette reached out for Max. "She hates me. Hates all of us. She'd like nothing better than to see us left penniless."

Max rose, sat on the bed and took his mother's hands. "Louis would never leave you penniless. You were the love of his life. I'm sure he left you well provided for. You and Mallory."

"And you, too, dear. You became a son to Louis."

He supposed she was right. In many ways he had become the son Louis never had. With each passing year, the two had grown closer. But there was no blood tie between them; he was not Louis's biological child, as were Jolie and Mallory.

Max didn't bother pointing out to his mother that even if Louis had left them penniless—something he never would have done—Max was now a wealthy man in his own right, perfectly capable of supporting Georgette and Mallory in the lifestyle to which they were both accustomed. Had she forgotten that he had inherited Philip Devereaux's shares in companies in both Mississippi and Louisiana and by shrewd business dealings had turned those practically worthless shares into a sizable fortune? Probably not. Georgette never bothered her pretty little head with business. Besides, she'd made it clear that she preferred not to dwell on the past, and that included her first husband, the man who had killed himself and left her a widow. Poor Philip. Had he embezzled from the businesses he and Louis had co-owned in Desmond County in order to pay for Georgette's elaborate spending? If so, he'd been a fool. No woman was worth such a risk.

Max kissed his mother's cheek, squeezed her hands, then released her. "Stop worrying. I'll handle all the arrangements for the funeral." He rose to his feet. "And if Jolie returns to Sumarville and tries to cause trouble, I'll handle her, too."

Georgette sighed deeply. "You must speak to Garland today."

"I'll phone him and set up a time for a formal reading of the will after the funeral."

Tears welled up in Georgette's eyes. "Oh, Lord, if anyone could hear us talking this way, they'd think all that mattered to us was Louis's money. But that's not true. You know that's not true. I loved Louis more than anyone . . . but—"

"Everything is going to be all right," Max assured her. "Finish your breakfast. I'll send Mallory up when I leave."

"Yes, dear, you do that. I really don't want to be alone. Not today."

Just as Max entered the hallway, he saw Aunt Clarice emerging from her bedroom. As always she looked neat as a pin, with her gray-blond hair arranged in fluffy curls atop her head and small gold-framed glasses shielding her hazel eyes. Her reed-thin body displayed the white linen slacks and billowy white silk blouse to perfection.

"Max. I'm so glad I caught you before you left."

He took a deep breath. He knew before she spoke what she would say. "Good morning, Aunt Clarice."

"How's Georgette this morning?"

"Coping," Max replied.

"I'll go in and sit with her for a while, later."

"I'm sure she'd like that."

"Max?"

"Yes?"

Clarice licked her bottom lip then bit down on it nervously. "If Jolie refuses to come home for the funeral, I want you to postpone it until we can persuade her. If necessary, you should go to Atlanta and bring her back here yourself."

"What?" He shook his head. "You can't mean you expect me to drag her back to Belle Rose kicking and screaming."

"No, of course not, but we have to do something. If

she doesn't come to Louis's funeral, she'll regret it for the rest of her life.''

Max gently grasped Clarice's shoulders. She lifted her face and smiled at him. ''Call her and tell her that you need her,'' Max said. ''If she'll come home for anyone, she'll do it for you. But just remember, that if she comes home, there'll be trouble.''

''You're quite good at handling trouble,'' Clarice said. ''You're a very strong, very commanding man, Max. I think you could handle just about anything, including Jolie.''

Max groaned. ''I've got to run.''

''Yes, yes. Go on, dear boy.''

Max released Clarice and headed toward the spiral staircase, then paused momentarily. ''When you speak to Jolie, tell her that there will be a formal reading of Louis's will after the funeral.''

''Oh. Yes. I'll tell her. But I don't think she'll be interested in any money Louis might have left her. You know she's quite a wealthy young woman.''

''Tell her anyway.''

Clarice had kept in touch with her niece during the past twenty years and had visited her often, especially after she moved to Atlanta. He knew only what Clarice had told them—that Jolie was a big-time fashion designer. Would it matter that Jolie didn't need Louis's money? If as Georgette suspected, he'd left Belle Rose to his elder daughter, was there even the slightest chance that she wouldn't throw everyone out, everyone except Aunt Clarice? Max didn't really know the woman Jolie had become, but if her thirst for revenge was as strong as her hatred, then they all had a great deal to worry about.

Jolie had been avoiding Aunt Clarice's calls the entire morning. Four calls in four hours. Damn, the woman was persistent. She could avoid her for only so long, then she'd have to speak to her and tell her that she wasn't coming back to Mississippi for Louis's funeral. It wasn't as if she didn't know exactly what tactic her aunt would use; she did. Aunt Clarice would try some version of her guilt trip persuasion that she'd tried in the past.

"If you don't come home, you'll regret it. I'm not getting any younger and neither is your father," Clarice had said numerous times. "You should forgive and make peace before it's too late. Please come home. I need you."

Now it was too late to forgive her father and make peace with him. She supposed a part of her regretted that fact; the little girl and teenager still alive within her, the daughter who had once adored her father. Before the events of that ungodly day! Before she'd seen him making love to Georgette Devereaux. Before her mother had been murdered and Jolie had begun wondering if Georgette had been somehow involved in the massacre at Belle Rose. Had the woman hired someone to kill Audrey Royale? Had she sent her son to do the horrific deed? Even now, after all these years, she couldn't bear the thought that Max might have committed the triple murders. At fourteen, she had thought herself madly in love with the brooding Max, so why had it been easier for her to believe him capable of the killings than to believe Lemar Fuqua was the gunman? Because she'd known Lemar all her life. The man had been practically family. Lemar had been kind, softspoken, gentle, and friendly. Just about everyone in Sumarville, both black and white, had liked Lemar.

To this day she couldn't understand how the local authorities had so easily ruled the three murders a double-murder and suicide.

Jolie pushed aside her sketch pad and pen, leaned backward in the cushioned swivel stool behind her drawing board and closed her eyes. The sleeping pill she'd taken last night had left her with a hangover that was only now, at one-thirty in the afternoon, beginning to subside. And despite the medication she'd taken before going to bed, she had suffered with nightmares. Cruel jumbled memories. Half-formed thoughts. Terror and pain. Caught in the dark trap of yesterday's tragedy.

"Coffee. Black and strong," the feminine voice said.

Jolie's eyelids flew open as she jerked in reaction to the unexpected sound. "God, Cheryl, you scared the bejesus out of me."

"Sorry. I knocked before I came barging in." Tall, model thin, with a mane of strawberry blond hair worn in a loose ponytail, Cheryl Randall extended her hand holding the bright purple mug. "You haven't stopped for lunch, so I thought maybe you needed a jolt of caffeine."

Jolie accepted the coffee. "Thanks."

"Your aunt called again," Cheryl said. "She's beginning to doubt that I'm telling her the truth about your being out of the office. She told me to tell you that if you don't take her next call, she's going to have someone named Max come to Atlanta and fetch you home." Cheryl chuckled. "I had no idea people still said things like that."

"Like what?"

"Like 'fetch you home.' "

Jolie sipped the coffee, then smiled at Cheryl. "That's because you're a Yankee."

Cheryl laughed. "Want to tell me what's going on? Why are you avoiding talking to your aunt? I know you adore the woman."

She and Cheryl had been friends for the past two years, ever since she hired the New York native to come to Atlanta and work as her assistant. But she hadn't shared all the gory details of her youth with Cheryl; only the highlights. They were more buddies, who swapped stories about men and enjoyed an occasional spa-day together, than best friends, who shared intimate secrets.

"My father died last night and—"

"Oh, Jolie, I'm sorry."

"Yeah, thanks. I'm okay. It's not as if he was really a part of my life. I told you that I hadn't seen him since I was fourteen."

"Bummer." Cheryl plopped down on the sofa in the corner. "So what's the problem about talking to your aunt?"

"She wants me to come home for the funeral."

"And?" Cheryl gazed at her, bewilderment in her expression.

"I don't want to go back to Sumarville. Not now or ever."

"Not even for your father's funeral?"

"Especially not for my father's funeral."

"There must be quite a story behind why you don't want to—"

"It's a story I'm not going to share with you today or anytime in the future."

Cheryl shrugged. "You could at least tell me who this Max guy is that your aunt is threatening to send to Atlanta to fetch you home."

"Max is my stepbrother. His mother married my father less than a year after my mother's death. Let's just say that in comparison to my wicked stepmother, all fairy-tale witches come off looking downright angelic."

"Ah-ha."

Jolie glowered at Cheryl.

"Don't give me the evil eye," Cheryl told her. "So you hate the stepmother and never forgave your father for marrying her. Do you hate Max, too?"

Heat rose up Jolie's neck and flushed her face. Her feelings for Max were complicated, perhaps more now than in the past. "I don't know how I feel about Max. I suppose I don't hate him, but—"

"There was something going on between you two. A little Southern-style incest maybe?"

"That's ridiculous! Your imagination is working overtime. I was fourteen the last time I saw Max and we weren't romantically involved. He was dating my best friend's sister at the time. And even if there had been something between Max and me, it wouldn't have been incest. We aren't blood related. And our parents weren't married then.''

Cheryl looked Jolie square in the eyes. "Do you realize that you're practically shouting?"

"What?"

"A fourteen-year-old girl can have the hots for a guy," Cheryl said. "I was just kidding about the incest thing, so there's no shame in admitting that you—"

"My big crush on Max Devereaux ended the day I realized that I suspected he was capable of murder."

Cheryl gasped. "Murder? Who? Who do you think he might have murdered?"

"My aunt and my mother."

Now isn't the time to panic. After all, there's no need to think Jolie Royale will return to Sumarville for Louis's funeral. And even if she does make a quick visit, staying for a few days and then returning to Atlanta, how much trouble can she cause?

I've been lucky—damn lucky—for twenty years. Back at the time it happened, perhaps a few people whispered my name, daring to consider me a suspect, but the authorities never seriously considered me. They had their man—Lemar Fuqua. His death was quite conveniently ruled a suicide. Even the slightest hint that there might have been an interracial romance between Fuqua and Lisette Desmond had been enough to make the man the chief suspect, and in the end, the only suspect.

Jolie was supposed to die that day. I shot her three times. Why didn't the damn girl die? Once she was in the hospital, I couldn't get to her to finish the job. Louis kept a guard at her door twenty-four-seven. Hell, even now, I break out in a cold sweat whenever I think about how I felt when she finally regained consciousness. At first she couldn't remember anything, then gradually her memory returned, until she recalled every detail of the day she'd been shot. She swore she never saw the person who shot her, had no idea if it had been a man or a woman, if it had been a black person or a white person.

But who's to say that she didn't block out that one memory. What if a visit to Sumarville unearthed that forgotten knowledge?

If she returns, I'll have to keep a close watch on her. And if she gives me any cause to suspect she knows the truth, then I'll have to finish the job I started twenty years ago. And this time, I'll make sure Jolie dies.

Chapter 4

Yvonne stayed discreetly in the background, quietly observing the mourners. No one would question her right to be here. As the family's housekeeper, she would be expected to be present at the visitation tonight at Trendall Funeral Home. She had asked Theron to stop by, to offer his condolences to the family, but he hadn't given her a definite answer. Surely he wouldn't disappoint her; she so seldom asked anything of him. If he didn't put in an appearance, Clarice would be upset. Clarice was especially fond of Theron, something he'd never questioned as a child but as an adult seemed to resent. Although she didn't want her son to forget their people's past and prayed that he would continue working for everything he believed in, she wished he could learn to forgive. She had considered telling him about the secrets from her past, wondering if it would help him understand her and perhaps himself. But what if the truth only fueled the anger inside him?

Yvonne silently watched the never-ending line of

mourners as they made their way closer and closer to
the family standing near the golden casket surrounded
by enormous floral arrangements. Every time someone
spoke to her, Georgette cried. Maybe Max should have
asked the doctor to give her a stronger dose of Valium.
Despite her sincere weeping, Louis Royale's widow
looked regal and undeniably lovely in her navy blue suit
and pearls, her jet-black hair fashionably styled and her
makeup flawless. At her left side, Mallory was a younger
version of Georgette, only her eyes were different. She
had Louis's dark azure blue eyes, which made for a
striking contrast to her ebony hair. Poor little Mallory
looked as if she'd rather be anywhere else on earth than
here. The girl was immature for eighteen and spoiled
rotten. Louis had lavished all the attention on her that
he had once given to Jolie.

Yvonne glanced at her wristwatch. Seven-thirty. They
were halfway through the three-hour visitation and still
no sign of Jolie. Clarice hadn't spoken to her niece
personally but had left her numerous messages. She
had tried to prepare Clarice for the possibility that Jolie
might not come home, not even for her own father's
funeral. But Clarice could not be swayed in her firm
conviction that her niece would put in an appearance.

Max stood to Georgette's right, his presence overpowering. Yvonne had sensed a unique strength in Max the
first time she'd seen him. He'd been a quiet brooding
little boy who had grown up hearing the ugly rumors
about his mother and the speculation about his own
legitimacy. He was not an easy man to like and didn't
seem to care what others thought of him. But people
tended to either admire or fear him. Yvonne admired
him. Over the years, she had watched him mature into
Louis Royale's right-hand man and had witnessed his
protective caring nature when it came to his mother,
his sister, and even to Clarice. He took his obligations
seriously. During the past five years, when Louis's health

had begun to deteriorate, Max had taken over the bulk of responsibilities for the businesses and the family.

Regardless of what others might think of Max, Yvonne had the greatest respect for him. He was accepted by the leaders of Mississippi society only because Louis had demanded it. Max had always been an outsider, an outcast who wasn't a true blue blood. She understood bigotry, whether it was directed at people because of the color of their skin or because of their lack of pedigree.

Despite the speculations of a few townspeople twenty years ago that perhaps an eighteen-year-old Max Devereaux had killed the Desmond sisters in order to clear the path for his mother to marry Louis, she had never taken those whispered innuendoes seriously. She believed in Max's innocence as strongly as she believed in her brother Lemar's innocence. Those rumors had died down less than a year after the murders, only to resurface again when Max's wife, Felicia, had mysteriously disappeared nine years ago. Her body was found months later by a couple of fishermen in a swampy area of lowland near the river. Felicia's murderer had never been caught and speculation had run wild in Sumarville that summer.

"Quite a circus event they've got going on here," Theron said, as he came up beside his mother. "I can just imagine what tomorrow's funeral will be like."

Deep in thought, Yvonne hadn't noticed her son approaching. She gasped softly, then grabbed his arm. "Thank you for coming."

"I'm here only as a favor to you. Otherwise, I'd steer clear of this sideshow."

She tugged on his arm. "Come with me. I want you to speak to Clarice and pay your condolences to Georgette and Mallory and Max."

Theron groaned, then glanced around the huge ornately decorated Magnolia Room. "So, Jolie didn't show up. Smart woman."

"It's not eight yet," Yvonne said. "There's still time for her to—"

"Why would she come back? What's here for her now?"

"Her family."

"Only Clarice. I'm sure she doesn't think of her stepmother, stepbrother, and half sister as family."

"No, she probably doesn't. She couldn't accept Louis's marriage to Georgette so soon after Audrey's death, but you'd think that once she grew up, she could have found it in her heart to forgive her father and at least come for a visit now and then."

"Louis Royale made his choices."

Yvonne sighed. "That's something you and Jolie have in common—your inability to forgive."

Yvonne led her son through the milling crowd that lingered in the Magnolia Room. Despite the air-conditioning, a stifling warmth permeated the area. Too many people crammed into a small space. Too much body heat on a hot June night.

"There's Clarice." Yvonne leaned closer to Theron as she whispered, "You be on your best behavior with her. Do you hear me? She's mighty fond of you and doesn't deserve anything from you but love and respect."

Clarice's face beamed the moment she saw Theron. She held out her hands. Yvonne nudged him in the ribs. He took Clarice's small lily-white hands in his big dark hands.

"Thank you for coming." Clarice squeezed his hands. "You've neglected to come around and see me since you've moved back to Sumarville."

"Yes, ma'am. Sorry about that, but I've been pretty busy getting settled in and setting up my practice."

Clarice removed one of her hands from Theron's grip and reached out to the tall muscular man beside her. "Nowell, this is Yvonne's son, Theron. He's a brilliant young lawyer and he's come home to Sumarville only recently." Clarice turned to Theron. "My dear boy, this is Nowell Landers, a very special friend of mine." Clarice giggled quietly, then covered her mouth with her hand, as if aware that laughter wasn't appropriate in the Magnolia Room. "I suppose I could say, as Mama would have, that Nowell is courting me."

Theron lifted his eyebrows, surprise evident in his facial expression. He nodded to Nowell. "How do you do?"

Nowell slipped a big arm around Clarice's waist. "Quite well, thank you kindly. And might I say it's a pleasure to meet you at long last. I've heard a great deal about you, from your mother and from Clarice. They're mighty proud of you."

"I'm afraid the ladies exaggerate. You know how mothers and . . . and family friends can be."

Yvonne tugged on Theron's arm. "You should speak to Max and—"

"By all means. Lead the way."

"We'll have to get in line," Yvonne said. "I think the end of the line is outside in the hallway. Earlier it was all the way outside and into the street."

"If we go to the end of the line, this could take a good twenty minutes."

"Mind your manners. Twenty minutes won't kill you."

She ushered him out into the hall. Several people glowered at them, but when a few smiled and spoke to Yvonne, the others seemed to relax. It wasn't that often that African Americans entered the doors of the Trendall Funeral Home.

"What's going on with Clarice and that guy?" Theron asked.

"You heard what she said—he's courting her."

"I take that to mean that they're dating?"

Yvonne nodded.

"What's he after? Hasn't somebody told him that all the money in the family belonged to Louis Royale?"

"Lower your voice. Someone might hear you."

"And do you think that everybody in Sumarville isn't laughing behind her back? A man doesn't *court* a fruit-cake like Clarice, unless he thinks he'll get something monetary out of it."

"Sh . . ." Yvonne cautioned, then lowered her voice to a whisper. "Max agrees with you and I must admit that I have my doubts, but Clarice refuses to listen to anything negative about Nowell."

Just as Theron started to reply, he glanced behind Yvonne and seemed totally hypnotized by whoever or whatever had captured his attention. Yvonne glanced over her shoulder. Dr. Sandy Wells and Dr. Amy Jardien entered the line directly behind them. Sandy and Amy were local general practitioners, partners in a clinic that served the poor in the community. Yvonne couldn't help thinking what an odd twosome the women made and how there had been a time when friendship between a white woman and a black woman was frowned upon in these parts. Unless of course, the black woman was the white woman's maid. Yvonne wondered what Sandy's father thought of his daughter's close association with the daughter of Sumarville's black undertaker? Just the thought of Roscoe Wells sent cold shivers through Yvonne. The man had once been a racist, a bigot, and a rumored member of the Klan. And despite his political promises that not only had he never been associated with the Klan and that he was now an advocate of progressive race relations, she didn't believe him. But others did, even some of the African Americans who had helped reelect him to the state senate four times.

"Hello, Mrs. Carter. How are you?" Sandy Wells asked.

Yvonne forced a smile as she turned to face the woman. Logic dictated that she be nice to Dr. Wells, who had never done anything to Yvonne, had never in any way been anything other than friendly and polite. But emotional reactions were something else altogether.

No matter how good a woman Sandy Wells might be, she was the spawn of the devil. And no matter how much Roscoe Wells declared himself a reformed racist, Yvonne would never believe a word out of the man's wicked mouth.

"I'm fine, Dr. Wells," Yvonne said. "And you?"

"Fine, but sad for Louis's family, of course. How is Georgette holding up?"

"She's rather shaky, but Max is taking good care of her."

"Naturally. Max is a rock, isn't he? Such a strong man."

Yvonne only nodded. She suspected that Sandy Wells was halfway in love with her former brother-in-law and perhaps always had been, even when her older sister Felicia had been alive.

Sandy looked up at Theron. "I had heard that you'd returned to Sumarville. Do you remember me from when we used to play together when I visited Jolie at Belle Rose?"

Theron nodded. "Yes, I remember you . . . and your brother."

Sandy lowered her voice. "Did Jolie come home for the funeral?"

"She hasn't arrived, yet," Yvonne said. Noticing the way her son was staring at Amy Jardien and she at him, Yvonne thought it best to introduce the two immediately. "Theron, you probably don't remember Mr. Nehemiah Jardien's youngest child, Amy. She's a doctor now."

Theron held out his hand to the young woman who tilted her head and smiled warmly at him. The girl was undeniably lovely, with coffee-colored skin and large black eyes that sparkled as she and Theron exchanged a lingering handshake.

"I'm Theron Carter, Dr. Jardien," he said, emphasizing the word *doctor*.

"Yes, I know who you are. Everyone's been talking

about your return to Sumarville. I'm pleased to finally meet you." Amy moistened her full lips nervously.

"The pleasure is all mine," Theron assured her.

"If y'all will excuse me, I'm going to break line," Sandy said. "I see my brother is up there ahead of us."

Yvonne kept her forced smile in place, then stood quietly as Theron and Amy continued their conversation. She watched and listened, realizing how very mutual the attraction between the two was. If it had been under any other circumstances, she would have left them alone. A man hardly needed his mother around when he was trying to impress a young lady. The best she could do was look the other way, backward toward the line that had formed behind them.

Every muscle in Yvonne's body tensed when she caught a glimpse of him only moments before she heard his booming Baptist preacher's voice. She froze to the spot, although every instinct within her told her to run. Roscoe Wells played the politician, shaking hands and exchanging pleasantries with his constituents. The stocky, ruddy-faced Roscoe's shock of white hair perfectly matched his thick white mustache. He swept through the crowd, his charisma capturing one and all.

Yvonne held her breath as he passed by, all the while praying that he would not speak to her. He paused momentarily and stared at her. She thought she would scream; indeed she was screaming quite loudly inside her mind. He smiled at her. The damn man actually smiled at her, then quickly moved on and into the Magnolia Room, totally disregarding the long line of waiting mourners. Roscoe Wells didn't wait in line, didn't adhere to the rules that governed others. After all, he was a Wells, and his family's roots were as deeply planted in Sumarville soil as were the Desmonds'.

Theron patted her arm. "Mama, are you all right?"

She took a deep breath. "Yes, I'm fine. Why do you ask?"

"Because the look you gave Roscoe Wells could have

curdled milk. I'm glad to see that you're capable of recognizing at least one white rattlesnake when you see it."

"Daddy thinks that man is only pretending to have had a change of heart," Amy said. "But for a long time now, folks have believed that he truly did repent from his past sins."

"That old bastard won't ever change," Theron said. "With his past history, I don't see how any of our people could put their trust in him."

Amen, Yvonne thought. If the African American community knew what she knew, he wouldn't be able to get elected as dog catcher.

Max's black Porsche sped down the country road away from Belle Rose and toward town. The night sky spread out overhead like a dark, diamond-studded, velvet canopy. Before he'd left, he had made sure everyone was accounted for and taken care of, to the best of his ability. Mallory had escaped to her room the minute they arrived home. But what should he have expected from her? She was just a kid. A spoiled little girl who was ill equipped to handle tragedy let alone lend comfort to others. In the days and weeks ahead she would need almost as much attention and pampering as his mother. Thank God for Yvonne. She was the only member of the household strong enough to actually be of help. She had given Georgette a mild sleeping pill and put her to bed. And when Max had abruptly asked Nowell Landers to leave, Yvonne had stepped in to soothe Clarice's rattled nerves.

He supposed he should have stayed at home, gone to bed, and prayed for sleep. But the tension inside him coiled tighter and tighter until he couldn't bear another minute trapped inside Belle Rose's ancient walls. He needed to escape, if only for a couple of hours, to a place where no one depended on him, no one asked

anything from him. For the past few years, he had found
an undemanding sanctuary in Eartha Kilpatrick's arms.
Sometimes he wondered why the woman put up with
him, why she allowed him to wander in and out of her
life without asking him for anything more than sex. He
supposed half the town knew about their relationship,
but he didn't give a damn and apparently neither did
Eartha. She was a good ole gal and deserved more than
he could ever give her. But he'd told her from the
beginning, been honest with her all along. He had no
intention of ever remarrying. And as far as loving
another woman—folks would be ice-skating in hell
before that would happen.

The tepid night air, heavy with warm moisture, settled
around Max as he zipped the Porsche into the parking
lot at the Sumarville Inn. Perspiration dotted his brow
and dampened his white shirt. In the distance a rum-
bling roar and a groaning whistle announced that a
freight train had just crossed the bridge over Owassa
Creek. After putting up the top on his car and locking
the doors, he kept his key chain in his hand as he
entered the inn's lobby. The clock on the wall behind
the check-in counter read twelve-twenty-three.

Max recognized the guy behind the counter. R. J.
Sutton. Young. Twenty-four at most, possibly younger.
Good looking in a low-class, dangerous sort of way. He
had a tatoo of a scorpion boldly displayed on his forearm
and a gold stud glimmered in his left ear. *Was this what
I would have looked like in my twenties,* Max wondered, *if
Philip Devereaux hadn't married Mama and brought us to
Sumarville before I was born?*

"Good evening, Mr. Devereaux." The guy nodded
and smiled. "Can I help you?"

"No, thanks. Ms. Kilpatrick is expecting me."

It was a lie, of course. He hadn't bothered to call
Eartha. Max didn't like having to explain himself to
anyone, least of all some minimum-wage flunky. He'd
have to speak to Eartha about this boy. There was some-

thing about him that made the hairs on the back of
Max's neck stand up. Instinct warned him that if the
guy stayed around too long, he was bound to cause
trouble. And God knew that was the last thing he needed
right now—more trouble.

As Max turned and headed down the corridor leading
to the rooms and suites on the first floor of the inn, he
singled out the key to Eartha's suite. Since her girls had
left town, she'd moved from her apartment into the
hotel. She'd given him a key this past winter. Tonight
when she had stopped by the funeral home, she had
squeezed his hand as she'd told him how very sorry she
was about Louis. And she'd given him that look, the
one that said she was hungry for him. Max didn't have
the slightest idea whether she had other lovers; he really
didn't care. But he suspected that although Eartha had
known more than her share of men, she was the type
who took them on one at a time.

He inserted the key in the lock. Lucky for him she
had left the safety latch undone. When he shoved gently,
the door eased open. She'd also left a light on in the
sitting area, a lamp beside the sofa. Max grinned. Had
she hoped he would come by tonight? The bedroom
door stood wide open. Max's sex swelled and throbbed.
He entered the room quietly. In the semidarkness he
saw only the outline of her body beneath the sheet. Her
left arm draped one pillow, her long red hair spread
out over the second, and a third teetered on the edge
of the bed. Lifting first one leg and then the other, he
removed his shoes and socks, then sat down on the bed
and pulled the sheet away from Eartha's body. Whimpering, she curled into a fetal position. Max eased down
alongside her, then took her into his arms. She came
awake with a jerk, her eyelids snapping open and her
mouth poised to scream. Max slapped his hand gently
over her mouth. She struggled momentarily. He nuzzled
her neck, then whispered into her ear.

"It's me," he said and the moment he felt her relax

against him, he slid his hand down her neck and over her chest to cup one large round breast.

"Max," she sighed against his mouth.

He kissed her, parting her lips and sliding his tongue inside. She rubbed rhythmically against him, then hurriedly ripped at his shirt until she pulled it from his slacks and undid all the buttons. He slipped his hand up inside her skimpy mint green teddy and cupped her slender hip.

"I'd thought you weren't going to make it," she told him, then ran a series of hot wet kisses over his chest and down his lean belly. While he continued caressing her hip and fondling her breast, she unbuckled his belt and unzipped his pants. With heated passion they rushed to remove the remaining barriers of clothing; then Eartha slithered down Max's body, her mouth and hands wild. She circled his erection and pumped him gently. He groaned deep in his throat. Positioning herself so that he could continue his attentions to her breasts, she began licking him like a lollipop. And when he thought he couldn't stand anymore, she took him into her mouth and closed her lips around him.

God, she was good at this! And unlike some women, she didn't seem to have a problem going down on a man; indeed she seemed to enjoy it.

He ached, needing release badly. Seeming to know exactly what he wanted, she continued, bringing him closer and closer to the brink. As the blood rushed through his body and echoed a deafening roar inside his head, he climaxed in her mouth. She swallowed and licked him clean, like a purring kitten washing herself.

Groaning, Max closed his eyes as his orgasm exploded through his nerve endings, tightening and then relaxing his muscles. When Eartha straddled him and laid her slender form on top of him, he took several deep breaths.

She kissed him tenderly. "Sleep for a while. I'll wake

you in a few hours and you can fuck me real good before you go home.''

The corners of his mouth lifted in a weak smile as he patted her naked butt before she slid to his side and lifted the sheet to cover them.

Jolie drove through Sumarville. Little had changed in twenty years. Most of the old buildings had been restored and a few had been torn down and replaced by ones she was sure met with the approval of the historical society. Strange how tiny the town looked to her now, after having lived abroad, in New York, and in Atlanta. Sumarville somehow had maintained that lazy, leisurely small town feel. At one-fifteen in the morning, there wasn't a sign of life anywhere in the downtown area.

She parked her Escalade in front of the Sumarville Inn. She could have flown and arrived sooner, but she had preferred to drive. She had needed those long hours on the road to build up her courage and to gird her loins for battle. Aunt Clarice and Yvonne would be the only two people happy to see her. They would welcome her with open arms. The Devereaux clan would no doubt prefer to shoot her on sight. Their animosity suited her just fine. There was no love lost between them.

But she had to admit that she wondered about her half sister. Did Mallory despise her the way Georgette and Max did? More than likely. But it didn't really matter, did it? After all, Mallory was really Max's sister, not hers.

Jolie removed a small suitcase from the back of her SUV, then locked the vehicle before heading toward the inn's front entrance. A young, lanky, model-handsome man sat in a chair behind the counter, his eyes closed and his mouth slightly parted. She cleared her throat. The man's eyes opened and he stretched. Slowly. Languidly. Then he smiled at her, and she wondered how many hearts this young stud had broken.

He stood and came toward her, only the counter separating them. "Yes, ma'am. Can I help you?"

"I'd like a room, please."

"Just for tonight?"

"No, for tonight and tomorrow night," she replied.

"Cash or credit card?"

"Credit card."

She unsnapped her shoulder bag, opened her wallet, and removed one of her Platinum cards. When he took the card from her, he read her name.

"Jolie Royale."

She nodded.

"Are you Mr. Louis Royale's daughter?" he asked.

"Yes. His elder daughter."

"Yes, ma'am." He went through the usual procedure to register her, then handed her a key. "Room two-oh-seven. Take the stairs to your left."

"Still no elevators in this place?"

"No, ma'am. Afraid not."

Jolie accepted the key he offered, picked up her suitcase, and walked away.

"Ms. Royale?"

"Yes?" She glanced over her shoulder.

"I'm sure sorry about your father."

"Thank you."

Jolie realized that she had to get used to accepting condolences. People would expect her to be in mourning. Damn, that was one of the many things she hated about living in a small town—having to live up to people's expectations. How many Sumarville residents actually endured *lives of quiet desperation?* How many generations of her own family had spent every waking moment constructing their day-to-day living according to society's rules and regulations, forever concerned about what other people would think of them?

Jolie didn't give a damn what anybody in Sumarville

thought of her, but Aunt Clarice would care. And so would Mama, if she were alive. Perhaps she owed it to her family—to the Desmonds—to at least act the part of a true Southern lady.

After making her way upstairs, she quickly found Room 207, unlocked the door, and went inside. She flipped on the light switch and was pleasantly surprised by the simplicity of the room's decor. Fairly typical for an economy-priced hotel/motel but clean and neat.

She tossed her suitcase on the bed to her left, then kicked off her sandals, removed her sundress, and fell across the bed to her right. Staring up at the ceiling, she thought about tomorrow. Her father's funeral. She couldn't—no, she wouldn't—pretend emotions she didn't feel. She had come home for the funeral. That would have to be enough. After all, she wasn't here to pay her respects to a father she had lost long ago; she was here to please Aunt Clarice.

And to find out if Belle Rose was hers now. "And if it is?" she asked herself aloud. Jolie smiled, thoughts of bittersweet revenge playing inside her head.

Chapter 5

Jolie wasn't surprised that Sumarville hadn't changed much in twenty years. But somehow she'd thought that Belle Rose wouldn't seem the same, that it would be different. How odd that it looked just as it had the day her father had sent her away all those years ago. The same winding drive led from the road. The same tall, white wrought-iron gates guarded the entrance. Only the security cameras were new. The grounds appeared unchanged: the same trees, same manicured lawn, the shrubbery and flowers identical to the ones she remembered. And the mansion was as it had been, a remarkable tribute to days gone by. Of course standing outside her SUV and looking in through the closed gates, she couldn't be sure that on closer inspection she wouldn't find minor differences. And there was no telling what Georgette had done to the interior of the house that had been in her mother's family since before the War Between the States. The very thought of that woman living in her mother's home, being the mistress of Belle

Rose and possibly sleeping in Audrey Royale's bed turned Jolie's stomach.

Her inner child longed to drive through the gates and go home to Belle Rose. Memories of her childhood flickered through her mind like faded scenes from a silent movie. Sitting in her father's lap as he read to her. Her mother coming into her room at night to brush her hair just before tucking her into bed. Playing "Chopsticks" on the piano with Aunt Lisette. Running through the house like galloping horses with Theron Carter when they were grade-school age. Aunt Clarice and she at the kitchen table, laughing and telling silly little jokes as they nibbled on Yvonne's freshly baked molasses cookies.

Jolie sighed and shook her head, then got back in the Escalade and started the engine. She could return to Belle Rose, but she could never go home again, never recapture those happy, carefree days before . . .

After she had been released from the hospital twenty years ago and her father had brought her home, she had felt terrified for weeks and unable to leave her room without someone staying at her side. Every time she walked out onto the landing, she could see Aunt Lisette's body sprawled at the top of the stairs. And downstairs she had balked at the kitchen door, refusing to go inside. She knew what she would see there—her mother's body. And she sensed exactly what she would feel. Sheer panic. The murderer had shot her three times and left her for dead there in the kitchen. And no matter how hard she had tried to remember something—anything—about the killer, her mind refused to cooperate. After all these years, she truly believed that she had never seen the person, that there was no way she could identify him or her. But three months after the Belle Rose massacre, someone had tried to drown Jolie when she'd gone swimming in the pond on the estate.

Someone had been afraid she might remember.

Jolie had sneaked out of the house that day, desperately wanting to be alone. It had seemed to her that she was watched every waking minute. Either Aunt Clarice or Yvonne or her father kept constant tabs on her; even the household day workers had, too. The employees had been curious about poor, crazy Jolie Royale, who had survived the brutal massacre only to lose her mind.

That day she wore her bathing suit under her clothes—a two-piece suit that had been a top seller in Aunt Clarice's downtown boutique. The July sun was unmercifully hot, so the cool spring-fed water of the pond felt refreshing. She swam the length of the pond a couple of times, oblivious to her surroundings, experiencing a freedom she hadn't known in months. No haunting memories. No watching eyes. But suddenly she heard someone enter the pond and dive under the water. Thinking perhaps it was Sandy or even Theron, who had not yet gone away to college, she didn't panic. Not at first. But when a hand grabbed her foot and yanked her under, she suddenly realized the murderer had returned to finish the job. She kicked and squirmed and somehow managed to free herself. She swam to the edge of the pond, hurried to gain her footing on the soft, mushy ground and then, leaving her clothes behind, ran as fast as she could through the woods. Not once did she look back, not until she reached Belle Rose and saw Yvonne hanging out sheets to dry in the fresh summertime air. To this day she had no idea how she'd been able to escape.

When she'd told her family what had happened, Yvonne and Aunt Clarice had gone to the sheriff, using the incident to try to convince him that the real killer was out there running around free, posing a threat to Jolie. But the sheriff hadn't been persuaded by the ranting of an unbalanced child. On the other hand, her father had taken the situation seriously and made immediate plans to send Jolie away—for her own safety. At the time she had believed the sincerity of his motives and hadn't put up a fuss when he'd sent her the very next week to stay with his cousin, Jennifer, and her husband, Paul Dean Underwood, an army colonel. Later in the fall, she had entered Ansley Academy, a private boarding school in Virginia. Exactly six months after her father sent her away, he'd married Georgette Devereaux and brought her and her son to live at Belle Rose. Jolie had never returned home. On breaks from Ansley, she had flown to whatever region of the world Jennifer and Paul Dean had resided at the time. When the couple had died in a plane crash when she was twenty-four, she had lost her true family.

She headed the Escalade down the road, intending to go back into town, but as she passed the old dirt lane that led onto the back side of the Belle Rose property and within walking distance of the pond, she slowed her SUV. Without properly thinking through her actions, she eased the sleek vehicle off the road and onto the bumpy overgrown trail. Feeling compelled to face one specific demon from the past, she parked, opened the door, and stepped down and onto the ground. If memory served her right, the pond was about a quarter of a mile through the woods. Was the old pathway still there, the one she, Theron, and the Wells offspring had forged when they were children?

She would never forget how outraged she'd been on Theron's behalf when Garland Wells, who'd been sixteen at the time, had told a fourteen-year-old Theron that he was now too old for it to be proper for him to play with and go swimming with the young ladies. The young ladies being Sandy and Felicia Wells, ten and twelve at the time, and ten-year-old Jolie.

Although she searched thoroughly for the pathway, she couldn't find it. No doubt it had been overtaken by the underbrush long ago. In all these years there had been no children's feet to trample the vegetation and keep the ground clear. Making her way as best she could, shoving aside low-hanging tree limbs, and stomping over decaying leaves and weeds, Jolie forged ahead, and realized she was going in the right direction when she heard the sound of running water. The spring trickled out of the earth, feeding the pond. Fresh sweet water that she had drunk as a child.

As she approached the spring, her pants leg caught on a briar bush and snagged the soft linen. She cursed softly, bent over to untangle herself, and in the process nicked her finger. She brought it to her mouth and sucked. She had lived in the city for too many years, had lost her familiarity with the country and the wilds of nature. Once free from the bush, she continued her trek until she neared the clearing. At the edge of the pond, a magnificent black Arabian stood, his head lowered to drink from the refreshing water. A saddled horse meant a rider, didn't it? Well hidden behind a tree and thick bushes, Jolie could see without being seen. Her gaze traveled around the area and within seconds caught sight of a dark-haired man. A tall, well-muscled man standing ankle-deep in the pond. As if mesmerized, she watched while he removed his shirt, tossed it on the ground behind him and bent to cup handfuls of water. He splashed the water on his head and let it trickle across his face and down onto his wide shoulders and over his back and chest. He repeated the process several times. Jolie sucked in her breath. The man was as magnificent as the horse.

She had come to the pond hoping she could force herself to recall the details of the day she'd been almost murdered for a second time, and perhaps remember something about her attacker. Not in all the years of therapy she'd undergone had she ever remembered anything important about either attempt on her life. Either the truth was buried forever within her subconscious or she truly didn't remember anything. If coming home could help her once and for all to free herself from guilt and stop blaming herself for what she didn't know, then this trip back to hell would be worth the price she would pay for the round-trip fare.

The man turned and walked out of the water, then sat on the damp ground. His wet black hair glimmered in the sunlight. Tilting back his head, he stared up at the crystal-clear azure sky and stretched his long lean body, reminding her of a big jungle cat spreading himself out in the sun. Jolie's breath caught in her throat. She recognized the man. He was no longer the beautiful, lanky eighteen-year-old he had remained in her memories; he was now larger, more muscular and the beauty of youth had matured into the rugged yet devastatingly handsome features of a man only two years shy of his fortieth birthday.

Maximillian Devereaux.

And God help her, the sight of him still created an untamed fluttering in her belly, a purely physical reaction unlike anything she'd ever felt with any other man. It was as if she were fourteen all over again and her teenage hormones had gone into overdrive.

Suddenly Max let out a loud howling groan that jarred Jolie's nerves. She watched in morbid fascination as he wept, his big body trembling with the force of his grief. And it was grief, she realized, that tortured Max so terribly. He was mourning her father. Odd how she envied him his ability to mourn, when there were no tears left inside her for Louis Royale.

Obviously Max had sought solitude by the pond, knowing he would be alone, knowing he could vent his frustration, his anger, and his pain without anyone seeing him. She felt an odd pang of sympathy. He seemed so alone, so totally, sadly alone.

She couldn't let him catch her spying on him. He wouldn't take kindly to her having witnessed him in a weak moment. Her smartest move would be to get the hell off Belle Rose property immediately. She'd have to face Max and the others soon enough. And when she came face-to-face with the new master of Belle Rose, she would meet him not as a member of the family but as an enemy. Max could never be anything else to her. In the battle to come, he would align himself with his mother and sister. If as she suspected, her father had deeded Belle Rose either to Georgette or Mallory, Jolie intended to protest. She'd hire a good lawyer, an expert in the field of breaking wills, and tie them up in court forever, if that's what it took to keep her mother's ancestral home out of the hands of that whore.

Jolie took one last look at Max and hated her body's unbidden reaction. With an iron will she had cultivated to protect herself from hurt, she turned and walked away, careful to move quickly and quietly. When meeting Max again, she would have to make certain that he never became aware of her physical attraction to him— now or in the past. He might try to use it against her, thinking she was the type of woman weak enough to allow a man to dominate her.

And she should never forget that there was always the possibility, however remote, that Max was the Belle Rose killer.

The First Methodist Church in Sumarville was filled to capacity, with the overflow spilling into the vestibule and outside, down the steps, and onto the sidewalk. Afternoon sunshine hit the stained glass windows like huge spotlights, flooding the interior with rainbows, and the melancholy moan of the church's organ resonated over the clatter of the packed house. The sweet overpowering scent of flowers permeated the warm air. Floral arrangements surrounded Louis's coffin, filled the pulpit behind the altar, and lined the sanctuary's walls from altar to vestibule. Max felt safe to surmise that there had never been a funeral in Desmond County to rival the one being held here today. Some of the most important people in the South were in attendance, including the governors of three states and various U.S.

congressional represenatives and senators. No other man in Mississippi had been as well-thought-of as Louis Royale. His business and political associations had been far-reaching. He had been respected by all who knew him and loved by his family and close friends. Naturally, his elder daughter's absence had been noted by several who had offered their condolences to Georgette, Mallory, and Max. When asked why Jolie wasn't here today, Georgette had been rendered speechless, thus prompting Max to respond. He'd said simply that Jolie had been notified and was expected at any time.

With his arm around his mother's shoulders, he all but dragged her away from the casket. Weeping pitifully, she clung to Max, her black gloved hands tightening on his forearm and wrist. He eased her onto the front pew, one of two on each side of the aisle that had been reserved for immediate family. When he pulled away from his mother, she reached out for him.

"Don't leave me," Georgette whimpered.

Max leaned over, took his mother's hands and whispered, "There are things I have to attend to." He glanced at his sister who sat as solemnly as a wooden statue on Georgette's left. "Mallory is right here with you, and I'll come back as soon as I can."

Georgette nodded, but Max felt the trembling in her hands just as he released his hold on her. His poor mother was going to be lost without Louis. Max looked at Mallory who stared back at him with a blank expression on her face.

"Take care of Mother until I come back." When she didn't respond, he said, "Mallory!"

"I heard you," she replied.

Max scanned the reserved pews. His mother and Mallory sat side-by-side on the first bench to the left. Uncle Parry, bleary-eyed but thankfully sober, kept his arm around Mallory's shoulders, occasionally patting her affectionately. A handful of Louis's distant relatives congregated in the second pew; some of the people Max

had never met. Aunt Clarice occupied the first bench
on the right, along with Nowell Landers. Yvonne Carter
sat on the other side of Clarice, her bright hazel eyes
ever watchful. He suspected she was as wary of Nowell's
attentions to Clarice as he was and was equally incapable
of dissuading her from continuing her relationship with
the man. Max had the greatest respect for Yvonne, who
was as devoted to Clarice as any mother or sister might
have been. He had no idea what deep bonds joined the
women, but he suspected that their abiding friendship
superceded the normal bounds of servant and mistress.
Indeed, he'd never seen the two act in any manner
other than as friends. Even when Yvonne waited on
Clarice and fussed over her, they acted and reacted as
if they were family.

On the second pew to the right various Desmond
relatives, none of whom bore the surname, sat proudly,
their southern aristocratic noses in the air. Not a one
of them were closer kin to Clarice than a second cousin
once removed.

As Max made his way up the aisle, he spotted the
Wells family—father and son—seated together. Roscoe
Wells was an old reprobate. A former Klansman who
had changed his ideology to adapt to modern times and
today's voters. At nearly seventy, he still tried to maintain
a level of authority over his two children, neither of
whom paid him much heed. Garland, affectionately
called Gar by his friends, resembled his father physically,
being short and stocky with a loud infectious laugh; but
he was a quieter, softer version of his charismatic father.
And a better man by far.

Sandy sat two rows behind her father and brother,
the distance between them making a bold statement.
Sandy was for all intents and purposes her now-deceased
mother's daughter, a friendly, outgoing do-gooder, who
had taken it upon herself to right many of the wrongs
her father had perpetrated before his well-known
change of heart. Max had always been fond of Sandy,

as was everyone who knew her, and a part of him regretted that he could never return the affection she felt for him. He'd known for years that she was in love with him or at least thought she was. She was absolutely nothing like Felicia. If only he had fallen in love with the younger Wells daughter instead of the elder. If he had, his life would have been so much simpler. And a great deal happier. But he'd been mad about Felicia, and she had used his wild passion against him. By the time she disappeared, shortly before their third anniversary, he had not only stopped loving her, he had grown to despise her. Felicia had been her father's daughter— a conniving, manipulative, self-serving monster.

As he passed the pew where Sandy sat on the end, she stood and held out her hand to him. He paused long enough to give her a hug and accept an affectionate kiss on the cheek, then he hurriedly broke away and continued down the aisle. Two o'clock was fast approaching and he wanted to double check with McCoy Trendall to make sure all the arrangements he'd made for today's service would be carried out just as he had instructed. Louis deserved only the best. Making sure his funeral was an unforgettable event was the last thing he could do for his stepfather—a final tribute.

A squad of talented bagpipers had been flown in to play "Amazing Grace" directly before the minister spoke. The choir from the black Sumarville Freewill Baptist Church would take turns with the white First Methodist's choir, both singing their own style of spirituals. Mississippi's governor would offer the eulogy.

McCoy met Max in the vestibule and pulled him aside. "We have things under control. No need to worry. I promise that everything will go off without a hitch."

"Do you have the outdoor loudspeaker system working?" Max gazed through the open doors to where a large crowd waited on the steps and sidewalk below.

"I've checked it myself. It's working just fine."

Max nodded, shook McCoy's hand, and made a mad

dash through the crowd in the vestibule. After being
forced to pause and shake hands with several people,
he escaped into the men's room. Thankfully, the room
was empty. He pulled his cell phone from his pocket,
along with a small black notebook, looked up the number he needed and dialed.

"This is Maximillian Devereaux," he said. "I'm calling to check on—"

The voice on the other end of the line assured him
that the New Orleans jazz band he'd hired to play at
the reception at Belle Rose following the funeral was
in fact already at the mansion. He breathed a sigh of
relief. Louis had loved jazz and the two of them had
often driven down to New Orleans for a boys night out.
Max thought it only fitting that the music played this
afternoon for Louis's mourners be the music he had
loved.

Max glanced in the mirror over the sink area and
noticed his tie was slightly crooked. He straightened his
tie, braced his shoulders, and swung open the rest room
door. In a few hours this would all be over, all the pomp
and circumstance, and then he would be faced with the
reality of Louis's death.

Just as Max returned to the sanctuary and was nearing
the front pew, he heard a buzzing hum rising from the
crowd. The hairs on the back of his neck stood up and
instinct cautioned him that something was wrong. The
murmurs grew louder until he distinctively heard someone say *Jolie.* His gut tightened. He stopped at the end
of the third pew to the left of the aisle and slowly glanced
over his shoulder. He swallowed hard and cursed softly
under his breath.

The woman, dressed in a simple beige linen suit,
walked down the aisle, her head held high, her expression solemn. She didn't look much like the plump teenager he remembered. But he would have recognized her
anywhere. This fashionably dressed curvaceous woman
bore a striking resemblance to her mother and her

aunts. She was without a doubt a true Desmond. Golden blond hair swept up into a French twist. A square jaw, full pouty lips, and an air of superiority that all but oozed from her pores. Only her eyes declared her a Royale. They were the same intense blue that Louis's had been and identical to Mallory's.

So, the prodigal had returned at long last and had managed to make a grand entrance. Every eye in the church kept watch as lips spread gossip like wildfire flying destructively through summer dry grass.

Do it whether you want to or not, Max ordered himself. *Everyone will expect it of you.*

As if his shoes held heavy lead weights, he turned around and took several tentative steps toward Jolie Royale, who didn't even glance his way. She was headed straight for her father's casket. Any minute now his mother would see her and so would Aunt Clarice. Their reactions would be totally different, poles apart, and yet each equally dramatic.

Forcing himself into action, Max moved directly in front of Jolie, halting her progress toward the altar. Pausing, she stared directly at him, her expression daring, her facial muscles tight.

"Jolie, I'm Max Devereaux, your stepbrother." He didn't touch her; he didn't dare. If he did, he might find himself wrapping his hands around her long white neck and strangling her.

She glared at him, pure animosity evident in her eyes. "I know who you are."

"Would you like to say a proper good-bye to your father?" he asked. "If you'd like, I can walk with you the rest of the way."

"How very nice of you to offer, but I think I can do this without your assistance." An icy tone edged her words.

"As you wish." He stepped out of her way, then added, "You will, of course, sit with the family for the service and ride with us to the cemetery."

Her lips curved into a fragile fleeting smile, so quickly concealed that he thought he might have imagined it. "Of course."

"And you'll come to the reception afterward at Belle Rose?"

Ah, he had her there. He could see the uncertainty in her eyes. If she came to Belle Rose, she would have to be civil to his mother and he knew how that would gall her.

"I hadn't planned on—"

"You might want to change your plans," he told her, then leaned over to whisper in her ear, "Garland Wells is going to read Louis's will to the family this evening. Don't you want to find out whether your daddy left Belle Rose to you or to my mother?"

Chapter 6

Jolie managed to make it through the funeral service. Seated between Aunt Clarice and Yvonne, both women overjoyed to see her, she drew strength from their love and concern. Aunt Clarice kept saying, "I knew you'd come home." The extravagant tributes to Louis Royale were probably well deserved, but the minister's condolences to her were wasted. In her mind and in her heart, she had buried her father long ago. If anyone questioned why she hadn't shed a tear, she wouldn't have a problem telling them. But then again, she didn't owe anyone an explanation. What the people in this antiquated one-horse town thought of her didn't matter. She'd be gone soon enough. Once the will was read.

Thankfully, Trendall Funeral Home provided two black limousines for the immediate family, so Jolie wasn't forced to ride to the cemetery with Georgette and her children. The chauffeur parked, then got out and opened the door for them. Yvonne emerged first, then Nowell Landers, who assisted Aunt Clarice. Jolie hesitated momentarily before joining the others. Not once had she given any thought as to where her father would be buried. Somehow she had managed to block the question from her mind. Would Louis Royale be laid to rest alongside his first wife in the Desmond family section of the Sumarville Cemetery? Or had other arrangements been made? Odd that she should care, but she did. What difference would it make now? Perhaps it mattered to Louis's new family, but certainly it shouldn't matter to her.

Within minutes, she realized that they had not stopped at the Desmond family's burial site. As she walked beside Aunt Clarice, she looked ahead to the dark green tent over the open grave. This was the Royale family plot, where Louis's father and mother were buried. A huge decorative stone, embellished with angels on either side, rested at the head of the open grave. As they drew closer, Jolie saw the inscriptions on the monument. Inscribed in the gray marble was her father's name and date of birth. Her heart sank when she read Georgette Royale's name beside his.

Joining Aunt Clarice and Yvonne, Jolie took her seat on the second row of folding chairs near the grave. Nowell Landers stood behind her aunt, his large tanned hands resting on Clarice's shoulders. Her father's second family occupied the first row—Georgette and her children. And even her brother Parry.

"Dear family and friends of Louis Royale, our hearts are heavy today," Reverend Arnold said, and went on to sing her father's praises, to list his many accomplishments and to offer condolences to the family as well as hope for a reunion in the hereafter.

Twenty years ago she had been in the hospital, hovering between life and death and unable to attend the funerals of her mother and aunt. In the years since, she had avoided funerals, finding excuses not to attend. But here she was at the funeral of a father she hadn't seen in twenty years. She would get through this final graveside service and make it through this day. Somehow. Some way.

While the minister continued his praise of a fine and honorable man, rays of the hot June sun bounced off the burnished gold metal casket. Once Reverend Arnold finished his oratory, he turned the service over to the Shriners, who proceeded to perform the Masonic burial rites for their brother who had at one time been a Potentate.

As the ceremony continued, Georgette's weeping grew louder, until she was finally unconsolable. Jolie carefully watched the black-clad widow, whose performance was quite convincing. Was it possible that Georgette had truly loved her husband for himself as much as for his money and social position? Odd, Jolie thought, that she should consider that possibility now, when she'd never before given the second Mrs. Royale the benefit of the doubt.

But what did it matter if Georgette had loved Louis? It changed nothing. The two had indulged in an adulterous affair before her mother's death and had married nine months after Audrey Royale had been murdered. Both acts were unforgivable.

"Poor Georgette," Clarice murmured softly. "She would never survive this loss if not for Max. He will be her strength and her comfort. He'll take care of all of us, just as Louis did."

Hearing Max Devereaux praised so highly by her aunt didn't surprise Jolie. She'd listened to Aunt Clarice singing the man's praises on numerous occasions over the past few years. *Max did this. Max said that. Max, the magnificent.*

The image of Max cooling himself in the pond this morning flashed through Jolie's mind. She cringed. *No more flights of fancy,* she cautioned herself. She would not fall victim to the spell Max apparently wove around every woman who knew him, young and old alike. She was no fourteen-year-old in the throes of her first mad crush on an older boy. Max Devereaux was *persona non grata* to her. As far as she was concerned, the man was the devil incarnate.

The pipers had come from the church to participate in the Masonic burial rites and now they played again as the family departed. The mournful wail of the Scottish bagpipes spread through the cemetery and lingered in the soul. Max ushered his mother, sister, and uncle into the first limousine, then stood by the car and glanced back at Jolie. Their gazes met and locked for a split second. The look he gave her chilled her to the bone. Did she have more to fear from Max than she thought? Was that hatred she'd seen in his eyes? Or had it been a warning?

"Come, dear girl," Clarice said from inside the second limousine. "We must go straight to Belle Rose and be there to greet our guests."

Jolie nodded, then hurriedly slid into the limousine beside her aunt. She would rather walk over hot coals or swallow a cup of glass slivers than participate in the postfuneral reception. Of course, she could skip the grand affair, make an excuse to return to the hotel and then come back later for the reading of her father's will. But what excuse could she give Aunt Clarice? No, it was too late to back out now, too late to have second thoughts about her return to Sumarville—and to Belle Rose.

So Jolie Royale had shown up after all, and looking enough like her mother and aunts so that everyone recognized her immediately. She'd grown up to be a beautiful woman, more beautiful than her mother or Clarice and every bit as beautiful as Lisette, who'd been the fairest of the Desmond sisters. In fact, her resemblance to Lisette was uncanny.

Why was she here? Why hadn't she stayed away? She had washed her hands of Louis, of Belle Rose, and of Sumarville

*years ago. Undoubtedly she expected to be named in the will,
perhaps given a huge slice of the Royale pie.*

*Damn her for coming back, for dredging up all those old
memories. People would start talking again, recalling the Belle
Rose massacre. Word had it that Yvonne's son Theron was
stirring up trouble, probing into the old murder-suicide case.
That boy needed to be stopped now before he stirred up a really
big stink. Handling him might prove difficult, but it could be
done. Handling Jolie Royale would be a different matter
entirely. It was possible, wasn't it, that she might already have
remembered something significant about the murderer? Was
that the real reason she'd finally returned to Sumarville? In
the past, two attempts on her life had failed. If another attempt
became necessary, failure wasn't an option.*

*What I did, I did because I had to. I had no other choice.
It had been the only way. God forgive me, I hadn't planned
to kill them all. But the others had gotten in the way. I couldn't
let them live, not when they knew what I'd done.*

Yvonne moved from room to room, her presence
subtle and nonobtrusive. Except for a warm hello from
a few people close to the family, she was ignored, as all
good servants were. It had long ago ceased to bother
her that outsiders considered her nothing more than a
housekeeper at Belle Rose. She had learned to accept
what could and could not be in her life—something
her son would never have to accept. Theron had no
limitations, no unholy moments from his youth to taint
his life or obligations that would hold him back from
achieving his goals. She only hoped and prayed that his
determination to prove Lemar innocent of the Belle
Rose massacre wouldn't ruin his political aspirations in
Mississippi.

Yvonne had hired the catering service from Vicksburg
that she'd used on numerous occasions, but despite
always having been totally satisfied with their work, she
kept a close watch on every aspect of today's reception,

from food preparation to the waiters' and waitresses' appearances and performances. She prided herself on perfection. She was good at her job. Clarice had pointed out to her once that with her managerial abilities she could have been a company CEO. Even now the thought made her smile.

Approximately two-thirds of the people who had attended the church service put in an appearance at the reception, filling the house to capacity. Of course, a few had already come and gone and more entered the front door every few minutes. The house would be a disaster once the crowd left, but she'd hired extra help to assist the daily maids to clean up tonight.

Clarice had already told her that she was expected to join the family when Gar Wells read the will. Yvonne supposed Louis had bequeathed her a small sum to show his appreciation for her loyal service. It would be expected. She sincerely hoped that he had left Clarice enough to live well for the rest of her life. Of course, Clarice still had some money of her own from when she'd sold her dress shop twenty years ago. Yvonne knew to the penny exactly how much. She and Clarice had no secrets. Not now. Not ever.

As she made her way through the back parlor, she heard Clarice's voice, slightly agitated, the pitch an octave higher than normal.

"But you must stay here," Clarice pleaded. "It's ridiculous that you checked into the Sumarville Inn when there's more than enough room for you at Belle Rose. After all, this is your home. Your old room is just the way you left it."

"There's no point in my leaving the inn," Jolie said. "I'm returning to Atlanta in a few days, maybe even tomorrow, unless something in the will requires me to stay on."

"Of course there will be something in Louis's will that will require you to stay on. You're his daughter. I'm sure he's left an equal share of everything to you."

"I doubt he did that. He had a new family to think about, to take care of. I'm sure he put their needs first in death as he did in life."

Clarice slipped her arm around Jolie's waist. "You're still so bitter." Clarice *tsk-tsked* and shook her head sadly. "Audrey was like that. Unable to forgive. Unable to understand human foibles. You mustn't be this way, dear, dear Jolie. Don't you know that in the long run hatred turns on you and causes you pain?"

"I'm sorry if you can't understand why I feel the way I do, but I can't accept the fact that Georgette took my mother's place in this house less than a year after her death or the fact that she took my mother's place in my father's bed before Mama died."

"Hush up!" Clarice tapped her index finger over her lips. "Someone might hear you."

Yvonne hated seeing Clarice upset, and if this conversation went any further, she'd have a difficult time dealing with Clarice later. Everyone in the household made an effort to keep things on an even keel for Clarice, to keep her content and smiling. She simply wasn't emotionally strong enough to deal with confrontation. Everyone here at Belle Rose was aware of that fact. Why wasn't Jolie? It was for this very reason that Max hadn't already kicked Nowell Landers's ass from here to Jackson and back.

"Clarice, Mr. Landers is looking for you," Yvonne said as she approached. A little white lie to calm the situation was in order.

"Nowell is looking for me?" Clarice's eyelashes fluttered, youthful flirtation in the gesture.

Yvonne hadn't seen Clarice react this way to a man since Jonathan. "Come on. Let me take you to him." She hoped that Nowell Landers wouldn't contradict her.

"But I haven't persuaded Jolie to stay here at Belle Rose. She's checked herself into the inn and says she's leaving Sumarville in a few days." Clarice hugged Jolie to her side. "Now that she's home again, we can't let her leave."

"I'll tell you what—you go find Mr. Landers and I'll talk to Jolie," Yvonne said. "How will that be?"

"Yes, of course. What a good idea. You have such a persuasive way about you." Clarice kissed Jolie's cheek, then released her and shook her finger in Jolie's face. "You listen to Yvonne. Do you hear me? You won't disappoint us, will you, sweet child?"

Jolie offered her aunt a weak half-smile. "I promise I'll listen to Yvonne."

That statement seemed to be enough to pacify Clarice, who waltzed off into the throng of partying mourners in search of her adoring suitor.

Yvonne turned to Jolie. "Would you like a breath of fresh air?"

"What do you have in mind?"

"I thought maybe we could escape to the back porch. Hopefully no one else has made it out that far, yet."

"Are we going to have a come-to-Jesus talk?" Jolie asked.

Yvonne smiled. "So, you remember those little talks I used to give Theron and you." She sighed. "Yes, I suppose that's exactly what I have in mind for you today. Don't you think it's past time for one?"

Georgette vacillated between teetering nervousness and pitiful sobbing. Max had tried his best to persuade her to go upstairs to her room an hour ago, but she had adamantly refused. His mother had been extremely proud to be Louis Royale's wife and had taken advantage of every opportunity to prove to the world that she was worthy of the title, so it was only natural that she would want to show everyone that she was truly the grieving widow. He didn't doubt for a second that his mother had loved Louis with great passion or that that passion often bordered on obsession. She had seemed to need Louis to survive the way she needed air to breathe.

Max had loved Felicia, had wanted her desperately, and in the end had allowed her to treat him shamelessly, but he had no idea how it felt for another human being to be the beginning and the end of his universe. The intensity and depth of that kind of love—the kind his mother and Louis had shared—frightened him in a way that nothing else ever had.

"Louis would have enjoyed this," Georgette said. "He did so love a good party."

"Indeed he did," Parry replied. "And he was no cheapskate when it came to paying for shindigs like this one. I always admired the way he enjoyed his money."

"My husband was a very generous man." She grasped Max's arm. "I'm feeling a bit faint. Perhaps I should sit down."

"Certainly, Mother."

Max separated a bevy of chattering women to clear a path to the Queen Anne chair in the corner of the front parlor. He helped his mother sit, then knelt before her.

"Are you sure you don't want to go upstairs for just a little while?"

She shook her head.

"Then how about something to drink? I'll find Yvonne and get her to make you a cup of mint tea."

"Yes, Max, that would be nice. A cup of tea. And be sure she adds three teaspoons of sugar. I like my mint tea very sweet."

"She never forgets," he said. "Coffee black. Tea very sweet."

Max glanced around, searching for Mallory. Having seen her only once since their return home, he suspected she was hiding away in her room. He needed to check on her. She had been unusually quiet and emotionally remote since Louis's death. His little sister was probably wondering, as was their mother, just how they could go on without Louis. Mallory had been his spoiled darling. After seeing to his mother's tea, he'd go upstairs in search of his sister and try to persuade her to come downstairs and keep their mother company.

Halfway to the kitchen, he encountered his uncle again, who had a fresh drink in his hand. Parry grabbed his arm. "Wait up."

Max paused, then gave Parry a hard glare.

"When are you going to throw this bunch of snobs out of here and get on with what's important?" Parry asked.

"And that would be?"

"Finding out what Louis's will says. We all need to know if we're going to get kicked out of this place." Parry leaned closer, his breath strong with liquor. "If he left anything to Jolie, you ought to protest. Get some big-time lawyer who specializes in breaking wills. That girl doesn't deserve a dime."

His mother's brother had been the bane of his existence and an embarrassment to Mallory and their mother for years now. But the man was family and despite his outlandish behavior, Parry could often be charming and even on occasion endearing.

"Do me a favor, will you, Uncle Parry?"

"Name it, my boy."

"Go upstairs and see if you can find Mallory and persuade her to come down and keep an eye on Mother."

"Consider it done."

Parry patted Max on the back, his touch rather forceful. Max drew in a calming breath; then when his uncle walked unsteadily toward the foyer, he continued on his way to the kitchen. He found the room buzzing with activity, but Yvonne was nowhere in sight. Had she, too, escaped somewhere upstairs?

"Can anyone tell me where Mrs. Carter is?" he asked the hired help working feverishly to replenish the food and wine trays.

"Mrs. Carter is on the back porch." An attractive young woman dressed in the white shirt and black slacks that made up the catering service uniform smiled warmly, giving him a flirtatious look.

"Thank you."

"Anytime, Mr. Devereaux."

Ignoring the girl's subtle come-on, Max marched through the kitchen and into the adjacent mudroom, then opened the back door and stepped out onto the porch. He heard them before he saw them—Yvonne and Jolie sitting side-by-side on the far end of the porch, their hips poised on the wide banister railing.

"Won't you even consider it, for Clarice's sake?" Yvonne asked.

Jolie shook her head. "Nothing short of my returning to Belle Rose on a permanent basis would satisfy Aunt Clarice, and that simply isn't going to happen."

"Then give her a few days. Surely you can put aside your dislike for your father's second family long enough to—"

"Dislike is too mild a word. I despise Georgette. And I don't trust Max. I'm afraid I can't disguise such strong emotions, not even for Aunt Clarice's sake."

"What about your sister? You can't possible hate Mallory."

"She's my half sister. And you're right. I don't hate her. With her having Georgette for a mother, I feel absolutely nothing for her but pity."

Max had two options—he could go back inside the house or he could make his presence known. Choosing the latter, he cleared his throat. The two women glanced his way. Yvonne slid off the banister railing. Jolie sat there staring at him.

"Yvonne, Mother would like a cup of mint tea," Max said. "Would you mind preparing it for her? She's in the front parlor."

"Yes, of course," Yvonne replied, then looked back

at Jolie. "You behave yourself. Remember you're a Desmond."

Yvonne passed Max and went straight inside the house. With Jolie's hostile gaze still boring into him, he moved toward her, one slow, deliberate step at a time. Before he reached her, she slid off the banister and onto her feet, then started to walk away. He reached out and grabbed her left wrist, halting her escape.

"Don't rush off," he said.

She jerked on her wrist, but he held fast. "Let go of me."

"Not just yet. Not until—"

She raised her right arm, lifting her hand in preparation for attack. Just as she swung at him, he grabbed her right wrist and manacled it to the left. They glowered at each other.

"My mother doesn't deserve your hatred and my sister doesn't need your pity."

She wriggled, trying to free herself, but to no avail. "I see I can add eavesdropping to your many sins."

"I don't care what you think of me or what you say about me," he told her, tightening his hold on her wrists and bringing them upward until he held them between their chests. "But if you hurt my mother or sister, you'll answer to me."

"Is that a threat?" She narrowed her gaze until her eyes were mere slits.

"Take it however you wish. I just want you to know that I protect what's mine."

"How very noble of you. Tell me, Max, does eliminating obstacles to your mother's happiness fall under the jurisdiction of protecting your own?"

Damn the bitch! She had all but accused him of murder. He released his tenacious hold on her. "You've learned to fight dirty, haven't you?"

"It's survival of the fittest in this world, isn't it? And believe me, I am a survivor. So, you'd better pray that my father didn't give me any power over your precious family, because if he did . . ." She smiled wickedly.

"A battle to the death?" he asked, already knowing the answer. Nothing would please Jolie Royale more than destroying his mother.

At eight o'clock that evening Garland Wells gathered the family in Louis's study. Yvonne served decaffeinated coffee and iced tea to those who wanted refreshments. When she started to leave the room, Gar reminded her to stay.

Every nerve in Jolie's body rioted. She wanted this night over with, and the sooner the better. Her father's will could change her life completely. It would either prove to her once and for all that he had cut her out of his life or it would give her the power to seek revenge.

Gar glanced around the room, then sat in the bourbon-brown leather chair behind Louis Royale's majestic Jacobean desk. "I believe we're all here."

"Are you saying that everyone in this room is mentioned in Louis's will?" Parry Clifton asked.

"That's right," Gar replied.

Jolie held her breath as Gar began to read the will, stopping occasionally to explain this or that. Louis Royale had left the bulk of his estate to his three children—Jolie, Mallory, and Max—to be equally divided among them. He had also left his business holdings to the three children, with the provision that Max continue in the leadership role he had held for several years now. He provided a fund for both Georgette and Clarice, sizable amounts to take care of all their needs for the rest of their lives. And to Yvonne, he had bequeathed the sum of one-hundred thousand dollars.

"And to my brother-in-law, Parry Clifton, I request that my stepson, Maximillian Devereaux, take care of his uncle as he sees fit, providing for him as is necessary."

"Why that old bastard," Parry grumbled.

"Shut up, Parry!" Georgette glared at her brother.

"You should be as outraged as I am," Parry told her. "Your husband should have left everything to you and you damn well know it. You gave him nearly twenty years of your life and this is how he rewards you—by leaving you a pittance!"

Max rose from his chair, grasped his uncle's arm, and said quietly, "Either sit down and be quiet or I'll take you out of here."

Parry looked Max square in the eyes, then reluctantly nodded. "Whatever you say, nephew. It seems that you're *The Man* now."

Max turned to Gar. "Continue."

"There are several charity donations and minor bequests," Gar said, "but the only other major bequest is Belle Rose."

A hushed silence descended over the room. Jolie wondered if it would be a sin to pray for something that could be the instrument of her revenge?

"Belle Rose was the property of my first wife Audrey Desmond's family for generations," Gar Wells read. "Upon my marriage to her, she and her sisters deeded the house to me in exchange for my restoring the house and grounds to their former glory. I have searched my soul and have come to the conclusion that the only fair and honorable thing is to bequeath Belle Rose—the house, furnishings, and acreage—to my elder daughter, Jolie Desmond Royale."

Chapter 7

"Dear Lord, no!" Gasping dramatically, Georgette clutched the bodice of her black silk dress, her hand centered over her heart.

"This is an outrage!" Parry Clifton rose to his feet, his face a bright red, his hands balled into tight fists.

"Daddy left our home to her?" Mallory glared malevolently at Jolie. "How could he do that?"

The room screamed with protests, filling the very air with indignation and disappointment. Jolie sat quietly, absorbing the reality of what Garland Wells had just said. Belle Rose was hers. In the end, her father *had* done the honorable thing.

"Oh, dear girl, Louis has given you a great gift," Clarice said, her cheeks slightly flushed and tears misting her eyes.

Jolie felt Max's gaze directed at her and was unable to resist looking at him. While his family ranted and raved at the injustice of Louis's bequest, Max sat solemnly, his body tense, his expression murderous. A shiver of apprehension quivered up Jolie's spine.

"Please, please," Gar called, and when the ruckus continued, he shouted, "There's a stipulation to this bequest."

Parry Clifton continued grumbling in a loud obnoxious tone. Georgette burst into tears and Mallory jumped up and headed for the door. Max shot out of his chair, grabbed Mallory before she could clutch the door handle, then whirled her around and shoved her back into her seat. After whipping out a white linen handkerchief from his pocket, he tossed it to his mother.

"Dry your eyes and blow your nose." He spoke to her with gentle authority, as if she were a child. Turning to his uncle, he clamped his hand on Parry's shoulder. "Sit down and shut up. Now." He emphasized the last word, his voice deep and low and commanding.

Immediately and obediently, Parry quieted, sat in the chair beside Georgette, then crossed his arms over his chest and stuck out his lower lip in a pouting, protesting gesture.

"Continue," Max told Gar. "What are the stipulations?"

Gar cleared his throat. "Louis left Belle Rose to Jolie Royale with the provision that his wife, Georgette, be allowed to live on the premises for as long as she lives."

Jolie's heart sank. Damn the old son of a bitch. He'd stuck it to her again. He'd given her what she wanted most, but he'd tied her hands to prevent her from wreaking havoc on his precious Georgette.

"And Mallory Royale and Maximillian Devereaux are to be allowed to remain on as residents of Belle Rose for as long as they choose." Gar drew in a deep breath, as if bracing himself for the next verbalization of righteous indignation.

Jolie had no intention of degrading herself with any sort of outburst. Let these low-class Cliftons reveal their lack of breeding. She was a Desmond and at this precise moment she had every intention of conducting herself as her female ancestors had done for generations—with pride and dignity. She needed time to think, time to speak to another lawyer, time to make decisions, time to deal with the intolerable situation in which her father had placed her.

"Does this mean we won't have to leave Belle Rose?" Georgette patted her damp face with Max's handkerchief.

"Yes, Mother," Max replied.

"Then even though she owns this place, she can't make us leave. Not ever. Is that right?" Mallory glared at Jolie, a triumphant smile curving her lips.

"That's right," Gar said.

Clarice rose from her chair, a soft pleasant expression on her face. "Isn't this wonderful? Everything worked out perfectly. We should celebrate Louis's wisdom and kindness."

Jolie stared at her aunt, uncertain whether to burst her happy we'll-all-live-together-harmoniously bubble or allow her to continue with the delusion. Poor Aunt Clarice. Maybe she was as loony as everyone else believed. If she thought for one minute that Jolie was going to share living quarters with Georgette's family— even on a temporary basis—then she was definitely living in a fantasy world.

Max helped his mother to her feet. "You've had a long day. You should go to bed early." He motioned to his sister. "Mallory, take Mother upstairs and help her get ready for bed."

"I'd be delighted." Mallory continued smiling at Jolie, obviously finding the irony of the situation quite delicious.

Parry Clifton headed for the door. Max called out to him, "Don't go running off to town tonight. I don't want to have to bail you out of jail again."

Parry's cheeks flushed. He grumbled under his

breath, then nodded and followed Georgette and Mallory out the door.

Clarice grasped Jolie's arm, then waved to Max. "Max, you must drive Jolie into town to the inn to pick up her car and her luggage." Clarice smiled at Jolie. "Your old room is all ready for you. Yvonne and I aired it out a couple of days ago and put fresh linens on the bed."

"Aunt Clarice, I won't be staying here tonight," Jolie said.

"Why ever not?"

"Clarice, I don't think Jolie is ready to come home to Belle Rose." Yvonne placed her hand between Clarice's shoulder blades and patted her soothingly. "Not quite yet."

"But this is her home. Louis willed Belle Rose to her." Clarice gazed at Jolie, puzzlement in her sad hazel eyes.

"Now don't pressure Jolie to do something she isn't ready to do," Yvonne advised. "Let her do things in her own way, in her own time."

"Well, I suppose . . ." Clarice's thin shoulders rose and fell as she sighed deeply. "It's just that I—"

Yvonne looked directly at Jolie. "Why don't you let me drive you into town after I see Clarice to bed and you can pick up your car and bags and come to my house tonight."

It was a compromise, one Jolie could live with and one that hopefully would pacify Aunt Clarice for the time being. She'd spend the night on Belle Rose property, just not in the house itself. "All right. Thank you, Yvonne. I think I will take you up on your hospitality."

"Good. Then that's settled." Yvonne patted Clarice on the back again. "You'll have her nearby tonight and you can see her in the morning." Yvonne gave Jolie a look that brooked no protest.

"Yes . . . yes," Clarice said. "I suppose that will be all right, won't it?"

"Jolie, why don't you wait for me on the back porch.

I won't be long." Yvonne took Clarice's arm and guided her toward the door.

Jolie nodded.

Gar Wells remained in the room, speaking quietly to Max. As she moved toward them, Gar turned to face her.

"It's good to see you again, Jolie," Gar said, extending his hand. "I just hate it was under these circumstances."

Jolie shook hands with him, then gasped when he put his arms around her and gave her an affectionate hug. He released her quickly and stepped back.

"It's good to see you again, too," she said. She couldn't blame Gar for the stipulations in her father's will. He would have had no choice but to obey his client's wishes. "Where's Sandy? I caught a glimpse of her at the funeral, but I didn't see her at the cemetery or at the reception."

"She had an emergency and had to rush off to the hospital right after the funeral," Gar said. "She took my car and is supposed to drop by tonight and pick me up. She phoned about an hour ago, so I'm expecting her any minute. You should hang around. I know she'd love to see you."

"I'd love to see her, too, but if I don't catch her tonight, tell her I'll call her."

Gar nodded. "I'll tell her." He glanced back and forth from Max to Jolie, then cleared his throat. "If either of you has any questions about . . . well, about anything pertaining to Louis's will, I'm at your disposal. Just let me know."

"I'll be in touch very soon," Jolie said.

The moment they were alone in the study, Max backed up to the desk, propped his hips on the edge, and crossed his arms over his chest. "So, where do we go from here?"

Pivoting around to face him, she huffed quietly. *Don't let him intimidate you,* she told herself. *Don't let him see your discomfort or your disappointment.* "I'm going to pick up my stuff at the inn and spend the night with Yvonne."

Max's lips twitched, as if he were going to smile but didn't. "And after tonight?"

"Why would I willingly reveal my battle plans to the enemy?" She smiled, the forced effort infusing her with determination.

Raising his eyebrows, he met her gaze head-on. "I take it that you don't see any way to compromise. You aren't willing to—"

"Accept the stipulations that your family be allowed to remain at Belle Rose?"

"This has been our home for nineteen years. This is the only home Mallory has ever known. Would you really throw your own sister out of Belle Rose?"

"Mallory is my half sister by blood, but she's your sister in every way that matters, not mine. I don't owe her anything. Hell, I don't even know her."

"And whose fault is that?" Max eased up and off the edge of the desk. "If you'd bothered to come home for a visit, you'd have had the opportunity to become acquainted with her. It's not too late, you know. It might take some effort on your part, but Mallory's a pretty good kid. Just a little spoiled, the way you were. You might find out that the two of you have quite a bit in common."

"I doubt that. Her mother is a Clifton. Mine was a Desmond." Jolie made the statement without giving it any thought whatsoever, then a moment later wished she'd controlled her vindictive response. Mallory couldn't help who her mother was.

The muscles in Max's jaw tightened; a vein in his neck bulged. "Twenty years away from Sumarville and as soon as you return you revert back to type, don't you? The high and mighty, better-than-everyone-else Desmonds." Max grunted. "Do you realize that Aunt Clarice is the only person living in Desmond County whose name is actually Desmond? You pure breeds are dying out fast and making room for us stronger, tougher mongrels."

"More's the pity." She practically spit the words at him.

He moved toward her, his gaze never leaving her face. Instinct warned her to run. Pure stubbornness forced her to stand her ground. If he thought she was afraid of him ... Maybe she was, but she'd never give him the satisfaction of letting him know. Jolie's heartbeat thundered in her ears.

He paused when only inches separated them. "Don't fuck with me, Miss Jolie, or you might wind up flat of your back and begging ... for mercy."

Heat rose inside her like flames from a roaring fire. Her muscles tensed; her nerves jangled. He was damn good at intimidation and there would have been a time, years ago, when she would have turned and run. But that had been a different Jolie. She didn't intimidate easily, not anymore. And she didn't run scared.

Jolie tapped her index finger in the center of Max's chest. "Don't bet any money on who's going to be doing the begging."

When she drew back her finger, Max suddenly circled her wrist with his big hand. Jolie resisted the urge to try to break free; instead she titled her head upward and leaned closer, her lips only a hairbreadth from his chin. Every feminine instinct she possessed became fully aware of Max's overwhelming masculinity. They stood there in her father's study, their bodies almost touching, their breaths mingling, their gazes locked in deadly combat—and neither of them would give an inch.

Like a couple of unyielding warriors daring each other, each determined to come out the winner, they tenaciously, stubbornly waited for the other one to surrender. Jolie thought she would scream, if he didn't break eye contact soon. A bold current of awareness sizzled between them. The tension wound inside her so tightly that she felt as if she'd fly apart, into a million pieces, with the least bit of provocation.

Moving unexpectedly, Max startled her when he grabbed the nape of her neck. She shuddered, as if he were the first man who'd ever touched her. Her mouth opened on a soft sigh.

She didn't know who moved first—and in the long run, it didn't seem to matter. He released his hold on her and they broke apart, each acting as if they had committed some horrendous crime. Perhaps they had. For one split second Max Devereaux had come very close to kissing her. And heaven help her, she would have kissed him back.

Jolie turned away from Max and forced herself not to run but to walk out of the room. *Don't you dare look back at him!*

Max didn't know what the hell had happened between Jolie and him, but whatever it was, he didn't like it. She'd been gone for a good five minutes and yet he still felt as if he'd been poleaxed square between the eyes. She was the last woman on earth he wanted to find attractive. Forget attractive. Alluring might be a better word. Or even seductive. What had he been thinking when he touched her? He might as well have jumped off a hundred foot cliff; it would have been less dangerous.

He'd wanted to kiss her. When he'd grabbed her by the neck, every primitive, masculine inclination within him had urged him to reach out and take her. The moment he touched her, he had known he'd made a mistake, a monumental mistake. He'd seen it there in her eyes—passion and acceptance. If he had kissed her, she would have returned his kiss.

"Why are you still in here?" Garland Wells stood in the study doorway. "Sandy just drove up. You should come out and say hello to her before we leave."

"Sure." Max stroked his jaw with his cupped hand.

By the time they reached the foyer, Sandy was coming through the front door. She smiled as she approached him, then opened her arms and enveloped him in a comforting hug. He wrapped his arms loosely around her.

"I'm so sorry that I didn't make it to the reception," she said. "I had a patient with a ruptured appendix. Things got dicey there for a while." Releasing her hold on Max, she reached down to clutch his hand, then glanced back and forth between Max and Gar. "So, how did things go here?"

"Louis did what he thought was right," Max said. "He tried to take care of everyone, but what he did was tie my family to Jolie from now until the end of our days."

"Oh?" She looked at her brother. "Where is Jolie?"

"Yvonne drove her into town to pick up her car and her suitcases," Gar said.

"Then she's coming back to stay at Belle Rose?"

"She's staying the night with Yvonne," Max explained. "What she'll do tomorrow is anybody's guess."

Sandy asked, "Want to tell me how Louis entangled Jolie with you and—"

"He willed Belle Rose to her." Max knotted his hands into fists, wishing he could smash something and partially vent his frustration.

"My Lord," Sandy said. "Does that mean y'all will be moving?"

Max shook his head. "Oh, no. Nothing so simple. Louis willed Belle Rose to Jolie . . . with the stipulation that Mother, Mallory, and I be allowed to remain in residence. And he split everything he possessed among Mallory, Jolie, and me."

Mallory came rushing down the stairs, then skidded to a halt when she saw her brother. "What's this, another legal pow-wow? I hope y'all are figuring out a way to make sure Jolie never sets foot in our house ever again."

Max surveyed his little sister from head to toe. She had changed out of her teal-green suit and into a pair of denim shorts and a yellow T-shirt emblazoned with the logo G.R.I.T.S.—Girls Raised in the South.

"I thought you'd be in bed by now," Max said.

"I couldn't sleep," she told him. "And before you ask, yes, I gave Mother a sleeping pill and stayed with her until she dozed off."

"Hello, Mallory." Sandy lifted her hand to wave.

"Hi, there." Mallory waved back at Sandy.

As his sister walked past him, he noticed a key ring in her hand. "Where do you think you're going?"

"For a ride. Okay? I need to get away for a little while. I thought I'd ride around. Get some fresh air. Get away from . . . I want to stop thinking about Daddy dying. And about how pitiful Mother is. And about how sorry for myself I'm feeling."

"I'd rather you didn't go out tonight," Max said. "It's after nine and—"

"Unless you hog-tie me, I'm going." Mallory gave him one of her determined, don't-try-to-stop-me stares.

"Don't be gone long," he told her. "If you're not home by eleven, I'll come out looking for you."

"Make it midnight, will you? I think you have more to worry about than my curfew. Big sister dearest is probably busy plotting ways to annihilate us." As Mallory passed Gar, she ran the tip of her bright pink fingernail over his cheek. "You'd better bone up on your law books before you have to face Jolie's high-powered Atlanta lawyer."

Mallory sashayed out the double front doors and onto the veranda. Within minutes Max heard the roar of her yellow Corvette as she gunned it and sped down the driveway.

* * *

R. J. had been in Sumarville just long enough to discover where the town's seedy underbelly was located. The backroom poker games. The cockfights. The phone number to call to buy a woman for a couple of hours. Life could be good for a guy like him, who'd just won two hundred bucks playing cards and had a hard-on he was looking to ease before the night was over. It was just a matter of finding the right dancing partner. He preferred his women experienced but not pros. He'd never paid a hooker in his life. He didn't need to; women usually flocked around him. Like bears to honey.

R. J. cruised down Main Street, the top off on his Jeep, the night air whipping his long hair into his face. He felt lucky. Damn lucky. He was twenty-three, healthy, and free as a bird.

Now, where could he find a good-looking gal on a Sunday night in Sumarville? The well-worn whores who frequented the hot nightspots weren't what he was looking for—not tonight. He wanted some sweet young thing with a knock-out body and just enough experience to know what she was doing.

The bright lights from the Dairy Bar a block up on the left, on Walnut Street, beckoned to him. Who knew, he might get lucky and find some preacher's daughter sipping a cherry cola and just hoping some dangerous man would take her for a wild ride.

R. J. turned right off Main Street and headed straight for the local teenage hangout, one of the few places in town open on a Sunday evening. He parked his Jeep, jumped out and ran a hand through his hair, then swaggered into the Dairy Bar. At the counter he ordered a burger, fries, and a Coke. All fluttering giggles, the girl who waited on him did everything to attract him, short of stripping naked and saying, "Take me now, big boy.'' She was definitely interested in him, but she wasn't his type. A bit too skinny and flat chested for his taste. He winked at her, figuring the harmless flirtation would make her day.

Taking his time in order to let the females look him over, he found an empty booth, set his food on the table, then slid into place. As he sipped on his cola, his gaze casually scanned the area. Already three good-looking babes were giving him the once-over. Two blondes and a redhead. What did he prefer tonight— vanilla or strawberry?

He could make the first move and take his pick, but the kind of girl he wanted was the kind who would come to him. So he waited. Acting cool, he began eating and made a bet with himself that he wouldn't finish his meal before one of the girls would come over and introduce herself.

In his peripheral vison he saw one of the blondes heading in his direction; the bosomy one with a heart tattoo on her shoulder.

''Hi, there.'' She all but purred as she sat down across from him. ''I'm Jamie Gambrell. I haven't seen you around before. You must be new in town.''

''Well, hello, there, Jamie.'' He flashed her one of his irresistible smiles. ''I'm R. J.''

''So, are you expecting somebody, like a girlfriend?'' she asked.

''I fly solo most of the time,'' he replied. ''It leaves me free to meet new people.'' He reached across the table and took one of Jamie's hands in his. ''Tell me, how old are you?''

She giggled. ''Nineteen. And I can prove it.'' She rummaged around in the small beaded bag draped over her shoulder and pulled out a driver's license. ''Here, take a look.''

R. J. checked out the license she handed him. He could usually spot a fake I.D. This one looked genuine.

Well, well, well. So, Miss Big Tits was legal. Yeah, he was lucky tonight and going to get luckier.

He tossed the license back to her. "There's not some burly country boy who's got a claim on you, is there?"

"There was," she said. "But we broke up a few weeks ago."

"Well, then, sweet thing, how'd you like to take a ride with me?"

"Where to?"

"I don't have to work tomorrow," he told her. "We could drive down to New Orleans and have us a real good time."

"New Orleans? You're kidding? Wow, I'd love to, but if I'm not home by one, my father would have the Highway Patrol out looking for me."

"Forget New Orleans. How about we ride around until we find someplace to park where we can look at the moon."

"Sure. As long as you have me home before one."

"No problem."

R. J. slid out of the booth, picked up his trash, dumped it, and then reached out and wrapped his arm around Jamie's waist. She waved to her friends who watched from a back booth.

"See y'all later," she hollered, then snuggled to R. J.'s side.

He was halfway to his Jeep when he saw *her*. Mallory Royale sat in her canary yellow Corvette, staring up at the sky, tears streaming down her cheeks. A damsel in distress, in need of a strong shoulder to cry on.

Remember, she's got a big brother who's already warned you to stay away from her. Yeah, yeah, sure. When had he ever been afraid of big brothers or fathers or boyfriends or even husbands? *But Max Devereaux is no ordinary big brother,* he reminded himself.

So, was he out of his mind? He already had a willing woman hanging all over him. If his guess was right, he'd have her panties off and her body penetrated five minutes after they parked on some dark secluded road. So why the hell did he want to take his chances with the princess over there? Because he liked a challenge and Jamie was easy prey?

R. J. stopped dead still and untangled himself from Jamie's clinging arms. "I see a friend of mine over there and she looks like she needs me." He gave Jamie a little shove toward the Dairy Bar. "Why don't you go back in there with your girlfriends and we can hook up another night."

"Huh?" Jamie stared at him, obviously puzzled by his sudden change of heart. "You mean Mallory Royale is a friend of yours?"

"Yeah, we're old friends."

"I thought you said you were new in town." Jamie planted her hands on her trim hips and glowered at R. J.

"I've been around long enough to make a few friends." He swatted her on the behind. "Go on. I'll look you up later."

Jamie swirled around and stomped back toward the Dairy Bar. R. J. sauntered over to the Corvette and stopped on the driver's side.

"Need some company, Miss Royale?"

Mallory gasped. By the surprised expression on her face, apparently she hadn't heard him approaching. "Mr. Sutton, is that you?"

"Call me R. J." He leaned forward just enough to reach her face, then wiped the tears from her cheeks with his fingertips. "You look like a lady who could use a friend right about now."

Mallory swallowed. Fresh tears gathered in the corners of her eyes. "I don't know what I need."

He opened the driver's door. "Get in the other seat," he said.

She stared up at him, then without questioning his request, she moved over the console and into the passenger seat. R. J. slid behind the wheel, turned the key in the ignition and revved the motor; then he fastened her seat belt before securing his.

"I know what you need," he told her. "You need me."

Chapter 8

Pleasant Hill had been in Garland Wells's family for six generations, the house built by slave labor in 1840, making it the oldest plantation house in Desmond County, predating even Belle Rose. As a boy Gar had loved living here, even if sometimes he hated being Roscoe Wells's son. Having a father despised by so many people had been difficult for Gar and Sandy when they were children. And as they grew to adulthood, their political and social views differed from those of their "former" white supremacist father, especially Sandy's. Once his baby sister left for college, she never lived at home again. Garland, on the other hand, had returned after law school to live in the family mansion with Roscoe, who had seemed terribly alone after Felicia's marriage to Max. Felicia had been their father's favorite child. Physically she had been as beautiful as their mother, but in every other way she had been her father's daughter. Sometimes it bothered Gar to think about the bad blood that ran in his veins—an insidious evil that went back generations. Somehow Sandy seemed to have escaped the curse of genetics, but Felicia hadn't. And Gar wasn't sure about himself.

Although he didn't kid himself that his father—the old racist leopard—had truly changed his spots, Gar liked to believe that if any small change of heart on Roscoe's part was genuine, it had been due to his influence. Gar considered himself a modern-thinking Mississippian, open-minded enough to accept that change was necessary, to realize that the great-great-grandchildren of slave owners had to coexist on equal terms with the descendants of slaves. That fact was simply part of a legacy that blacks and whites alike had to accept.

Sandy pulled her Lexus up in the driveway but didn't kill the motor. Garland undid his seat belt, then turned to his sister. With her short brown hair, dark brown eyes, and slender figure, Sandy was attractive, but not in the breathtaking way Felicia had been. However, what Sandy lacked in beauty, she made up for in brains and temperament. He had no doubt that the youngest Wells child had turned out far better than her elder siblings. Gar supposed he was a decent enough fellow, but he didn't possess Sandy's good heart. And Felicia, rest her soul, had been a first-class bitch.

"Aren't you coming in for a few minutes?" Gar asked.

Sandy harrumphed. "When pigs fly."

"It wouldn't hurt you to just come in and say hello," Gar told her. "After all, he is your father. And he's not getting any younger."

"You've tried that tactic numerous times. It hasn't worked before and it isn't going to work now or in the future. I washed my hands of that old reprobate a long time ago. I'm sorry that you're stuck with him, but that was your own doing."

Gar nodded, then leaned over and kissed Sandy's cheek. After opening the door, he stepped outside, then bent over and peered back into the car. "The inability to forgive your fathers for their sins is something you and Jolie seem to have in common."

"Jolie always was a smart girl." The corners of Sandy's lips lifted into an almost smile. "I hate I missed getting to talk to her after the funeral." Sandy sighed. "God, I remember when we were kids. Jolie and I were so close. I loved her—and liked her—far more than I ever did Felicia. She's one of the best friends I've ever had."

"If you befriend her now, you'll find yourself making an enemy out of Max. You'll have to choose sides."

Sandy nodded. "Yes, I know."

"We haven't loved wisely, have we?"

Gar slammed the door. As Sandy drove away, he stood in the driveway, watching her hasty departure. He didn't envy his little sister. As the attorney for both Louis Royale and Max Devereaux, the choice had already been made for him. Until he'd seen her again, he hadn't realized how much he'd hate not being on Jolie's side in this matter. But for Sandy, the choice would be even more difficult. Sandy had kept in touch with Jolie all these years and had visited her in Atlanta several times. And he was well aware of Sandy's feelings for Max. The poor girl had been in love with him for as long as Gar could remember. He'd never forget how bravely she'd faced Max's wedding to Felicia. Hell, she'd even served as Felicia's maid of honor.

But Sandy's feelings for Max weren't reciprocated and never would be. Gar understood, only too well, how tormenting love could be, especially a hopeless love. Sometimes it seemed to him that all three of the Wells siblings had been cursed at birth.

The double front doors opened onto the portico and light from the foyer blended with the two torchlights on either side of the entrance. Gar took a deep breath, then turned to face his father. Still wearing his white shirt and black trousers that had been part of his funeral attire, Roscoe inclined his head toward the fading red taillights of Sandy's Lexus.

"That girl was in a damn hurry to leave, wasn't she?" Roscoe cleared his throat, then spit into the nearby shrubbery. "You'd think, considering the way her mama raised her, she'd have the good manners to at least come in the house just to see how I'm doing."

Having learned in the past not to respond to his father's comments about Sandy, Gar climbed the steps to the front portico and laid his hand on his father's shoulder.

"Have you taken your medicine?" Gar asked.

"Yes, I've taken all those damn little pills that Mattie laid out for me. I swear she's the most aggravating woman. I'd fire her again, but I know it wouldn't do any good. You'd just hire her back the way you have the last five times I fired her."

Gar's firm touch urged Roscoe to turn and enter the house. "Mattie's a good, honest woman who does her job well. She'd be difficult to replace. Good housekeepers don't grow on trees."

"When I was a boy, families like ours had their pick of nig—" Roscoe laughed. "I've been trying to break myself of the habit for years and stop using that word, even in my own home. Don't want it slipping out at an inappropriate time. Might lose me some of my black voters." Roscoe entered the house, Gar at his side. "What I was saying is that when I was a boy, you had your pick of black women to do the domestic work. Most folks with our kind of money usually had at least four or five house servants. And in my papa's day, men in his position could get all the pussy they wanted from those gals."

Gar closed and locked the front door. "Those times are long gone, Daddy."

"Yeah, don't I know it." Roscoe sighed loudly.

"Are you going up to bed now?" Gar headed toward the stairs. No use correcting his father. No use wishing for the impossible.

"Hold up, there."

Gar glanced over his shoulder. "Do you need something?"

"Yeah. I need to know what happened at Belle Rose tonight," Roscoe said. "How did Louis divvy up things? And is that Miss Jolie Royale going to be staying around these parts for long?"

Gar slumped his shoulders. He could claim client/attorney privilege and refuse to answer, but Roscoe knew as well as he did that the terms of Louis's will would be common knowledge by this time tomorrow.

"Louis equally divided everything among Max, Mallory, and Jolie. He provided a trust fund for Georgette and Clarice. And he left Yvonne a hundred thousand dollars."

"Well, won't she get even more uppity than ever," Roscoe said. "That gal's always thought she was better than she was."

"Who are you talking about?" Gar asked.

"Yvonne Carter!" Roscoe spoke the name with contempt.

"Daddy, I don't know where you got such a notion. Yvonne is a nice woman and—"

"I know more about that pale-skinned, hazel-eyed witch than most folks." Roscoe waved his hand, dismissing the subject. "Enough about that. What did Louis do with Belle Rose?"

"He bequeathed it to Jolie."

Roscoe let out a long, low whistle. "Well, shit's going to hit the fan now. She'll kick the whole kit and caboodle of 'em out. Everybody except Clarice."

"She can't. There's a stipulation in the will that allows Georgette, Max, and Mallory to stay on at Belle Rose. Jolie can't kick them out."

Roscoe laughed. "I'll be damned. But maybe some good will come of it. Jolie won't stay in the house with Georgette, so she'll probably go back to Atlanta where she belongs."

"What difference does it make to you where Jolie lives?"

Roscoe rubbed his chin. "Personally, it don't make me no never mind. But Max is my son-in-law and I'd hate for that gal to cause him any trouble."

"Yeah, sure." Gar headed up the stairs, all the while wondering why his father wanted Jolie to leave Sumarville. What was the real reason? Not for one minute did he buy the explanation that Roscoe felt any great attachment to Max. Had the old scoundrel forgotten that when Felicia came up missing, he'd been the first one to accuse Max of murdering her?

R. J. turned the yellow Corvette off the main highway and onto a backroad that led to the river. A couple of weeks ago when he'd been exploring Desmond County, he'd found an ideal spot for parking. He'd already tried out the place a couple of times and found the women he'd brought here had thought the old picnic area was romantic. What was it with women that they had to pretend sex was the same thing as love and romance? Of course, he'd learned at a young age to use his knowledge about women's weakness for romance to his advantage. Moonlight, soft music, and a few well chosen words usually did the trick. Amazing how when you told a woman she was beautiful and that you'd never felt about another woman the way you felt about her, she'd spread her legs for you quick as a wink.

"Where are we going?" Mallory asked.

"Haven't you ever been down here? Haven't any of your boyfriends brought you parking at the river?"

"I don't go parking. My boyfriends take me to the movies or out to eat or they come to the house for supper. And if we want to be alone, there's all sorts of places at Belle Rose where two people can get off by themselves."

R. J. eased the 'Vette to a stop between two old cracked

concrete picnic tables that flanked the dirt road. "I don't think I'd be welcome at Belle Rose."

"Why do you say that?"

He shrugged. "I figure I'm not the type of guy your folks would let you date."

Mallory turned to him, her face lit by the moonlight, and R. J.'s sex tightened. Damn, she was gorgeous. With that black hair and those blue eyes she looked sort of exotic. He unsnapped his seat belt, leaned over, and brushed a flyaway strand of her hair away from her face. Allowing his fingers to linger, he caressed her neck and knew he'd hit pay dirt when he heard her indrawn breath.

"I guess all the guys tell you how pretty you are, don't they?"

She nodded. "My daddy says I'm his pretty little doll." She swallowed the emotion lodged in her throat as tears gathered in her eyes.

Hell! He hadn't brought her here to listen to her talk about her father. The kind of comforting he wanted to give her was the kind that would put a smile on his own face. Good loving always helped any bad situation, didn't it? It wasn't as if he were being totally selfish. He'd make sure she enjoyed it, too.

R. J. got out of the Corvette, rounded the trunk and opened the passenger door. "Your old man was right. You are a doll. A living doll."

She smiled. A crazy sensation hit R. J. square in the middle of his gut. He undid her seat belt, reached inside the car, and grabbed her hands, then tugged.

"Come on. Let's take a stroll by the river. If you want to talk, we can talk," he told her, while in the back of his mind he thought about finding a grassy spot where he could lay her down for some sweet loving. "And if you need a shoulder to cry on"—he patted his left shoulder—"I've got one available."

She went straight to him, right into his waiting arms. With one hand R. J. reached around her and closed the car door while his other arm circled her waist. He drew her to him, her breasts pressing against his chest.

Her breath caught in her throat as she gazed into his eyes. Ah, she was his for the taking. All he had to do was reel her in. Slowly. Carefully. An uncertain little fish like Mallory could be easily scared off. R. J. planted a lingering kiss on her forehead, a ploy to make her feel at ease, but also to make physical contact so that later when he tasted her lips, she wouldn't be taken by surprise.

Tilting his head, he gazed up at the night sky. "Just look at that moon. Another few days and it'll be a lover's moon."

Mallory glanced heavenward. "When I was a little girl, Daddy and I used to sit outside and study the stars. He knew the names and the locations. We hadn't done that in a long time." She grasped R. J.'s biceps tightly. "Nobody understands. I love Mother, but . . . not the way I loved Daddy. He always took care of me, but Mother needs taking care of herself."

With one arm draped around her waist, R. J. prompted her to start walking. As they strolled along the riverbank, Mallory continued talking, pouring out her heart, and R. J. made every effort to appear attentive and concerned. He told himself that she would remember, later on, how caring and comforting he'd been.

"Max just doesn't understand that I can't be strong the way he is," Mallory said. "He kept telling me that Mother needed me, that I should stay with her and take care of her. But how could I? Just being with her, listening to her cry and say over and over again that she doesn't know what she'll do without Daddy drove me crazy. Heck, I'm the child and she's the mother. Isn't she supposed to be the one looking out for me?"

"Yeah, that's usually the way it is," R. J. agreed. "But sometimes we get the short end of the stick when it comes to mothers."

Mallory paused, her gaze riveted to the dark flowing

river, the Mighty Mississippi that never slept. "Nobody else could possibly understand how I feel about losing Daddy. He wasn't really Max's father, you know. Just mine."

"I heard you had an older sister," R. J. said. "Don't you think she knows how you feel?"

Mallory jerked away from him, pulling completely free of his hold. "Don't call her my sister. Jolie hated Daddy because he married my mother. And I hate her. So does Max. She's probably glad that Daddy is dead." Mallory burst into tears.

Acting instinctively, without any thought of making brownie points, R. J. wrapped her in his arms and stroked her back tenderly. "Go ahead and cry. Get it out of your system."

He couldn't remember ever feeling so protective of another person. God help him, he wished he could ease her pain, take away the hurt. For the first time in his life, R. J. Sutton actually put someone else's needs before his own.

Damn it to hell! Things weren't turning out the way he'd planned, but the night didn't have to be a total waste. He could lay the groundwork for the future, maybe for a night next week when Mallory would be less inclined to talk and more inclined to make love. When he wanted something—and he wanted Mallory Royale badly—he was willing to wait.

The mantel clock struck ten times, the sound reverberating throughout Yvonne's small cottage. Jolie set her suitcase on a chair in the corner of the guest bedroom, a small space filled with antiques, several of which had belonged to the Desmond family in the past. An intricate vine-and-leaf design formed the headboard of a metal bed that had once been Jolie's great-grandmother's when she was a girl. Then there was the tall narrow highboy, its mahogany wood polished to a glowing shine; and the gilt-frame mirror in which she caught a glimpse of herself.

After kicking off her heels, Jolie lifted her skirt, grasped the waistband of her pantyhose, and tugged them down and off. She kicked them aside, then started to unbutton her jacket.

Yvonne knocked on the bedroom door, then called, "Jolie?"

"Yes?"

"I've poured us up some tea. Do you want me to bring yours to you or do you want to come out on the porch and sit with me for a while?"

What Jolie really wanted was to go to bed and get some sleep. But she knew that sooner or later, she'd have to talk things out with Yvonne. Might as well get it over with. "I'll be right out."

When she opened the door, Jolie found that Yvonne had already returned to the living room and now stood by the front door, a glass of iced tea in each hand. As Jolie approached her, Yvonne turned and smiled.

"It's cooled off quite a bit and there's a breeze stirring. Let's go outside and sit a spell."

"Sure." Jolie accepted the glass of tea Yvonne offered, then, barefoot, followed her outside onto the porch.

"Why don't you take the swing," Yvonne said, as she sat in one of the two wicker rockers. "I remember how you loved my swing when you were a little girl."

Jolie backed into the swing, eased down, and settled in. Just as she lifted the iced tea to her lips, she saw a car's headlights and then heard a vehicle coming up the long drive from the road. Yvonne watched the car's approach, an expression of concern on her face; but when the Ferrari came to a full stop at the side of the house, she sighed and smiled as she rose to her feet.

"It's Theron." Yvonne rushed to the edge of the porch and made it down two steps before her son got out of the car and met her.

"I wasn't expecting you," she said.

"I thought maybe I should drop by and see if you're angry with me for not making it over to Belle Rose this afternoon."

"I'm not angry," Yvonne told him. "But I am disappointed. Clarice kept asking where you were."

Glancing past his mother, Theron's gaze met Jolie's. He grinned when he recognized her. "I see somebody else has an aversion to Belle Rose."

Jolie set her glass on the nearby windowsill, then stood and rushed forward to greet Theron. He'd been her childhood friend, more like an older brother or a favorite cousin than the housekeeper's son. But by the time Gar Wells had warned Theron to keep his distance from Jolie and Sandy and Felicia, she and Theron had become aware of the vast differences not only in the color of their skins but also in their social positions in Sumarville. And once Theron left for college and she'd been shipped off to boarding school, they hadn't kept in touch.

When Jolie walked to the edge of the porch, Theron stepped up and held out his hand to her. She opened her arms and hugged him, prompting him to respond with equal affection.

"Never thought you'd come back to Belle Rose," he said, holding her hands between them and looking her up and down. "Little Jolie Royale all grown up. And looking like a Desmond."

"I am a Desmond," she replied.

"Half Desmond, half Royale." He studied her face for several minutes. "You look like your Aunt Lisette."

"Thank you. She was a beautiful woman."

"That she was."

Yvonne handed Theron her glass of tea. "You two sit and talk. I'll be right back. I'll get myself another glass of tea and bring out some cookies."

Theron refused the tea. "No, thanks."

"Well, I'll get the cookies anyway. I'm sure Jolie would like some to go with her tea."

The minute his mother went inside, Theron laughed. "She thinks we're kids again. Giving us orders and serving us tea and cookies."

"I'm glad you showed up when you did," Jolie admitted. "I'm pretty sure I was fixing to get another one of Yvonne's famous come-to-Jesus talks."

After releasing her hands, Theron followed Jolie to the swing and sat beside her. "Then I've saved you from a fate worse than death. Nobody, and I mean nobody, can give you a talking-to like Mama can. She has a way of making me feel about two inches high sometimes."

"Maybe you can help me. She's going to try to persuade me to make peace with that bunch of trash Daddy brought into Belle Rose. She and Aunt Clarice want me to play nice and act like a lady."

Theron chuckled. "Don't tell me that Jolie Desmond Royale grew up to be anything other than a lady."

"I'm my own kind of lady," Jolie said. "I'm not as socially conscious as the Desmond sisters were . . . as Aunt Clarice still is. I live my life the way I want to live it, with apologies to no one. And I'm afraid that I'm fixing to stir up trouble around these parts that's going to upset a lot of people."

"You sound just like Theron." Yvonne opened the screen door and came outside onto the porch. "My son has similar plans."

"Now, Mama, don't start in on me."

Jolie looked directly at Theron. "Just how do you plan to stir things up?"

"You first," Theron said. "What are you going to do, contest Louis's will?"

"For starters."

"Mercy, girl, why would you want to do that?" Yvonne asked. "You got a third of everything and one-hundred percent of Belle Rose. How much more do you want?"

Theron whooped and slapped his knee. "You mean you got Belle Rose? Heaven help Georgette Devereaux."

"Don't I wish," Jolie said. "Unfortunately, I can't

make her and her offspring vacate the premises. It seems Daddy put a stipulation in his will that they can remain at Belle Rose as long as they choose to.''

"What you need is a smart lawyer to figure out a way to make that stipulation go away.''

Jolie smiled broadly. ''Do you happen to know a smart lawyer who might be interested in representing me?''

"Stop this nonsense right now." Yvonne set her glass and the small plate of molasses cookies down on the wicker table beside her rocker, then turned and glowered back and forth from Jolie to Theron. "No good will come from the two of you plotting together." She narrowed her gaze on Jolie. "You should respect your father's wishes in this matter.''

"My father didn't respect my wishes, and he certainly didn't respect my mother's memory, did he, when he married Georgette?''

"Mark my word, the both of you, there's nothing but trouble ahead if y'all follow through with your plans." Yvonne shook her head sadly.

"I have a feeling your mother's talking about something other than your agreeing to act as my lawyer in this case," Jolie said. "Just what dastardly deed are you plotting?''

"Something that might be upsetting to you," Theron told her. "I don't want to hurt Mama or you or Clarice, but it's past time we all found out the truth.''

Adrenaline pumped through Jolie's body, preparing her for the worst. "The truth about what?" But she knew before he replied—the truth about the past, about the day her mother and aunt were murdered. The day Lemar Fuqua died. The day someone shot Jolie in the back and left her for dead.

"I'm going to do everything in my power to have the Belle Rose massacre case reopened. I intend to prove that someone other than my uncle Lemar was the real murderer, that he, too, was a victim.''

Suddenly Jolie realized that fate had played a hand

in her return to Sumarville. She had wavered between attending her father's funeral and simply sending an Atlanta lawyer to handle things for her. But at the last minute, something deep within her had urged her to make the trip. For the past twenty years she had strived to put the past behind her, to erase the memories of that day from her mind, to accept the fact that she would never remember anything more about those horrific events. But after all these years, it was what she didn't know that caused her the most anguish.

"I'll make a deal with you," Jolie said. "If you'll help me find a way to gain full control over Belle Rose, I'll stay in Sumarville and do everything I can to help you prove that Lemar didn't kill Mother and Aunt Lisette. You know I've always believed in his innocence."

Theron sucked in a deep breath. "You do realize that the real killer might still be alive, might still be living in Sumarville? He ... or she ... isn't going to take kindly to our investigating a murder that he thought he got away with."

"I understand what you're saying—you're warning me that the real killer might come after us, after me in particular."

"It's a dangerous thing you're talking about doing," Yvonne cautioned them again.

"Mama's right," Theron said. "Not only will we have the whole town against us, people who want to let sleeping dogs lie, but we could be risking our lives."

Did she have the courage it would take to stay in Sumarville, to face the ghosts from her past, to risk her life?

"I realize the danger," she said.

"So, do we have a deal?" Theron searched her face for an answer.

With steely determination, Jolie looked Theron squarely in the eyes. "We, my old friend, most definitely have a deal. So what do we do first?"

"The first thing you do tomorrow morning is move

into Belle Rose," Theron advised. "Move in, take over, and shake things up a bit. I'll speak to Gar Wells and get a copy of Louis's will, just to make sure, but I'd say you're within your legal rights to do anything you want with or to the land, the house . . . and the residents. Short of throwing them out."

A sadistic glee rose inside Jolie at the thought of making life a living hell for Georgette. Having Jolie living at Belle Rose, assuming the ownership in a personal way, was bound to upset the entire household. "Okay, that's the first step in my acquiring full control of Belle Rose, so what's our first step in getting the murder case reopened?"

"I've already done some preliminary work. I have a meeting set up with the D.A. and the sheriff tomorrow afternoon," Theron told her. "If you go with me, your presence alone should carry a lot of weight with both men."

"Tell me the time and the place and I'll be there."

Theron smiled. "Ms. Royale, I think you and I will make a formidable team."

"Mr. Carter, I agree wholeheartedly."

When the two shook hands, Jolie caught a glimpse with her peripheral vision of the horrified look on Yvonne's face.

Chapter 9

With visions of sweet revenge swirling through her thoughts, Jolie hadn't been able to fall asleep until well after midnight. Admittedly she had mixed feelings about moving into Belle Rose, even if only for a few weeks—a month at most. She hoped that if Theron hadn't been able to find a way to legally remove the trash from her ancestral home by then, her deliberately annoying presence would have prompted them to leave. Executing a thousand-and-one demented little torments would give her great pleasure and no doubt send Georgette screaming from the house. Patience, she cautioned herself. Rome wasn't built in a day, and getting rid of vermin would take time and effort.

Jolie popped the last bite of an apple-and-raisin muffin into her mouth, then washed it down with a sip of coffee. She'd slept later than she had intended, but at least she'd missed another lecture from Yvonne, who undoubtedly still arrived at Belle Rose by six-thirty every morning, just as she had in the past. But she'd left Jolie coffee, muffins, and a note.

> *Think long and hard before you follow through with your plans to remove your father's family from Belle Rose. I'm afraid that you'll be the one to suffer in the end, and I can't bear the thought of your discovering, too late, that you were wrong.*

Dear, sweet, forgiving Yvonne, so much like Aunt Clarice. She was the type of person who would do almost anything to avoid trouble, to maintain peace. But peace came at too high a price for Jolie—and for Theron. By combining forces they could, hopefully, achieve two goals: return full control of Belle Rose to the youngest remaining Desmond descendant and prove that someone other than Lemar Fuqua was responsible for the Belle Rose massacre.

Jolie tossed her suitcase into the back of her Escalade, then hopped in the driver's seat and started the engine. Reaching inside her purse, she felt around until her fingers encountered the small, sleek cell phone. She punched the button to dial Cheryl's home number, placed the telephone to her ear, then shifted the SUV's gears into reverse. By the time she turned the vehicle around and headed down the road to her family's plantation house, Cheryl answered on the fifth ring.

"Hello."

"I'm glad I caught you before you left for work," Jolie said.

"Jolie?"

"Yes. Now, listen. I'm not returning to Atlanta today as I'd planned. As a matter of fact, I'm going to be stuck here for a few weeks, and I need for you to handle things in my absence."

"What's wrong?"

"Nothing really. Just a snag that's going to take some time to fix."

The back side of the mansion came into view as Jolie turned the curve in the paved road. Twenty years ago the path from Yvonne's cottage to the main house had been gravel. Admittedly, she felt strange and somewhat out of place being back in Sumarville. But an eerie familiarity suddenly possessed her.

She was going home. Moving in. And taking over!

Was she really prepared to give up her life in Atlanta, even temporarily—her friends, her daily contacts at the office, her hands-on approach with her business—to right the wrongs from twenty years ago? Why couldn't she just let Georgette stay on at Belle Rose? And what did it matter now, after all this time, whether Lemar had been framed for murder? Was she insane to put her life on hold for the chance to wreak havoc on her stepmother? And was she truly brave enough to face the possibility that Lemar was innocent, and out there somewhere the real murderer might do anything to stop Theron—and her—from instigating a new investigation?

"I'll set up a home office as soon as possible," Jolie told Cheryl. "I'll be working from Belle Rose until . . ." *Until I run Georgette out of my mother's house. Until Theron can convince the district attorney to reopen the case.* "I'm hoping I won't be here longer than a few weeks, but if necessary, I'm prepared to stay a month . . . or two." *Please, God, not that long!*

"A month or two!" Cheryl all but screamed. "What the hell is going on? You didn't even want to go home for your father's funeral and now you're telling me that you're going to move in with your stepmother. What's wrong with this picture?"

"I've got to go," Jolie said, as she parked her SUV in the drive at the back of the house. "I'll call you

tomorrow and fill you in on all the details. Right now,
I'm fixing to claim my property.''

The entire family, even Uncle Parry, was at the table
when Mallory dragged herself downstairs and into the
dining room. Her mother insisted that meals always be
served in the dining room, something Aunt Clarice had
told her was proper etiquette. As much as she loved the
old loony bird, as Uncle Parry called her, Mallory wished
that her mother didn't set such great store by what
Clarice Desmond deemed appropriate or ruled unsuit-
able. She had once complained to her father about how
Aunt Clarice, who really wasn't her aunt, wasn't even
any blood kin to her, seemed to make all the rules.
He'd hugged her and reminded her that her mother
had always been insecure because she'd been born very
poor and that more than anything Georgette longed to
be a genteel Southern lady.

How ridiculous! She'd thought so then and she
thought so now. What difference did it make what other
people thought? The Royales were rich, weren't they?
Her daddy had been one of the most powerful men
in Mississippi, hadn't he? And this was the twenty-first
century, not the nineteenth. Family lineages, Civil War
ancestors, and traditions from a world long since gone
weren't what people thought was important these days.
Money and power were what mattered. Why couldn't
her mother understand that? Max understood. He'd
once told her that he'd learned from her daddy that
people overlooked a lot of deficits in a man's background and personality if he wielded enough power.
Now that Daddy was gone, Max would take over her
father's powerful position, wouldn't he?

"You shouldn't come down to breakfast in your pajamas, especially such skimpy pajamas," Georgette
scolded.

Skimpy? A see-through teddy was skimpy. A pair of butt-floss panties was skimpy. A bikini that was little more than a thong and pasties was skimpy. Mallory yawned and stretched, then glanced down at her satin boxer-shorts and camisole top. With a smart-aleck remark on the tip of her tongue, she suddenly felt Max's heated glare zeroing in on her. She glanced at him, saw the expression of forewarning on his face, and quickly rethought her response. Of course Max was right— her mother deserved respect. And Georgette was more fragile than usual now, so soon after Daddy's death.

"I can go back upstairs and put on something else," Mallory offered.

"That's all right, dear," Georgette said. "We'll overlook it this morning."

"Thank you, Mother."

Mallory stared directly at Max. His lips twitched, the corners lifting slightly. He'd come very close to smiling at her. Poor Max. He didn't smile much, especially not lately.

"So, when are you meeting with Gar to see about getting something done about Louis's will?" Parry asked his nephew, then filled his mouth with a spoonful of grits.

Mallory felt the tension at the table. From Max. From her mother. And from Aunt Clarice. She wished that Jolie Royale would drop off the face of the earth. Why had Daddy left a third of everything he owned to her? Why had he left Belle Rose to her? Jolie had been cruel to Daddy, treating him badly all these years, refusing to ever come visit.

"I think Gar should explain to a judge how Jolie treated Daddy, that she's been mean and spiteful ever since Daddy married Mother." Mallory sauntered over to the buffet, where the silver serving trays filled with breakfast items awaited her. "She has no right to anything, least of all Belle Rose. This is my home, not hers."

"Technically, this house is hers," Max said. "Not only did Louis bequeath it to her, but the home originally belonged to her mother's family."

"What difference does that make?" Parry split a biscuit and dribbled honey over the two halves. "This place would have rotted down years ago if Louis hadn't put a lot of money into restoring it. Louis should have given this place to Georgette."

"No, he shouldn't have," Georgette said. "I wouldn't have felt right if he'd left Belle Rose to me. But . . . well, I had hoped that perhaps he'd leave it to Mallory."

Mallory placed two strips of bacon on a small plate, then poured herself a tall glass of orange juice and returned to the table. "I agree with Uncle Parry. Daddy should have given the house to you, Mother. After all, you were his wife." Mallory plopped down in the chair beside her brother. "You are going to make sure Jolie doesn't get to keep Belle Rose, aren't you?"

Clarice cleared her throat. All eyes turned to her. Oh, shit! Mallory had forgotten that Jolie was Aunt Clarice's niece, her real niece, and that it was her family that had once owned Belle Rose.

"Sorry, Aunt Clarice," Mallory said. "But that's the way I feel."

"Of course you have a right to your opinion." Clarice folded her white linen napkin and laid it beside her plate. "But before y'all take any steps to have Louis's will contested, you might want to consider the fact that Jolie could well be contemplating doing the same thing."

"What?" Georgette shrieked.

"She wouldn't dare," Parry said.

"What would she have to contest?" Mallory asked.

"Our family's right to remain living here at Belle Rose." Max lifted his cup and took a sip of coffee. So calm. So cool and unemotional. That was her big brother. He never let anything get to him. Sometimes she wondered if he was susceptible to normal human emotions the way the rest of them were.

"Damnation! I wouldn't put it past her, the vindictive little bitch." Parry speared his scrambled eggs with his fork. "She'd just better think again if she thinks she can run us off."

"Really, Parry, such language." Georgette groaned. "And in front of Mallory."

"Don't mind me." Mallory grinned. Her mother often treated her as if she were still ten years old.

"I don't appreciate your referring to Jolie in such terms." Clarice frowned at Parry. "I don't agree with my niece's opinion of Georgette, but I do understand why she feels the way she does. I believe if y'all will meet her halfway and give her a chance to get to know each of you, she'll realize how wrong she's been all these years. And if that happens, there won't be any need for y'all to protest Louis's will."

Poor Aunt Clarice. She always thought the best of everyone. Mallory doubted if Clarice had ever disliked anybody. But didn't she realize it was too late to mend fences with Jolie? There had been a time when Mallory had longed to meet her older sister, had even dreamed of the two of them becoming friends. But that was before she'd learned the truth about what Jolie thought of their father's second family.

Jolie entered the house through the back door, but instead of going into the kitchen, she paused in the mudroom and peeped inside at Yvonne. Busy cleaning up from breakfast preparation, Yvonne didn't notice her, so she mimicked a cough, which instantly gained her Yvonne's attention.

"Jolie!" After wiping her hands on her apron, Yvonne hurried across the room to the open door. "What are you doing slipping in the back way?"

"I want to surprise the family. Are they still at breakfast?"

"As far as I know everyone is in the dining room."

"Then there's no time like the present for me to say hello and tell them that I'm moving in this morning."

"Theron shouldn't have advised you to move into the house and cause trouble. I think you're making a big mistake."

Jolie shrugged. "Maybe. But I don't think so."

"At least let me warn them that you're here," Yvonne said.

Jolie grabbed her wrist. "No need to do that." When Yvonne gave her a condemning look, she immediately let go of her. "I'll announce myself."

Jolie smoothed her hands over her hips before squaring her shoulders and taking a long deep breath. As she released her indrawn breath, she deliberately avoided the kitchen—a room she preferred to never enter again—and instead exited the mudroom through the door that led into the hall. The dining room was only a few steps away, on the left. Low voices flowed down the corridor. Unfamiliar voices. Then suddenly she heard a deep baritone that she vividly recalled.

"Louis put all of us, including Jolie, in a bad situation. I'm sure he thought he was doing what was best for all of us," Max said. "You know how Louis was, always wanting to take care of everyone he cared about and to make sure his actions were fair."

"Was it fair for him to leave Belle Rose to Jolie?" Mallory asked.

Jolie realized that now was the ideal moment to make them aware of her presence. Mallory had given her the perfect cue. Jolie crossed the threshold and walked into the dining room as if she lived there, as if they should have been expecting her to join them for breakfast.

"Yes, I think it was quite fair that Daddy left Belle

Rose to me." Jolie smiled when they all gasped in unison and turned to glower at her. Everyone except Max. Such a delicious sensation to see the shock on Georgette's face, the hostility in Parry's expression, the surprise in Mallory's eyes, and the cold, controlled anger etched in Max's strong features as he finally turned to look at her. "What I think was unfair is that he gave me no choice but to allow all of you to stay on here, regardless of how I might feel about it."

"Jolie!" Clarice scooted back her chair and jumped up. "My dear girl, we had no idea you were here."

Her aunt came forward to greet her, arms open wide. Jolie offered Clarice an affectionate embrace, then released her and strolled over to the buffet. With a silly little smile on her face, Clarice returned to the table. Totally disregarding the others, Jolie lifted a plate and filled it with bacon, eggs, fried potatoes, and two biscuits. Then she poured steaming black coffee in a china cup and added a liberal amount of cream. She recognized the china and silverware; both had belonged to her family for well over a hundred years.

Jolie wasn't the least bit hungry, but what did that matter? She intended to start her takeover of Belle Rose the right way—by *breaking bread* with her deadly enemies. Despite how much she loathed the idea of dining with this bunch, she had every intention of joining them for all the family meals, which was sure to curb everyone's appetite.

"Well, you've got your nerve." Narrowing his gaze, Parry directed his attention directly on Jolie. "Nobody invited you for breakfast."

Jolie placed her plate and cup on the table. "Now, now, *Uncle* Parry, with that tone of voice someone might think you don't like me." She pulled out the chair next to Clarice. "Besides, I hardly need an invitation to have breakfast in my own house."

"Naturally, Jolie is welcome here at Belle Rose."

Georgette looked directly at Jolie and smiled. "We're delighted that you could join us for breakfast this morning."

Mallory groaned. "Honest to God, Mother, give the Southern belle routine a rest, will you?" Mallory scowled at Jolie. "What are you doing here? What do you want?"

Under different circumstances, Jolie would have admired Mallory's spunk, a trait they shared. But the fact that they were half siblings didn't alter another more important fact: Mallory was one of them—the enemy. "My, my, little sister, where are your manners?"

"Screw you." Mallory stuck her tongue out at Jolie. Such a childish act. Jolie laughed.

"Behave yourself," Max told Mallory, his tone even and totally unemotional; then he glanced at Jolie. "Disregarding Mother's oversolicitous attitude and Mallory's hostile one, would you mind telling us exactly what you're doing here?"

Jolie sat, picked up a fork and took several bites from her plate. After swallowing, she offered Max an eat-dirt-and-die smile. "Why, I'm eating breakfast, of course."

"Other than the obvious, why are you here?" Max asked.

All eyes focused on Jolie. Oh, she had them worried. Every last one of them. Even the cool-and-collected Maximillian. His unruffled attitude didn't fool her. He despised her as much as the rest of his family; he was just more adept at masking his feelings.

Jolie lifted the cup to her lips and sipped Yvonne's delicious coffee. Eyeing Max over the rim of the gold-trimmed china cup, she said, "I've decided to move in with y'all. I've got my suitcase outside in the car."

"You can't move in!" Mallory cried.

"Call Gar immediately!" Parry shouted.

"You intend to stay here with us?" Georgette's

cheeks flushed. "Of course, you're welcome. You're Louis's daughter and this has always been your home." She glanced at her son. "Max, you must go outside and get Jolie's luggage." She looked back at Jolie. "You'll probably want to stay in your old room, won't you?"

Mallory shot up out of her chair, stomped her foot and growled. "Damn it, Mother, stop this right now! Why are you being so polite to her? She has no right to stay here. This is our home."

Jolie continued sipping her coffee. When no one replied to Mallory's outburst, she turned and ran from the dining room.

"Hell, Max," Parry said, "do something."

Max eased back his chair, stood, walked around the table, and yanked back Jolie's chair, just enough so that he could grab her arm and pull her to her feet. Tilting her chin upward, she glared at him, but made no effort to jerk free of his tenacious hold. He was spitting mad, but only the slight throbbing of a vein in the side of his neck even hinted of the rage boiling inside him. Provoking Max was like poking a stick at a rattlesnake—sooner or later he'd bite you if you didn't kill him first. But God help her, she loved irritating the man. Loved seeing him sweat, albeit invisibly.

"I think we need to talk," Max said. "Privately. In the study."

Jolie looked pointedly at her wrist trapped in his grasp. "Do you intend to drag me there?"

"If necessary."

She would call his bluff if she thought he was bluffing; but he wasn't. There was no doubt in her mind that he'd pick her up and carry her out of the dining room, if she didn't go with him peacefully.

"Then by all means, let's talk privately." She tugged on her arm.

He didn't release her immediately, as if weighing his options, trying to decide the wisest course of action. He loosened his hold just enough for her to pull free. With a wide, gracious sweep of his hand, Max urged her into action. Taking the lead, Jolie headed for the doorway, Max only a few steps behind her.

"Kick her ass out of here," Parry called after them.

"Parry, will you, please, stop being so hostile," Clarice said. "You're not helping the situation with your ugly outbursts."

Once in the hallway, Jolie kept walking, but couldn't resist saying, "Is that what you intend to do—kick my ass out of here?"

"Believe me, that's what I'd like to do," Max told her. "Unfortunately, you have every legal right to live in this house. I just can't figure out why you'd want to."

Jolie rounded the corner, opened the study door, and breezed into the room that had once been her father's private domain. Even now, with Louis Royale dead and buried, this paneled den was filled with his spirit, as if at any moment he might return to sit behind the massive desk or smoke his pipe while resting in one of the huge wing chairs. Memories of childhood moments in this room washed over her, moving her swiftly through time, back to when she'd been her daddy's little darling. Jolie shook her head, attempting to dislodge such senseless reminiscing. *This is what you'll be up against, if you stay here. Memories from the past, both good and bad. The kitchen where you found your mother's body is still there; the room where you were shot and left for dead. And upstairs, the landing where Aunt Lisette died is waiting for you when you go up to your old room.*

"Sit or stand?" Max asked.

"What?" Her mind was still fuzzy with thoughts of the past.

Max shrugged. "We'll stand."

She nodded. Max looked as if he belonged in this

room, as if it were as much his as it had been her
father's. Aunt Clarice had told her that Max had
become a true son to Louis. How happy that must
have made Georgette.

"Why are you moving in here?" Max asked.

"Truthfully?"

"That would be nice."

Jolie smiled. "Why am I moving into Belle Rose
today?" She laughed, the sound a throaty mocking
chuckle. "Because I can. And there's nothing anyone
can do to stop me."

Chapter 10

Max had the overpowering urge to grab Jolie and shake her until her teeth rattled. He remembered her as a girl, running barefoot all over Belle Rose, riding her mare bareback, swimming in the pond on hot summer days. She'd been little more than a child, just a rebellious, pampered, undisciplined teenager—a great deal like Mallory. Both of them had been spoiled at a young age by a father who adored them. How many times had he listened to Louis talking about Jolie, always with a mixture of joy and sadness? She had broken her father's heart by refusing to ever see him again after he remarried. Over the years, Max had grown to dislike Jolie intensely. He thought of her as an uncaring daughter who hadn't matured enough to understand and forgive human frailties. The more he'd loved Louis, the more he'd hated Jolie.

Now, here she was, home at Belle Rose, where Louis had longed for her to be. But she hadn't returned to make an old man happy. Too late for that now. No, she was here for revenge. And apparently she was still spoiled and undisciplined—with no regard for the feelings of others.

"You do realize that while you're making everyone else miserable, you're not likely to be anything but miserable yourself."

Jolie shrugged. "It's the price I'll have to pay."

"What's wrong with you?" he asked. "Is your life in Atlanta so dull and meaningless that you'd rather stay here, live at Belle Rose, just to disrupt our lives?"

"What makes you think that my decision to live at Belle Rose has anything to do with you ... or with anyone else who lives here?" Jolie plopped down in one of the wing chairs, making herself right at home.

"Give me one good reason, other than the one I've stated?" Max sat on the edge of the desk, then crossed his arms over his chest.

"Oh, my. So big and bad and dangerous." Jolie placed her open palms on her cheeks and rounded her eyes, mimicking fear. "You're so intimidating. Should I be trembling?"

"You have no idea how dangerous I can be."

"Is that a threat?" Jolie met his menacing gaze head-on.

Damn her, she was daring him to prove himself. He was unaccustomed to having others stand up to him. Usually his killer stare was enough to make even the biggest, meanest son of a bitch back down. After all, Maximillian Devereaux had a reputation as a man you didn't dare cross. So why was this sassy-mouthed woman unafraid? Didn't she realize that he could break her in half with his bare hands?

Max eased off the desk, stood and walked over to her, then leaned down and grasped the chair arms on either side of Jolie. She swallowed hard, a hint of uncertainty in her eyes; but she didn't break eye contact, nor did she show any sign of real fear.

"It's a warning. I will not allow you to torment my mother or constantly aggravate my sister."

His gaze clashed with Jolie's. What he saw in her eyes was bullheaded determination. They were going to do battle. War between them was inevitable. His gut instincts warned him that she was no more likely to give an inch than he was, so this would be a fight to the finish. *To the death.*

She lifted her face until they were eye-to-eye, their noses almost touching, only a hairbreadth between them. "Just how do you plan on stopping me? By killing me? I've heard the rumors, you know. About your killing your wife. Poor Felicia. And about how some people believe you might have killed my mother, so yours could marry my daddy and move into Belle Rose. Tell me, Max, have you already tried to kill me once?"

She realized, too late, that she'd gone too far in her taunting. Pure rage burned in Max's blue-gray eyes. Anger stained his cheeks. His nostrils flared and he snorted, like a bull preparing to charge. She opened her mouth to speak, to admit that she'd overstepped the bounds; but before she could utter a word, Max grabbed her by the shoulders, lifted her out of the chair and shook her. Roughly. Several times. She gasped for air, then finally managed to cry out as his big hands bit into her upper arms. Instantly he loosened his grip and shook her one last time, but with less force. Tears lodged in her throat, threatening to erupt at any moment; but she willed herself to remain calm and not show him any fear. Her gaze connected with his and what she saw in his eyes at that moment surprised her. Pain. An agonized, tortured expression.

Had she hurt him with her thoughtless accusations? Was it possible that Max Devereaux was capable of ordinary human feelings? If you pricked him, would he actually bleed?

"Damn you!" His chest lifted and fell heavily with his labored breathing.

"Max, I—"

He released her so abruptly, shoving her slightly in the process, that she almost lost her balance. "Move into Belle Rose at your own risk."

"Another warning?" Now, why hadn't she just kept her mouth shut? What was it about Max that made her want to antagonize him? Was it because, despite the fact that she intensely disliked him, hated his mother and resented his whole damn family, she'd never gotten over her teenage infatuation? *Face it, you find him devastatingly attractive, but you know that he's the last man on earth you should want.*

"Keep it up, *chère*, and you'll find out." Without another word, Max turned and walked out of the room.

Jolie released a long strained breath, feeling as if she'd narrowly escaped the full effect of Max's wrath. Sooner or later things would come to a head between them. Later, she hoped. She needed time to build her strength, to prepare herself. During the years she'd lived away from Belle Rose, she had fought more than her share of battles, many of them emotional; as a businesswoman, she had faced, fought, and bested worse bastards than Max. But she had never locked horns with an opponent who was capable of murder.

But was Max really a murderer? Did she truly believe that he was responsible for the Belle Rose massacre? And what about the unsolved mystery surrounding Felicia's death? Twenty years ago she would have defended Max with her whole heart. But she had been young, foolish, and hopelessly enamored with the brooding bad boy. Now she was older and wiser and didn't put her trust in others so easily. Just because she was still attracted to Max didn't mean she should let down her guard. She had no reason to believe in his innocence, no reason not to consider him a prime suspect.

* * *

"Well, what did he say?" Parry demanded as he paced the floor in his sister's sitting room. "Does he have a plan to get rid of her? Has he contacted Gar?"

Reclining on the white silk-tufted chaise longue in her white-and-beige sitting room adjacent to the bedroom she had shared with her husband, Georgette sipped leisurely on her afternoon iced tea. On these hot, humid summer days, she did so enjoy these little luxuries. Ignoring Parry, she glanced around, taking note of her opulent surroundings. She'd have to redecorate these rooms soon, once an appropriate amount of time had passed. Louis's presence was unbearably strong in her boudoir.

"Are you listening to me?" Parry asked.

Georgette did so wish that Parry would leave her alone. She'd had a most disturbing morning and her nerves were simply frayed. But knowing her brother as she did, she didn't doubt that he'd keep pestering her until she responded. In some ways, Parry was like a pesky mosquito buzzing around, driving a person crazy. Naturally she loved Parry. He was her only sibling. And growing up more or less orphans in New Orleans—with their mother dead and their father a worthless drunk—they had found ways to keep body and soul together. They had done what they'd had to do. She was horribly ashamed of her past and prayed that no one would ever learn the truth about Georgette Clifton, who'd been a whore at thirteen. When she was eighteen, one of her clients, Philip Devereaux, who visited New Orleans several times a year, fell in love with her. She had been fond of Philip, but she'd been incapable of loving anyone. Not then. Not until years later. Not until Louis.

"Answer me, damn it, woman!" Parry got right up

in Georgette's face. "Jolie Royale is the fly in our honey. We've had it made all these years. Louis was a generous man. And completely devoted to you. But mark my word, that gal is trouble. She wants us out of Belle Rose and she won't stop until she's taken away everything we've got."

"But she can't take away . . . Louis protected me . . . protected all of us. He left my children two-thirds of his estate."

As if he hadn't even heard her, Parry grumbled, "Max needs to get rid of her. I'd be more than happy to help him dispose of her body. Maybe toss her in the river. She'd make good fish food."

"Parry! You're talking crazy. Max would never . . . Just hush up such nonsense. If anyone should hear you, it might resurrect all those ugly speculations that surfaced when Felicia died."

"What do you think, Georgie? Do you think your son killed his not-so-loving and unfaithful wife?"

"No, I most certainly do not. Max is a good man. A devoted son. He may have a violent temper, but he keeps it under control."

"Yeah, he controls his temper . . . most of the time. But I've seen him come close to losing it completely, and so have you. When he gets all closed-off and brooding, don't you ever wonder if he inherited a weakness for evil from his father?"

"Philip Devereaux was kindness personified," Georgette said. "The man didn't have an evil bone in his body."

A hint of scorn tinted Parry's loud boisterous laughter. "Hell, Georgie, I wasn't referring to Philip. I was talking about Max's biological father."

"Philip was—"

"Philip was the sap who married you and made an honest woman of you, but he didn't sire that Black Knight son of yours and we both know it."

Georgette would not listen to another word. How dare Parry bring up ancient history. Now, of all times, when the family should stand united, presenting themselves in the most favorable light possible. To the community. And to Jolie.

"Hush up such stupidity," Georgette told her brother. "What if someone should overhear you? I've forbidden you to ever discuss anything about our lives before we came to Sumarville. And you promised me you'd keep our secrets."

"I've never breathed a word. Not to a soul. Not even when I've been . . . when I've had a little too much to drink. At least as far as I know." He chuckled, a mirthless, guttural *haw, haw, haw.* "Hell, you don't think I'd want people knowing what I did when I was a kid, do you?"

Georgette reached out and grasped Parry's soft smooth hand. The hand of a man who hadn't done any physical labor in many years. Neatly manicured nails proclaimed him to be a gentleman. But she knew better. Beneath the polished exterior that Parry presented to the world, her baby brother was gutter scum, just as she was.

"Max has gone to the office today," she said. "He's meeting Gar for lunch to discuss our options. And until we have some legal way of dealing with Jolie, we are going to make her welcome at Belle Rose. Do I make myself clear? She is Louis's daughter and I will not allow anyone in this house to mistreat her."

"You really mean that, don't you?" Parry gazed at her, puzzlement in his eyes. "You know, Georgie, sometime during the past forty years you've turned into a lady. A real lady."

Just because Jolie was back in Sumarville, there was no reason to panic. Even if she stayed for a while, what difference would it make? She doesn't remember seeing me that day. She has no way of knowing what I did. If she could have, she would have identified me years ago. If there had ever been any evidence linking me to the crime scene, that evidence is long gone. Thank God, the local authorities had been more than willing to believe that Lemar Fuqua had murdered the Desmond sisters and then killed himself. The damn fools hadn't looked any further, hadn't even considered the possibility that someone else might have had motive and opportunity. And at the time Louis Royale had been so focused on whether Jolie would live or die that he'd seemed unconcerned about who had killed his wife and her sister. Or maybe he'd been glad that Audrey was dead, glad someone had removed the one obstacle that stood between him and the woman he loved.

I was lucky and my luck has held for twenty years. All I have to do is continue on as I always have. I have nothing to fear. Nothing except memories. Memories of that bloody day. Memories that won't leave me alone, that have haunted me. I hadn't planned on killing anyone. Why did I have to overhear her talking about me? Why hadn't I realized sooner what a manipulative bitch she was? She forced me to do the unthinkable. It wasn't my fault. It was her fault. She gave me no other choice. Damn the woman. I had hoped her soul was rotting in hell, but after seeing Jolie, I know now that Lisette's evil spirit has come back to haunt me.

Now, look what you've done to yourself. Your hands are trembling. You're feeling queasy. Why do you upset yourself this way? Because Jolie's back, because she's the only other person alive who was there that day. But she didn't see you. She swears she never saw the person who shot her.

But what if she remembers something? What if . . .

Stay calm. Don't lose control. You can wait her out. She'll go back to Atlanta sooner or later, with no harm done. Except to your nerves.

Clarice met Nowell in the gazebo. Her heart raced as she approached him. He wore his usual faded jeans and cotton knit shirt. He'd pulled his shoulder-length gray hair into a ponytail. Sweat dampened his face; a trickle slid from his temple and down his cheek. Even she was perspiring slightly. Moisture dampened the undersides of her breasts.

She felt guilty being so happy today, so alive and so in love. It wasn't right that her life was rich and complete, not with poor Louis buried only yesterday. And dear little Jolie, so hurt and angry, and so determined to wreak vengeance.

Clarice knew that people whispered behind her back, saying terribly ugly things about her and about Nowell. She wasn't as dense as everyone thought. She had suffered from a nervous condition since she was eighteen, an emotional affliction that had worsened twenty years ago. But the Valium she took helped soothe her. After the doctors here in Sumarville had refused to give her the medication she needed, she'd found a man in New Orleans—a special doctor—who understood her problem. The medicine kept the ghosts at bay, even though sometimes at night, in her dreams, the memories returned. Blood everywhere. The stench of death. Sightless eyes staring up at her. The faint beating of Jolie's pulse.

Don't think about it! Don't relive that horrifying day. Jolie's alive and she's come home; reason enough to celebrate. Let the past stay buried. No need to dredge it up.

Nowell took her in his arms and held her. She loved the feel of being held, enjoyed the gentleness of this kind man. Despite his coarse appearance, he was such a gentleman. And he never treated her as if she were crazy, not the way so many others did. People thought of her as that poor, pitiful Clarice. *She's lived such a tragic life,* they said. *Lost her fiancé when she was just a girl and never quite got over his death. And then she was the one who found the bodies of her sisters and that black man at Belle Rose. She's been touched in the head ever since.*

Clarice clung to Nowell, embracing his strength,

absorbing his masculine power, taking his vitality into her, believing in the impossible—that he loved her. Everyone had warned her against him. And at times even she wondered why a man such as he would be interested in her.

Nuzzling her neck, Nowell whispered, "How long can you stay?"

"Long enough," she said. "Georgette thinks I'm taking my afternoon nap."

"I've brought you something."

Keeping one arm draped around her, Nowell reached down and lifted the flower off the built-in bench behind him. When he presented her with a perfect yellow rose, she sighed dreamily and accepted his gift.

"Is everything all right?" he asked. "When you phoned and asked me to meet you here, I thought I heard worry in your voice." He kissed the tip of her nose. "I don't want you worrying about anything. So, tell me what's wrong and let me make it right for you."

She groaned. "If only you could."

This wonderful man made her happy to be alive, but he was no miracle worker. He couldn't erase the past, couldn't undo what had been done. And only a miracle could make things right. It would take an act of God to ease the tension between Jolie and Louis's second family, to change hatred and distrust into love and understanding.

"Is it about Louis Royale's will?" Nowell asked. "Was there some problem?"

"Louis's will?"

Yes, of course, Nowell would be interested in Louis's will, wouldn't he? If they were to marry, as Nowell wanted, he would share in any inheritance she received. People thought Nowell's only interest in her was her money. Some assumed she had much more money than she did; others thought she had much less. She wasn't rich by Louis Royale's standards, but neither was she poor. With the trust fund Louis had left her, added to her tidy savings, she was a millionaire.

Clarice took Nowell's hand and led him to the bench where they sat down, side by side. Looking into his beautiful dark eyes, she relished his adoring expression. Could a man fake such loving devotion? she wondered.

"Louis left me a million-dollar trust fund," she told Nowell.

"Why, Clarice, my dear, you're a very rich woman."

"Richer than before, that's for sure."

"I knew that Louis would do right by you. He was a good man."

"Yes, he was. A very good man." Clarice stroked Nowell's smoothly shaved cheek. He was so hairy. His arms, legs, and chest. *Jonathan had been hairy.* When Nowell had first arrived in Sumarville, he'd been sporting a beard and mustache. But when Clarice had asked him to shave, he'd done so immediately and had been clean shaven ever since. "My darling, you've asked me several times to marry you and I've put you off, but Louis's death has shown me that it's foolish to wait for happiness. None of us has any assurance that we'll be alive tomorrow."

"Clarice? Are you saying what I think you are?"

She nodded. "Yes, I'll marry you, if you still want me."

Nowell's smile warmed her heart. He grabbed her, kissed her passionately, then whispered in her ear. "I'll make you happy every day of our lives. I promise you that. You'll never have a reason to regret marrying me."

She prayed that she wouldn't be proven wrong, that her trust in Nowell wasn't misplaced. He acted like a man in love. Every touch. Every whispered endearment.

"How do you think your family will react to our news?" Nowell asked. "Max has made it abundantly clear that he dislikes and distrusts me."

"Naturally, I'd like Max's blessings. I'm hoping that during the next year, you'll find a way to bring him around. All he wants is for me to be happy. Once he understands that you *are* my happiness, he won't stand in our way."

"What do you mean, during the next year?"

"During our engagement, of course." She ruffled Nowell's silver gray hair. "We must have a proper engagement and a year seems quite appropriate."

"But Clarice, honey, I had hoped we could marry right away." He gazed pleadingly into her eyes. "I want you to be my wife as soon as possible. I don't want to wait."

"Patience. Patience." She kissed his mouth tenderly. "We can't marry now, not so soon after Louis's death. It wouldn't be proper."

"No, of course not. I understand. But a year is such a long time to wait."

"We'll be waiting only for the ceremony that will make our relationship legal. There's no need to wait to consummate our love," she told him, as she slipped her hand down his chest, over his belt, and cupped her palm over his crotch. "You've turned me into a wicked woman. There's no reason why we can't be lovers, is there? I long for you so, Jonathan."

Nowell cringed. This wasn't the first time she had called him by another man's name and it probably wouldn't be the last. But what did it matter that she often confused him with the fiancé she had loved and lost so long ago? The first time she had called him Jonathan, he'd wondered if she knew the truth, but soon realized she couldn't possible know. How would she have reacted if he'd been totally honest with her the way he'd planned on being when he'd first come to Sumarville? But seeing how emotionally fragile she was, he'd realized that the truth might destroy her completely. Instead of honesty, he'd chosen subterfuge. It had been easy enough to take on the persona of the one man she would never forget. If Clarice wanted Jonathan, he would give her Jonathan. He'd do anything—absolutely anything—to persuade her to marry him. And soon.

Chapter 11

"My advice is for you to talk to Jolie." Garland Wells sliced into his medium-rare T-bone steak. "Make a deal with her—you won't contest Louis's will if she agrees to do the same."

Max's meal remained untouched in front of him. Not that the food at the Sumarville Inn Restaurant wasn't good; it was. But ever since Louis's death, Max hadn't had much of an appetite. What he needed was some positive feedback from Gar, not a suggestion that he compromise with Jolie.

"I'd prefer to not contest the will, but Mother and Mallory won't be able to endure having Jolie living at Belle Rose. Not for very long. Something has to be done as soon as possible."

Be honest with yourself, Max—you need Jolie gone from your life just as much as, if not more than, anyone else in your family.

Gar chewed slowly, swallowed, and pointed his fork at Max. "I put together an ironclad document for Louis.

He wanted to make sure that his wishes were carried out in this matter." Gar sliced another piece of steak. "Believe me, I tried my best to talk him out of setting things up for Belle Rose the way he did, but he was adamant. And you know how Louis could be."

"What was he thinking? He had to know that Jolie wouldn't accept having my mother living at Belle Rose, if there was any way she could force her to move out."

"She can't make Georgette move."

"No, but she can make Mother's life so miserable that she'd prefer leaving Belle Rose than staying there and enduring Jolie's revenge."

"Then it's up to you to see to it that your mother doesn't cave in and give Jolie what she wants. Just wait her out." Gar ate another piece of steak. "By the way, Theron Carter phoned me bright and early this morning. He wants a copy of Louis's will. It seems he's representing Jolie now."

"What?"

"Mm-hmm. There's something smelly about their association. Theron must think Jolie can do something for him. Or it could be that he has a personal interest in Jolie. I remember when we were teenagers. I had the audacity to tell him that he shouldn't be hanging around my sisters and Jolie, not after we all reached a certain age. He hated my guts after that. Of course, I can't say I blame him. And I can't believe that by that time I hadn't learned anything from my father's mistakes."

"Maybe the guy wants something else from Jolie," Max said. "I've been hearing rumors that Carter would like to see the Belle Rose massacre case reopened. If that's true, he might think he needs Jolie's help."

"Damn! You're right. If Jolie joined forces with him in trying to get that old case reopened, then Katie-bar-the-door. With her being one of the victims, not counting that she's a Royale and a Desmond, her opinion would carry a lot of weight with certain people."

"That's just what we all need, just what this town

needs—reopening old wounds that could rip Sumarville apart. Right down racial lines." Max knew that if the case was reopened, the past would come to life again. Old rumors would resurface. Rumors about him having been the murderer. Rumors about his mother and Louis's adulterous affair. Everyone he loved would be hurt. His mother. Mallory. Uncle Parry. Even Aunt Clarice. How could Clarice deal with having to relive that horrible day when she discovered the bodies? But if his guess was right and Jolie had joined forces with Theron Carter, then obviously she didn't care who got hurt in the process. All that mattered to Jolie was wreaking havoc on Georgette and her children. God, how she must hate them!

"I sure don't want to see that happen." Gar washed down another bite of steak with a big swig of iced tea. "Those were some dark days for Sumarville. I don't think anyone went unscathed by what happened at Belle Rose. It didn't seem possible that something so horrible could have happened here, where folks didn't even lock their doors at night."

Max remembered that Yvonne had begged the sheriff's department to look for other suspects. She had been so sure her brother couldn't have committed the murders. At the time, Max hadn't really cared if Lemar Fuqua did it or not, hadn't cared about Yvonne's convictions, because he hadn't known her then. He'd just been thankful that the law hadn't gone after him. They had questioned him, as they had Uncle Parry, but nothing ever came of it. Both he and Uncle Parry had told the sheriff where they were and what they were doing that day. Thank God, no one had ever checked out his alibi.

"Have you ever had any doubts about Lemar Fuqua's guilt?" Max asked.

"No. Well, not really. I feel certain that Sheriff Bendall followed the proper procedures. He even called in the Criminal Investigation Bureau. Mostly because the victims were Desmonds and one of them was married to Louis Royale." Gar lifted his cup. "Old Horace Madry, our county coroner at the time, ruled it a double murder and suicide. And the CIB's guy backed Horace up. I remember Daddy saying at the time that nobody could come back later and claim Lemar Fuqua had been unjustly accused." Gar sipped on his coffee.

"Well, I have to admit that I've had some doubts," Max admitted. "I always thought it odd that those rumors about Lemar Fuqua and Lisette Desmond didn't really take hold and circulate until after the murders. You'd think if the two had been carrying on an affair for years, somebody would have known about it sooner."

"I never believed that rumor about Lisette. She wasn't in love with Lemar, and she wasn't having an affair with him."

Max looked directly at Gar, whose facial features hardened and skin splotched with color. "How would you know for sure?"

Gar's gaze clashed with Max's. He cleared his throat and glanced away hurriedly. "I don't know for sure, of course, but . . . I remember Lisette. She was the most beautiful woman I'd ever seen. I suppose I just don't like the idea that she was as promiscuous as people said she was."

Max suddenly realized the truth. "You had a crush on her."

Gar huffed softly. "Yeah, I guess I did."

"Maybe she wasn't the way folks said she was. People say a lot of things that aren't true. They've said an awful lot of nasty things about my mother."

"And Jolie still believes every one of them." Gar picked up his knife and fork, sliced several pieces off his steak, then laid the silverware on the edge of his plate. "I wanted to ask you something . . . something about Jolie."

"What would that be?"

"I was wondering how you'd feel about my asking

her out while she's staying in Sumarville. I wouldn't, of course, if you decide to follow through with your plans to contest the will, but if—"

"I'm not going to make any snap legal decision," Max said. "But whom you date is your own business."

"Then you don't object?"

Max studied Gar for a moment. "I know Jolie looks a lot like her aunt Lisette . . . but you need to remember that she's not Lisette. She has an agenda all her own for staying in Sumarville. I wouldn't want to see you get hurt. I get the distinct impression that Jolie looks out for Number One and to hell with anyone else."

Gar shrugged. "Who knows, she might turn me down . . . especially if there is something personal going on between her and Theron."

Max didn't like the idea of something personal going on between Jolie and anyone in Sumarville. He didn't want her forming attachments that might prolong her stay. He wanted her gone. And the sooner the better.

Jolie didn't recognize the district attorney's secretary, but then why should she? She hadn't lived in Sumarville in twenty years and anyone new to the area would be a stranger to her.

"If y'all will just take a seat in Mr. Newman's office, he'll be with you shortly," the slender, middle-aged blonde instructed. "He's been delayed, but should be here within the next fifteen minutes. He asked me to extend his apologies for keeping y'all waiting. Would anyone care for coffee?"

"Thank you, Ms. Cunningham. And no, I wouldn't care for any coffee." Flashing her his wide, thousand-watt grin, Theron used only a fraction of his considerable charm, but it was just enough to elicit a smile from the woman. He glanced at Jolie and then at the sheriff. "Would either of you care for coffee?"

Six-three, barrel-chested, ebony-skinned Ike Denton,

who'd been a linebacker for Mississippi State a good fifteen years ago, shook his head.

"No, thanks," Jolie said.

Sharla Cunningham left the door partially open when she returned to her desk in the outer office. Jolie wandered around the room, taking note of the items on the walls: Larry Newman's law degree, photos of him with prominent people, an antique saber, and a pair of old flintlock pistols. She barely remembered Larry. He'd been years older than she, a high school senior when she'd been in grade school. So how old would he be now—in his early forties? She did recall that his mother had been a Martin and had come from a family of schoolteachers. And hadn't his father been a Sumarville policeman?

Ike sat in one of the two matching leather chairs facing the large oak desk. With his massive shoulders slightly slumped, he dropped his hands between his knees and nervously patted one foot on the tiled floor.

"He's playing with us," Ike said. "Keeping us waiting this way."

Theron crossed his arms over his chest and grinned. "I don't think so. He knows that the outcome of this meeting will be the same whether we talk now or later."

"You sound awfully sure," Jolie said. "What do you know that we don't know?"

"I know it's a foregone conclusion that we'll get what we want. The district attorney can't refuse our request."

"What makes you so sure?" Ike eyed Theron inquisitively.

"Because I've learned how the system works. And I've done my homework on this case." Theron sauntered casually to the door and called out to Ms. Cunningham, "I've changed my mind. I think I would like a cup of coffee. Black. Two sugars."

Ms. Cunningham glanced up at him and smiled. "Certainly, Mr. Carter." After rising from behind her desk, she peered into her boss's office. "Anyone else want coffee?"

"Yeah, okay," Ike said. "Black."

"Nothing for me." Jolie noted the way Theron watched Ms. Cunningham as she left the outer door open when she headed down the hall.

The moment the secretary was out of earshot, Theron turned around in the doorway. "I put in a call to the state's attorney general early this morning. When we discussed the situation, I told him that Louis Royale's daughter, who'd been the only victim who survived, wanted to see the case reopened as much as I did. Bill Sanders assured me that he would call Larry Newman and persuade him to let us take a look at all the files on the Belle Rose massacre. And if we can come up with anything—and I mean anything—that indicates the Belle Rose massacre wasn't a double murder and suicide, then he'll see to it that the case is officially reopened."

Ike chuckled softly. "I'll be damned." He glanced at Jolie, cleared his throat and said, "Excuse me, ma'am."

"No need to apologize for your language," Jolie assured him, then looked directly at Theron. "You've come a long way, baby." Smiling, she winked at Theron, who winked back at her. "Your uncle Lemar would be very proud of you."

"I hope so. He's the reason I became a lawyer, the reason I've worked hard, did my time in Atlanta and Memphis. Reopening this case has been a major goal in my life, and achieving that goal has been a long time coming."

"You've spent twenty years preparing for this day," Jolie said. "And I've spent twenty years running away."

"You're not running now," Theron told her.

"No, I'm not. I'm staying. I have a lot of unfinished business to take care of before I leave town."

* * *

Using his digital phone, Lawrence Newman punched in the numbers for Roscoe Wells's unlisted private line. The phone rang four times.

Wells answered, "Yeah?"

"It's me," Larry said.

"I thought you had a meeting with Yvonne Carter's boy this morning."

"I did. I mean I do. He's probably waiting in my office right now. I told Sharla to serve them coffee and tell them I'd been delayed."

"Why put it off?" Roscoe chuckled. "You're going to tell that young hotshot lawyer that there's no need to reopen a twenty-year-old case when there's no new evidence."

"It's not that simple."

Roscoe growled. "What do you mean? I told you what to do, how to handle it. That's simple enough."

"I got a call from Bill Sanders before I left my house this morning."

"Hm—mm. And just what did our attorney general have to say?"

"I'm to let Carter and Ms. Royale take a look at the case files, and I'm to instruct Ike Denton to assist them in any way he can."

"Shit! Bill Sanders is a prick, but he's an ambitious prick. He's planning on running for governor. Did you know that? He's smart enough to realize he'll need the black vote if he wants to get elected in Mississippi. I guess he thinks pacifying Theron Carter will win him a few points with Carter's people. Looks like I'm going to be forced to contact some old friends I haven't associated with in years."

"You do see that I don't have any choice in this matter," Larry said, hoping Roscoe understood.

"Do what you have to do," Roscoe told him. "And I'll do what I have to do."

Larry hit the OFF button, slipped his phone into the inside pocket of his sports coat, and left the seclusion of Desmond Park. He had no idea whether Roscoe Wells had been involved in the Belle Rose massacre, and he didn't want to know. That event had occurred years ago and had nothing to do with him. He'd been in college when it happened. But he'd worked long and hard to get where he was today and he was smart enough to know that in Mississippi, especially in Desmond County, you didn't cross Senator Roscoe Wells. Larry had been elected Desmond County D.A. with Roscoe's backing. Hell, he owed the man more than one favor. So, if Roscoe said, "Jump," Larry knew he'd better ask, "How high?"

Sliding a finger under his tight collar, Larry loosened the knot in his tie. He didn't know why Roscoe had been adamantly opposed to letting Theron Carter and the Royale woman take a look at those old records, but his gut instincts warned him that if Roscoe had taken an interest in the situation, there would be trouble ahead.

R. J.'s Jeep came bounding up the dirt road toward the back of the Belle Rose property line. Mallory had given him directions and told him to meet her at two-thirty and to bring his bathing suit. No one at home had questioned her taking Splendor out for a long ride. If Max knew she was meeting R. J., he'd be furious. But what Max didn't know, wouldn't hurt him. After all, what was the big deal? So R. J. wasn't a local guy from one of the upstanding families in Desmond County; she didn't care. She liked R. J. He'd been kind and understanding last night, when she'd desperately needed someone to care about her, to put her needs first. And it didn't hurt that the guy was a real hottie. She'd spent an hour on the phone this morning telling her two best friends—Lindsey Castle and Ashley Wilson—all about R. J.

When he pulled his old green Jeep off the road near the dilapidated barbed-wire fencing, Mallory lifted her arm and waved. A crazy, unexpected fluttering turned her stomach inside out. She'd had several boyfriends in the past couple of years—her parents hadn't allowed her to date until she was sixteen—but not one of them had ever made her feel the way R. J. did. There was something exciting and maybe even a little dangerous about him. And he was older than she. At least five or six years older and no telling how many years older in experience.

R. J. jumped out of the Jeep and waved at her. Tall, lanky and toned like an athlete, his knockout body looked great in cutoff jeans and a sleeveless white T-shirt. Add to that his thick blond hair pulled back into a short ponytail and you had most girls' dream lover. He bounded over the section of fence that lay on the ground, then stopped and waited for her to come running to him. She was so glad to see him. With R. J., she could escape the morbid sadness inside the walls of Belle Rose. She could forget that her daddy was dead, buried only yesterday, and that her mother seemed unable to cope with his death. She'd heard her mother crying during the night. When she'd peeped in on her, Max had been sitting at her bedside. Sometimes she wished she could be more like Max, so strong and in control, so able to take care of himself and those he loved. But she wasn't like Max. She needed comfort, needing petting and reassurance that her life could go on without her daddy.

Oh, Daddy! Why did you have to leave me?

She shouldn't be thinking about Daddy, not when it hurt so much. He wouldn't have wanted her to be sad all the time. She could almost hear him now, *"Don't you cry, sugar. Whatever's wrong, tell Daddy and I'll fix it for you."*

Pushing the memories out of her mind as she blinked the tears from her eyes, Mallory grabbed R. J.'s hands and said, "Come on. The pond is close by. Did you bring your swim trunks?"

"Will I need them?"

Blushing profusely, Mallory giggled. "Don't kid me like that."

R. J. slipped his arm around her shoulders, all casual like. She loved the way it felt being so close to him. His touch wasn't at all threatening. Some of the boys she'd dated had possessed more arms than an octopus. God, she hated having to fight off a boy who wouldn't take no for an answer. R. J. wasn't anything like any of the immature, suitable guys Max approved of. He was better—in every way.

He followed where she led, through the thick woods, so dense in spots that the towering treetops almost blocked out the sun.

"Just a little farther," she told him. "See, through there." She pointed the direction.

Afternoon sunlight glistened on the surface of the water, creating small flashing circles dancing on the pond. A humid breeze rustled through the trees and bushes, only slightly easing the summer heat. A few yards from the pond, set up underneath an old willow tree, a quilt was spread out and on top of it rested a large wooden picnic basket. She had arrived early and prepared the perfect romantic scene.

"What's this?" he asked.

"Lunch," she replied. She had sneaked around in the kitchen while Yvonne had been overseeing the daily cleaning crew upstairs. And she'd stashed the picnic basket in the mudroom, under a bottom counter near the back door.

"You think of everything, don't you, honey? A picnic under the trees, a pond to swim in and—" he pulled her into his arms—"a beautiful girl to share the afternoon with. What more could a man want?"

Instinctively she lifted her arms and circled his neck.

"I'm so glad you came today. I was afraid you might change your mind."

"Now why would I do that?" He nuzzled her nose with his. "There's no place on earth I'd rather be."

Mallory's heart did an erratic *rat-a-tat-tat*. "Want to swim first or eat first?"

He eased one hand between them and reached up to skim his fingers over her cheek. "I'm kind of eager to see you in your bathing suit." When she sucked in her breath, he smiled. His fingers loosely cupped her jaw, while his thumb slid across her lips, stopping in the center when she sighed. "Let's swim first and eat later."

Mallory's body responded to his touch in a way she didn't quite understand. How could she be hot and cold at the same time? Using his thumb, R. J. pulled down her bottom lip. Without even realizing what she was doing, she licked his thumb. He grinned. She whimpered as a tingling sensation radiated from the apex between her legs and spread through her entire body.

"I . . . uh . . . I think we should swim now," she said.

He eased her arms from around his neck and stepped back just enough to put a couple of inches between them. While she stood there staring at him, he tugged his T-shirt over his head and stripped out of his cutoffs. Mallory gaped at him. In nothing but a pair of black body-molding briefs, R. J. could hide nothing from her. He was very obviously aroused. And she had aroused him! That knowledge gave her a heady sense of power.

Stop staring at him, she told herself, and hurriedly removed her shorts and tank top. She'd specifically chosen her bright blue bikini, the one Mother had forbidden her to wear. She'd bought it during a shopping trip to Memphis with Lindsey. Max had told her to get rid of the thing, but she'd simply hidden it away in the bottom of her closet. Now she was glad she'd kept it. She wanted to knock R. J. for a loop.

"What do you think?" she asked.

"Wow!"

R. J. surveyed her from head to toe, letting his gaze linger over her barely concealed breasts. She wasn't big, but she filled out a B-cup. And her breasts were high, round, and perky. She knew she had a good body. She'd been told often enough—by her girlfriends and by lots of guys at school.

Pivoting slowly, she allowed him to take a good long look. "You like?" she asked.

"I like," he replied.

Smiling, feeling more alive than she'd felt in ages—not since before Daddy went in the hospital weeks ago—Mallory turned, ran to the pond and jumped in. The cool water engulfed her, chilling her, tightening her nipples into protruding pebbles. She shuddered as she stood up, waist deep in the pond.

"Come on in." She motioned to R. J. "I'll race you to the other side and back."

He quickly joined her. "What do I get if I win?"

"What do you want?" she asked.

"I want you, Mallory."

Chapter 12

Larry Newman breezed into his office, a politician's smile on his long narrow face. Jolie noted that his looks were nondescript. Medium height and build. Medium-brown hair and faded brown eyes. He was a man who'd get lost in the crowd, easily forgotten. He held out his hand to Theron. The two exchanged a quick handshake, then Larry turned to Ike for the same cordial greeting before zeroing in on her.

"Ms. Royale, may I offer my sincerest condolences on the death of your father. His passing is a great loss for Sumarville, indeed for the state of Mississippi."

"Thank you, Mr. Newman."

Larry glanced around the room, viewed the empty coffee mugs, and smiled as he positioned himself behind his desk. "Please, everyone have a seat and we'll get right to business. I apologize for having kept y'all waiting, but I had to handle a minor town problem." He looked directly at Jolie. "Ms. Royale, I understand that y'all want permission to take a look at the Belle Rose massacre files, is that correct?"

"Yes, that's correct." Catching a glimpse of Theron's tense expression, she realized he had taken affront at Larry Newman's dismissal of him in favor of directing the conversation to her. "Mr. Carter and I want access to all the files pertaining to the murders of my mother, my aunt, and Lemar Fuqua."

"Lemar Fuqua committed suicide, after murdering your mother and your aunt," Larry said. "I can't believe that you actually want to put yourself through the ordeal of reading all the details, looking at the snapshots taken at the scene, reliving such a tragic event in your life. Surely you haven't bought into Carter's supposition that someone other than his uncle committed that horrible atrocity."

"Let us take a look at everything, all the files on the case, and I'm betting that we'll come up with something that was overlooked," Theron said. "Deliberately overlooked."

D.A. Newman leaned forward, spread his arms wide and placed his hands, palms down, on his desk. "Are you accusing the Desmond County Sheriff's Department and Mississippi's Criminal Investigation Bureau of withholding vital evidence in the case?"

Larry's expression contained just the right amount of outrage, but Jolie sensed his reaction was nothing more than a performance. However, Theron's tense jaw and narrowed gaze was not an act.

"I'm not accusing anyone of anything," Theron said. "Not yet."

"I'd think you would want to cooperate with us," Jolie told Larry Newman. "After all, if a miscarriage of justice occurred, if Lemar Fuqua was innocent, then as the current district attorney, it would be your job to reopen the case and to find and convict the real murderer. If what we suspect is true, and you cooperate with us, think of all the positive publicity you'd get out of it.''

Larry's cheeks flushed. He cleared his throat. "I hate to see you waste your time. But if y'all are damned and determined, then by all means, take a look at the files." He glanced at the sheriff. "Denton give Ms. Royale and Carter access to all files pertaining to the Belle Rose massacre.''

"Yes, sir," Ike replied, his lips lifting in a restrained smile. "I'd be glad to.''

"First thing tomorrow morning, y'all may—'' Larry said.

"Today." Theron glared at the D.A.

Larry nervously cleared his throat again. "Why the hurry? Those files have been collecting dust for twenty years. They aren't going to sprout legs and run off before tomorrow.''

"You never know what might happen by tomorrow," Theron replied. "Besides, the sooner we start going over the records, the sooner we can get the case reopened.''

"Hm—mm. Well, by all means, go ahead and start today." Larry looked downright uncomfortable.

"Thanks, we will,'' Theron said.

When Jolie followed Theron and Ike to the door, Larry Newman came out from behind his desk and called to them. "I'd consider it a courtesy if—and that's a big if—you find anything noteworthy, you'll contact me before getting in touch with Bill Sanders. No need to bother the attorney general unless there actually is enough evidence to reopen the case.''

Jolie absolutely loved Theron's reaction. He flashed the D.A. his wide dazzling smile. "Sure thing, Larry. I wouldn't think of doing anything else, considering how helpful you've been.''

Jolie barely controlled the laughter bubbling up inside her until they reached the sidewalk. "Did you see the look on his face?''

"He's scared shitless that we'll dig up something,''

Theron said. "If he's so damned sure Uncle Lemar was a murderer, why would he be worried? He knows something about the case."

"How could he know anything?" Ike asked. "He wasn't involved in the case. Twenty years ago, he'd have been a college kid."

"He wasn't involved. Not originally. Not until I contacted Bill Sanders. Getting a phone call from the attorney general put the fear of God into Newman. He realized that he had no choice but to give us permission to look over the old files. And our esteemed D.A. knows that somebody doesn't want us looking at those files."

Jolie curved her hand over Theron's forearm. "Are you saying that you think someone is pulling Larry Newman's strings, someone who doesn't want the case reopened?"

"Yeah, that's exactly what I'm saying," Theron told her.

"If that's true, then we can narrow it down to only a few people," Ike said. "Not many men have the power to dictate terms to the D.A."

"A couple of names come to mind immediately." Theron glanced from Ike to Jolie. "Roscoe Wells . . . and Max Devereaux."

An odd sensation quavered in Jolie's stomach. *Not Max.* Her immediate reaction surprised her. Why had her gut instinct instantly defended a man she so thoroughly despised?

R. J. relaxed, flat on his back, on the blanket spread out beneath the huge willow tree. He and Mallory had frolicked in the pond like a couple of kids, then feasted on cold fried chicken, tangy lemonade, and fried peach pies. Good food, laughter, and a beautiful girl. A guy could do a lot worse. Of course that didn't mean he was willing to settle for the kisses and mild petting Mallory allowed. He wanted to screw her so bad he was nearly eaten alive with the need to toss her on her back, spread her legs, and ram into her. But every time he thought he had her maneuvered into the right frame of mind, she'd start talking about her daddy. Damn her daddy!

Mallory lifted her head off R. J.'s outstretched left arm and looked at him. "What are you thinking?"

Hell, why did all females ask the same question? Why were they so determined to know what a man was thinking? If she had any idea what he was really thinking, she'd be shocked. And hurt and disappointed.

"Just thinking about how glad I am to be with you."

Smiling as if she'd just won the lottery, Mallory leaned down and kissed him on the mouth. A sweet fleeting kiss that left him wanting more. He tangled his fingers through her hair, cupped his hand over the back of her head, and held her in place for a ravaging response. His other hand slid down her back and into her bikini bottoms. He caressed her buttocks, the feel of her smooth flesh arousing him unbearably. Then suddenly she pulled back, ending the pleasure that had only just begun. She sat up, wrapped her arms around her waist in a comforting gesture, and gazed at the sky.

When he rubbed his hand up and down her arm, she shivered. "I'm sorry, baby. Did I frighten you just then?"

"No, you didn't frighten me. I knew you wouldn't hurt me." She continued staring at the sky, deliberately avoiding direct eye contact with him. "I didn't want to lead you on, to let you think I was willing to . . . to go all the way. I like you too much to tease you and then say no."

For some damn reason, Mallory had given him the role of good guy and trying to wear that false mantle cramped his style. He'd never been a good guy. He'd been a bad boy all his life and most women seemed intrigued by that fact. But here was little Miss Innocence thinking he was some sort of damn hero. She trusted him. *I knew you wouldn't hurt me.* How could she be so damn naive? No, he wouldn't hurt her physically; he wasn't into beating up on women. But he could hurt her emotionally, and unless they stopped seeing each other, he probably would.

Hey, man, it's your own fault that she thinks you're such a nice guy, he told himself. Hadn't he played it cool last night down by the river? Hadn't he been understanding and sympathetic, thinking it would win points for him that he could collect later? And today, for the past couple of hours, he had flirted with her outrageously and even gotten to first base, sexually speaking, but he hadn't pushed her further than she seemed willing to go. So, why the hell hadn't he pushed her? If she'd been any other girl, he'd already be on top of her, pumping into her like crazy. But not Mallory.

All right, Sutton, don't go thinking she's different from any other girl, from any of the women you've known. She's just classier than your usual honey. And far more innocent and trusting.

"You aren't angry with me, are you?" she asked.

R. J. lifted himself up and scooted over beside her. He didn't touch her, didn't look at her. Instead, he looked up, the way she was still doing.

"I couldn't ever be angry with you," he told her.

She looked at him then, just as he knew she would. God, she was so predictable. And she had no idea that he was playing her like a fiddle. She wasn't quite willing to spread her legs for him, not yet. But it was only a matter of time. Ordinarily he wouldn't wait around. He'd just move on to a more willing woman. He wasn't by nature a patient man.

Mallory reached over and laid her small open palm over his hand. "I'm so very glad you're here."

Disturbed by a niggling little feeling he didn't quite understand, R. J. didn't respond immediately. Hell, how was he supposed to react to such a syrupy sweet statement?

"I'm glad I'm here, too."

She grasped his hand and squeezed tightly. "I've been

so frightened, so unhappy and worried, ever since Daddy went into the hospital and the doctors told Max that it didn't look good. I couldn't believe that Daddy might die. But he did."

R. J. turned her hand over in his and brought it to his lips. When he kissed her hand, she sighed and laid her head on his shoulder. Casually, loosely, he slipped his arm around her waist.

"Max has been so busy taking care of Mother and making all the plans for the funeral and doing all the things he usually does, that he hasn't realized how much I need him. He doesn't understand how I feel. My whole world is falling apart. My daddy is dead. My mother is unraveling before my very eyes. And my half sister has moved into Belle Rose and is going to make our lives a living hell."

"It's all right, baby." R. J. smoothed his lips over her temple. "I'm here. Lean on me. Let me make you feel better."

"Oh, R. J."

She responded, just as he knew she would, by turning to him, flinging her arms around his waist and burying her face against his chest. He wrapped her in a gentle embrace, his manner comforting and nonthreatening. Her tears dampened his naked flesh.

"That's it. Let it all out. Keep on crying." He kissed the top of her head, then rested his chin there.

"Please, don't leave me." She held on to him for dear life. "Don't leave Sumarville. Stay. Please, please stay forever. I need you so much."

"I'm not going anywhere," he assured her.

After all, why would he want to leave town? At least not yet. He had a good job, a decent place to live, and a potential lover whose innocence and trust aroused him more than he liked to admit. He'd have to be very careful to not get himself all tangled up in Mallory's sweet seductive snare.

* * *

"Sorry about this mess," Ike Denton said. "Looks like somebody tried to bury those files where they'd never be found."

Jolie knelt down beside Theron as he prized open a rusty file cabinet in the basement of the sheriff's department located in the courthouse. "I can't believe Sumarville didn't computerize their files until six years ago."

"I can," Theron grumbled. "Sumarville is about half a century behind. Some people around here think it's the nineteen-fifties." When he jerked the creaking cabinet open, dust flew everywhere and a couple of small bugs scurried across the top of the files.

"With no more manpower than we have and such a limited budget, we haven't been able to put all the old records on computer," Ike explained. "Nellie's been working on it diligently whenever she can find time, and we've got the past ten years' worth of information computerized, but she's doing double duty as our computer expert and our dispatcher. And she's our only female officer, so occasionally we need her to handle some of the women we arrest."

Theron glanced over his shoulder at Ike. "Is there a desk and some chairs down here in the basement? It would save us time if we could start looking over files down here instead of having to tote them upstairs."

"There's a table down here," Ike said. "I'll move it over here, then go get y'all a couple of chairs."

"Need any help with that table?" Theron asked.

"I can get it," Ike replied. "You just keep searching for those files."

Theron grabbed a handful of dusty, slightly moldy file folders and handed them to Jolie. "Start with these while I go through the next batch."

She nodded, then clasping the dirty folders to her chest she glanced around for a place to lay them. With a small square wooden table held in front of him, its legs protruding straight out, Ike came toward her, then set the battered desk down on the concrete floor a few feet away from her.

"I'll get y'all some chairs and bring a rag to clean off that table," Ike said as he turned to leave.

Jolie dropped the folders on top of the desk, creating another minor dust storm. She sneezed.

"Gesundheit," Theron said.

They both laughed.

"I guess it would have been asking too much for the files from twenty years ago to be on the computer," Jolie said.

"That would have made this much too easy," Theron replied.

"Well, you'd think that the records of the only double murder . . . make that, triple murder . . . in Sumarville would warrant special treatment."

"By the time all the tension settled and all the rumors died down twenty years ago, most people in Sumarville, black and white, were ready to put the incident behind them and move on."

"I don't understand why Daddy didn't demand a more thorough investigation. He knew the kind of man Lemar was," Jolie said. "And yet he accepted the sheriff's decision to close the books on the case."

"I think, maybe more than anyone, your daddy wanted the whole thing put behind him." Theron dumped a stack of folders on the opposite end of the desk, sending dust particles flying. "All he seemed to care about in the first few weeks after the killings was whether you'd recover. And even if he was having an affair with Georgette at the time, Mama can tell you that he was pretty broken up about your mother's death."

"He recovered soon enough." It had taken Louis Royale less than a year to recover fully—recover enough to take a new bride.

Jolie tried to make out the typed heading on the first file folder in front of her, but mildew had destroyed the ink. She flipped it open and hurriedly scanned the report. A bank robbery. She checked the date. Nineteen years ago. She flipped through several other files, noting the dates.

"Check the dates on your files," she told him. "These all seem to be from nineteen years ago."

Theron hurriedly went through a dozen folders. "Same with all of these. They're all nineteen eighty-three."

"Then we're close. The ones dated nineteen eighty-two must be in another cabinet." Her gaze rested on the tall cabinet beside the one Theron had opened. "Maybe that one."

Just as Theron turned and reached out for the handle on the next cabinet, Ike reappeared carrying two metal folding chairs. A large white rag hung out of his pants pocket.

"Here's a couple of chairs." He set the chairs on either side of the desk, then whipped out the rag and ran it over the tabletop, sending billows of dust dancing in every direction.

"If y'all need to take a break, you know where the rest rooms are and where the coffeepot and vending machines are." Ike glanced at the stack of musty folders. "Find anything yet?"

"Not yet," Jolie replied, "but at least we're in the right decade."

"Okay, then. I'll get back to work. But if there's anything I can do to help out, just let me know."

"Thanks, Ike," Theron said. "I appreciate your being so cooperative. I realize that if we're able to find something to warrant reopening the Belle Rose massacre case, it could wind up making your job a lot more difficult. Tempers could flare. Old prejudices could resurface. And if it gets too bad, national news services are bound to swarm the town."

"Let's just take this thing one step at a time." Ike laid his meaty hand on Theron's shoulder. "You two find what you need to get the case reopened and I'll deal with any local rumblings.'' Ike gave Theron's shoulder a squeeze. ''I remember Lemar quite well. He was a nice man. Everybody liked him. For a time, he dated my aunt LaKora. Every time he came around to the house, he'd always give me a piece of peppermint candy.''

Jolie smiled. ''I think Lemar kept his pockets filled with peppermints just for us kids.'' Sighing softly, she looked at Ike. ''Was he dating your aunt that spring? If he was then—''

Ike shook his head. ''They dated a year before that and Auntie ended their relationship when she up and ran off with another man.''

''Do either of you know if Lemar was involved with someone at the time of the murders?'' Jolie asked.

''If he was, not even Mama knew anything about it,'' Theron said. ''But she swears that he and Lisette Desmond were not romantically involved. Not ever.''

''Yvonne should know.'' Jolie swished her hands together, removing the dust. ''What I don't understand is how the rumor about Lemar and Aunt Lisette ever got started in the first place.''

Ike eyed Theron, as if contemplating Theron's reaction before he spoke. Ike coughed a couple of times. ''Folks talk, you know. A black man and a white woman being friends used to be punishable by death in these parts and even now, it's frowned on. Black folks in Sumarville always said that Lemar had better watch out hanging around the Desmond sisters the way he did, especially Lisette and Clarice.''

''Lemar and Yvonne grew up at Belle Rose,'' Jolie said. ''They were like family.''

''Yes, ma'am, I know that, but . . . Heck, there's no point in my going over old gossip when y'all have got more important stuff to do.'' Ike glanced at the folders.

''You're right,'' Theron agreed. ''Old gossip won't help us find evidence to clear Uncle Lemar's name.''

When Ike turned to leave, Jolie grasped his arm.

"Humor me, would you, Sheriff Denton?" He shrugged. "Tell me what old gossip you were talking about?"

Ike eyed Theron again. "It probably wouldn't have any bearing on the case. But . . . well, folks used to say that Lemar and Yvonne were treated like family by the Desmonds because they were family?"

"What?" Jolie and Theron said in unison.

"It was just gossip. Like I said before, you know how people talk. They said Mr. Sam Desmond and Sadie Fuqua were . . ." Ike looked down at the floor.

"People thought that my grandmother and Mr. Sam were lovers?" Theron's eyes widened in surprise. "That's the most ridiculous thing I ever heard of. Mama would have told me if—Hell, that would mean that Lemar was Lisette's half brother." Theron stomped around the dank musty basement, his feet pounding against the cold concrete floor. He kept shaking his head as if trying to dislodge an unwanted thought. "It can't be true. Tales about white men and pretty black servant girls are as plentiful as cotton bolls in these parts."

"I told y'all it was just gossip," Ike said. "And it doesn't pay to listen to gossip."

Ike made his escape while Theron continued pacing the floor. Jolie allowed her mind to assimilate the information, to weigh the possibilities. If it were true, if Lisette and Lemar had been half siblings, then why hadn't Mama or Aunt Clarice ever told her? Why hadn't Yvonne told Theron?

"I don't believe it's true," Theron said. "Mama would have told me. She would never have kept something like that a secret from me."

Theron stopped, grasped the back of the metal chair nearest him, and looked down at the file folders. "We're wasting time even thinking about such nonsense." He reached out, scooped up the folders, and returned them to the file cabinet, then did the same with the folders in front of Jolie.

While he worked to open the top drawer on the next cabinet, which seemed to be stuck, Jolie tried the cabinet on the other side. The drawer opened easily, but she soon discovered that the files were from 1984. Just as she started to speak to Theron, he managed to open the warped drawer. She moved to his side and watched while he scanned the first couple of files.

"Nineteen eighty-two," he said. "Jackpot!"

"You take half, and I'll take half," she said.

He lifted an armful of folders, leaving the drawer empty, and dumped the files on the table. The stench of mold and mildew irritated Jolie's nose.

"Phew, these things stink." But she didn't allow the smell to stop her from taking several folders and looking through them.

Twenty minutes later, Theron replaced the folders. His broad shoulders slumped. A weary disappointed expression crossed his face when he turned to Jolie.

"Nothing. Absolutely nothing." He slammed his fist down on top of the table, shaking the unstable legs. "I knew this wouldn't be easy, but . . . What if someone destroyed those files? What if they've been gone for years?"

"We can't give up," Jolie said. "Not yet. Not until we've searched every file in this damn basement!"

"Are they still at the sheriff's department?" Roscoe asked.

"Yes, sir, they're still there," Templeton Blair replied.

Roscoe had called an old friend, a man who also had been a Klan member back in the old days. His friend knew the right people to contact if you needed somebody for a certain kind of job. Templeton Blair, an expert at dealing with unpleasant situations, came highly recommended.

"Hell, it's nearly nine o'clock. What are they going to do, stay there all night?"

"What if they find what they're looking for?"

"They won't. And that's the problem." Roscoe had been paying former sheriff Aaron Bendall *hush money* for twenty years. He was still sending him a check every month. He'd made a mistake trusting Bendall to get rid of those files. Oh, he'd removed them from the sheriff's department, but he hadn't destroyed them. Bendall had made copies of the Belle Rose massacre files and kept them, along with the originals, in various safety deposit boxes.

"If there's something in the basement you don't want anybody to find, why didn't you just have somebody set fire to that old building years ago?" Templeton asked.

"I had my reasons." Because there had been no need to destroy the building. Not then. He'd never figured anybody would go snooping around, not after all these years.

"When do you want me to—"

"As soon as possible. I want that uppity son of a bitch stopped. Take him out of the picture first. That should make Jolie Royale think twice. But if she keeps on snooping, then you'll have to deal with her, too."

"Yes, sir. Leave everything to me."

Roscoe slammed down the receiver. Hellfire! Why had Theron Carter come back to Sumarville? Why hadn't he stayed in Memphis at that big fancy law firm? And Jolie Royale! Who'd have thought Louis would leave Belle Rose to her? He'd have laid odds that Louis would have left the old plantation to Georgette. The man had been a fool over that New Orleans whore.

When Theron and Jolie didn't find the files, when they realized those particular files were missing, they'd figure out that somebody deliberately got rid of them. But that wouldn't stop them; it would only add fuel to the flame. They'd keep digging. And once they found out that Bendall was still alive, they'd try to find him. He couldn't allow that to happen.

Roscoe kicked the wastepaper basket beside his desk

and sent it sailing across the room, scattering debris as it rolled to a stop.

A soft knock sounded on the closed door. "Daddy, are you all right? I thought I heard a noise." Gar opened the door.

"I'm fine, Garland," Roscoe said. "Just accidently knocked over the wastebasket."

"Don't worry about it. I'll clean it up."

The minute Gar bent to lift the basket, Roscoe bellowed, "Leave the damn thing. That's what Mattie's for. I pay her enough money to clean up after me."

"All right," Gar said. "I'm going up to bed now. Do you need anything before I retire for the night?"

Did he need anything? Hell, yes, he needed those damn files destroyed. He should have known once Theron moved back to Sumarville that he was up to something. If only he'd sent someone to tear that damn basement apart months ago and destroy a bunch of old files. Then there would be an explanation for why those Belle Rose files were missing. Of course it wouldn't have been an easy thing to accomplish, not with the new sheriff, that big gorilla Denton, being a straight-arrow kind of man. If he could be bought off, Roscoe would have already done it. But Denton was an honest lawman—the kind Roscoe hated.

"Daddy, is something wrong?"

"Huh?"

"You seem miles away."

"Yeah, well, just thinking about a speech I've got to give. You go on up to bed, son. I don't need anything."

Garland said good night, then closed the door behind him when he left Roscoe's study. His son was a good man. A little naive about the way things should be done—the in-and-outs of politics—he'd made a few mistakes. One big mistake in particular. But he was a good man nevertheless. Garland had stood by him when no one else had. Roscoe would do anything to protect his only son and his son's potential political career. He'd even kill to protect him. There was no reason anyone should ever know the truth. He'd make sure of that.

Chapter 13

Nowell followed Clarice into his apartment, then closed and locked the door. She hadn't felt this giddy, hadn't known this mixture of excitement and uncertainty in nearly forty years. Not since the first time she and Jonathan had made love. She'd been twenty-three then and living in Memphis, working at a dress shop, learning her trade. On a rainy Tuesday a young soldier, home on a month's leave, came into the shop looking for a birthday gift for his mother. They had taken one look at each other and it had been love at first sight. Jonathan had been handsome, dashing, ardent. He'd simply swept her off her feet. Within two weeks of their first meeting, they were engaged. And the night he put the ring on her finger, he made love to her for the first time. Those had been the happiest days of her life. Three short weeks. Five months and a hundred love letters later, Jonathan had been killed in Vietnam.

Nowell slipped his arms around Clarice and drew her back up against his chest. While nuzzling her neck, he whispered, "I love you, Clarice. I love you more than life itself."

She turned slowly, the warmth of his embrace, the tenderness in his expression enveloping her in a loving cocoon. His adoring gaze told her more than the words he had spoken what his true feelings were. She never should have doubted him. But she'd been confused since the first day Nowell Landers walked into her life. He'd just shown up one day at Belle Rose and asked to see her.

"I don't mean to disturb you, ma'am," he'd said. "I'm Nowell Landers, and I was a friend of Jonathan Lenz. We were in the same outfit in Nam. I—I was with him when he died."

She hadn't been as instantly attracted to another man since Jonathan, so was it any wonder that she kept finding similarities in the two men? Same height and similar builds, although Nowell was heavier, broader, probably the results of aging. Same piercing dark eyes. But there were differences, too. Enough so that she could usually differentiate between the two. Yet sometimes, when Nowell and she were alone together, like now, her heart longed for them to be the same man. Of course, that wasn't possible, was it? Jonathan was dead.

"I don't like that sad look on your face." Nowell rubbed his index finger across the frown lines on her forehead.

"Sorry, I was just thinking about . . . It doesn't matter." Standing on tiptoe, she kissed him. Sweet and fleeting, just a brush of lips against lips.

"You were thinking about Jonathan, weren't you?"

Clarice grabbed Nowell's hand. "Don't be jealous. I loved Jonathan dearly, but he's been gone a long, long time."

"You still love him," Nowell said.

"I . . . yes. But I love you, too. And I never thought I'd ever love again."

"It's all right, honey." He cupped her face with his

big hands. "I don't mind if you love both of us. Your heart's big enough for that."

"How kind you are. How understanding." She tugged on his hand. "I thought you brought me back here to your apartment after our dinner date so that you could ravish me."

He smiled. "I want to make love to you. But only if it's what you want, too."

"It's what I want," she told him. "More than anything."

Nowell scooped her up into his arms. Sighing with delight, she draped her arm around his neck and laid her head on his shoulder. He carried her through the small living room and into the bedroom, then placed her in the center of the bed, on the brown quilted spread.

"I haven't been with anyone in years," she told him. "Not since . . ."

"No one?" he asked. "No one since Jonathan?"

"No one . . . until you."

"God, Clarice."

She was both surprised and yet deeply touched by the tears in Nowell's eyes. Crying seemed so out of character for the big burly man. Opening her arms in welcome, she said, "Make love to me."

His gentleness mixed with passion, showing her by heated romantic words and nerve-tingling caresses that she was precious to him. "Precious beyond words," he said as he removed her beige silk blouse and unlatched the front hook of her bra.

Shouldn't I feel the least bit embarrassed? she wondered. Shouldn't I worry that he will be disappointed when he sees my thin sixty-year-old body? But she felt neither embarrassment nor worry as Nowell slowly, tenderly removed her clothes, caressing her, kissing her, praising her each step of the way. When she was completely naked, he rose up and off the bed and quickly divested himself of his own clothing. Clarice watched with fascination as he stripped down to bare skin. He was big, thick chested, and very hairy. His chest hair was almost white and the rest was mixed with gray. She studied him, admiring his raw masculinity. And another comparison came to mind. He looked like Jonathan there, too. Although her experience was limited, she knew enough about men to know they weren't all equally endowed.

"You keep staring at me that way, honey, and I won't be able to wait. And I want to wait. I want to take a long time with you."

Clarice swallowed. Her nerves sang a high-pitched melody of great expectations.

Nowell came down over her, bracing his weight so that he didn't crush her. His lips moved over her face, down her throat and stopped to pay homage to her small breasts, her taut nipples. She quivered, the sensation an unbearably painful pleasure. While he acquainted himself with every inch of her body, every curve, every indentation, she caressed him—his shoulders, his hairy chest, his large biceps, his stomach, his penis. When she circled him, he drew in a deep breath, but made no move to stop her when she began pumping him. Odd how familiar everything was, the taste of him, the feel of him, the sound of his heavy breathing. *Making love must be like riding a bicycle,* she thought, *you never forget how to do it.*

With intimate lunges, Nowell's tongue explored between her open thighs. When he laved the kernel of sensitive flesh between her feminine folds, Clarice's hips bucked upward to meet his mouth. And then before she realized what was happening, she climaxed. While shudders of release racked her body, Nowell tested her readiness and found her moist from her orgasm. He lifted her hips and entered her, slowly, carefully, inch by inch embedding himself deeper inside her. When he'd taken her fully, she wrapped her legs around his hips and participated passionately as he thrust and retreated. Within a couple of minutes, he came, his roar of completion like that of a jungle animal.

"God, Ricie, I love you." He eased off her, sliding down beside her on the bed.

Although she was in a state of shock, she didn't protest when he pulled her close and held her. She lay there, her heart beating wildly, her mind filled with chaotic, incomprehensible thoughts. He had called her Ricie, but apparently wasn't aware that he had. Jonathan had called her Ricie. No one else. Only Jonathan. There was a logical explanation for why he'd used Jonathan's pet name for her. There had to be. But she couldn't imagine what that explanation might be. She couldn't believe that Jonathan would have shared something so personal, so intimate with anyone else, not even a comrade in arms. But what other explanation could there be? Unless . . . *Oh, Clarice, you mustn't do this to yourself. Stop thinking crazy thoughts. Accept Nowell for who he is and be grateful that you've found love again. Don't ask for the impossible.*

Tired, dirty, and feeling slightly waterlogged after drinking God only knew how many cups of coffee, Jolie dropped her head onto the old desk in the basement of the sheriff's department and groaned loudly.

"Okay, I give up," she said. "We've gone over every inch of this basement, looked through every damn file cabinet, every shelf, every drawer, in every nook and cranny. There are no Belle Rose massacre files."

Theron cocked his chair backward, up on two legs, stretched his arms, entwined his fingers, and cupped the back of his head. "Either someone took them, probably years ago, or someone destroyed them. It really doesn't matter. Either way, we're screwed. Without those files—"

"Don't say it." Jolie lifted her head just enough so that she could look at Theron. "There has to be another way to get the case reopened. Just the fact that the files are missing should prove something."

"Prove what?" he asked. "Prove incompetence? Files get misplaced all the time. We have no proof that they were destroyed or taken. All we have is my gut instinct."

"Then we'll just have to find another way to gather evidence. Find Sheriff Bendall, if he's still alive. Talk to his deputies. It's only been twenty years ago. Most of them probably still live around here. And there's always the CIB report. The agent who came to Sumarville to investigate had to have filed a report. We need to find out his name and where he lives now."

"I'm too tired to think about it tonight." Theron checked his wristwatch. "Damn, it's nearly eleven o'clock." He scooted back his chair and stood. "Come on. Let's go home. We can come back tomorrow and straighten up this mess. After a good night's sleep, we'll plot our new strategy."

Jolie rose to her feet, arched her back, and groaned. "I'm not used to sitting that long. My neck, shoulders, and back are sore."

As they headed for the stairs, Theron clamped his hand on Jolie's shoulder. "Take a long soak in the tub before you go to bed. Then sleep until I phone you in the morning. Bright and early tomorrow, I'm going to make some calls and also talk to Ike to see if I can find out the whereabouts of everyone involved in the investigation. As soon as I have something to go on, I'll call you."

"Sounds like a plan to me."

Upstairs they said good night to the deputies on the evening shift, then headed outside to their cars. Just as Jolie unlocked and opened the driver's side door of her Escalade, Theron called to her.

"You realize that Ike was right about it taking somebody with money and power to pull Larry Newman's strings, don't you? The same holds true for whoever saw to it that those records disappeared. And since we have no way of knowing if those files have been missing for years or only for months—"

"What are you trying to say?"

"If the files were *misplaced* in the past few months or even the past few years, then I'd say either Roscoe Wells or Max Devereaux is the man behind the scenes."

"And if they were misplaced twenty years ago?" She held her breath, knowing the answer, but needing to hear Theron say it.

"Then it would be either Roscoe or . . ." he hesitated a split second, "or Louis Royale."

She released the breath she'd been holding, suddenly feeling like a deflated balloon. "Why would Daddy . . . Oh, my God. To protect Georgette."

"Or Georgette's son."

Georgette lay awake in her bed. Alone and afraid. She'd never been afraid when Louis was with her. He always kept the demons at bay. Nothing would ever be the same without him. He had known her so well, understood her completely, and loved her unconditionally. Now that Louis was gone, Max would try his best to take care of her. But her son didn't know the woman she'd once been, so he couldn't truly understand her well enough to help her fight the monsters that lived inside her.

The room lay in shadows. The night-light in the corner didn't banish enough of the darkness. She reached out and flipped on the bedside lamp. A creamy glow illuminated the room. Georgette slipped out of bed, grabbed her thin silk robe from the chaise longue, and went to the French doors that opened out onto the upstairs balcony at the front of the house.

As a young girl she had dreamed of living in a house like this, with servants to wait on her, and more money than she could spend in a lifetime. While she earned her living by giving her body to any man with the right price, she had kept her heart untouched. And dreamed of the day her prince would come. Philip Devereaux had been her prince. One of her customers for several years, using her services whenever he visited New Orleans, Philip had fallen in love with her. She had given Philip a little piece of her heart when he married her and took her with him to live in Sumarville. His home had been nice, better than anything she'd ever known, but it was nothing in comparison to Belle Rose.

The first time she saw Louis Royale, she knew that he was unlike any man she'd ever known. And the first time he touched her, she had felt that she was destined to be his in a way she had never belonged to another man. She had given her whole heart to Louis, loving him more than she'd ever thought possible. And he had loved her, with his body and his heart and even with his very soul.

But I had no soul to give you, did I, my love? Georgette whispered the words as she opened the French doors and walked out onto the balcony. *Once you've killed, once you've taken another person's life, you lose your soul.*

Chapter 14

Theron started the Ferrari's motor, powered down the windows to release some of the stale oppressive heat that had accumulated inside the vehicle during the afternoon, and upped the air-conditioner setting. Glancing in his rearview mirror, he watched Jolie's SUV pass by behind him. She threw up a hand and waved good-bye. Odd that a friendship forged in childhood and left unattended for years could remain so strong. Of course, discovering they had a common purpose—righting the wrongs of the past—bound them together now. But was that the only reason he felt a connection to Jolie? *It was just gossip. You know how people talk. They said Mr. Sam Desmond and Sadie Fuqua were . . .* Ike's word played over in his mind, like a needle stuck in a groove on an old record. He didn't want to believe it was true, that Sam Desmond had fathered his grandmother's twins, that his mother was a half sibling to the Desmond sisters. He couldn't deny that he'd wondered about his mother's light skin and her hazel eyes, eyes he had inherited from her. But he had thought that whatever white blood flowed in her veins came from generations ago.

But if it were true, why hadn't his mother told him? And why hadn't he ever heard the rumor before today?

Theron removed his cell phone from the belt clip, fished in his shirt pocket for the number he'd written down this morning, and punched in the digits. She had told him to call anytime before midnight.

She answered on the fifth ring. "Hello."

"Amy, I apologize for calling so late at night, but—"

"That's all right. It's not midnight. I hadn't gone to bed."

He loved the sound of her voice. Soft, light, slightly high-pitched, like a little girl's. But Amy Jardien was no little girl. She was all woman. Beautiful, intelligent, and successful. The kind of lady he liked.

"I suppose it's too late for me to drop by," he said.

She laughed, a sweet tinkling sound that aroused him. "Yes, I'm afraid it is."

Theron touched the button that lifted the windows closed, then he put the gears into reverse and backed out of the parking place. Bracing the phone between his ear and his shoulder, he put both hands on the wheel as he headed down Main Street.

"What about tomorrow night?" he asked.

"What about it?"

"How about dinner? Around six-thirty?"

"I usually start my rounds at the hospital at six. But if you'll make it seven-thirty, then we have a date."

"Seven-thirty it is." As Theron turned off Main and onto Oak Avenue, he noticed headlights behind him. A vehicle had made the same turn a couple of minutes after he did. "Do you have any preferences for dinner? Italian? Chinese? Downhome cooking?"

"I'll let you choose," she told him. "I'm not picky and I'm afraid my indiscriminate appetite shows on my hips."

"Your hips look fine to me." He smiled when he heard her sigh. "As a matter of fact, everything about you looks fine to me. Mighty fine."

"My, my, Mr. Carter, I had no idea you were such a sweet-talking man. But I should have suspected you would use words to your advantage, since you're a lawyer."

"I've found that words can be used to hurt, to heal, to seduce . . . Amy?"

"Yes?"

Theron turned again, off Oak Avenue and onto Pinewood, the street where his rented duplex apartment was located. Instinctively he glanced in the rearview mirror. No sign of headlights. A sense of relief eased through him. Hell, why had he been concerned? *You didn't think somebody was following you, did you?*

"You've lived in Sumarville all your life, so I was wondering . . ." He paused. Should he bring up the subject of old hometown rumors? "Nah, just forget it."

"What? What were you wondering?"

Theron pulled his car into the driveway at the side of his duplex. "I heard a rumor today . . . an old rumor. About my grandmother."

"Oh?"

"Ike Denton happened to mention that . . . Have you ever heard people say anything about my mama being Mr. Sam Desmond's daughter?"

Amy sucked in a deep breath.

"Amy?"

Theron undid his seat belt, opened the car door, and got out; then he closed and locked the door behind him.

"You mean you don't know if it's true or not?" she finally responded. "If it's true, wouldn't your mother have told you?"

"You didn't answer my question." Using the streetlight to see by, Theron jiggled his key chain, seeking his door key.

"No, Theron, I've never heard that rumor. But come to think of it, I do remember my mother saying something I thought was rather odd at the time."

"What was that?" He walked up the sidewalk toward his front door.

"I overheard Mama and Daddy talking not long after the Belle Rose massacre and Mama said that if it had been anyone else, she wouldn't have believed it, but that Lisette Desmond was just the type of woman who would have taken her own brother as a lover. I wondered what Mama meant because the Desmond sisters didn't have a brother."

"My God!"

"You shouldn't jump to conclusions," Amy said. "Ask your mother. She'll tell you the truth."

Theron started to insert the key in the deadbolt lock on his front door. Hearing a car drive by, he glanced over his shoulder in time to see a dark sedan pull over to the curb and stop in front of the duplex.

"Amy, will you hold on for a minute," Theron said. "I'll—"

Three men emerged from the car. Three white men.

"Amy, call the police station and tell them to send a patrol car to my house, 118-B Pinewood."

Theron's hand shook as he tried to insert the house key into the lock. Three trailer-trash white guys trooping toward his duplex had to mean trouble. Big trouble. For him.

"Theron, what's wrong?"

"Just do it!"

The damn key was upside down!

Leaving the phone on, he slid it onto his belt clip and turned to face the threesome coming right at him. He didn't have time to unlock the door, get inside, and deadbolt the door.

"Good evening," one of the men said, the tallest of the three, the guy in the middle.

"Evening," Theron replied, trying for a show of bravado. "What can I do for y'all?"

They hadn't tried to disguise their appearances, had done nothing to prevent him from recognizing them and identifying them at a later date. That meant one of two things—either they had no intention of physically harming him or they were going to kill him.

Jolie stopped at the closed gates, rolled down the window, reached out, and punched in the code numbers Aunt Clarice had given her. She had memorized the codes for the gate and for the house. When had her father installed the security system at Belle Rose? Not immediately after the murders, so it must have been sometime after he sent her away. Had he been afraid that someone might harm his new family?

As she approached the house, she noticed that lights were still on downstairs, but the upstairs was dark. Did that mean someone—probably Aunt Clarice—had left the lights on for her?

She parked her SUV in the drive. Tomorrow she'd have to inform Max that she expected a place in the garage to be vacated for her Escalade. It didn't really matter to her whose car would have to be removed to make room for hers. Preferably Georgette's Mercedes. But she suspected Max would leave his Porsche outside before he'd dream of upsetting his mother. After locking the Escalade, she kept the key chain in her hand as she headed up the steps to the front veranda.

Just as she started to insert the key in the lock, a voice said, "Coming home kind of late, aren't you?"

After gasping and jumping simultaneously, Jolie jerked around, seeking the man who had spoken. Dropping her keys into the pocket of her linen jacket, she strolled across the veranda. With one leg crossed over the other, looking completely relaxed and right at home, Max sat in one of the big rocking chairs on the side porch. Light coming through a nearby window silhouetted the chair and its occupant. His blue shirt was completely unbuttoned and hung loosely around his hips. She scanned him from his damp hair—apparently he'd just showered—to his chest, lightly dusted with dark hair, over his faded jeans, then hurried past his crotch, and down over his legs to his bare feet.

"Waiting up for me, stepbrother dear?"

"Perhaps."

He glanced up at her. Because she couldn't see his eyes clearly, she felt at a disadvantage. She'd found that the best chance of discerning Max's reaction was to study his steel blue eyes.

She removed her wrinkled linen jacket, hung it on the back of the rocker beside the one Max occupied, then sat down beside him. "Has everyone else gone to bed?"

"Mother and Mallory are in their rooms," he replied. "Uncle Parry stays in town several nights every week. And Aunt Clarice isn't home yet. She's still out on her date with Nowell Landers."

"You don't like Mr. Landers, do you?"

"I don't trust the man."

"Why not?" Jolie began rocking back and forth.

"He wants something from Aunt Clarice. I just haven't figured out what it is. Money probably."

"Have you ever thought that the man is who and what he presents himself to be and all he wants is Aunt Clarice herself?"

"I had no idea you were such a romantic."

She sensed rather than heard the humor in Max's voice. "I'm not a romantic, not by any means. But I'm not totally pessimistic either. I don't question everyone's motives . . . unless they give me a reason."

He turned his head in her direction. The interior light hit his face just right so that she saw the hint of a smile. "Maybe I should turn Aunt Clarice over to you, let you be her keeper while you're here at Belle Rose."

"I don't believe Aunt Clarice needs a keeper. She's a bit more high-strung than most, but she's not crazy. Not the way people think."

"I didn't say I thought she was crazy. But she is vulnerable and easy prey for a con man claiming to have been with her beloved Jonathan when he died."

If she didn't know better, she'd swear that Max actually cared about Aunt Clarice. But that wasn't possible, was it? Not Max Devereaux, the heartless bastard.

"Maybe Nowell Landers really was with Jonathan when he was killed."

Max shook his head. "About a month ago Louis asked me to run a check on Nowell Landers. There was no one by that name in Jonathan's outfit. No one named Nowell Landers was even in Vietnam the same year Jonathan was."

"Oh." She allowed her gaze to meet his in the semi-darkness. "Did you tell her? Does she know he lied to her?"

"I told her. And she told me that I must be mistaken, that the information was incorrect."

"Have you confronted Mr. Landers with the truth?"

"Not yet. I've been distracted by other things that required my immediate attention. Louis's illness and death, to name two."

Ah, yes, Max was Louis Royale's right-hand man, the son he'd always wanted and never had. The heir apparent to her father's power and prestigious position in the realm of Southern business and politics.

"I'm surprised, considering how close you two became that you didn't call him Daddy or Father or Papa."

"I was nearly nineteen when he married my mother," Max said, his tone even and without emotion. "Besides, I'll always think of Philip Devereaux as my father."

"Hm—mm. I remember Philip. A quiet shy man. Very sweet." She leaned over the arm of her chair and gazed straight into Max's eyes. "What happened to all that hatred you felt for my father? You made no secret of the fact that you believed if Daddy hadn't informed the police that Philip had embezzled money from their jointly owned businesses, the insurance company and the stove foundry, that Philip would never have killed himself."

Max remained silent for several minutes. The cicadas' stridulous buzz surrounded them, reminding Jolie of childhood summer nights spent on the porch with her family or in the yard chasing lightning bugs. A hoot owl's cry blended with the other nocturnal sounds. But above the familiar summertime chorus, she could hear Max breathing. A peculiar sensation deep inside her made her shiver. She felt an overpowering urge to reach out and touch him, to lay her hand over his chest and feel the steady pumping of his heart.

"I did something for Louis that you refused to do for my mother," Max said, his deep voice low and oddly soft.

"And what was that?" She sensed sorrow and pain radiating from him, but it was such a subtle realization that she knew she could be imagining it.

"I gave myself the chance to get to know my step-parent, to find out just what sort of man he was. When our parents married and my mother begged me to come to Belle Rose with her, I came. I did it for her. And with each passing year, the hatred I'd once felt for Louis changed to begrudging respect and then to liking and finally. . . . The only dishonorable thing your father ever did was have an affair with my mother, while your mother was still alive."

"And while Philip Devereaux was still alive."

"No, the affair began after Philip died."

"How do you know?"

"Mother and Louis told me that their affair began after Philip's death."

"And you believed them?"

"Yes. Louis never lied to me. Not ever."

"He lied to my mother, every time he betrayed her with Georgette."

Jolie rose from her chair, leaving it rocking. She walked to the edge of the porch and leaned against one of the white columns bracing the upstairs balcony. All the anger and pain and the terrible sense of betrayal she had felt that day when she'd watched through the dirty windowpanes of the cottage in the woods overwhelmed her. It was as fresh and raw as the moment it happened, as vivid in her memory—the sight of her father's naked butt moving up and down as he pumped into Georgette Devereaux.

"I saw them," she said, her voice whispery with emotion.

"Who?" Max asked.

"Your mother and my father. In the old cottage, deep in the woods. You know, where you used to take Felicia. Sandy said Felicia told her about the cottage."

Max rose from his chair and came up behind Jolie. She felt his heat, his overpowering masculine presence.

"You saw Louis and my mother making love?" he asked.

"Yes. I saw them. I saw them fucking . . . the day of the Belle Rose massacre. And when I regained consciousness at the hospital, I told Daddy that I'd seen them."

His big hands clamped over her shoulders, but his touch was unbelievably gentle. "And you were how old—fourteen? And had never even been kissed. You must have been shocked senseless by what you saw." His grip tightened ever so slightly as he drew her backward toward his body. "And you went straight home to . . . to do what? Tell your mother? And that's when you found the bodies. That's when you were shot and left for dead."

His warm breath grazed her neck, making her unbearably aware of his presence. So near. So very near.

Tears lodged in her throat, threatening to choke her. She sucked in air between her clenched teeth.

"It was a Saturday," she said. "He should have been home—home with *my* mother, not hiding away in some shack screwing *your* mother!" Jolie whirled around, her actions releasing her from his tentative hold. She glared at him. "If my father had been home with his wife that day, home where he belonged, he could have stopped the murderer. He could have saved Mama and Aunt Lisette and—"

Max grabbed her upper arms with brutal force, his fingers biting into her flesh. "You've blamed them all these years, blamed them for what happened that day here at Belle Rose."

"Yes, I blamed them. If they hadn't been together, if Daddy had been here . . . If Georgette had stayed away from him, if she'd left him alone, Daddy would never . . . He loved my mama."

Max's gaze collided with Jolie's. She found that she could not break eye contact, could not look away. His hot gaze held her spellbound, trapped with no means of escape.

"I'm sure he loved your mother when he married her," Max said, his voice taking on an oddly sensual quality. "But things happen in a marriage. People change. Feelings change."

"They're not supposed to. If you truly love some-one—"

"Louis didn't love Audrey Desmond the way he loved my mother. I've never seen two people more passion-ately in love than Louis and Mother. She once told me that they were as essential to each other as the very air they breathed. Do you have any idea how that feels? Do you know what a man and woman with that type of hunger would do to be together?"

"No." Every nerve in Jolie's body shrilled a warning. "Do you know? Was that the way it was with you and Felicia?"

"God, no! That bitch never loved anyone except herself." Max ran his hands up and down Jolie's naked arms.

Heat exploded inside her as she swayed toward Max, her body just barely touching his. Her hand lifted of its own volition and came down in the center of Max's chest, directly over his thundering heart. A low growl escaped his lips. They glared at each other. He lowered his head.

A telephone rang. Max froze. Jolie held her breath. The phone kept ringing.

"It's the phone in the house," Max said. "I'd better get it."

She managed to nod her head. He released her, turned, and hurried into the house through the open French doors leading into the front parlor. Jolie gasped huge mouthfuls of air the minute he was out of sight. *Dear God, what just happened?* she asked herself. *Had Max been about to kiss her? And more important, had she wanted him to kiss her?*

"Jolie!" Max called from the doorway.

She forced herself to face him. "Yes?"

"That was Yvonne. She was nearly hysterical. It seems Theron has been in an accident. The police just notified her."

"Oh, dear God, no!"

"I told Yvonne that she was in no condition to drive herself, that you and I would be right over to get her and take her to the hospital."

"Yes, of course." Jolie lifted her jacket off the chair, then moved toward Max as if she were in a trance. Indeed she felt as if she were.

She stood just inside the front parlor, watching him hurriedly slip on the socks and shoes he must have discarded there earlier before he went outside on the porch. He buttoned his shirt and stuck the ends inside his jeans, then grabbed Jolie's arm, pulling her farther into the room before he closed and locked the French doors. She staggered slightly when he released her.

"We'll take your SUV," he told her, while he opened the mahogany secretary, removed pen and paper, and began writing furiously.

"What are you doing?"

"Writing a note for Mother and Mallory and Aunt Clarice, to let them know where we've gone."

She nodded. Leaving the note lying on the open secretary, Max manacled Jolie's wrist and pulled her with him, through the parlor and out into the foyer.

"Give me your keys," he demanded.

"Why?"

"Don't argue, just give me the damn keys. We're wasting time."

She pulled the keys out of her jacket pocket and handed them to him. "Was it a car wreck?"

"What?" Max punched in the security code on the pad by the front door, then shoved Jolie out onto the porch. He closed and, using her keys, locked the double doors behind them.

"Theron's accident—was he in a car wreck?"

"No." Max paused long enough to look directly at her. "Yvonne said the police told her that it appears Theron was beaten . . . beaten almost to death."

Chapter 15

Jolie hated hospitals and had religiously avoided them since she'd spent over a month here at Desmond County General twenty years ago. Hospitals had their own unique scents and sounds, and a special atmosphere, except on the maternity floor, that projected visions of suffering and death. She would rather be just about anywhere else on earth. Although the facility had been modernized, enough of the original remained to give Jolie an eerie feeling of familiarity.

While Max parked the Escalade, Jolie and Yvonne rushed into the ER, only to be told that Theron had been taken to surgery moments after arrival. By the time they absorbed the information, Max was there, taking charge, leading them into the hospital corridor and straight to the nearest elevator.

"Max, please, find out what happened." Yvonne clutched Jolie's hand. "The person who called—I can't remember his name—said that Theron had been badly beaten." With her facial features pinched in a mother's agony, Yvonne moaned, an obvious effort to keep herself from becoming hysterical.

"I'll handle everything," Max assured her. "As soon as we get to the surgery waiting room, I'll speak to the nurse in charge and find out how extensive Theron's injuries are." He reached out and curled his big hand over Yvonne's shoulder, patting her comfortingly. "And I'll contact Chief Harper and get a report on exactly what happened to Theron."

"Thank you." Yvonne whispered, her voice racked with emotion.

The elevator doors swung open. Jolie moved swiftly to keep up with Yvonne's urgent pace as she followed Max's lead down the hall and into the small dark waiting area. He flipped the wall switch and overhead lighting illuminated the room. A pair of twin sofas flanked the walls to the right and left of the entrance and a couple of chairs, with a table positioned between them, occupied the back wall, directly beneath a wide window covered with aluminum blinds.

"Y'all stay here," Max said. "I'll see what I can find out."

No sooner had Max spoken than a policeman appeared in the doorway. "Mrs. Carter?" the young black officer asked.

Yvonne jerked around to face him. "Yes, I'm Mrs. Carter."

"I'm sorry about your son," he said.

Jolie read the officer's name tag: T. CURRY. "Could you tell us what happened? Was Theron really beaten? Where did it happen? Who would have done something so—"

"Let Officer Curry speak." Max placed his hand in the small of Jolie's back.

His casual touch should have set off alarm bells inside her, but it didn't. For some peculiar reason his hand resting gently on her back seemed quite natural, as if they were old friends. Or old lovers.

Curry shook his head, avoiding eye contact with Yvonne, then he looked directly at Max. "We received a call from Dr. Jardien at eleven-twenty-five—"

"Amy Jardien?" Yvonne asked.

"Yes, ma'am," Officer Curry replied. "Mr. Carter had called her on his cell phone and they were still connected when it happened. He told her to call the police immediately but didn't tell her what was wrong. Then she heard a scuffle, heard some rather explicit language, a few racial slurs . . . she's pretty sure there were several voices. At least two, maybe three, other than Mr. Carter's."

"Oh, dear Lord." Yvonne entwined her hands in front of her face in a prayer-like gesture.

Max inclined his head toward the door. "Why don't we step outside, officer."

"No!" Yvonne grabbed Max's arm. "I want to hear the rest. I want to know what happened."

"Are you sure?" Max asked. "I could—"

"Yes, I'm sure," she replied.

Curry swiped his hand across his mouth and down over his chin. "When we arrived, we found Mr. Carter lying on the ground in front of his apartment. At first we thought he was de"—Curry cleared his throat—"but he was only unconscious. We saw right away that he'd been beaten. He was bloody and . . . The ambulance arrived a few minutes after we did and they rushed him here to Desmond County."

"What about the men who attacked him?" Max asked. "Did you apprehend them?"

Curry shook his head. "No, sir. There was no sign of anybody when we arrived, just the woman who lives in the other duplex. She'd heard a racket and looked out her window. She said she saw three white men running to a car parked by the curb. She couldn't give us a description of the men or of the car. The streetlight is across the street on the corner, so her vision was limited.

And Mrs. Fredericks wears glasses and didn't have them on. She'd just gotten out of bed to check on the noise."

"I was afraid something like this would happen," Yvonne said. "I told him"—she glared at Jolie—"I told both of you the risk you'd be taking."

"What were you afraid would happen?" Max asked. "What did Theron and Jolie do to put themselves at risk?"

"Yvonne, you can't be sure there's any connection," Jolie said.

"Of course there is!" Yvonne told her. "I just didn't think it would happen this soon."

"Would you mind telling me what you're talking about?" Officer Curry asked. "It might help us in our investigation."

Yvonne walked away, across the room, and sat down in one of the chairs by the window. She closed her eyes, laid her hands in her lap, and moved her lips silently. *She's praying,* Jolie thought.

Jolie looked directly at Curry. "Theron is convinced that his uncle, Lemar Fuqua, was not the Belle Rose massacre killer. He intends to prove that someone else killed my mother and aunt . . . and Lemar, too."

Max groaned. Slanting her gaze sideways, Jolie offered him a searing glance.

"Are you Ms. Royale?" Curry asked. "Jolie Royale, the only survivor of the Belle Rose massacre?"

"Yes, I am. And I agree with Theron that Lemar Fuqua wasn't a murderer. Theron and I both want the old case reopened. We want the real murderer found and punished and Lemar's name cleared. Yesterday afternoon, D.A. Newman gave us permission to look at all the files pertaining to the Belle Rose case. Theron and I worked together until after eleven last night in the basement of the sheriff's department, going through all the old files."

"Are you saying that there's a connection between

the Belle Rose massacre and what happened to Theron Carter?" Curry asked.

"I can't say for sure," Jolie said. "But there very well could be."

"Why do you think there could be a connection?" Max asked. "Did y'all find something in those files that would prove Lemar innocent?"

Jolie snapped her head around and glowered at Max. "We didn't find the files. They weren't there. But maybe you already knew that."

"Damn, how could I have known?" Max squinched his eyes to mere slits.

Like two gunfighters in an old Western movie, Max and Jolie squared off, bodies tense, gazes riveted.

"Look, Ms. Royale, we'll probably need a statement from you." Curry's comment momentarily reduced the tension radiating between Max and her. "I'll pass the information you gave me along to the chief and see what he thinks. In the meantime, I'd like to check with the officers who went over the crime scene. I'm hoping they found something that will lead us to Mr. Carter's attackers." Curry turned to leave, paused, and glanced over his shoulder. Nodding sideways to indicate Yvonne, he spoke to Max. "Tell Mrs. Carter that we'll do everything we can to find the"—he glanced toward Jolie—"the bastards who attacked her son."

The minute Curry disappeared down the hall, Jolie rushed to Max, grabbed his arm, then gave him a non-too-gentle shove toward the door. "I want to talk to you. Out in the hall."

Max obliged her without comment. Once they were in the corridor, several feet away from the surgery waiting area, he stopped, leaned back against the wall, and casually crossed his arms over his chest.

"Let's have it," he said.

"Theron and I found out two things today. One: somebody is pulling Larry Newman's strings. Two: somebody stole all the files pertaining to the Belle Rose massacre case."

"And just what does this information have to do with me?"

"Only two men in Desmond County have the power to control the D.A. and make those files disappear."

Max shrugged.

"Damn you!" Jolie glowered at him. "Those two men are Roscoe Wells and Maximillian Devereaux."

Max's expression didn't change, didn't reveal the least bit of emotion. But there was a glimmer of something in his eyes. Something sinister? Or was it simply controlled rage?

"I didn't even vote for Newman in the last election. And I don't know anything about your missing files."

"Do you expect me to believe you?"

"I don't expect you to do anything except cause trouble. That seems to be the one thing you're good at doing. Dredging up old memories, stirring up a stink, putting people through the misery of reliving a past better left forgotten."

She took a tentative step toward him, pausing when only a few inches separated their bodies. "Do you honestly think that anyone involved could ever forget about those brutal murders? If you'd been shot and left for dead beside your mother's lifeless body, would you ever be able to forget?"

"Probably not," Max admitted. "But you have no proof that the snooping you and Theron were doing is in any way connected to those men attacking Theron."

"I don't need proof. I know in here"—she slapped her clenched fist on her belly—"that somebody wanted Theron stopped before he unearthed any information that might force the D.A. to reopen the Belle Rose case. And so help me God, I'm going to find out who the son of a bitch is. Theron might not be able to continue searching, to keep digging for the truth, but I can. And I will."

Max uncrossed his arms and eased away from the wall. "If what you believe is true, then you could wind up getting yourself hurt, maybe even killed."

"Is that a threat?"

Groaning, Max rolled his eyes toward the ceiling. Then before Jolie realized what he intended, he grabbed her upper arms, whirled her around, and pushed her up against the wall. Her heartbeat accelerated. Wide-eyed and mouth parted on a shocked gasp, she shivered as he splayed his big hands on either side of her head.

"I don't make threats. I learned from Louis to make promises and to always keep those promises."

"What else did you learn from my father? Did you learn to lie and cheat and betray people who loved and trusted you? Did he teach you how to manipulate the law and to keep the truth hidden?" *That's it, Jolie, keep staring right into those cold blue eyes. Show him that he can't intimidate you.*

"My God, listen to yourself." Max's scowl fixed menacingly on Jolie's face. "You're implying that Louis was somehow involved in the Belle Rose massacre."

"Only indirectly. He would have protected Georgette. If your mother had hired someone . . . or if she had persuaded you to—" The fiery wrath burning in Max's eyes silenced her. She suddenly felt as if she were trapped at the summit of a volcano that was on the verge of erupting.

Without saying a word, Max lifted his hands from the wall and moved away, then strode down the corridor. Not until he turned the corner and was completely out of sight did Jolie breathe again. Heaven help her, she had goaded a fire-breathing dragon. Now, she couldn't help wondering if it were only a matter of time before his searing anger burned her alive.

* * *

Even Aunt Clarice had been unable to persuade Yvonne to leave the hospital, so they had banded together and set up a flexible schedule for themselves to make sure she would never be alone. Aunt Clarice took the day shift; Amy Jardien took the evening shift; and Jolie took the night shift. Nowell Landers kept Aunt Clarice company and watched over Clarice and Yvonne like a guardian angel. The more Jolie got to know Nowell, the better she liked him. If he wasn't in love with Clarice, then he deserved an Academy Award for his performance. Members of Yvonne's church—the Freewill Baptist Church—visited regularly, checking on Yvonne, joining Reverend Chapman in several prayer vigils and bringing meals to the hospital for Yvonne and Clarice.

Sandy Wells had agreed to be on call in the evenings so that Amy didn't have to deal with patients during her shift at Yvonne's side. Ike Denton came by around eight every evening and had stayed until midnight the past couple of nights, not leaving until Yvonne and Jolie bedded down on the sofas in the ICU waiting room. The first night Ike came by, Jolie had told him that she planned to continue the investigation into the Belle Rose case, but after seeing how upset her declaration made Yvonne, she made sure that Yvonne didn't hear her future conversations with Ike.

The police had come up with a big fat zero as far as identifying Theron's attackers. Chief Harper swore that the Sumarville Police Department would, in his own words, "leave no rock unturned, because surely the men who had brutalized Theron must have crawled out from under a rock somewhere." The local papers gave the case front page headlines daily and the local TV station was running a piece about racial hate crimes on their ten o'clock broadcast every night. A representative of the NAACP had dropped by the hospital to see Yvonne on two separate occasions. And Morris Dees, founder of the Southern Poverty Law Center, had phoned Yvonne.

Jolie knew for a fact that Max came by the hospital twice a day and called to check on Theron several times between visits. But since her confrontation with Max, he had avoided her like the plague. Aunt Clarice said that Max slept at home each night but timed his arrival after Jolie left for the hospital at ten-thirty each night and then made sure he was up and gone before Jolie returned to Belle Rose around eight-thirty each morning. The time she spent at the house involved little more than taking a nap, eating lunch and dinner, and checking in with Cheryl Randall to keep tabs on her Atlanta-based design firm. Since Theron's accident, Georgette had started taking her meals in her room, which kept the substitute housekeeper running up and down the stairs. Jolie had the pleasure of dining with Parry and Mallory, both totally sympathetic to Theron, and each blaming her for his condition. She tried to ignore them, but that was easier said than done.

"If you hadn't joined forces with Yvonne's boy, I doubt anything would have ever come of his plans to get the old Belle Rose case reopened," Parry had said. "You could have saved everybody around here a lot of trouble if you'd just gone back to Atlanta after Louis's funeral."

"I wish you'd been the one they attacked!" Mallory had told Jolie. "Nobody wants you at Belle Rose. You have no right to be here. We all hate you!"

Mallory was a brat. God, had she been that much of a smart-mouthed know-it-all at eighteen? And Parry Clifton puzzled Jolie. He vacillated between vaguely disguised hostility and some sort of weird flirting, apparently unable to decide whether he despised Jolie or desired her. She supposed she could write off his unnerving flirtation to the fact that she resembled her aunt Lisette. Perhaps sometimes Parry looked at her and saw Lisette. That was the only explanation for his odd behavior.

Five days had passed since the brutal attack on Theron. Although his prognosis had improved—the doctors now believed he would live—he hadn't come out of the coma.

When the elevator doors swung open, Jolie stepped out and headed straight for the ICU waiting room. She'd brought a thermos of decaf coffee and a half-read paperback with her. Often she found it difficult to sleep at the hospital and needed something to pass the long hours while Yvonne rested.

She stopped dead in the doorway. The waiting room was empty. She checked her watch. Ten-fifty. The last visiting time for ICU was at ten o'clock. Where were Yvonne and Amy? Where was Ike? *No need to keep wondering,* she told herself. After placing her thermos and book on the sofa in the waiting room, she headed straight for the closed ICU door. She lifted her hand to knock, then through the glass pane in the center of the door, she saw a nurse coming toward her.

The door opened and the nurse—Connie Markham, a plump, petite brunette with a Moon Pie face—smiled at Jolie. "Ms. Royale, please come with me. Mrs. Carter said to bring you right on back the minute you arrived."

"What is it? What's wrong?"

"Nothing's wrong," Connie replied. "Mr. Carter is responding. When his mother went in to see him at ten, he squeezed her hand."

"Then he's conscious?" Jolie asked. "Has he said anything?"

Connie shook her head. "His eyes are open and he's squeezing his mother's hand and Dr. Jardien's hand. But he hasn't moved or spoken. We put in a call to Dr. Bainbridge about thirty minutes ago and he's on his way here."

The minute Jolie reached Theron's ICU cubicle, Ike Denton stepped out to greet her, a wide smile on his face.

"You go on in, Ms. Royale. Mrs. Carter won't leave his side and the nurses are being very considerate, but

I don't think they'll allow four of us in there at the same time."

"Thank you." Jolie patted the sheriff's arm as she passed him and went over to where Yvonne stood by Theron's bed. She draped her arm around Yvonne's shoulder.

Even though he looked better than he had right after surgery, Theron still looked as if he'd been run over by a transfer truck. His nose, several ribs, both arms, and both legs were broken. His face and other areas of his body were bruised and discolored. He had suffered a severe concussion and extensive internal bleeding. Dear God, he was lucky to be alive. Just the sight of him filled Jolie with rage. She wanted the men who had done this to him caught and punished. Hell, what she really wanted was each of those men to be beaten within an inch of his life.

Yvonne eased her arm around Jolie's waist. "He's getting better. He can hear what we say to him and he can respond. He squeezes my hand once for yes and twice for no." Yvonne nudged Jolie closer to the bed. "Say something to him. Ask him a question."

Jolie reached down and took Theron's limp hand. "Hey, there. It's about time you quit sleeping and let us know you're okay." He lay there, seemingly lifeless, his eyes open, but he appeared not to see anything. "Are you in pain?"

He squeezed her hand once.

"Can't they give him anything?" Jolie asked Yvonne.

"He's on the medication prescribed by Dr. Bainbridge," Amy Jardien, who stood on the other side of the bed, explained. "As soon as his doctor examines him and concludes that Theron is conscious and responsive, then he'll alter the medication."

Theron's grip on Jolie's hand tightened. "What is it?" she asked. "Is there something you want me to do for you?"

He squeezed once.

How would she ever know what he wanted? Was there any point in playing twenty-questions. Probably not, but what choice did she have?

"Do you need something from your apartment?"

Two squeezes.

"Does it have anything to do with Yvonne?"

Two squeezes.

"Is it about the night you were attacked."

No response.

"Is it about why you were attacked?"

One squeeze.

"The Belle Rose massacre case?"

One squeeze.

Yvonne and Amy both leaned in closer, their eyes glazed with tears.

"Maybe you shouldn't go any further," Yvonne suggested. "We don't want to upset him."

Theron squeezed Jolie's hand twice, paused, and then squeezed twice again. He repeated the two negative squeezes over and over again.

"I think he's trying to tell me not to stop questioning him," Jolie said.

He squeezed once. Jolie smiled. Yvonne gulped a gasping sob.

"You want me to do something for you about the Belle Rose massacre case?" Jolie asked.

One squeeze.

"You want me to go ahead without you and try to get the case reopened."

One squeeze.

Letting out a relieved sigh, Jolie glanced up at Yvonne. With tears streaming down her face, Yvonne nodded. Jolie lifted Theron's hand and rubbed it against her cheek.

"I promise you that I'll get the case reopened. Just as soon as you're better, I'll—"

He squeezed twice.

"You don't want me to wait, do you?"

Two squeezes.

"Okay. I'll start first thing tomorrow. I promise."

One squeeze, then he uncurled his fingers, showing his apparent exhaustion. Jolie released her hold on his hand, turned and walked out of Theron's unit and straight to Sheriff Denton who still waited outside the cubicle.

"Did you hear?" she asked.

"Yes, ma'am."

"Are you willing to help me?"

"In any way I can," Ike said. "Tell me what you want me to do."

"I want to start by talking to all of the deputies who worked in the sheriff's department twenty years ago. And I'd like to find out if Sheriff Bendall is still alive and if so, where he lives now."

"I can get you a list of the people who worked for the sheriff's department in the early Eighties, and if Bendall receives a pension from the state, it should be easy enough to find out where those checks are sent."

"Great." She held out her hand to Ike. "Tomorrow we move forward with the investigation."

She and Ike shook hands.

Connie Markham took a bathroom break fifteen minutes later. When she entered the nurse's lounge, she checked it out thoroughly, making sure she was alone before using the telephone. Situated where she could keep an eye on the door, she lifted the receiver and dialed the number.

A growling voice answered the phone. "Who the hell is calling so late?"

"It's me, Connie. Connie Markham over at Desmond County General."

"Ah. Have you got news on Theron Carter?"

"Yes, sir. He's conscious. He can't move or speak, but he's able to respond by squeezing someone's hand."

"Damn! He was supposed to die."

"He's recovering. And . . . and tonight he was able to relay his wishes to Ms. Royale. He wants her to continue trying to get the Belle Rose massacre case reopened."

"Son of a bitch."

Connie heard footsteps out in the corridor. Her heart ceased beating for a millisecond.

"I want her stopped and I want Carter out of the way."

"But Mr. Wells, I've already told you that I won't kill Theron Carter. I'll do anything else you ask, but I will not commit murder for you."

"Calm down, Connie. I'm not suggesting you take care of it yourself. Although I could make you do it, couldn't I? You know what will happen if you don't cooperate. One word from me and your brother will never get out of the pen alive."

"Please, Mr. Wells . . ."

"You just do what you've been doing—keep me informed. If Carter continues to improve, I'll send someone to take care of him. But for now, Jolie Royale is my immediate problem."

"Not so wonderful," Nellie corrected.
post office box in Dothan.

Chapter 16

Ike Denton handed Jolie a cup of iced tea. Looking up at him from where she sat behind his desk, she smiled. "Thanks."

"Now, don't get discouraged," he told her. "We've still got Linden Singleton to question. He'll be here any minute now. And we know Willie Norville moved to Oklahoma to live with his daughter, so we can call him later, as soon as Nellie gets us his number."

Jolie rubbed the perspiring cardboard cup against her warm cheek. "Two deputies have died, one lives in Oklahoma, and the two we've questioned didn't give us any information that could help us."

Standing outside the open door, Nellie Keenum cleared her throat, then stuck her head in and said, "Got an address for where Aaron Bendall's retirement checks are sent."

"Oh, Nellie, that's wonderful." Jolie set the tea on a Post-it notepad atop Ike's desk.

"Not so wonderful." Nellie grimaced. "They go to a post office box in Dothan."

"Shit!" Ike mumbled under his breath.

"I don't see the problem. If his checks go to Dothan, then that must mean he lives there, right?" Jolie glanced from Nellie to Ike.

"Wrong." Ike looked at Nellie. "Have you already—"

"Yep. I ran a check. No Aaron Bendall in Dothan. No phone. No utilities. No paper trail of any kind."

"What does that mean?" Jolie asked.

"That means somebody picks up Bendall's check every month and forwards it to him," Ike explained. "Could be a relative or could be somebody he pays to do it. Whichever doesn't matter. What's important is that apparently Bendall doesn't want anybody to know where he's living. Now, why would he care, unless he doesn't want to be found?"

"And why doesn't he want to be found?" Jolie smiled. Finding out the secretive nature of Aaron Bendall's whereabouts was the first break they'd gotten today. She'd known finding information that would clear Lemar in the twenty-year-old double homicide case wouldn't be easy, but without the case files it might be impossible.

Nellie hovered in the doorway. "Anything else y'all want me to do?"

"Yeah," Ike replied. "See if you can get a phone number for Willie Norville. He lives in Oklahoma with his daughter. I think her name is Merry Watkins. First name spelled like Merry Christmas."

"I'll see what I can do." Nellie left, but was back in five seconds, a small thin man at her side. "Linden Singleton is here."

Ike met the wiry old man before he entered the office, shook his hand and projected a friendly demeanor. "Come on in, Lin. Have a seat. Nellie, get Lin some coffee. How do you take your coffee?"

"Cream, no sugar." While eying Jolie, Linden sat

down in one of the two chairs in front of Ike's desk. "You're Louis Royale's gal, ain't you?"

Ike shooed Nellie with a swish of his hand. She closed the door before scurrying off.

"Yes, I'm Jolie Royale."

"Good man, your daddy." Lin studied Jolie intently. "You look like your aunt. Like Lisette Desmond."

"Yes, sir, so I've been told."

"Prettiest woman I ever saw in my life." Lin looked at Ike. "What's this all about? When Nellie called, she said you needed some information about an old case I worked on back when Aaron Bendall was sheriff."

"That's right." Ike took the seat beside Lin. "The Belle Rose massacre case."

"Damn, what a bad time that was. They named that case right—it was a massacre. You know, I was one of the deputies who took the call. Me and Earl Farris." Lin looked point-blank at Jolie. "Miss Jolie, are you sure you want to hear about this?"

"Yes, Mr. Singleton, I want to hear."

Lin nodded. "If Earl was alive he could tell you just what we found. I'll never forget. Not as long as I live."

"Mr. Singleton?" Jolie interrupted.

"Yeah?"

"Do you remember who made the call to report the murders?" She'd been told that Aunt Clarice had come home from work and found the bodies, but she was curious to see if Linden Singleton remembered that day any differently.

"Thought you knew that Miss Clarice found 'em. She's been touched in the noggin ever since, poor soul." Lin tapped his head. "Don't know how she was able to make that phone call. But she did, somehow. She told the dispatcher to send an ambulance. When we found her, she couldn't even talk. Totally zonked out. Her eyes were all funny looking and she was just staring off into space.

"Anyhow, we went in through the back door—the

front door was locked—and walked straight into the kitchen. That's when we saw Miss Audrey—Mrs. Royale—lying by the table and Miss Clarice sitting on the floor on the other side of the table. She was holding you up, Miss Jolie, your head against her chest, and she was stroking your face. Poor thing had blood all over her dress and on her hands.''

Jolie swallowed hard. No one had ever told her any of the actual details about that day, about the events that occurred after Aunt Clarice had found the bodies.

"Once we saw that Miss Jolie was still alive, just barely"—Lin's gaze met hers and she saw the pity in his eyes—"we got on the horn and told them to rush that ambulance. Earl, he stayed with Miss Clarice and Miss Jolie and called for backup while I started searching the rest of the house. I gotta admit that I was mighty scared that the killer was still in the house.''

"But you didn't see anyone else? Anyone alive?'' Ike asked.

"Nobody.'' Lin shook his head. "I found Miss Lisette lying on the landing. Even dead she was beautiful.'' Lin sighed loudly. "And then I found *him*, in her bedroom, in the doorway. He was lying there, facedown, with the gun in his hand. If the son of a bitch hadn't already been dead, I'd have probably killed him with my bare hands.''

"Tell us something, Lin, have you ever doubted that Lemar Fuqua murdered the Desmond sisters and then committed suicide?'' Ike Denton asked.

"Wasn't no reason to doubt it. All the evidence pointed directly to him.'' Lin glanced at Jolie. "Meaning no disrespect to Miss Lisette, but she shouldn't been fooling around with—'' Lin looked up at Ike, then looked away quickly. "Well, folks said that if she hadn't been messing around with Lemar Fuqua, she'd still be alive. Her and her sister.''

"Why do you think he killed my mother, too?'' Jolie asked.

"Ain't it obvious? Because she was there at the house and knew he was there, upstairs with Miss Lisette. She probably heard the shot and—" Lin scratched his chin. "You know there was something I always thought odd. He didn't kill Mrs. Royale in the kitchen. He killed her outside and carried her body inside. Her blood was on his hands and all over his shirt. He must have killed Miss Lisette, then tried to run away and ran into Mrs. Royale on his way out."

"Then why take my mother's body into the kitchen before going back upstairs and killing himself in Aunt Lisette's bedroom?"

"Don't know," Lin admitted. "Like I said, I always thought it was odd."

"What did Sheriff Bendall think about this information?" Ike asked.

"Aaron? I don't recall him ever saying anything about it one way or the other."

Nellie knocked, opened the door and brought Lin a cup of coffee. "Cream, no sugar." She glanced at Ike. "I got that phone number you wanted."

"Thanks. I'll take care of that matter later." Ike dismissed her, then turned back to Lin. "Is there anything else odd you remember about the case?"

"Nothing really, except . . . well, Mr. Louis Royale seemed to have some doubts about Lemar Fuqua's guilt. But he was the only one, except Lemar's sister. And I heard that later, when she was able to, Miss Clarice Desmond made a statement that she believed he was innocent. But everybody knew Lemar did it."

"Daddy had doubts about Lemar's guilt?"

"Yeah, but the sheriff told Mr. Royale flat-out that the evidence showed plainly that Lemar was guilty and that there was nobody else could have done it."

"Were any other suspects questioned?" Ike asked.

Lin shook his head. "Weren't no other suspects. Not really."

"Did the sheriff question anyone else about the case?" Ike tried a different tactic.

"Well, sure he did. And so did that CIB agent. Can't recall his name. Sanderson, Henderson, something like that. They had to call in the CIB and get some help. Our sheriff's department and our police department wasn't equipped to handle anything like the Belle Rose massacre. Anyway, the CIB came to the same conclusion as Sheriff Bendall." Lin lifted the mug to his lips and sipped on the hot coffee.

"Who was questioned?" Jolie asked.

"Who?" Lin sat there and thought for a few minutes. "Well, you were questioned, Miss Jolie. While you were in the hospital. And of course, Miss Clarice, but she was completely off her rocker for a while. I think her doctor kept her doped up all the time. Mr. Royale was questioned and—" Lin became suddenly quiet, his gaze darting back and forth from Jolie to Ike.

"And who else?" Jolie pressed him.

"Ma'am, it ain't something you ought to hear." Lin looked to Ike for help.

"I don't think you'll be telling Ms. Royale anything she doesn't already know," Ike said. "Everybody in Sumarville heard about Mr. Royale's alibi that day."

"Don't be concerned, Mr. Singleton," Jolie said. "I know that my father was with Georgette Devereaux when my mother was killed."

"Ain't a man alive hadn't been tempted at some time or other," Lin said. "Your daddy wasn't no bad man. He just gave in to temptation. And Lord knows Georgette Devereaux was a mighty tempting piece of—"

Ike cleared his throat.

Lin darted an apologetic glance at Jolie, then looked sheepishly down at the floor. "Yeah, well, Mr. Royale and Mrs. Devereaux were questioned. And so was Parry Clifton, since he was engaged to Miss Lisette. Lucky bastard." Lin shook his head and *tsk-tsked* sadly. "Never seen a man so broke up. Parry sure did love Miss

Lisette." Lin took a few more sips of his coffee, then leaned over and set the mug on Ike's desk. "And they questioned Max Devereaux, too."

"Did Max have an alibi?" Jolie asked.

"Can't say as I recall. Don't guess it mattered. Nobody really took those rumors about him killing your mama to clear a path for his mama very seriously."

"Lin, is there anything else you can tell us that you think might have been the least bit odd?" Ike flopped his big hands down on top of his thighs in a well-does-that-about-cover-it? gesture.

"Nope. That's about it. So, you gonna tell me why you're wanting all this information about a twenty-year-old case that was solved at the time it happened?"

"Theron Carter—I'm sure you heard about what happened to him," Jolie said. Lin Singleton nodded.

"He believes that Lemar Fuqua was innocent. And I agree with Theron. We think he was murdered by the same person who murdered my mother and aunt."

Lin let out a long low whistle. "You're opening up a can of worms. A stinky can of worms. People don't like remembering bad times."

"All we want is to find out the truth," Jolie said.

Lin looked at Ike. "Have you questioned any of the other deputies about the case?"

"We talked to Carl Bowling and Ernie Dupuis before we did you, and we're going to call Willie Norville later." Ike stood and stretched his legs, moving restlessly around his office.

"You ought to talk to Earl Farris's widow," Lin suggested. "She might know something. Earl was the only deputy who questioned Lemar's guilt. After the sheriff told Earl that there was no room for doubt and not to be stirring up unnecessary trouble, Earl kept his mouth shut. But he might have told his wife something about his suspicions before he died. Now, mind you, I don't think Earl was right, but if you're determined to rake over the past, you ought to talk to Ginny."

Ike held out his hand to Lin. "I want to thank you for coming in today and talking to us."

Lin shook Ike's hand, then nodded to Jolie. "You might ought to be careful, Miss Jolie. Sometimes it's better to just let sleeping dogs lie. You never know, you might dig up something you'd rather not know."

With that said, Lin turned and left Ike's office. When Jolie opened her mouth to speak, Ike held up a restraining hand, then closed the door.

"I say we get Willie Norville's number from Nellie and call him right now," Ike said. "Let's see if he's as talkative as Lin."

"Ike, when did Earl Farris die?"

"Huh?"

"Earl Farris. When did he die?"

"I don't know. Years ago."

"How many years?"

"Fifteen, twenty years . . . What are you thinking?"

"You don't know exactly when he died or how he died?" Jolie rose from the swivel chair behind Ike's desk.

"I've got no idea. I wasn't around back then. I was away at college for several years, then I worked out of state for a few years after that."

"Ask Nellie to find out for us when Farris died and how. ASAP."

Ike nodded. "Why didn't you just ask Lin before he left?"

"Because I think Mr. Singleton was beginning to sweat. I believe he's had a lot of years to go over things in his mind and he's afraid that maybe Earl Farris was right to have had doubts about Lemar's guilt. If Earl was killed to keep him quiet, then anybody who talks too much, even now, might be in danger."

"And your imagination could be working overtime." Ike walked to the door. "I'll get Norville's phone number and ask Nellie to see what she can find out about Earl Farris."

* * *

"Yes, sir, Mr. Wells," Willie Norville said. "Sheriff Denton called me and asked me a bunch of questions about the Belle Rose massacre case. And Jolie Royale herself talked to me."

"What did you tell them?"

"Not a damn thing."

"What sort of questions did they ask?"

"They asked me if I remembered anything odd about the case, about the investigation."

"Who else have they talked to?" Roscoe Wells asked.

"All the deputies who are still alive. Bowling and Dupuis and Singleton."

"Nobody else?"

"Like who?" Willie asked.

"Like Ginny Farris."

"Ginny Pounders. She got married again about five years after Earl was . . . after Earl died. But I think she's divorced now."

"Yes, that's right. Ginny Pounders. Well, maybe I need to send somebody around to talk to Ginny, make sure she remembers to keep her mouth shut."

Jolie parked her SUV on the cracked concrete driveway directly behind a black Honda Civic, then removed the folded paper from the sun visor she'd used as a paper clip. She held the address in her hand and double-checked the address: 132 Sunrise Avenue. She had phoned ahead to set up a time that was convenient for Ginny Farris Pounders, who worked at Shop Rite Foods and didn't get off work until six. Jolie glanced at her wristwatch. Precisely seven o'clock.

"Come by around seven," Ginny had said. "That'll give me time to change clothes, fix me some supper, and relax a few minutes."

"I appreciate your talking to me," Jolie had told her.

"I'll talk to you. I think you got a right to know. But I'm not telling the law nothing and if you get the case reopened, I'm not testifying."

What did Ginny Farris Pounders know? And who was she afraid of?

The one-story, yellow frame house, adorned with dark green shutters, sat back off the street, giving the property a large front yard, but practically no backyard. Neatly trimmed green grass, low round shrubbery, and a couple of old oak trees added curb appeal to the residence. A neat house on a street of small neat houses dating back to the Forties. A thickly wooded area ran behind the house. Hobo Woods. Jolie recalled her father saying people named the woods that because the old railroad tracks were on the other side of the woods and during the Depression years, hobos had often lived temporarily in the shallow caves nearby.

Jolie got out of her Escalade, the straps of her bag over her shoulder, and made her way across the stepping-stone walkway to the front porch. Behind the storm door, the dark green front door stood wide open, which, to Jolie, meant Ginny had been watching for her arrival. But when she reached the door and peeped inside, she didn't see a sign of anyone. She rang the doorbell and waited. *Quiet neighborhood,* she thought. Not even a dog barking. Where was Ginny? Jolie rang the bell again. *Damn!* Had the woman changed her mind? Was she afraid to tell anyone about her first husband's suspicions concerning Lemar Fuqua's innocence?

After ringing the bell a third time, Jolie wondered if she should leave. Instinctively she reached out and yanked on the door handle. It wasn't locked. *Should I or shouldn't I? Yes, you should—go in and see if you can find Ginny.*

Jolie entered the small living room, well lit from the double windows that let in the early evening light. "Mrs. Pounders?"

No response.

"Ginny, are you here?"

Silence.

A niggling sense of uncertainty crept up Jolie's spine, but she disregarded it, telling herself that there was nothing to fear. She called out for Ginny several times as she made her way from the living room, through the dining room and into the kitchen. The aroma of meat cooking filled Jolie's nostrils. Glancing at the stove top she saw pork chops frying in an iron skillet on the large right-front stove eye and potatoes boiling in a pot on the left-back eye. Ginny was cooking supper; that meant she was here. Somewhere.

Through the half open back door, Jolie could see a small screened-in porch. Had Ginny gone outside for some reason?

"Ginny?"

Jolie stepped onto the back porch. She blinked several times, telling herself that her eyesight was playing tricks on her. A woman lay on the wooden floor, her sightless eyes wide-open, and a bright red ring of fresh blood circled her neck from ear to ear. A bloody butcher knife stuck straight up in the wooden floor beside her. Jolie opened her mouth to scream. Nothing came out. *Ohmygod! Ohmygod! Run! Now!*

When she turned to flee, back into the house, she caught a glimpse of someone hidden in the shadows behind a rusty metal baker's rack filled with flower pots. Ginny's killer! Spurred into action by sheer terror, Jolie ran into the house. The man followed her, his heavy footsteps pounding behind her. As she passed through the kitchen, she grabbed a chair from the kitchen table and flung it to the floor, directly in her pursuer's path. While rushing into the dining room, she heard the loud crash as the chair hit the kitchen wall where no doubt the murderer had thrown it.

"You can't get away from me, bitch."

Jolie could almost feel his hot breath on her neck. Ike Denton had offered to come here with her, but

Ginny had told Jolie to come alone, that she wouldn't talk to the sheriff. Why had she been so foolhardy, thinking there wouldn't be any danger in simply talking to the woman? Hadn't Nellie checking on and finding out the date of Earl Farris's death been just a hint that somebody might not want her talking to his widow? Deputy Farris had died right in the middle of the Belle Rose massacre investigation. He had accidently shot and killed himself while cleaning one of his guns.

Jolie made it to the living room before *he* reached out and grabbed her. His hand clamped down on her shoulder. Jolie tried to scream. A hoarse warble came out instead. She cleared her throat. He dragged her backward, knocking her bag off her shoulder. She caught a glimpse of the side of his face. Ruddy complexion. Pockmarked cheek, scarred by acne. Long brown sideburns. Jolie opened her mouth again and this time the terror she felt found a voice. She screamed. He slapped his glove-covered hand over her mouth.

Oh, God, I'm going to die!

The storm door flew open, almost ripped from its hinges. Another man charged toward her, pure rage etched on his features. Max Devereaux lunged forward. She wasn't quite sure how, but in the ensuing struggle, she was shoved to the floor. On hands and knees, she crawled away from the two men locked in deadly hand-to-hand combat. Ginny's killer managed to land a solid blow to Max's stomach, reeling Max backward for a couple of seconds and giving the guy time to escape. But Max immediately pursued him.

Jolie sat on the floor in the living room, unable to move, knowing if she tried to stand, her legs wouldn't hold her. With trembling fingers, she reached out, grabbed the strap of her bag lying a couple of feet away and dragged it to her. *Call for help*, she told herself. As she tried to undo the zippered pouch on her bag that held her cell phone, she heard thundering footsteps, the back door slamming . . . and then a gunshot.

Max! She managed to stand. With her nerves rioting, fear eating away at her insides like acid, Jolie hurried back through the house. She paused in the kitchen, looked around for something—anything—she could use as a weapon. She chose one of the heavy iron skillets hanging on the wall behind the stove. With her weapon raised, ready to strike, she cautiously crept out onto the porch.

Max stood in the backyard near a maple tree, his right hand clutching his left shoulder. Jolie raced down the wooden steps and out into the yard, straight to Max.

He turned, grunted, and then said, "Call the police."

Blood oozed out from between Max's fingers.

"You've been shot!"

"Call the goddamn police!"

She nodded, dropped the iron skillet to the ground, then unzipped the pouch and grabbled in her shoulder bag. With her hands trembling, she pulled out her cell phone and dialed 911. As soon as she made the call, she barreled toward Max, almost colliding with him.

"They're sending an ambulance." Her fingers tightening around his, then pulled his hand away from the wound. "Oh, Max. I didn't realize he had a gun."

"Yeah, he whipped it out and started shooting at me, then ran like hell down the alley and into the woods. He probably parked his car in there." Max watched her grimace when she inspected his shoulder. "I don't need an ambulance. The bullet only grazed me."

"He could have killed you. You're lucky he—"

"Me? Hell, he could have killed you. And he would have, if I hadn't gotten here when I did."

She nodded, realizing the truth of his words. "Why *did* you show up when you did?"

"I was looking for you. I thought we needed to talk, to clear the air between us, so I started calling around trying to locate you. I spoke to Ike Denton and he told me you were meeting Earl Farris's widow at seven."

"Did you know I'd be in danger?" Jolie jerked her

blouse from the waistband of her slacks and ripped several inches of soft cotton material from the hem.

"Sheriff Denton seemed nervous, like he was worried, so I asked him a few questions and he told me what y'all had found out from Linden Singleton. I didn't like what I heard."

Jolie grasped the tear in Max's shirt from where the bullet had slashed through the material and through the flesh beneath. Yanking the linen apart as much as the sturdy material would give, she wadded the strip off her blouse into a makeshift bandage and stuffed it inside his shirt, over his bleeding wound.

"Damn, take it easy," Max said.

"Sorry."

"You should have had better sense than to come here by yourself."

"I know that now. And it should be obvious to everyone that somebody doesn't want the Belle Rose massacre case reopened." Jolie added gentle pressure to the cloth over Max's wound.

"Yeah, it would seem so. And that somebody tried to kill Theron the other night and now you tonight."

"Max?"

"What?"

"I'm sorry that I suspected it might be you."

He simply stared at her for a moment, then they heard the shrill drone of sirens howling off in the distance. Jolie eased her arm around Max's waist and together they walked from the backyard into the front yard to wait for the police and the ambulance.

Chapter 17

"I'd like for you to stay overnight for observation,"
Dr. Andrews said.

The ER physician seemed genuinely concerned about
Max, which in turn made Jolie more concerned than
she already was. And she had every right to care about
Max's health—after all, the man had saved her life
tonight.

Max slid off the examination bed in the ER cubbyhole. "The damn bullet didn't enter my shoulder, it
just sliced off a small chunk of meat as it passed through.
I'm perfectly all right. And I'm going home."

"Even so, you lost quite a lot of blood and there's
always a possibility of infection, though the—"

"I'm leaving!"

When a bare-chested Max marched out of the cur-
tained cubbyhole, Jolie rushed after him, but paused
momentarily and glanced back at the doctor. "I'm sorry.
He's very stubborn. But I promise I'll look after him

and make sure he takes the antibiotic and the pain medication, if he needs it and—''

"Let's go," Max growled.

"Oh, I see now that he's going to be the ideal patient." Jolie gave the doctor a faint smile and ran to catch up with Max.

Sheriff Denton and Police Chief Harper halted Max just inside the electronic glass double-door entrance to the ER. Jolie paused a few feet behind them. Although Ginny Pounders' house was officially within the city limits and therefore within the Sumarville police's jurisdiction, the sheriff's department definitely had a vested interest in Ginny's murder. Jolie and Max had given the police officers who arrived on the scene a condensed version of what had happened, and Max had been able to give them a description of the man who'd shot him. Then Jolie had insisted Max needed immediate medical attention. He had refused to ride in the ambulance but had reluctantly agreed to let her take him to the hospital.

"Did the doctor give you the okay to leave?" Ike Denton eyed Max's partially undressed state.

"Yeah. Sure." Max cut Jolie a sidelong glance, his expression daring her to contradict him. He rubbed his hand over his bare chest. "I told them to throw my shirt away. Damn thing was ruined."

"I don't know what's happening to our peaceful little town." Chief Harper shook his balding head. "There hasn't been a murder here in five years, and now in less than a week, we have a man beaten nearly to death in front of his own home and a woman's had her throat slit. And one of our leading citizens gets shot."

"Maybe Sumarville is just now paying the price for having allowed the truth about the Belle Rose massacre to be covered up all these years, for allowing an innocent man to be condemned as a murderer." Jolie looked squarely at Leon Harper.

"Ike, what do you know about this mess?" Leon asked.

"About Ms. Royale here claiming that Theron Carter was beaten up to stop him from trying to get that old case reopened. And now she's saying that the guy who killed Ginny Pounders did it to stop her from revealing some sort of secret information Earl Farris knew about the case."

"I know that the evidence seems to back up Ms. Royale's assumptions," Ike said. "I think it bears looking into."

"What do you think, Mr. Devereaux?" Leon focused his attention on Max. "Do you believe any of this stuff?"

With her gaze fixed on Max, Jolie held her breath, waiting for his reply. Her stepbrother's opinion carried a great deal of weight in Desmond County.

"I think Theron Carter needs around-the-clock protection," Max said. "I'd like the local law to provide a guard tonight. I'll contact a private security agency in Memphis first thing tomorrow and have them send a couple of their men down here."

Jolie's mouth dropped open. Had she heard him right?

"Of course, Mr. Devereaux." Leon all but bowed to Max.

"I'll stay tonight," Ike said. "And one of my deputies can relieve me in the morning and stay until your security men can get here from Memphis."

"Now, Ike, that won't be necessary," Leon said. "I can have my officers take shifts outside the ICU until Mr. Devereaux makes other arrangements."

"Ike can stay tonight," Max said. "In the morning, y'all can work out something. I just want to make sure that Theron is protected."

"You can count on it," Leon said.

Max and Ike looked at each other, unspoken promises passing between them.

Jolie slipped her arm around Max's waist. "Come on. Let's get you home."

The corners of Max's mouth lifted slightly, just a hint of a smile. "Bossy, isn't she?"

"You're damn right about that." Jolie urged Max into movement. "And you might as well just shut up and do what I tell you to do. When a man gets shot saving my life, I feel obligated to see to it that he takes proper care of himself."

Ike grinned. Leon Harper's eyes rounded as he glanced from Max to Jolie.

Guiding Max outside, Jolie kept her arm around his waist and gauged her pace according to Max's gait. He moved a little slower than normal and her guess was that he was in a lot more pain than he'd let on to the doctor. Of course Max was the quintessential macho man and everyone knew that a real man didn't feel pain. She'd never understood why acknowledging pain or fear or sadness was paramount to admitting you were a wimp.

Just as Jolie pressed the button on her key chain to unlock her SUV, a Harley "Hog" whizzed into the parking lot, followed by a silver Mercedes. The two vehicles parked side-by-side. Jolie groaned. Max froze to the spot.

"Oh, great," Jolie said under her breath.

"Damn!" Max closed his eyes, as if praying for patience, and moved slightly away from Jolie.

Nowell Landers dismounted from his big metal stallion, assisted Clarice from her perch behind the driver's seat and helped her remove her metallic red helmet. Jolie just barely restrained herself from laughing out loud. The sight of her petite, immaculately groomed, Southern belle aunt climbing off a motorcycle was, at the very least, comic. Clarice rushed toward Max and Jolie. Nowell removed his helmet and hung both helmets on the bike's handlebars.

"Max, are you all right? When we were notified you'd been hurt, we came as quickly as possible." Clarice hovered over him, her hands fluttering all about, but she didn't touch him. Her gaze settled on the large square of gauze bandaging his shoulder. Already fresh blood stained the center of the dressing. "What happened to you, dear boy? The policeman who drove your car out to Belle Rose said there had been some sort of altercation, and it involved a shooting."

Nowell walked up behind Clarice, his massive body standing guard over the small nervous woman. "She's been beside herself with worry."

Mallory emerged from the Mercedes and broke into a run. Skidding to a halt when she saw Max's shoulder, she gasped. "My God, what happened? Were you really shot? The policeman told us you'd gone to the emergency room." Mallory's gaze zeroed in on Jolie. "What did you do to him?"

"Calm down, calm down." Max reached out and pulled his sister to him. She laid her head on his chest and wrapped her arms around him. "I'm all right. It's just a little wound. Nothing serious. No need to worry."

No need to worry your pretty little head, Jolie mentally finished Max's sentence. *Mercy no, don't let spoiled, selfish Mallory worry about anything or anyone!*

Georgette, a lace handkerchief pressed against her cheek, charged forward, only a couple of minutes behind Mallory. Tears dampened Georgette's face. Parry brought up the rear, his lumbering gait hampered by his inability to walk a straight line. Drunk as usual.

"What the hell happened?" Parry demanded.

"I was shot," Max said.

Mallory lifted her head from Max's chest, glowered at Jolie and screamed, "You shot him! Why aren't you in jail? How dare you—"

"Oh, heaven help us." Georgette swooned. Max had his hands full at the moment with Mallory, and Parry seemed oblivious to the fact that his sister was on the verge of fainting. Jolie caught her wicked stepmother around the waist just in time to prevent her from hitting the pavement.

"Jolie didn't shoot me." Max gently shoved Mallory aside and reached out for his mother.

"I've got her," Jolie said, although her voice sounded strained, even to her own ears. Georgette was a slender woman, but Jolie was no weight lifter either. "I don't want you reopening that wound. It took twenty stitches to close it up."

Without saying a word, Nowell came over to Jolie, lifted a sagging Georgette into his arms and carried her to the Mercedes.

Max looked directly at Mallory, who grimaced, then said, "I know, I know. You want me to go see about Mother. But not before you tell us who shot you . . . if it wasn't her?" Mallory's gaze hurled daggers at Jolie.

"I have no idea who he was." Max nodded toward the Mercedes. "I'll tell y'all everything when we get home. I'm getting a little groggy from the shot the doctor gave me, so I need to get off my feet. Mallory, I want you and Uncle Parry to get in the car and see about Mother. I need to talk to Jolie." When neither his uncle nor sister moved an inch, Max said, "Go on. Check on Mother."

Clarice patted Jolie's back. "I'll see you later, at home."

Jolie nodded, then Clarice walked over to where Nowell hovered in the open back door of the Mercedes, speaking softly to Georgette as she slowly revived. When Parry and Mallory responded to Max's request to leave, he turned to Jolie.

"I should ride home with my family," Max told her.

"Sure." For the life of her, Jolie couldn't explain why she felt rejected. She actually wished that Max would stay with her, that he'd get in her Escalade and allow her to drive him to Belle Rose. *What's the matter with you?* she asked herself. *This is Max Devereaux for whom you're feeling all these fluttery little feminine emotions. Your stepbrother. Georgette's son. Your enemy.*

No, he wasn't her enemy, not any longer. Max was

the man who had saved her. He had risked his own life to protect her. She'd never thought that the day would come when she'd think of Max Devereaux as her knight in shining armor.

When Jolie started walking away from Max, he grabbed her wrist. She waited, her back to him, her breath caught in her throat.

"Y'all go on home," Max called to the others. "Jolie's going to take me to the Wal-Mart pharmacy before they close. I've got a couple of prescriptions I should get filled tonight."

A euphoric high swept through Jolie. *Get a grip,* she told herself. *Rein in all those let-me-kiss-it-and-make-it-better feelings before you say or do something really foolish.*

"Let's go," Max said. "Before they have time to protest."

Jolie unlocked her SUV. Within seconds she and Max were settled inside and she was revving the motor.

"You realize that Theron isn't the only one who needs a bodyguard, don't you?" There was an uncustomary gentleness in Max's voice.

Jolie backed out of the hospital parking lot and drove directly onto Milton Avenue. "You believe my life is in danger?"

"Very possibly."

She took a left off Milton onto Dearborn, which would take her straight to the Wal-Mart Super Center on the outskirts of town.

"Do you think I should hire myself a bodyguard?"

"That won't be necessary," Max replied. "Until you're out of danger, I'll make sure you're safe. From tonight on, consider me your personal protector."

Roscoe Wells gripped the telephone with white-knuckled ferocity. "Goddamn you fucking son of a bitch! What were you thinking? I told you to scare her, not kill her."

"She didn't scare none too easy. And when I started slapping her around, she fought me. Hell, she tried to stick me with a butcher knife, so I just turned around and used her knife on her."

"Did Devereaux and the Royale girl see your face?"

"Don't think the girl got a good look, but the guy did."

"And you let them both live, you stupid asshole."

"Hey, man, that Devereaux guy took me off guard and I couldn't get to my gun while he was trying to beat my brains out. How'd I know he wasn't armed? How'd I know that if I stuck around to try to kill them, that he wouldn't have whipped out a gun and shot me first?"

"So you ran like a scared rabbit and now the police have a description of you."

"Yeah, well, I'm long gone. A good hundred miles out of Sumarville. Don't you worry none. I know how to lay low. Nobody's gonna find me unless I want to be found."

"Might not be a bad idea for you to get out of the country."

"I'm way ahead of you."

The dial tone hummed in Roscoe's ear. Hellfire, where were the smart men, the ones who knew how to follow orders and keep a low profile? What happened to the men who could move in quickly, do the job, and never get caught? He didn't know this guy, another recommendation from an old friend. They'd never met. He called himself Wesley, but that might not be his name. The guy had come highly recommended, but then pickings were slim these days when it came to redneck hoodlums willing to do anything for the right price.

"Daddy, what have you gotten yourself into now?" Garland stood just inside the doorway to Roscoe's den.

Damn, he hadn't heard his son enter, hadn't realized his conversation with Wesley had been overheard.

"What did you hear?" Roscoe asked.

"Just you telling someone that it might not be a bad idea if he got out of the country."

Roscoe sighed with relief. "It's nothing. A minor irritation. Don't worry about it."

"But I do worry about you. I worry that sooner or later you're going to get caught doing something illegal. I know, despite what you profess to the world, that you've still got ties to some rather ruthless people. I'd hate to see everything you've worked for all these years destroyed by a stupid mistake."

"Yeah, well, the mistake won't be mine. I cover my tracks. You know that." Roscoe eyed Garland. His only son. His heir. "Tell me, boy, have you given any more thought to my idea of your running for the U.S. Congress? I've got all the wheels in motion. All I need is a word from you and we'll start laying the groundwork."

"I don't know, Daddy. I'm not sure I'm suited for the life of a politician."

"Nonsense. Politicking is in your blood. Hell, your great-great-granddaddy was the governor. There's been a Wells involved in Mississippi politics since before the War Between the States."

"I know. And I promise I'll think seriously about taking a shot at the congressional seat that Tom Watkins is vacating."

Roscoe rounded his desk and walked over to Garland, whopped him heartily on the back, and smiled. "You do that. You do that. And stop fretting about me. I can take care of myself." *And I can take care of you, too. I always have and I always will. There's nothing I wouldn't do for you.*

"Promise me that if you need my help . . . legal help—"

Roscoe laughed. "Everything's going to be just fine. Stop worrying. I got myself a little problem to solve, but it's nothing I can't handle and it's nothing that needs to concern you." *No, this needn't concern you, son. Everything I have done—in the past and in the present—to bury the true facts about the Belle Rose massacre, I'd do all over again. There's no need for anyone to even suspect you were involved in any way.*

Jolie couldn't sleep. Couldn't even lie in bed and rest. She paced the floor, back and forth in front of the French doors that opened onto the balcony. Her mind kept replaying the events at Ginny Pounders' house. Even with her eyes wide open, she could still see the woman's slashed throat. And the blood. So much blood.

An eerie tingling radiated from the base of her spine upward. She could almost feel the killer's hands grabbing her. She shuddered, closed her eyes momentarily, and shook her head, trying desperately to dislodge the fear. She could have died tonight, been murdered just like Ginny Pounders had been. If Max hadn't shown up. If Max hadn't fought off her attacker. If Max hadn't risked his life to save her.

Earlier tonight, Max and she had gotten his prescriptions for the antibiotics and Percocet filled at the Wal-Mart pharmacy. The downtown pharmacy that the Royale family normally used closed promptly at six each evening. On the ride home to Belle Rose, both had been quiet. Max had actually dozed on and off.

"Why don't you stop fighting the effects of the shot the doctor gave you," she'd advised him.

"Bossy woman."

Yes, she was bossy. She was used to being the one in charge, the one giving orders. But in this case, she would have had to fight Max's family in order to control the situation. The minute they had arrived at Belle Rose, the whole lot of them had come swarming out of the house, Georgette and Clarice fussing over Max as if he were a six-year-old who'd skinned his knee. At least Parry had done something constructive. He'd helped her get a slightly woozy Max up the steps and into the house, despite Parry's own wobbly condition.

Once inside the foyer, Mallory had all but shoved Jolie out of the way. "I'll help Uncle Parry take Max up to bed. I think you've done more than enough."

Sarcastic little bitch, Jolie had thought. "Here's his prescriptions." She'd held out the white paper sack to Mallory, who had grabbed it quickly and done her best to ignore Jolie.

That had been hours ago, even though it seemed more like days. She'd tossed her bloody clothes in the bathroom wastebasket and taken a nice long shower, scrubbing herself thoroughly from head to toe. She'd chosen a pair of thin cotton pajamas and then crawled into bed. She'd dozed off for about an hour, then woke with a start, thinking she'd heard Max calling her name. It had taken her several minutes to realize she'd been dreaming.

Admit it, she told herself, *you want to check on Max. You want to see for yourself that he's all right. Yes, damn it, yes, that's exactly what I want to do!*

What would it hurt? Who would ever know? The entire household was asleep. Max was probably still drugged from the injection he'd been given in the ER. She could go quietly down the hall, open the door to his room, and peep in, just to make sure he was resting peacefully. If she did that, then maybe she could get some rest herself.

After slipping on her white terrycloth house shoes, she crossed the room, opened the door, and walked out into the hall. Quiet. Still. Only those dead-of-the-night muted rumblings peculiar to very old houses. She crept silently down the long wide corridor that led from her room to Max's. Hesitating outside his door, she let her hand hover over the crystal doorknob. She glanced up and down the hall. No sign of anyone. She grasped the knob and opened the door just a fraction. Darkness lay beyond, but moonlight pouring through the long wide windows washed a path over the wooden floor and across the foot of the big oak four-poster.

Jolie felt as if her heart were going to beat its way out of her chest. She eased open the door a little farther and took several tentative steps. Max lay on his side, his back to the door. The covers rested at the foot of the bed, leaving his large body exposed. When Jolie tiptoed closer, she realized that he wore nothing except a pair of dark silk boxers. Sexual excitement stirred in her belly. *No, don't do this,* she told herself. *Don't let yourself care about Max Devereaux.*

She moved to the side of the bed and looked at him. She wanted to touch him. Wanted to caress his back, his uninjured shoulders, his chest, his . . .

Listening to his even breathing, she sighed. He was resting comfortably, probably still in the depths of a drug-induced sleep. He'd never know if she touched him, never realize that she'd been here in his room.

Her hand moved of its own volition, her fingertips caressing his thick dark hair.

He moaned.

Jolie jerked her hand away.

Max flopped over, reached out, and grabbed her wrist. She gasped.

"Sleepwalking, *chère?*" he whispered, then jerked her down and into the bed on top of him.

Chapter 18

Taken totally by surprise, Jolie didn't respond verbally, only stared at Max, her gaze seeking his in the semidarkness. Her heartbeat trumpeted in her ears, obliterating every other sound. She lay on top of him, leaning slightly to the side. The thin material of her pajamas did little to protect her from the heat and solid strength of Max's naked chest or his hairy legs—or the undeniable firmness of his erection. Her body betrayed her, melting against Max, molding itself around him. After releasing her wrist, he wasted no time in recapturing her with a swift move, shooting his fingers through her hair and gripping the back of her head with his big hand. Tension vibrated between them so intensely that it was almost visible, like tangible electrical currents connecting in the heavy, sensual atmosphere.

Her lips parted, whether to speak or to sigh she wasn't sure and wasn't given the time to decide. Max pushed her head downward and held her in place as he took her mouth with hungry passion. She responded instantly, as ravenous for the kiss as he was. Wild, screaming-and-clawing need exploded inside her, unlike anything she'd ever known. When his tongue delved inside, she reciprocated with manic thrusts, taking him as surely as he was taking her. He loosened his grip on her head and moved his hand down her neck, across her back and over her hips. His sex throbbed against her belly; she ached almost unbearably at the apex between her thighs.

When they came up for air, their breaths ragged, their bodies damp with perspiration, Max nuzzled her neck with his nose.

"I'm not in the best shape for this," he told her.

"Oh, Max—your shoulder!" She eased off him and onto the bed.

He reached out to caress her cheek. "Ah, *chère*, what are we going to do?" Cupping her chin, he ran his thumb over her bottom lip. "We don't even like each other."

Her breathing settled, yet she felt as if a heavy weight suddenly dropped on her chest. "I know. Until last night I hated you. Or I thought I hated you."

He glided his hand down her throat, his fingers like rough silk, creating tingles that tightened her nipples and moistened her.

"There is too much . . . past history . . . between us, isn't there? Too many strong emotions that involve our parents as well as ourselves. It would be difficult for us to indulge in a simple little affair."

She heard what he was saying, understood perfectly that they would be fools to begin a sexual relationship. But her body didn't comprehend why it couldn't have what it so desperately wanted. Every feminine compulsion she possessed craved this one particular man.

"I didn't come to your room for . . . because I thought we'd . . ."

"You came because you couldn't stay away." His fingertips toyed with the top button of her pajamas.

"I needed to check on you, to make sure you were all right." She lifted her hand and touched his face. "You saved my life."

"A potent aphrodisiac."

She smiled. "Yes, something like that."

"You're a smart woman. You must know that I can be dangerous for you." He leaned over to place a kiss in the hollow between her breasts. She gasped. "That's the way it is between us. I want you. And you want me."

"Yes, I know."

"You can save yourself if you leave now. My willpower will last for only so long."

"You want me to—"

He dropped his index finger over her lips. "Once it's done, there will be no going back. This is no mild flirtation between us."

Oh, God! He was right. Damn him! "I don't want this," she said. "It's the wrong time. You're the wrong man."

He moaned softly. "I understand. It's the same with me."

Jolie forced herself up and off the bed. She hovered at his side. "I—I'll see you in the morning."

"Of course. We have a great deal to do. Plans to make."

She nodded, then hurried to the half-open door. Just as she eased through the door, he called her name.

"Jolie?"

She glanced over her shoulder.

He lifted himself up on one elbow. "Do you suppose they felt this way, in the beginning, when they first realized how much they wanted each other?"

"Who?" she asked but knew the answer.

"Your father and my mother."

She shook her head. "I don't know. I don't know."

Jolie turned and ran down the hall, back to her own room. Once safely inside, she pressed her shoulders against the door, leaned back her head, and gasped for air. This couldn't be happening. It just couldn't! She didn't want to feel such powerful emotions for Max Devereaux. And she didn't want to believe that this type of gut-wrenching hunger had motivated her father's love affair with Georgette. If it had, then he must have felt as helpless as she was feeling right now. But most of all, she didn't want to put a label on her feelings. God help her, it couldn't be love. A kind of all-consuming, animalistic, primitive love that made people do anything to be together.

Even kill?

Jolie went downstairs late, after everyone had eaten breakfast and left the dining room. Feeling slightly queasy, she poured herself a cup of coffee, added a liberal amount of cream and sipped the hot liquid as she went out into the hall. She had stopped by Max's room before coming down and had seen that it was empty, his bed already neatly made. She had to find him. They needed to talk. After getting several hours of restless sleep, she had awakened knowing that she could not allow anything serious to happen between Max and her. No matter how tempted she was—and God knew she was—he definitely was the wrong man for her. Even on a temporary basis.

Instinct told her that, if he were still at Belle Rose this morning, he would be in her father's study. Max's study, now.

The temporary housekeeper stood in the hallway near the kitchen, giving instructions to the daily maids. Jolie paused, waited until the maids went about their duties, then spoke to Mrs. Tanner.

"Is Mr. Devereaux here?" she asked.

"Yes, ma'am. He's in the study."

"Thank you."

"Ms. Royale?"

"Yes?"

"He asked that when you came down, you join him," Mrs. Tanner said. "I see you found the coffee. I cleared away the breakfast items at ten, just as Mrs. Royale requested, but if you'd like for me to fix you something, I could—"

"Thank you, no."

Mrs. Tanner smiled.

Jolie took her time, sipping her coffee, strolling leisurely, as if she were in no hurry. Her emotions warred with her common sense. She longed to see Max again, wanted to rush into his arms and kiss him. But logic warned her to be cool, even distant, and to get straight to the point when she spoke to him.

The study door was closed. Should she knock? No, why should she? This was her house wasn't it? Yes, but common courtesy required her to knock. She lifted her hand and knocked softly several times.

"Come in," Max said.

Her heart raced wildly. Damn! She opened the door and entered the study. Max glanced up from where he sat in the big tufted-back leather chair. When he saw her, he jumped to his feet.

"Come on in. Did Mrs. Tanner tell you—"

"Yes, she said you wanted me to join you in the study."

He came out from behind the desk, looking hail and hardy, not like a man who'd been shot fifteen hours ago. He wore a pair of charcoal gray trousers and a burgundy linen shirt, the top two buttons undone. Casual elegance. Odd, how that term fit Max perfectly. Even when he wore jeans, he exuded an air of elegance. But no matter how well dressed or well behaved he was, an aura of danger always surrounded him.

He paused in front of the massive Jacobean desk. "Did you sleep well?"

"Probably about as well as you did," she replied.

A smile played at the corners of his mouth. "You're awfully far away, all the way over there by the door."

"It's safer over here."

He grinned. "Feeling as if you've been run over by a steamroller, *chère?*"

Jolie closed the door behind her but didn't venture any farther into the room. "We need to talk about . . . I can't deal with whatever is going on between us. There are too many other things more important . . . things that need my immediate attention."

"I need your immediate attention."

He took a step toward her; she backed up against the door. When she saw that he was still moving toward her, she held up both hands in a gesture for him to halt. He paused.

"It's all right, Jolie. I won't come any closer." He returned to the desk, sat on the edge, and crossed his arms over his chest. "I realize that we'd be fools to pursue anything of a truly personal nature. Our relationship is already too complicated. Sex would only muddy the waters even more. Besides, you still despise my mother. You still want my family out of Belle Rose. Nothing has really changed. Except now you've switched your focus from seeking revenge to unearthing the truth. You've taken Theron Carter's cause and made it your own."

Jolie blew out a dramatized huff. "I see that mind reading is one of your many talents."

"I did pretty well in stating your feelings, didn't I? Everything I said to you is what you'd planned to say to me, right?"

She nodded. "I'm glad you see things the same way I do."

"Not about everything." He studied her closely. "But for the time being, I agree that finding out what really happened the day your mother, your aunt, and Lemar Fuqua died here at Belle Rose comes first on our agenda."

"Our agenda?"

"Someone hired three goons to kill Theron, but he's tougher than they thought he was. And my guess is that one of those hired assassins killed Ginny Pounders, would have killed you, and shot me. There's no doubt that whoever is behind these events does not want anyone digging into the Belle Rose massacre case. And this person knows you're going to keep digging, so your life is still in danger."

"What about your life? You saw the killer's face."

"He was a hired underling," Max said. "Long gone by now. In Mexico or South America for an extended vacation. I'm no threat to whoever is pulling the strings behind the scenes—not yet—but you most definitely are."

"Then if you don't involve yourself any further—"

"I am involved."

"Because you were shot?"

"No, *chère*. Because someone tried to kill you."

"Max . . ."

"I told you once that I protect my own."

"But I'm not . . . I'm not—"

"Aren't you?"

He stayed seated on the edge of the desk, not making a move toward her, and yet she felt his heat from across the room.

"You said we weren't going to . . . we agreed that . . ."

Max eased off the desk. She held her breath, thinking he would come toward her. Instead, he rounded the desk, picked up the telephone receiver, and dialed.

"Chief Harper, please. This is Max Devereaux."

She walked into the room, moving a little closer to Max.

"Yes, Chief, Ms. Royale and I will be coming down to give our official statements this morning." He checked his Rolex. "Around eleven-thirty."

Max returned the receiver to its base, then glanced at Jolie. "I've already contacted a private security firm in Memphis and they've dispatched two of their best men for around-the-clock protection for Theron. And I have a private detective looking for Aaron Bendall.

Once we find Bendall, I have a strong hunch that he can tell us what happened to those missing files.''

"You've already done all that this morning? What time did you get up?"

"Six o'clock."

"You're actually going to help me, aren't you?"

"I already have," he said.

"Yes, I know. You saved my life last night and I'm grateful."

"I wasn't referring to that. I was talking about the fact that I contacted someone I know with the CIB to find out about the investigator who came here twenty years ago to help out the local sheriff's department with the Belle Rose massacre case."

"What did you find out? Will they let us take a look at their files?"

"I found out that the investigator was a man named Kirby Anderson. He's seventy now, lives in a nursing home and is suffering from Alzheimer's."

"Guess that rules out questioning him. But what about the files?"

"Would you be surprised to learn that the CIB's files on the Belle Rose massacre are missing?"

"Damn!"

"That means that Anderson was probably hand-picked by someone to represent the CIB and that Anderson misplaced those files years ago."

Jolie took several more steps in Max's direction, pausing a few feet from where he stood at the side of the desk. "I suppose I can rule you out as a suspect, now."

"I'd appreciate that." He didn't smile, but humor twinkled in his eyes.

"My father could have been responsible for the cover-up twenty years ago but not now. So who does that leave? Roscoe Wells is the only name left on my short list."

Max eased closer to Jolie. "Why would Roscoe want to cover up what really happened here at Belle Rose?"

"He wouldn't, unless he was somehow involved," Jolie said. "But why would he want to kill my mother and Aunt Lisette and Lemar? What possible motive could he have had?"

"Good question. Roscoe is a wily old fox, with a mean streak a mile wide, but personally murdering three people in broad daylight isn't his style."

"Then what could it be? There isn't anyone else with the power and money to have manipulated a CIB agent and the local sheriff."

"And possibly the county coroner."

"I hadn't thought of that. Who was the coroner back then? Wasn't it Dr. Madry?"

"Dr. Horace Madry," Max told her. "I double-checked this morning to make sure he was the county coroner back in Eighty-two. He was. But Horace is dead. Died two years ago, at the ripe old age of eighty."

"What if we went to see Roscoe and—"

"Bad idea." Max shook his head, then took another step closer to Jolie. "He's not going to admit anything. He'll deny any guilt, any connection, hollering his denial at the top of his lungs. And we could tip our hand, if we accuse him outright. What we need is evidence. Something in black-and-white."

"The files that are missing. There has to be something in those files that would point to him."

"I wouldn't put anything past Roscoe, but for the life of me, I can't think of any reason he'd murder two of the Desmond sisters. Or have them murdered. He's always considered the Desmond family to be Mississippi royalty, on an equal footing with his own family."

"How did Roscoe react when Felicia told him she was going to marry you?"

"Don't you mean why did he allow her to marry a bastard without a family pedigree?" Max snorted. "She didn't tell him until after we were married. We eloped."

"That's right. I seem to remember Aunt Clarice mentioning that she and your mother were terribly disappointed because you and Felicia didn't have a huge formal wedding.''

"We needed to get married in a hurry," Max said.

"Oh?"

"Felicia told me she was pregnant."

"Pregnant?"

"She wasn't. She lied. Of course, I didn't find out the truth until a few months later."

"Oh, Max, why would she lie to you about something so important?"

"Because she'd used sex to blind me to her true nature, and she knew that sooner or later, I'd find out what a conniving bitch she really was, what a self-centered little whore. So she decided to trap me before I saw her for who and what she really was."

Jolie heard the anger in his voice, but she also caught the hint of pain. Without thinking about the consequences, she reached over and laid her hand on his cheek.

"I'm so sorry, Max. Did you love her terribly?"

Max cradled his big hand over her small one and pressed her caress deeper. "Yes, I loved her. But it didn't take her long to destroy any tender feelings I had for her. By our first anniversary, I loathed her."

"Do you still?"

He shook his head. "When I think of her, I don't feel much of anything. Bitterness, maybe. That's all."

They looked deeply into each other's eyes. Mirrors to the soul, someone had once said. What she saw in Max's eyes had nothing to do with the past, nothing associated with a lost love.

He pulled her hand away from his cheek and brought it to his mouth, then planted a kiss in the center of her palm. Self-preservation instincts warned her to flee, but the primeval mating call ruled supreme. When he took her in his arms, she went willingly. His mouth covered hers. She threw her arms around his neck as he cupped her buttocks and brought her closer, pressing her against his erection.

Neither of them heard the door open. Lost in the heat of passion, consumed by a need that rode them hard, they didn't even hear the loud startled gasp.

"What the hell is going on?" Mallory demanded. "Max, have you lost your mind?"

Jolie and Max broke apart, their breaths ragged, their faces flushed. When she glanced toward the doorway, Jolie saw the horrified look on her half sister's face.

"You should knock before you enter a room," Max said. "It's the polite thing to do."

"Screw being polite!" Mallory's gaze bored into Jolie. "Want to explain why you were eating *her* face off? You can't be that hard up for a woman."

"Mallory, I think you've said enough," Max told her.

"I haven't even started."

Mallory smiled, but only malevolence shined in her blue eyes. Eyes identical to Louis Royale's. *Eyes identical to my own,* Jolie thought.

"You've started and finished," Max said. "Whatever you think you saw going on between Jolie and me is none of your business."

"Like hell it isn't. She's the enemy, remember? And only a fool sleeps with the enemy. I never thought you were a fool, big brother."

"Mallory, I'm warning you." Max glared at her.

Disregarding Max's threat, Mallory zeroed in on Jolie. "You don't mean anything to him, you realize that, don't you? He has other women. One in particular. Somebody he sneaks off to screw around with whenever he feels the urge. A woman who probably knows a lot more about pleasing a man like Max than you ever could. Want to know who she is . . . this woman Max likes to fuck?"

"Mallory—" Max clenched his teeth.

"Eartha Kilpatrick. Remember her? The big-boobed

redhead who owns the Sumarville Inn? He's been messing around with her for a couple of years now."

Max lunged forward, grabbed Mallory's arm and marched her out of the study and into the hall. Jolie stood frozen to the spot, feeling strangely numb. What difference did it make to her that Max had been having an ongoing affair with Eartha Kilpatrick? She had no claim on Max. *Oh, God, then why does it hurt so much to think of him making love to another woman?* Her mind reeled with thoughts of Max lying naked in bed with the voluptuous redhead.

She heard Max's voice, low and edged with steel, as he spoke to his sister in the hall. And she heard Mallory's bitter tirade. But their words bled together into a confused garble.

Suddenly Max returned to the study, slammed the door behind him and came straight to her. She met his gaze head-on.

"Eartha Kilpatrick and I are friends," he said. "I suppose if it were fifty years ago, people would say she's been my mistress for the past few years."

Jolie nodded. *I don't care. I don't care. I don't care.*

"Our relationship is . . . Eartha and I know we don't have a future together. I don't love her and have no intention of ever marrying her."

Jolie nodded again. *Damn you, Max. Damn you for making me care.*

"Say something, dammit."

"What do you want me to say?"

He forked his fingers through his hair, huffed loudly, and turned away from her. She held her breath.

"Hell, tell me to stay away from you. Tell me not to ever touch you again. Tell me you hate my damn guts."

"I hate your damn guts!"

Jolie ran out of the study, leaving Max cursing none too quietly.

Chapter 19

R. J. Sutton woke to a relentless pounding on his door. Who the hell? He glanced at the digital clock on the nightstand. Eleven-fifteen. Late in the day for most people to still be sleeping, but not for a guy who worked the evening hours he did. Some nights after his shift as the restaurant's bartender, if the regular front desk clerk at the inn didn't show up, he took over and worked until seven, which he'd done this morning.

"R. J., please let me in," Mallory Royale cried as she kept beating on the door.

"Mallory?"

R. J. jumped out of bed, then remembered he was naked. What the hell was she doing here? He grabbed his jeans off the floor where he'd tossed them around seven-thirty this morning, yanked them on, and walked across the carpeted floor in his bare feet.

The second he opened the door, Mallory threw herself at him, then lifted her arms up and around his neck. Her hot wet tears dampened his naked chest.

When he awoke he'd already had a woody, as he did most mornings, so just the instant touch of her body against his stiffened his John Thomas into action.

"What's the matter, honey?" He wrapped his arms around her, then kicked the door closed. "What's got you so upset?"

"I don't want to talk about it," she told him. "I just want you."

"You've got me, sugar. I'm all yours." He kissed the top of her head. "Stop crying. Whatever's wrong, we'll work it out."

She lifted her head off his chest and gazed up at him. "Make love to me, R. J. Make love to me, right now."

"You came here to ask me to make love to you?"

"Yes." She swiped at the tears spilling from the corners of her eyes, then wiped her face with her fingertips.

"Are you sure?" *Hell, Sutton, what's wrong with you? When did you ever look a gift horse in the mouth? The woman says she wants you to screw her, and you know damn well you're ready, willing, and able to accommodate her.*

Mallory nodded. "I'm very sure."

He hadn't been with a virgin since he'd been a virgin himself and made out with Valerie Hovater in her bedroom one night when she'd been baby-sitting her two younger brothers. Of course over the years, he'd had his share of young, fairly inexperienced girls, but no one like Mallory. Despite his determination never to get emotionally involved with any of his conquests, he knew he already felt something for Mallory that he'd never felt for anyone else. Not love, but something more than just wanting to get into her pants.

"Come on in." He took her hand and led her deeper into the room, straight toward his bed.

"I'm not on the pill or anything," she told him, her voice indicating a hint of nervousness.

"It's okay. I've got protection. I'll take care of you."

A fragile smile trembled on her lips. "I—I think I'm in love with you."

Damn! "Do you?" He looked her over from head to toe. A walking, talking, living doll. *Don't let your conscience get in the way*, he told himself. *If it wasn't you, it would be some other guy. You just happen to be the lucky one.*

"Mm-hmm." She gazed at him with those big blue eyes of hers, suddenly filled with uncertainty.

R. J. ran the back of his hand over her cheek, down her neck, and across the pink crop-top she wore. She sucked in her breath when his fingers spread out across her naked skin directly below her breasts.

"I love everything about you," he said. "Your beautiful blue eyes." He stared directly into her eyes. "And your long black hair." He skimmed her hair with his fingers. "And your sweet body. And the way you make me feel when we're together." He knew all the right things to tell a woman, all the compliments that softened her up for the kill.

When he grasped the hem of her shirt and pulled it up over her breasts, she lifted her arms so that he could easily remove the garment. Before she had a chance to change her mind, he caressed her buttocks, then unzipped her shorts. She sucked in a deep breath, but didn't try to stop him. A second later, she stood before him in a pair of pink bikini panties and a matching pink satin bra.

He let out a wolf whistle. "Damn, baby, you're gorgeous." And she was. No pretense on his part.

She surveyed him hurriedly. "You're gorgeous yourself. I've never known anyone like you."

"That makes two of us." He kissed her, thrusting his tongue into her mouth, while he slid his hands inside her panties and kneaded her round firm butt.

By the time they came up for air, he was hard as a rock and hurting in the worst way. Keeping her attention focused on his kissing, he nibbled on her ear, then kissed her neck before adeptly undoing the catch on her bra and sliding the soft satin down her arms and off. He jerked her up against him, letting her naked breasts crush into his chest. For a couple of seconds, he thought he might lose it right then and there. He hadn't touched another gal since he'd been seeing Mallory and he was needing some pussy real bad.

She shuddered and whimpered. He eased her toward the bed until the back of her legs encountered the mattress, then he toppled her over and onto the bed. Lying there almost completely naked, she looked up at him and smiled. Damn little vixen. She knew how much he wanted her. Forgoing any pretense at gentleness, he grabbed hold of her panties, ripped them down her legs and tossed them on the floor, then quickly removed his jeans.

"Wow!" Mallory stared at his erection.

"Like what you see, honey?"

"Yes."

She almost choked on the word and R. J. wished she were choking on his dick. *All in good time,* he thought. *Basics first.*

"It's all yours," he told her. "Do you want it now?"

"I—I . . . yes."

R. J. opened the nightstand drawer, took a condom out of the box he kept there, and sheathed himself. He went down over her, bracing himself so all his weight didn't land directly on top of her. He nudged her with his sex, letting the tip dip between her closed thighs.

"Open up and let me come in." He lowered his head and took one tight nipple between his teeth.

When he shook his head, tweaking the nipple, she gasped and spread her legs. His mouth opened over her nipple and began sucking, while his penis sought entrance into her body. He probed. God Almighty, she was tight!

When he shoved halfway into her, she tensed and cried out. Hell, she was already wet and he had the job fifty percent completed. He wasn't about to stop now. No way. He didn't think he could, even if he wanted to—and he didn't.

"Take it easy, honey. It's going to hurt a little this first time."

"R. J. don't—"

He lifted her hips and rammed into her, popping her cherry as he took her completely. She meowed like a scalded cat and clawed at his back with her sharp little nails.

"It hurts," she told him.

He withdrew a couple of inches, then rammed back into her. She grabbed his shoulders, her fingers biting down hard.

"Dammit, I told you that it hurts."

He lay on top of her, his sex buried in her body. "You wanted this and I'm giving it to you. Try to relax. Next time, I promise you'll enjoy it."

"Next time?"

Why didn't she just shut up? A couple of more lunges and he'd come. If she could just wait, he'd be able to go again and he'd make sure she got her cookies off. Ignoring her whimpers, her scratching nails, and the tension in her body, R. J. pumped into her repeatedly. Within a couple of minutes his release jetted into the condom. Because he was embedded to the hilt inside Mallory, his climax nearly took off the top of his head. The only way it could have been any better was if he'd taken her raw, without the rubber.

Maybe next time. After all, she'd been a virgin, so there was no chance she could give him the clap, or anything more deadly for that matter. But she wasn't on the pill, so he could get her pregnant. But hell, what were the odds he'd knock her up if he didn't use a rubber just once?

"Where's Jolie?"

Yvonne's eyelids popped open the moment she heard Theron speak. She'd closed her eyes to pray just a moment ago.

"Theron?" She lifted his hand and looked into the eyes focused on her face.

"Mama." His voice was raspy and hoarse.

"Oh, thank you, dear Jesus." Tears welled up in her eyes and spilled from the corners.

"Where is Jolie?"

"Jolie? She's at Belle Rose," Yvonne replied. "Do you want me to call her?"

Theron nodded. "Call her. And call Ike."

"Ike Denton?"

The day-shift bodyguard Max had hired peered inside the ICU cubicle. "Is everything all right, Mrs. Carter?"

"Fine, thank you. Actually more than fine. My son is able to speak." She smiled at the big, broad-shouldered man in the nice navy blue suit who wore a large gun on his hip. His presence bothered her greatly, but she was thankful he was here protecting Theron.

"Who's he?" Theron asked.

She debated whether to tell him the truth, then said, "He's a private bodyguard. Max hired him."

"To guard me?"

"Yes."

"Why?"

Yvonne smoothed her hand over Theron's cheek. "Don't upset yourself. You need to rest and heal."

"What's happened? Why did Max think I needed a bodyguard?"

"Nothing's happened," she fibbed. "It's just that Max is concerned someone might try to harm you again."

"Call Jolie. I want to see her."

"I'll call her."

"Do it now."

Georgette and Parry sat side-by-side in matching wicker rockers in the sunroom. She sipped on fresh-squeezed orange juice and he guzzled a Mimosa, liberally laced with expensive champagne. Over the years, she and her brother had become accustomed to the best money could buy. Fortunately, Louis had never quibbled about money. Her beloved husband had been a very generous man. Not only with her, but with Parry and even more so with Max and Mallory.

"You're mighty quiet today, Georgie."

"Just thinking."

"About what? Max getting himself shot saving Jolie last night?"

"Hm—mm. There's something between them," Georgette said.

"Max is a man. She's a beautiful woman. He probably wants to screw her. To be honest, I'd like to screw her myself."

"Parry! Must you always be so crude?"

"I'm not always crude," he told her. "But I thought I could be myself around you, just as you can be with me. We don't have to put on false faces and pretend to be something we're not when it's just the two of us."

"I could be myself with Louis. He didn't mind that I wasn't born a lady. As a matter of fact, I think he rather liked it when I let down all my defenses and acted like a tramp."

"You miss him something awful, don't you?"

No one could begin to imagine the pain she endured just getting through each day without him. If God were truly merciful, he would have taken her the very moment he took Louis. Her soul longed to be with his.

"It's as if I died the night Louis died," she said. "And somehow I'm trapped in this body that's still alive."

"Lord, Georgie, I wish you wouldn't talk that way. You give me the creeps."

"You've never loved anyone the way I loved Louis, never had someone love you as passionately in return."

"I loved Lisette." He downed the remainder of his Mimosa, then set the flute on the table to his right.

"Did you really? I always wondered. I thought perhaps you only loved the fact that she was Desmond County royalty and by marrying her you believed you'd gain respectability."

"That might have been part of it. But I did love her. And I'd have made her a fairly decent husband, if I'd had the chance."

Georgette reached out over the chair arms and grabbed Parry's hand. "I know, darling, I know." She squeezed his hand. "Promise me something."

"What do you want me to promise?"

"Promise me that no matter what happens, even if they find out Lemar Fuqua didn't kill Audrey and Lisette, you won't let anything bad happen to Max. We have to protect him."

Parry leaned over, kissed her cheek, and said, "Georgie, Max didn't kill them. You haven't been thinking all these years that he—"

"I believe I know the truth," Georgette said. "I think perhaps I've always known that Lemar Fuqua didn't kill Audrey and Lisette."

"And how do you know that?"

"Because I think I know who killed all three of them."

"Do you, Georgie? Do you really?"

"Yes, Parry, I do. I really do."

Mallory had tried to leave, but R. J. wouldn't let her go. She had fought him until she wore herself out and then she cried and pleaded, but to no avail. She had come to him, needing him. Needing comfort. Wanting somebody to care about her. Love her. But all R. J. had done was take her ruthlessly, not caring if he hurt her. How could she have misjudged him so badly? She thought he cared about her, that he was the one person she could trust not to betray her.

"Come on, honey." R. J. swooped her up into his arms. She didn't have the strength to fight him, so she let him lift her and carry her into the bathroom.

He took her with him into the shower, then set her

on her feet and turned on the water. His body shielded hers from the initial blast of cold liquid; only when the water warmed did he reverse their positions so that the spray hit her full-force. Her body ached, probably more from the fact that she had tensed her muscles when R. J. invaded her so roughly than from the sex itself. And she burned between her legs. Damn, why did people have sex all the time if it was so horrible?

R. J. lathered a washcloth and ran it over her back and buttocks, lathering her skin. And when he parted her legs and washed her intimately, she made no protest. He turned her around carefully and lathered her breasts and belly. She couldn't bring herself to look at him. She hated him for what he'd done to her, for how terribly he'd disappointed her. But when he dropped the washcloth and gently pushed her against the tiled wall, she gasped and her gaze locked with his.

"You're pretty mad at me right now, aren't you, honey?"

She swallowed the emotions lodged in her throat, anger mixed with unhappiness.

"I can make it better," he told her.

She glared at him.

"Don't believe me?" he asked.

She shook her head. She despised him! How could he undo what he'd done? He couldn't change anything, least of all the cruelty of his actions.

R. J. didn't wait, didn't ask her permission. He just kissed her. An open mouth, tongue-lunging, wet kiss. Whimpering a protest, she squirmed to free herself, but he manacled her wrists, held them above her head and deepened the kiss. Despite how much she hated him right now, her body responded. Her nipples peaked and pressed against his chest. Her feminine core throbbed. How was it possible that she could want him after the way he'd mistreated her?

His hand slid between them, over her belly to cup her mound. When he pried her thighs apart, she moaned, but he forged ahead and managed to slip a couple of fingers inside her.

"Are you sore, baby?"

"Yes, I'm sore, damn you."

He chuckled. "I'm going to make it feel good any minute now."

He slipped his fingers out and began an assault on her aching core. Then he whispered shockingly crude words in her ear moments before his tongue teased first one nipple and then the other. As he caressed her intimately and suckled at her breasts, Mallory's body hummed with every stroke until she began feeling a bone-melting pleasure.

Lifting his head, R. J. grinned. "Feeling better?"

"Mm-hmm."

"Relax, baby, and let it happen. You're going to come for me. You're going to shudder and shake and cry out." He kept stroking her, harder, deeper, faster. And all the while the warm water showered their naked bodies. "The next time I'm inside you, it's going to feel like this, only better. Come on, baby, come for me."

She wriggled and squirmed, riding his hand while his fingers worked their magic. The whole world fell apart, shattering all around her as she climaxed. The aftershocks went on and on as she fell into R. J.'s arms and pressed her head on his shoulder.

"That's my good girl."

He shut off the shower, helped her out and onto the tiled floor, then wrapped her in a towel and sat her on the commode until he dried himself with another towel. She crossed her arms over her waist and hugged herself tightly, not sure she understood what had just happened. And while she was in the process of trying to figure it out, R. J. jerked her up off the commode seat and dragged her back into the bedroom. He whipped the towel from her body and pulled her into the bed with him. This time he lifted her until she sat astride his hips.

"Again, Mallory. Only this time, you're going to like it. I promise."

Tell him no. Tell him you're not going to let him stick his big, hard dick inside you and hurt you again. But before she could form the words of protest, he maneuvered her up and around until the tip of his penis teased her feminine folds. Instinctively, she tensed. He grabbed her hips, lifted her, then brought her down on his jutting sex, impaling her. She gasped at the sensation of fullness inside her and waited for the pain. But there was no pain. Only a slight irritation. And when he moved in and out several times, she experienced a tingling enjoyment.

He moved her hips up and down in a slow steady rhythm, his sex rubbing back and forth over her hard little kernel and striking a sensitive area inside her with each lunge. Soon she took over and moved of her own volition, riding him with an urgency she knew would lead to another climax. With one hand on her hip, he lifted the other to tease her nipples, pinching and flicking, keeping them tight and ultra-sensitive.

"Oh, God, R. J."

"Faster, baby, faster."

She accelerated the pace, but it apparently wasn't fast enough to suit him. Once again he grabbed her hips and pumped her up and down until she exploded in a mind-blowing orgasm. His release followed hers a second later.

Wet with perspiration and breathing wildly, Mallory dissolved on top of R. J., melding her body to his.

"Better the second time, wasn't it, honey?" He nuzzled her neck.

She sighed. "Yes. Much better."

It wasn't until later, when she and R. J. had sex for a third time, that she realized he hadn't used a condom the second time. Oh, well, nothing she could do about it now.

"Use a condom this time," she told him.

He sheathed himself, then eased into her. She kissed him, wanting him, needing him, longing for more and more of this newly awakened passion she'd just discovered.

"Teach me things," she told R. J.

"What do you want to learn?" he asked.

"Everything."

"That could take awhile. Days, weeks, months."

"Fine by me, as long as you give me another lesson right now."

Chapter 20

"Isn't this the most wonderful news." Clarice hugged Yvonne, then clasped Yvonne's hands and beamed cheerfully. "God has answered a lot of prayers. He's given us back our precious Theron."

"Come on in and say hello," Yvonne said.

"Oh, I shouldn't disturb him, if he's resting. We don't want to tire him out."

"Nonsense. He wants to see you." Yvonne tugged on Clarice's hand, then glanced at Clarice's constant companion. "You don't mind waiting out here, do you, Nowell?"

"Not at all," he replied. "Clarice has been awfully worried about Theron. It'll do her good to see him and have him talk to her. Maybe she'll stop fretting so much once she sees for herself that he's improving."

When they entered the ICU cubicle, Theron lay flat on his back, his body still attached to an assortment of tubes and wires that monitored his vital signs and administered the nourishment and medication his body needed. The moment Clarice and Yvonne approached his bed, he opened his eyes and smiled oddly, then glanced back and forth from one to the other, as if studying them. Yvonne's heartbeat quickened. Why was he looking at them that way? she wondered.

"I don't know why I never saw it before." Theron's voice, unused for days, was still a bit hoarse and slightly scratchy.

"What didn't you ever see before?" Clarice asked.

"How much you and Mama resemble each other."

Yvonne gasped. Her hand flew to her mouth.

"Well, of course we favor each other," Clarice said, as if stating the obvious. "Yvonne and I both look a lot like our daddy. Whereas Audrey and Lisette looked more like my mama, and Lemar resembled his mama."

"Theron, let me explain . . ." Yvonne had kept the truth hidden from her son all his life, uncertain how he would react if he knew. And here Clarice had proclaimed them sisters as if she'd been discussing nothing more unusual than hot weather in July.

"What's there to explain?" Theron's gaze connected with Yvonne's.

"I didn't tell you because—"

"Because you thought I wouldn't want to know that my grandfather was white."

"Well, I wanted to tell you," Clarice said. "I wanted you to know that I was your aunt, just the way I was Jolie's aunt. I hope you believe me when I tell you that I've always loved you just as much as I loved Jolie."

A fine mist glazed Theron's hazel eyes. Eyes that were a biological inheritance from Sam Desmond. "I—I didn't know," he said. "But I should have. You always treated me as if I were special to you. I have to admit that your affection for me bothered me once I got older. It just didn't make any sense to me. And it bothered me that you and Mama were so close. I didn't understand."

There was a great deal her son didn't know about her, far more than simply her white heritage. There was one thing in particular Yvonne prayed he would never find out. The one other secret she shared with Clarice. A secret that bound them together as deeply as sisterhood. A terrible secret that they had sworn they would take to their graves.

"People suspected the truth about Yvonne and Lemar being Desmonds," Clarice said. "But we all promised Daddy, when he lay dying, that we'd keep the truth within the family. Among us five siblings." Clarice lowered her voice. "He didn't want folks thinking less of Sadie, you know. After all, he was married to my mama when Yvonne and Lemar were born. And our daddy was such an honorable man. He didn't want Sadie or Mama to be disgraced."

"How can you say he was an honorable man when he not only committed adultery, but he took advantage of his housekeeper?" Theron's gaze darkened; his brow wrinkled.

Clarice's eyes widened in horror. "He didn't take advantage—"

"Mr. Sam and Mama loved each other," Yvonne cut in quickly.

"You can't possibly believe that," Theron said. "No matter what Grandma told you—"

"Mr. Sam told me." Yvonne met her son's gaze without blinking an eye. "Before he died, he told me that he'd cared deeply for Miss Mary Rose, but that my mama had been the love of his life."

"It's true," Clarice said. "But even after Mama died, Daddy couldn't marry Sadie. That was back in the late forties and interracial marriages were illegal."

"Uncle Lemar *was* Lisette's half brother." Theron closed his eyes.

"You're tiring yourself out." Yvonne caressed his cheek.

"There was no love affair between Lisette and Lemar," Clarice said. "They knew they were brother and sister. And they'd been friends all their lives, since they were little children. They had a special fondness for each other. But nothing sexual. Not ever."

"Why didn't y'all tell the sheriff about this during the Belle Rose massacre investigation?" Theron opened his eyes and pinned his mother with his sharp gaze.

"I did," Yvonne said. "I told him, but he acted like he didn't believe me. He told me that I would say anything to clear my brother's name."

"And months later, when I was able to, I collaborated what Yvonne told Sheriff Bendall." Tears trickled down Clarice's cheeks. "But nobody would pay any attention to either of us. The sheriff said it didn't make any difference, that even if Lisette and Lemar were half siblings, that only made their affair all the more abhorrent."

"The sheriff didn't want to hear the truth," Theron said. "He wanted Uncle Lemar branded a killer."

"But why—" Yvonne said.

"Did you call Jolie?" Theron asked.

"I called her," Clarice said. "She's on her way here. And she said to tell you that y'all have a new ally."

"Who?"

"Well, Max, of course," Clarice replied.

Jolie and Max had just left the Sumarville Police Department when her cell phone rang. The moment she had heard Aunt Clarice's voice, she immediately thought of Theron, knowing that her aunt was probably at the hospital.

"Come quickly, dear girl. Our Theron is talking. And wanting to see you."

When she'd told Max the good news, they had rushed to Desmond County General. Just as they arrived, a red Taurus pulled out of a parking place right in front of the entrance. Max whipped his Porsche into the empty slot, then killed the motor. When Jolie reached for the door handle, he leaned across the console and grabbed her wrist. Glancing over her shoulder, she glared at him.

"What?"

"It's not going to work," he said.

"I don't know what you're talking about."

"The silent treatment you've been giving me. All the way into town and from the police station over here to the hospital. You haven't said anything except to answer yes or no when I spoke to you."

"What is there to say?" She yanked on her wrist. He released her. "We agreed that I hate you and that nothing else has changed just because we seem to have the hots for each other."

"So, your plan is to ignore it and it'll go away?"

"Yeah, something like that." She opened the door and got out, then headed toward the hospital entrance, not waiting on Max.

He got out, locked the Porsche, and caught up with Jolie in the lobby. Falling into step beside her, he easily kept up with her fast-paced walk as she headed for the elevators. She watched him in her peripheral vision, thankful that he didn't look at her or try to touch her. Learning about his ongoing affair with Eartha Kilpatrick had given her the perfect excuse to reject him. Putting another woman between Max and her own desperate desire for him was the best solution she could think of at the time. Actually, she wasn't nearly as upset about Max's "mistress" as she pretended. She hadn't actually thought a man such as he would be celibate. Hell, sexuality practically oozed from his pores.

Jolie punched the UP arrow and waited. Almost instantly the elevator doors opened and three people emerged, leaving the interior empty. Max followed her into the elevator, then punched the floor number for the ICU. A deafening silence hung between them. Within minutes, the elevator doors opened and Jolie bolted out into the hall and practically ran toward the ICU. As eager as she was to see Theron, her hectic escape had more to do with her not wanting to be alone with Max, even for one more minute.

She found Yvonne, Aunt Clarice, and Nowell Landers in the ICU waiting room. The moment she entered, Yvonne and Clarice stood and rushed toward her.

"Don't upset him when you see him. He's already upset enough," Yvonne said. "He says that he can identify all three men who attacked him. Chief Harper is on his way here to personally take Theron's statement."

Jolie grasped Yvonne's hand. "I'm going to tell him what happened to me and to Max. He needs to know everything that I know, including the fact that someone killed Ginny Pounders to keep her quiet."

"I understand that you have to tell him." Yvonne squeezed Jolie's hand. "Just try your best not to let him get too excited. He may be able to talk now, but he's still got a long way to go until he's fully recovered."

Clarice put her arm around Yvonne's shoulders. "Jolie cares about Theron. She's not going to do anything to harm him." Clarice glanced at Max, who stood just outside the open doorway. "You must go in with her to see Theron. The nurses shooed us out because he got so agitated, and they asked that when you arrived, for y'all to wait until the next visiting time."

"When will that be?" Max asked.

"Not for another hour," Yvonne replied. "But Theron demanded to see Jolie immediately. He threatened to tear the hospital down, brick by brick, if he wasn't allowed to see her as soon as she got here."

"Then maybe we shouldn't keep him waiting." Max's gaze met Jolie's. She nodded agreement. "Let's go see if they'll let us in."

While Jolie told him all about Ginny Pounders' murder, her own narrow escape, and Max being shot, Theron noticed the way Max hovered over Jolie, like some sort of protective guardian. He wanted to ask her what was going on between her and her stepbrother, but he could hardly voice the question with Max in the room.

"Thanks for hiring the bodyguard," Theron said. "I can pick up the tab myself. Just have the agency send the bills to me."

"Let me worry about the bills," Max told him. "You worry about getting well."

"Max is right." Jolie sat in a chair at Theron's bedside, his hand held firmly in hers. "We'll take care of everything. You just concentrate on recovering. Max and I aren't going to stop digging until we find out what really happened at Belle Rose that day. He's as convinced as we are that Lemar didn't kill my mother and aunt."

Theron's gaze locked with Max's. "You're going to take care of Jolie, aren't you? You won't let anything happen to her?"

"Keeping her safe is my top priority," Max said.

Jolie snapped her head up and glared at Max.

"If you let her get hurt, you'll have to answer to me," Theron warned him. "After all, she and I are . . . we're like family."

"I understand." Max nodded, then settled his gaze on Jolie, who instantly glanced away.

"You'll keep me informed every step of the way, won't you?" Theron asked.

"You'll know what we know," Jolie promised. "After all, you're the one who started the ball rolling. This is your case. Max and I are just going to do the legwork."

"Be careful," Theron cautioned. "Don't take any unnecessary chances."

"Look who's talking," Jolie kidded him.

"Yeah, and see where it got me."

A tall and commanding middle-aged black nurse entered the cubicle. "I'm afraid I'll have to ask y'all to leave. Chief Harper is here to take Mr. Carter's statement, and I will not allow half of Sumarville in here at one time."

Jolie stood, leaned over, and hugged Theron very

gently and very carefully, then kissed his cheek. "You behave yourself and don't give the nurses too hard a time."

Theron grasped her wrist. "Be careful and don't do anything foolish." He almost ended his sentence by calling her cousin. It would take awhile to get used to thinking of the Desmonds as family. His mother's family.

That night Max and Jolie gathered the clan, including a sulking Mallory, in the front parlor. Jolie couldn't help wondering how they'd all react to being questioned, especially Georgette and Parry. After all, it was possible, wasn't it, that one of them knew the truth, that one of them had been responsible for the murders?

"What's this all about?" Parry demanded as he took a seat beside Georgette.

"Yes, dear boy, please tell us what's going on." Sitting together on the sofa, Clarice placed her hand in Nowell's. She had insisted her fiancé stay, since he would soon be a member of the family.

Max had tensed at the mention of marriage between Clarice and Nowell, but when Jolie had given him a warning glance, he'd kept quiet. One problem at a time was all they could handle.

Mallory sneered at Jolie. "Since Aunt Clarice is planning on marrying her overaged hippy, I suppose you two are fixing to announce that y'all want to make it a double wedding."

"Shut up, Mallory," Max said. "Sit down and keep quiet."

"Yes, sir!" Mallory saluted him, then flopped down on the huge velvet ottoman in front of Georgette's chair.

"Hush, dear." Georgette leaned over just enough to pat Mallory's back several times.

Max glanced around the room before his gaze settled on Jolie. "As y'all know, Theron Carter and Jolie decided to try to have the Belle Rose massacre case reopened and—"

"And Theron wound up in the hospital and Jolie nearly got herself killed," Parry stated the facts quite adamantly.

"And don't forget that Max got shot," Clarice added.

"The point is that by this time y'all have to realize that someone is trying to prevent any further investigation into the old double murder case. Which, I would think, means that someone other than Lemar Fuqua murdered Audrey Royale and Lisette Desmond."

"I've always believed Lemar was innocent," Clarice said.

"What Max and I want from y'all is any information you can give us about that day." Jolie purposefully avoided looking at her stepmother.

"I can't see where that could help y'all . . ." Georgette glanced pleadingly at Parry.

"Georgie's right." Parry frowned, his gaze directed at Max. "What good's it going to do to rehash everything?"

"I—I don't want to remember." Clarice shook her head. Nowell draped his arm around her shoulders protectively.

"Please, Aunt Clarice," Jolie said. "If I'm willing to try to recall all the details of what happened to me that day, then surely you can. If only I had even a vague memory of who shot me."

Clarice whimpered. "Blood. So much blood. I parked in the back, where I always did, and came in through the kitchen." Clarice's eyes grew wide, a trancelike expression glazing them. "I saw Audrey's body. She was dead. And then I saw Jolie. At first, I thought she was dead, too. But thank the Lord, she was still alive. I suppose I called the police. I don't remember exactly. I sat down in the floor and held Jolie in my arms." Clarice sighed heavily. "The next thing I remember clearly, it was weeks later."

"Then you never saw Aunt Lisette or Lemar?" Jolie asked.

Clarice shook her head. "I never went beyond the kitchen."

"Aunt Clarice, there wasn't any truth to the rumors that Lisette and Lemar were having an affair, was there?" Max asked.

"Mercy no. Lemar was our brother, you know. Our half brother."

A hushed silence fell over the room. An eerily comforting atmosphere of wonder and relief that the truth had finally been brought out into the light of day.

"Lemar and Yvonne were Granddaddy's children?" Jolie asked, surprised, but not shocked. It was as if on some level she had always known and yet never consciously suspected.

"Oh, my, yes." Clarice's lips curved into a fragile smile. "So, you see, there was no love affair. Only a family attachment."

"Then what would Lemar's motive have been to kill his two half sisters?" Max asked. "If not jealousy, then what? Hatred?"

"No, no, no," Clarice insisted. "Lemar didn't hate anyone, least of all Lisette. And everyone who knew Lemar knew he couldn't hurt a fly. He was such a kind and gentle man."

Max turned to Parry. "Did you suspect Lisette of having an affair?"

"Huh?" Parry seemed taken aback by the question. "I . . . er . . . of course not. We were engaged to be married. We loved each other and were planning a future together."

"I'm sorry to speak ill of the dead," Jolie said. "But I've been led to believe that my aunt Lisette was rather promiscuous, that she'd had numerous lovers before you two became engaged."

"Lisette was a wild carefree spirit," Parry said. "And

I loved that about her. She wasn't some straightlaced Goody-Two-shoes."

"I see." Jolie looked point-blank at Parry. "So, you had no reason to be jealous?"

"I wish you wouldn't say such hateful things about Lisette." Clarice's thin shoulders tensed, even under Nowell's comforting caress.

"I'm sorry, Aunt Clarice." Jolie took a tentative step in her aunt's direction, then paused, and said, "But we have to figure out who might have had a motive to kill Mama and Aunt Lisette."

"Well, I resent the fact that you've practically implied I might have had a motive," Parry huffed, his cheeks swelling like a bullfrog's.

Max came up beside Jolie and for a split second she thought he was going to place his hand on her shoulder, but he didn't. "We aren't accusing anyone of anything. But Jolie's right. The more we know about what was going on back then, the better our odds of finding out who the real killer was and stopping him before he tries to stop us a second time."

"Oh, dear," Georgette gasped. "Why must we go through that nightmare all over again? My poor Louis was devastated." She looked at Jolie. "He wouldn't leave the hospital for days. He stayed there, waiting and praying that you would live. And I couldn't be with him, couldn't comfort him. I had to stay away."

Jolie hated hearing the love and caring in Georgette's voice, hated having to admit the possibility that her stepmother had truly loved her father. "What we need to know is if any of you can think of something—any-thing—that might cast suspicion on someone other than Lemar."

"Someone besides Max?" Parry asked.

"What do you mean by that?" Silent for quite some time, Mallory demanded an explanation for her uncle's comment.

Parry shrugged. A rather wicked grin played across

his face. "There were rumors, lots of rumors. People thought maybe Max killed off Audrey Desmond to clear the way for Georgie to marry Louis."

"That's a dirty, filthy lie!" Mallory screamed. "Max would never—"

"No, of course he wouldn't," Jolie agreed. "Someone, perhaps the real killer, started that vicious lie, just as someone started the lie about Lisette and Lemar being lovers."

Staring at Jolie, a startled expression on her face, Mallory quieted. "Then maybe you'd better find out who started the rumors."

Georgette rose from the sofa. Wringing her hands anxiously, she walked toward Jolie. "Your father believed Lemar was innocent. He spoke to Sheriff Bendall about it, but the sheriff assured Louis that no one else could have committed the murders. For years afterward, Louis would occasionally get in an odd mood, worrying about Lemar's innocence. And I'm afraid I'm guilty of having persuaded him, more than once, to let the matter drop. I couldn't bear to see Louis hurting the way he did every time he relived that day.

"We both felt so terribly guilty." Georgette came right up to Jolie and looked directly at her. "All these years I've wanted to tell you . . . to say that I'm so terribly sorry about what happened to your mother. Louis and I . . . we loved each other and wanted to be together, but not that way, not at the expense of Audrey's life."

Jolie stiffened, every muscle in her body rigidly taut. Emotions overwhelmed her, but she fought them, momentarily conquering the tears threatening to weaken her resolve to hate Georgette until her dying day.

"Mother . . ." Max spoke softly, comfort and concern in his voice.

"It's my fault that Louis didn't pursue the matter, that he never insisted on reopening the case, in proving to himself Lemar murdered Audrey and Lisette."

Georgette held out her hands to Jolie. "Please, forgive me. And forgive your father. He never stopped loving you. Never stopped hoping you would come home."

Tears gathered in Jolie's eyes, tears she could no longer control. *God, make the pain stop. Make it go away.* She couldn't bear hearing the truth and knowing in her heart that she had wronged her father.

"No . . . no . . ." Jolie turned and ran from the room. Blinded by her tears, she could hardly see where she was going but somehow managed to make it outside onto the front veranda. Feelings long suppressed broke free.

"Jolie!" Max called.

She leaned her forehead against the porch column, then clutched it with trembling hands. Max came up behind her, turned her around and enfolded her in his embrace. She clung to him, weeping uncontrollably.

"Ah, *chère*."

He held her fiercely, protectively. Clinging to him with all her might, Jolie hoped that Max would never let her go.

Chapter 21

Over the past eight days, Jolie and Max had instigated a full-fledged investigation, with the unofficial help of Sheriff Ike Denton. Chief Harper simply looked the other way, neither assisting nor hindering their efforts. At first, people in Sumarville, both black and white, had been reluctant to talk about the murders that had rocked the small town twenty years ago. But a few people had been persuaded to recount those unsettling days when the town had divided bitterly along racial lines. The blacks believed Lemar to be innocent; most whites still believed him to be guilty. But not one person of either race had known one bad thing about Lemar.

The residents of Belle Rose had cooperated with Max and Jolie by recalling the events of that long-ago day and sharing their memories of the people and the events prior to and after the murders. Jolie felt almost guilty that she couldn't remember seeing the killer, that she had no memory of a face that should have haunted her to this day. *But I didn't see him; I only heard his footsteps.*

And as much as she hated to admit it, Jolie came to realize the extent of Georgette's love for her father. The look in her eyes, the expression on her face, the tone of her voice when she spoke of Louis Royale revealed the depth of her feelings for him. Of course, that didn't lessen the crime of their affair or change the fact that her father had married Georgette so soon after her mother's death.

And as poor Aunt Clarice wept while recounting the events of a day almost too painful to remember, Nowell Landers had remained at her side, caring, supportive, and protective. Jolie's instincts told her that this man loved her aunt, that he had no ulterior motives for wanting to marry her. Max disagreed. But then Max was a pessimist by nature.

Parry had been reticent at first to discuss his relationship with Lisette, but after coaxing from Max, he had opened up, even admitting that because of her promiscuity, more than one man in Sumarville might have wanted to kill the youngest Desmond sister.

"We were two of a kind," Parry had said. "But I think we could have made a marriage between us work, if—if she hadn't been killed."

After all was said and done, they weren't any closer to proving Lemar Fuqua innocent than they'd been in the beginning. But she would not give up. And neither would Max. They hadn't discussed his motives, not since he had implied that his possessive feelings for her were why he had made her quest his own. In all honesty, she would prefer not to look too closely at Max's motivation.

Jolie thought it rather interesting, perhaps even revealing, how well Max and she worked together, how in tune with each other's moods they were. She had never felt such a strong physical and mental connection to another person. But she kept an emotional distance between them, allowing herself only an occasional glance and an infrequent touch. She didn't dare let herself give in to the longing seething just below the surface. No matter what happened in the days and weeks ahead, when all this was over, they would go their separate ways. When she left Sumarville for good, she wanted to make sure she walked away with her heart and her pride intact.

Theron's condition had improved and the doctors ordered him moved into a private room. Jolie gave him daily updates on the investigation and could tell how much he wished he could be directly involved. Yvonne returned to her position at Belle Rose, with the stipulation that she be allowed to go into town to visit Theron twice every day. The bodyguards Max had hired continued their around-the-clock duties. And Yvonne, too, had gone over her memories of that long-ago day and had given them a sister's insight into the kind of man her twin had been.

Despite their determination to come up with enough evidence to warrant reopening the Belle Rose massacre case, so far, no other incidents of violence had occurred, no major roadblocks had been put in their path. But Jolie knew that Max felt a certain amount of anxiety, just as she did. While they kept digging for information, they waited and wondered when and where the next strike would occur.

Two days earlier, Jolie had flown to Atlanta to take care of a work-related emergency and to make arrangements with her attorney for Cheryl to sign checks and make decisions in her absence. In only a few weeks' time, the focus of her life had changed from her present to her past. There was no way she could go back to her life and career in Atlanta until she discovered the truth about the Belle Rose massacre—and, once and for all, laid the past to rest.

On the flight back to Sumarville, all she'd thought about was seeing Max again; so it was no surprise that when she stepped off the plane at the Sumarville airport, Max Devereaux's face was the only one she saw in the small crowd awaiting the incoming passengers. As she

approached him, she walked faster. When he caught
sight of her, he all but ran toward her. As they came
together, each had to screech to a jerky halt to keep
from colliding.

"Good flight?" he asked.

"As good as you get on one of those"—she inclined
her head toward the twin-engine airplane sitting on
the runway—"crop dusters that fly between here and
Atlanta."

He took her small vinyl bag, slung it up on his shoulder, then slipped his arm around her waist. "Come on.
We have an early dinner date."

"We?"

"The two of us are meeting Sandy and Gar Wells for
supper at the Sumarville Inn restaurant."

"We are?"

They exited the small airport terminal and walked
out into the oppressive heat of a summertime afternoon
in the Delta.

"Since we've ruled out questioning Roscoe Wells
directly—"

"You ruled out questioning him directly." Jolie kept
pace with Max as he headed toward the parking lot.

"Whatever." Max opened the Porsche's trunk and
dumped Jolie's bag inside. "The point is that Sandy
adamantly opposes everything her father has ever
believed in and even Gar disapproves of his father's
history."

"Your point?" When Max opened the passenger
door, Jolie slid in and then looked up at him. "How
does the fact that Roscoe's children have different moral
and political views than their father affect our investigation?"

Max got in on the driver's side, started the engine,
and glanced over his shoulder before backing out of
the parking place. "If we question Sandy and Gar about
the possibility that Roscoe might somehow have been
involved in a cover-up twenty years ago and might be

connected to the attacks on Theron and you, I believe they'll be honest with us and tell us if they know anything."

As the hot breeze whipped the flyaway strands of Jolie's hair about her face, she stole a glance at Max. Gorgeous, sexy Max, who had become far too important to her in a very short period of time.

"Okay, I agree that Sandy will be up front with us," Jolie said. "But are you sure Gar won't go straight to Roscoe and tell him that we suspect him?"

"If I ask Gar to keep the conversation in confidence, I'm reasonably sure—"

"You should question Sandy," Jolie interrupted. "And I should question Gar."

"What?" Max snapped around and glared at her for a millisecond, then returned his gaze to the road.

"I'm sure it's no secret, not even from you, that Sandy would walk over hot coals for you, so it stands to reason that she'll tell you if she knows anything."

"Sandy's a fine woman, but . . . There's never been anything between us other than friendship." Max paused, apparently waiting for her response, but when she didn't comment, he went on. "I hadn't realized that you'd picked up on the fact that Gar is interested in you."

"He is?"

"Yes, he is. The evening after Louis's funeral, right after the reading of the will, he asked if I'd mind if he invited you out, once our legal problems were settled."

"That's nice. I like Gar, but I didn't have any idea that he . . . well, that he's interested in me personally. I just thought that because we were childhood friends, he might—"

"Don't flirt with Gar."

"Excuse me?"

"I said do not flirt with Gar tonight."

"Why shouldn't I?"

"Because I don't want him taking you seriously. He might wind up getting hurt if you have to reject him."

"Maybe I won't reject him."

"Don't try to use him to make me jealous. It wouldn't be fair to Gar. Besides, he'd have no idea how to handle a woman like you."

Of all the nerve! To imply that the only reason she'd flirt with Gar would be to make Max jealous. "He wouldn't know how to handle me, but you would. Is that it?" She glowered at Max.

A quirky grin lifted the corners of his lips, but he didn't even glance her way when he said, "I believe the answer to that question is obvious."

Jolie huffed loudly, then kept quiet. Something told her that she couldn't win this argument with Max.

As the sun hovered on the western horizon, a vivid yellow-orange ball of flame, Yvonne and Clarice sat on the side porch in the big white rockers, each sipping lemonade that Yvonne had prepared fresh that afternoon. This was truly the first day in nearly two weeks that Yvonne had allowed herself to relax, to forgo worry and concern about Theron and what the future held for all of them. God only knew what ugly truths were on the verge of being discovered.

"Sure been hot today," Clarice said, fanning herself with the antique lace fan that had once belonged to her mother.

"Likely to be the same tomorrow," Yvonne replied.

Clarice took another sip of lemonade, then placed the nearly empty glass on the table between the rockers. "Maybe they'll let you bring Theron home tomorrow."

"Could be. Dr. Bainbridge said tomorrow or the next day."

"I thought Theron took it pretty well, learning about our being kinfolk and all."

Clarice's gaze met Yvonne's and the two women smiled at each other. Loving, bittersweet smiles that encompassed more than friendship—even more than sisterhood.

"Much better than I thought he would," Yvonne said. "Of course once he's had time to think about it more, he might—"

"He can't deny his heritage anymore than the rest of us can."

"Guess not."

Sitting there quietly for several minutes, they continued rocking. The humid evening breeze began to cool ever so slightly.

"That wind's getting up." Yvonne sniffed the air. "And it's cooling off some. Must be coming off a rain close by."

"Yvonne?"

"Hmmm?"

"I'm sure Jolie and Max think Roscoe's involved."

Yvonne's heart lurched as if it would burst right through her chest. Just the mention of that man's name had a way of reminding her of things she'd rather forget.

"I hope they can prove it," Yvonne said. "I'd like to see his lily-white hide nailed to the barn wall. I'd even doing the nailing myself."

"Guess you would." Clarice kept fanning. "And I'd help you."

"A man like Roscoe would be capable of just about anything, even murder. Somebody needs to expose him and show the world that he's the same racist hate-monger he was forty years ago. He needs to be punished for . . ." Yvonne wrung her hands. If Jolie and Max could somehow prove that Roscoe was involved in manipulating the investigation of the Belle Rose massacre, then maybe that heartless monster would finally be punished. It really didn't matter to her which of his many sins he would have to pay for, just as long as he paid. Preferably with his life. There had been a time when she'd considered killing him herself.

Yvonne sighed. "I've often wondered if we did the right thing. If we'd told Mr. Sam about what—"

"We swore that we'd never tell anyone, that it would be our secret forever. We made a pact."

"Times have changed. People might believe us now. We could—"

"No!"

Yvonne nodded. "You're probably right. Best we keep it to ourselves. Besides, our telling about one crime Roscoe committed wouldn't prove he took part in another. We'll just have to let Jolie and Max dig up the evidence against him."

While Theron had hovered between life and death, Yvonne hadn't had time to think of anything except her son. Her days and nights had been spent praying and waiting. But now that Theron was recovering, she had begun thinking about who had paid those men to kill Theron. Only one name came to mind. Even Jolie and Max thought there was a good possibility Roscoe Wells was somehow involved.

Maybe times had changed; maybe people would believe them if they chose to tell their story now. Even if it would be her word and Clarice's against Roscoe's, proclaiming the truth to the world would probably end the bastard's political career. Maybe she needed to remind Roscoe, even threaten him. She wouldn't go see him, wouldn't put herself inside his home, but she could telephone him. She could make him squirm.

Yvonne and Clarice sat together in silence for a good fifteen minutes before the roar of Nowell Landers's Harley shattered the stillness.

Clarice jumped up from her rocker and rushed to the edge of the porch, then grasped the banister railing and looked down the road.

"I've got a secret," Clarice said.

"What sort of secret?" Yvonne immediately knew that *the secret* must have something to do with the man sitting astride the motorcycle just now pulling to a stop in the driveway. "Something about Nowell?"

"We've always shared all our secrets, haven't we?"

"Yes," Yvonne replied. "All our secrets, all our lives."

Clarice turned to Yvonne, rushed over to her and grabbed her hands, urging her to stand. When Yvonne came to her feet, Clarice fidgeted, her whole body dancing with delight.

"You'll never guess who Nowell Landers really is." Tears of happiness flooded Clarice's eyes.

"Who is he?" A pang of apprehension jolted Yvonne's stomach.

"He's Jonathan, of course. My sweet Jonathan come home to me at last."

Jolie glanced across the table at Garland Wells. He smiled. All through dinner it had been apparent that Gar was under the misimpression that Max had set up a double date in order to bring Gar and Jolie together. And Max whisking Sandy off and onto the dance floor only added evidence to the case Gar had already built in his mind.

"Gar, we need to talk."

He reached over the table and grasped her hand where it rested on the white linen tablecloth. "I suppose Max told you how I feel about you."

Oh, shit! "He mentioned that you'd thought about asking me for a date."

Gar turned her hand over, palm up, and caressed it tenderly. "I'm glad to see you and Max on speaking terms. After all, he's not only a client but a good friend. I wouldn't want—"

"I'm not interested in dating anyone right now," Jolie

said, doing her best to project a friendly caring tone. "Max and I have joined forces, more or less out of necessity, to do everything in our power to have the Belle Rose massacre case reopened. We've been questioning everyone that might know anything about what happened that day."

"I'm afraid I don't understand what you're getting a⸱ " He released her hand hurriedly, his own hand jerking in the process.

He seems unnaturally nervous, Jolie thought. The color drained from his face as if he'd suddenly taken ill.

"Are you all right?" she asked.

"This dinner tonight, it wasn't a double date, was it?"

She shook her head. "No. And I'm sorry if Max led you to believe it was."

"Poor Sandy." Gar shook his head.

Jolie glanced at the people on the dance floor, quickly focusing on one couple in particular. Sandy was smiling at Max, a lovesick expression on her face. Dear God, did he have that effect on all women? Sweeping her gaze across the restaurant, she paused on the redhead behind the bar. Eartha Kilpatrick watched Max and Sandy, a forlorn expression on her face. Not jealousy. Not anger or hatred. More a look of heavyhearted acceptance. Another of Max's conquests realizing how futile loving Max was, how unlikely it was that she would share a future with him.

"Funny thing," Jolie said, "when we were kids, I had no idea that Sandy had a crush on Max. We were best friends, but that was one secret we never shared."

"She knew you had a crush on Max, too," Gar said. "That's why she never told you."

"She knew? But how did—"

"You weren't very subtle. Every time Max was anywhere around, you'd moon over him. He never knew, of course. But Felicia suspected and she used to torment

Sandy about it, telling her that Max would never want her, not when he could have his pick of either Felicia or you."

"Felicia was cruel to have treated Sandy that way."

"Felicia was a cruel person." Gar sighed. "I always regretted that I didn't try to warn Max before he married her."

Jolie suddenly felt guilty. Guilty that she'd been in Max's arms. Guilty that she had kissed him. Guilty because she knew he wanted her in a way he would never want Sandy.

"Loving someone who doesn't love you is a real bitch," Jolie said, more or less mumbling to herself.

"Yes, it can be," Gar agreed.

Jolie looked directly at him, a stricken feeling knotting her insides. *Oh, please, God, please, don't let him mean that he's in love with me.*

A pitiful smile tweaked the corners of Gar's lips. "Don't look so upset. I wasn't referring to you. I had a major crush on someone once, years ago. She was older, more experienced, and I fell madly in love with her."

"Oh, Gar, what happened?"

"She died." He closed his eyes as if the pain was still fresh.

"I'm sorry."

Gar shrugged. "It was a long time ago. Besides, she didn't love me. She was engaged to someone else." Gar opened his eyes and stared at Jolie. "You remind me of her. Physically. You look so much like she did then. I guess you're about the same age she was twenty years ago."

"My God! You're talking about my aunt Lisette. You— you were in love with Lisette?"

Gar snorted. "Yeah, me and half the men in Desmond County."

Jolie's mind whirled with a myriad of puzzle pieces that didn't quite fit. But one thing fit: Roscoe Wells was somehow connected to the Belle Rose massacre. And Roscoe's son had been in love with one of the victims. Meaningless? Maybe. Maybe not.

"I hate to ask this, but . . ." Jolie hesitated. "Did you and Aunt Lisette have an affair? And if you did, did your father know about it?"

"I've never told anyone. Not even Max."

"Then you were lovers?"

"Yes, we were lovers, but . . . What are you implying?"

"I'm not implying anything," Jolie assured him. "Just trying to fit some puzzle pieces together. So, you and my aunt had an affair, but she wasn't serious about you. She planned to marry Parry Clifton and you—"

"Wanted her to marry me, but she laughed when I asked her. She told me that I was just a kid, that we'd had fun together, but . . ." Gar closed his eyes and shook his head slowly. "I didn't kill her, if that's what you're wondering. I couldn't have harmed a hair on her head."

"What about your father?"

"Daddy? He didn't know anything about Lisette and me."

"Are you sure?"

"You think— My God, you and Max think my father had something to do with the Belle Rose massacre, don't you?"

"We believe he was involved in the cover-up, in the disappearance of the old files from the sheriff's department, and—"

Sandy and Max returned to the table before Jolie could finish her explanation. Max seated Sandy, then took the chair across from her, beside Jolie.

Sandy glanced back and forth from Jolie to Gar. "Well, I'd say you two had the same conversation Max and I did." She looked at her brother. "So, what do you think, brother dear, is our father capable of murder?"

"Probably," Gar said. "But what motive would he have had to kill Lisette and Audrey? Their families had been friends for generations."

"That's what I asked Max." Sandy focused on Jolie. "God knows I'd never defend the old bastard if I thought he was guilty, but in this case, I can't figure out a motive."

A tense silence fell among the four of them. Jolie's heartbeat drummed noisily in her ears. Even if Gar was wrong and Roscoe had known about his affair with Lisette, that wouldn't have given him a motive to murder her. No, no, that wasn't it. There had to be something else. But what? What small significant piece of information were they all missing in their calculations?

Suddenly Max's cell phone rang. Jolie gasped. Sandy jumped. Gar groaned.

"Excuse me." Max removed the phone from his pocket. "Devereaux here."

Jolie waited while Max listened and then grunted a few times. He kept glancing at her during the one-sided conversation. Finally he said, "Yes, thanks. This could be the break we've been looking for."

"Max?" Jolie grabbed his arm.

"Wait a minute." Max took a small notepad and pen from the inside pocket of his sport coat and scribbled something down, then returned both items to his jacket.

"Well?" Jolie glowered at him.

"Just a business call."

Gar rose to his feet. "It's been . . . interesting. But I'm ready to call it a night. How about you, sis?"

Sandy nodded. "Sure, me, too. I think I'll drop by the hospital and see Theron. I'm sure Amy's there. She's been spending a couple of hours with him every evening since he went into a private room."

When Sandy stood, Max got up. She kissed his cheek, then leaned over and hugged Jolie. "I hope you two can find out what really happened the day Miss Audrey and Miss Lisette were killed. And I pray to God that my daddy didn't have anything to do with it."

Gar shook hands with Max, then patted Jolie's shoulder. "Be careful, you two."

The minute Sandy and Gar were out of earshot, Max grabbed Jolie's arm and jerked her to her feet.

"What the—"

"The call that just came in on my cell phone—that was Hugh Pearce, the private investigator I hired," Max told her. "He's found Aaron Bendall."

Chapter 22

Max hired a private plane to take them straight from Sumarville to Key West. They left after breakfast the next morning and arrived in the Keys before lunchtime. They had agreed to share their news with Theron and Yvonne and no one else, letting Yvonne explain to the family only that they'd gone out of town together as part of their ongoing investigation. It wasn't that they distrusted anyone at Belle Rose, but if somebody accidently let it slip that they were on their way to Key West to question Aaron Bendall, that information could easily find its way to Roscoe Wells.

The hot tropical sun, the humidity, and the ocean breeze welcomed them to Key West. A rental car awaited them, along with directions to their hotel, an inn in the heart of Key West's historic "Old Town" district. The manager, a thin, hollow-cheeked, leather-brown man of indiscernible age, greeted them graciously; and it quickly became apparent to Jolie that he knew who

Maximillian Devereaux was. Or at the very least, Mr. Fritz knew how wealthy Max was.

"Your suite is ready, Mr. Devereaux. If there's anything you need, don't hesitate to let us know immediately. I'm at your service twenty-four hours a day."

The decor of their two bedroom suite was Caribbean with rattan and bamboo furniture, the walls pastel shades of green, yellow, and blue. Paintings of local scenes hung on the walls, probably done by Key West artists. Bouquets of lush tropical flowers resided on every table. Everything worked to create a cool, serene, vacation-perfect atmosphere. Only they weren't here to lounge on the beach or scuba dive or rent a catamaran.

The bellhop deposited Max's bag in the bedroom to the left and hers in the room to the right. By the time Jolie had visually inspected her bedroom and opened the doors leading to the balcony, laced in gingerbread trim befitting the Victorian structure, waiters were bringing in lunch and setting it up on a white linen-covered table in the lounge between the two bedrooms.

"Just something light," Mr. Fritz said, motioning the waiters away. "Fruit salad, Key Lime bread, grilled shrimp, and a bottle of Chablis."

Jolie checked the wine. *A 1999 Francois Raveneau Chablis Montee de Tonnerre.* Only the best for Max Devereaux. Mr. Fritz personally uncorked the bottle of *grand gru* Chablis.

"Thank you." Max shook hands with the manager. "And I'll need directions to get from here to Maloney's Marina. After lunch, Ms. Royale and I plan to visit a friend who keeps his cruiser docked there."

"The marina is very easy to find and only minutes from here. I will jot down the directions for you and have them waiting at the front desk." Mr. Fritz all but bowed as he left the suite.

Jolie eyed the delectable lunch items. Max lifted the bottle of Chablis and filled two crystal flutes.

"We could have gone straight to the marina," Jolie said.

"You barely touched your breakfast," Max told her. "And it could be quite some time before we eat dinner, so I thought it best for us to have a light lunch before we go in search of Mr. Bendall."

"When we find him, what are the odds that he'll tell us anything?" Jolie allowed Max to seat her, then she lifted the white linen napkin from the table and spread it across her lap.

"If our assumptions are correct and someone, probably Roscoe Wells, paid off the former sheriff, then I'd say it's possible that, for the right price, he'll tell us whatever we want to know."

"You're saying we'll have to pay him for information." Jolie lifted her fork, speared a piece of fruit and lifted it to her mouth.

"Oh, we'll have to pay him all right," Max said. "The only question is how much."

An hour later, Max parked the rental car at Maloney's Marina; then he and Jolie got out and began their search for the *Mississippi Magnolia*, a small cruiser, where Aaron Bendall reportedly lived. A wide variety of yachts, ranging from top-of-the-line beauties that would sleep a dozen to cruisers that bunked two, lined up in the slips along the pier.

The *Mississippi Magnolia* turned out to be a twin-engine, midpriced cruiser that slept four, which would have cost at least a hundred and fifty thousand. Not too shabby for a retired sheriff from Desmond County, Mississippi. A large heavyset man, with a scraggly gray beard, wearing a faded red baseball cap, a loose-fitting floral shirt and baggy cutoff jeans stood on deck.

"Aaron Bendall?" Max called.

The man turned, looked at them and grinned, then threw up his hand and waved. "Well, as I live and

breathe, if it's not Max Devereaux and Jolie Royale."
He motioned to them. "Come on board. I've been
expecting y'all."

Theron closed his eyes and pretended to be asleep,
knowing it was the only way he could get his mother,
Aunt Clarice, and Amy to stop hovering over him. The
minute the threesome tiptoed out of the bedroom, he
breathed a sigh of relief. Not that he didn't enjoy having
three women waiting on him hand and foot, but enough
was enough. After his release from the hospital this
morning, his mother had insisted he stay at her house
until he was fully recovered, and considering the fact
that he could do little more than feed himself and use
a wheelchair to get to the bathroom, he didn't argue
with her. But he thought he'd lose his mind if any one
of them asked him again if he needed anything.

With the bedroom door half-closed, he could make
out most of what they were saying.

"I'm going to run on, Mrs. Carter," Amy said. "I'll
be back tonight."

"You come for supper," Yvonne told her.

"It'll be after seven," Amy explained.

"Whenever you get here will be fine," Yvonne said.
"Just your being around seems to cheer Theron a lot."

The front door closed quietly, then the roar of a car's
engine told him that Amy had started her Mustang.

"She's such a sweet young woman," Clarice said.
"And you can tell she's just crazy about our Theron."

"I think he's fond of her, too." Yvonne sighed. "Nothing would make me happier than to see him married
to a fine girl like Amy. It's high time I had me some
grandchildren."

"Oh, wouldn't that be wonderful. Babies at Belle Rose
again."

Theron closed his eyes, letting the drone of his mother's and aunt's voices lull him into a semiconcious state.

It would take some getting used to, this notion that his mother was a half sister to Clarice Desmond, that his grandfather had been a white man, the descendant of slave owners. As he let his mind wander back to his childhood, he managed to bring to the surface a vague memory of his grandmother, Sadie Fuqua. She'd been a slender, small-boned woman, with fine features and large black eyes. He remembered her singing to him. He couldn't recall the tune, but he could feel the laughter inside him bubbling up from the memory. Mr. Sam Desmond had died before Theron was born, but he'd seen the portrait of him in the front parlor at Belle Rose. A large commanding man, with brown hair and bright hazel eyes.

Theron sighed and let his mind continue wandering through his childhood. Fuzzy, hazy thoughts. Lethargy claimed him. And moment by moment he drifted off into a light sleep.

Later in the day, Theron woke, rousing slowly, languidly. He could hear his mother's voice. She was speaking quietly to someone. Was Aunt Clarice still here? He gazed out the window and noted that the sun was shining, which meant it was still daytime, then he glanced at the clock on the bedside table. He chuckled to himself. He'd slept only an hour. Using the techniques the physical therapist had taught him, Theron managed to maneuver himself out of bed and into his wheelchair. Someone had closed the bedroom door while he slept; that's why he couldn't make out what his mother was saying or to whom. After opening the door, he eased the chair from the bedroom and into the narrow hallway. His mother stood in the middle of the living room, the telephone to her ear.

"Yes, this is Yvonne Carter."

He wheeled closer, intending to let his mother know he was awake and up, but before he caught her attention, her next words froze him in place.

"I'm not afraid of you," she said. "But you should fear me."

Who the hell is she talking to? Theron wondered.

"You're wrong if you think I won't do whatever is necessary to keep my son safe. I can't prove that you hired someone to kill him, but I promise you this—if anyone tries to hurt him again, Clarice and I will go to the sheriff and press charges against you."

Theron had never heard his mother speak to someone so fiercely, with such anger and hatred in her voice. His mind whirled with questions, but he tried to quiet his puzzled thoughts so he could eavesdrop on her conversation.

"I'm talking about another crime," Yvonne said. "One where Clarice and I were the victims."

Theron's heart leaped to his throat.

"No, it won't be your word against mine. It will be your word against my word and Clarice Desmond's word."

What the hell was his mother talking about?

"It doesn't matter that people think Clarice is touched in the head or that I'm just a *colored woman* with a racial ax to grind. Even if you never serve a day in a jail, do you think any black person would ever vote for you again, if they knew what you did? And quite a few white folks would doubt your innocence. Your political career would be over. And any future hopes you have for Garland would come to an end."

Garland? Garland Wells? Good God Almighty, his mother was talking to Roscoe Wells. And she knew about something he'd done that could put him in jail, something she and Clarice had witnessed.

"You think long and hard about what I've said." Yvonne slammed the receiver down on an end table by the sofa.

Her hand shook as she removed it from the telephone. Theron wheeled into the living room. When she heard him, his mother gasped, then turned to face him.

"I—I didn't know you were awake," she said, her gaze meeting his, her eyes questioning him.

"Who were you talking to?" he asked.

She hesitated, and he wondered if she would lie to him.

"Roscoe Wells," she replied.

"Why would you talk to that son of a bitch?"

"I called him to warn him."

"Warn him about what?"

"I told him that if he'd hired those men to kill you, that he'd better not try it again."

"Why would Roscoe Wells be afraid of you? What do you and Clarice know about him that could put him in jail?"

Yvonne tensed so suddenly and so solidly that she seemed to have turned instantly to stone. Even her breathing slowed.

"Mama?"

No response.

"Answer me."

Silence.

"I heard you say that it was a crime where you were one of the victims. What the hell did Roscoe Wells do to you?"

"I've got to get back up to Belle Rose and start dinner." Yvonne turned toward the kitchen. "But I need to put on a pot roast for us before I leave. Amy's coming to eat with us. Do you need anything before I—"

Theron caught up with her, reached out, grabbed her wrist, and said, "Dammit, tell me what he did to you!"

"Please, don't use bad language when you speak to me."

"Mama . . ."

"I'll send one of the day girls down here to stay with you until I get back. I won't be gone long."

"I don't need anybody," Theron said. "I'll be all right alone for a couple of hours."

"All right. But call me if you need me."

Yvonne walked off into the kitchen. Theron balled his hands into fists and scrunched his face in a frustrated frown. He knew his mother well enough to realize that she was not going to tell him what he wanted to know. Not now or ever. Not unless and until she wanted to.

He wheeled over to the phone, lifted it and dialed.

"Royale residence." A voice he didn't recognize but assumed to be one of the daily maids answered.

"May I speak to Clarice Desmond, please."

R. J. thrust into Mallory, the tension within him winding tighter and tighter with each lunge. Since he had initiated her into the pleasures of sex, the girl had been wild for it. And he sure as hell wasn't fool enough to turn her down. When she came, she moaned and groaned and squeezed every ounce of feel-good out of her orgasm. Within seconds, he climaxed.

"Ah, baby." He grunted as the aftershocks rippled through him.

Mallory lifted her head just enough to bite his neck. "Again," she murmured. "I want to do it again."

"Sweet Jesus, Mal, give a guy a few minutes to recover, will you?" He rolled off her and onto his back.

Mallory rose up and over him, then slithered down the side of his body, stopping when her mouth aligned with his penis. "Need some encouragement?"

"You go down on me now and you'll get a taste of our cum," he told her.

"You'd like that, wouldn't you?"

He grabbed the back of her head. "Are you playing games with me?"

"No games."

She lifted his semierect penis and sucked several inches inside her mouth, then closed her lips to hold him in place. Her tongue danced over the bulbous tip, laving the most sensitive area. R. J. bucked up, then shoved her head down so she was forced to take him completely. She gagged a couple of times before he began moving in and out of her. When he grew hard again, she stopped. He groaned. She licked him from scrotum to tip, then ran kisses from his navel to his neck.

"Fuck me again," she told him. "You're ready."

"Damn you, Mallory."

She crawled on top of him, positioned herself in a rider's mount and leaned forward just enough to give him access to her breasts. They went at it again, like a couple of wild animals. And this time, when they came, Mallory lay quietly on top of him, murmuring his name. Within minutes she fell asleep. He stroked her long black hair and wondered how the hell he'd let himself get so deeply involved with an eighteen-year-old kid.

She was hot and wild. Sweet and funny and full of life. He'd never known anyone like Mallory Royale. She made him feel like he was somebody special. He'd never felt that way, not with anyone else, not ever. And it scared the hell out of him.

Except for the second time they'd had sex, he'd been careful to use a rubber without fail. Until today. She'd told him that she had gone to the doctor and was now on the pill. He had to admit he was glad. Fucking without a rubber was great. But R. J. knew he was skating on thin ice. Mallory was no good-time gal. She might love sex, but she loved him, too. And for the first time in his life, he worried about how the hell he was going to leave a woman without breaking her heart.

"Come on aboard." Aaron Bendall invited them with a sweep of his meaty hand.

Max followed Jolie across the gangplank and onto the walk-a-round. Bendall lifted a couple of beers from a cooler and held them out to his guests.

"No, thank you." Jolie shook her head.

Max accepted one of the chilled cans, popped the lid, and took a swig, then focused his gaze on Bendall. "Why were you expecting us?"

"Oh, I've got friends all over, and I keep in touch with one or two folks back in Sumarville," Bendall said. "I was told you two have been asking a lot of questions about me." He popped the lid on the other beer, then saluted Max with it before downing half the can in one long guzzle. He belched, then wiped his mouth with the back of his hand. "You even hired yourself a private dick to find me."

"It took him awhile," Max said. "You weren't an easy man to find."

"Didn't want to be found."

"Why not?" Jolie asked.

Bendall guffawed, a loud boisterous rumble from his chest. "Now, Ms. Royale, there's no need to play dumb with me. I know that you know there are some pretty important documents missing from the sheriff's department. Files pertaining to the Belle Rose massacre."

"Then you did know they were missing?" Jolie glowered at the red-faced, slack-jawed man.

"Of course I knew. Who do you think took them?" Bendall slurped his beer.

"Then you admit you stole those files?" Max lowered his aviator sunglasses just a fraction, enough to allow Bendall to see his eyes.

"Let's just say I know where the original files are and where copies can be found." Bendall finished off his beer, crushed the can, and tossed it on top of the cooler.

"What would it take for us to get our hands on the original files?" Max asked.

Bendall *tsk-tsked*. "The original files wouldn't come cheap."

"How much?" Jolie's heartbeat accelerated.

"The original files are in a safety deposit box and so is one set of the copies. My lawyer's got the other set."

"The lady asked you how much." Max lifted his sunglasses back in place.

"I've got me a comfortable life here—a retirement check from the State of Mississippi and a supplemental check every month from an old friend."

They didn't really need to ask who that "old friend" was. Who else could it be other than Roscoe Wells?

"Name your price, Bendall." Max's voice had a deadly edge.

"A million dollars." Bendall laughed again, not quite as loud or self-confident and just slightly uncertain.

"I can have that amount wired to me at a local bank by tomorrow morning," Max said, as if it were pocket change. "Name the bank and the time. I'll have the money for you, if you have the files for me. And let me warn you that if you try to screw me, it'll be the last thing you ever do."

"With a million bucks, I can disappear again. Go farther south."

"Name your bank."

"First State Bank on Whitehead Street, at eleven tomorrow morning."

When Bendall stuck out his hand to shake on the deal, Max glanced at the man's large dirty hand. "Eleven tomorrow at First State Bank." Max didn't shake his hand.

Max grasped Jolie's arm, his motion urging her into movement. Neither of them glanced back as they disembarked.

"Since y'all were so accommodating, I'll give you a freebie," Bendall hollered.

Max and Jolie stopped dead still but kept their backs to him, neither moving an inch.

"When you're looking over the files, don't miss the most important clue of all." Bendall paused for effect. "Lisette Desmond was pregnant. And you'll never guess who the daddy was?" Bendall's bawdy laughter mocked them.

Jolie started to turn around, but Max jerked on her arm. "Don't," he whispered.

When they were several yards away, Jolie said, "I never heard anything about Aunt Lisette being pregnant. Do you think we can trust him or trust anything he says?"

"No." Max kept walking.

"Then why—"

"He's greedy. He'd sell his mother for a million dollars."

"Max, that's an awful lot of money. I can come up with a million in cash, but it could take me a few days, maybe weeks."

At the edge of the dock, Max stopped, turned and reached out to cup her chin in the cradle between his thumb and forefinger. "I can have the entire amount here tomorrow morning. Consider it a gift from your father. Without his guidance, I wouldn't be a very rich man today."

"Max, you don't have to—"

His thumb lifted to caress her lips. "Haven't you figured it out, yet, *chère*? I'd do anything for you."

Chapter 23

He'd had it good—really good—for the past fifteen years. After retiring as sheriff of Desmond County, Mississippi, he had, for all intents and purposes, disappeared off the face of the earth. He'd moved around a lot those first few years, but when he realized he was relatively safe, he'd settled in Key West. Roscoe Wells had paid him monthly "hush money," nothing big, but enough to live well. He hadn't tried to bleed Roscoe dry because, truth be told, he was just a little bit afraid of the old buzzard. Yeah, he had the Belle Rose massacre files, with copies in his lawyer's safekeeping; but with the kind of ties Roscoe had to some powerful but unsavory people, a man couldn't be too careful. Now, suddenly, everything had changed—maybe for the better. Who would have ever thought that Jolie Royale would join forces with Max Devereaux to dig up the past and try to get the old case reopened? And they were willing to pay him a million dollars for the files. With that much money a man could get lost in South America or on a

Pacific island and live like a king. He doubted that even Roscoe could reach out that far to find him. Anyway, by that time, the son of a bitch would be rotting in jail, along with his precious son.

Now, now, let's not be too hasty. Let's weigh all our options. Why not contact Roscoe and let him know that there's a bid on the table. Who knows, he might up the ante. Wouldn't that be sweet? Possibly a mil and a quarter? And I wouldn't have to be looking over my shoulder, worrying that one of Roscoe's goons might catch up with me someday. Yeah, make that call and see what he says. After all, if his answer is no, I can collect the million from Devereaux and be long gone from Key West before Roscoe can find out where I've been living all these years.

Clarice practically ran the entire way from the mansion to Yvonne's cottage. She had waited until Yvonne arrived and was busy in the kitchen before she left Belle Rose through the front door. After all, Theron had told her that he wanted their conversation to be private. She imagined he had all sorts of questions to ask her about his grandfather. Oh, the stories she could tell him about Sam Desmond. Her daddy had been quite an interesting man, ahead of his time in many ways. As she approached the cottage, she saw Theron sitting in his wheelchair on the front porch. She threw up her hand.

He waved back and called to her, "Thanks for coming."

Clarice stepped up on the porch, went to Theron, bent down, and kissed his cheek. She felt him tense ever so slightly. "You sounded so eager to speak to me, so naturally I rushed right over as soon as Yvonne became occupied in the kitchen."

"Sit down, won't you . . . *Aunt* Clarice." He motioned to the rocker beside his wheelchair.

Theron had called her Aunt Clarice again. How wonderful! She had thought perhaps it would take awhile before he'd be comfortable claiming her as family.

She took a seat at his side. "Now, what's this all about? What are you so eager to know? I'm a fount of information about the Desmond family. Ask me anything."

"I . . . uh . . . what I want to ask you about has nothing to do with the Desmonds—only with you . . . and Mama."

Tiny nervous butterflies twittered in her stomach. Apprehension. Uncertainty. "I know you never understood or approved of how close Yvonne and I have always been, but—"

"It's more than the fact that y'all are half sisters, isn't it?"

"I'm afraid I don't know what you mean." Clarice wrung her hands. *Surely Theron didn't suspect the truth.* "We've been close since we were childhood playmates. We're friends as well as sisters."

"I understand that," Theron said. "But what I want to know is what else binds the two of you together? What secret do you share?"

"Secret?" *He doesn't know,* Clarice told herself. *There's no possible way he could have found out about what happened. Only three other people knew—Yvonne and Roscoe. And Jonathan.*

"Mama called Roscoe Wells earlier today and threatened him."

Gasping, Clarice patted her hand over her heart. "I didn't think she'd really do it." She had suspected that Yvonne would take whatever actions she thought necessary to warn Roscoe off, to make sure that if he'd been behind Theron's beating, there would be no repeat performances. *But why didn't Yvonne share her plans with me?*

"You knew she was going to call him?"

"I thought she might, although she didn't actually tell me that she would. But since Jolie and Max suspect Roscoe of being behind the attempt on your life, I'm not surprised."

"Aunt Clarice . . . what did Roscoe Wells do to my

mother? What crime did he commit that you witnessed?''

"How do you know anything about . . . You eaves-
dropped on her conversation, didn't you?''

He nodded. "I need to know the truth. What did
Roscoe do?''

"Did you ask Yvonne?'' Clarice rose to her feet and
paced frantically, wringing her hands and murmuring
to herself in a hushed voice. "He can't know. No one
must ever know.''

"I asked Mama and she refused to tell me. As a matter
of fact, she changed the subject immediately.''

"I can't tell you. Can't tell anyone. Ever.''

She had feared this day would come. Secrets had a
way of being revealed sooner or later and often causing
more harm and even greater destruction, after the fact.
Forty-two years ago, Yvonne and she had made what
they considered the best decision for all concerned. If
they had told Sadie she would have told Daddy. And
Sam Desmond, being the man he was, would have no
doubt killed Roscoe and wound up spending the rest
of his life in prison. And if Yvonne and she had not
taken that little trip to New Orleans, on the pretense
of a shopping trip for Clarice, they would have been
forced to remember on a daily basis what had happened
the day when, as young teenage girls, they'd gone blackberry picking.

Theron wheeled over to where Clarice stood at the
end of the porch, reached out and grasped her wrist.
"All you have to do is answer yes or no. Did Roscoe
Wells rape my mother?''

Closing her eyes, Clarice whined like a child in pain.
Don't ask me. Don't ask me. I can't tell you. I can't.

"Clarice!''

"No, no, no. I can't tell. I can't ever tell. It's our
secret. We swore to never tell a living soul as long as we
live.''

"God! It's true. I knew it. I knew it when I heard her

talking to that bastard." Theron slammed his fist into the palm of his other hand. "When ... when did it happen? What year?"

When? What year? Why did that matter? Whimpering, Clarice tugged on her wrist. "Secrets. Secrets. So many secrets."

"There's something I have to know. Please, Aunt Clarice. Tell me ... is Roscoe Wells my father?"

Mattie brought the portable phone out to the patio where Roscoe lounged by the pool. He glanced up as she approached.

"Phone call for you, Mr. Wells."

"Who is it?"

"He didn't say. Just said it was important."

"A man can't get any peace and quiet around here." He held up his hand to accept the telephone. The minute he took it, Mattie scurried away. Damn insolent woman. "Yeah, this is Roscoe Wells."

"Hello, Roscoe. How are you doing?"

"Who the hell is this?"

The man chuckled. "Don't you remember me? I'm the guy you've been sending monthly checks to for the past fifteen years."

"Bendall! Where the hell are you? You'd better be buried so deep that nobody can find you."

More chuckling. "There are only so many places a man can hide, unless he's a lot richer than I am."

"Meaning?"

"Meaning Max Devereaux got his money's worth out of the private eye he hired to find me," Aaron Bendall said. "Devereaux and Jolie Royale showed up in my neck of the woods today ... and they made me a mighty fine proposition."

"What kind of proposition?"

"Devereaux offered me a million dollars in exchange for the original files on the Belle Rose massacre."

"Son of a bitch!"

"He's having the money wired to me first thing in the morning. We've set up a time and a place to exchange our goods."

"If you turn over those documents to Max, I'll see to it that you don't live long enough to enjoy a dime of that million."

"You could make it easy on both of us," Bendall said. "Make me a counteroffer . . . one I can't refuse."

"You asshole." Why hadn't he realized twenty years ago that Aaron Bendall couldn't be trusted? Why hadn't he arranged for an accident to befall the sheriff, then had those damn files destroyed before the bastard stole the files and started blackmailing him?

"Are you willing to go higher than a million? For the sake of your future? For the sake of Garland's future?"

"Shut your damn mouth!" All his life, he'd covered his tracks, making sure none of his unlawful deeds would come back to haunt him. But it hadn't been his crimes he'd been covering up all these years, not his own sins that he'd paid dearly to keep secret.

"Times a wasting. Do I hear a million and a quarter?"

"A million and a quarter."

"By ten o'clock tomorrow morning," Bendall said.

"I'm not sure I can arrange—"

"I'm meeting Devereaux at eleven, unless I get your money by ten."

"You'll have your damn money by ten." Roscoe rose from the longue chair and began pacing restlessly. "But I want those files. And all the copies."

Before this ended, he'd have more than the files. He'd have a few scalps to add to his belt. There was fixing to be several *accidents*. He planned to start with Max and Jolie. Then he'd deal with that damn bitch, Yvonne Carter, and her uppity son.

* * *

Max watched her from the balcony of his bedroom as she dove into the pool. Oddly enough she was only one of four people using the hotel pool this afternoon, but then the hotel wasn't all that big. Only thirty rooms. A lot of the guests were probably out shopping, on the beach, deep-sea fishing, or scuba diving.

Trim and toned, Jolie's body possessed a sweet voluptuousness, every rounded inch of her totally feminine. The bathing suit she'd bought in the hotel gift shop was a simple black one piece and the fact that her body was adequately covered made her all the sexier. He wanted her. Wanted her more than he'd ever wanted another woman. When he'd first realized how he felt about her, he had been mildly surprised by the depth of his passion. He had once loved Felicia and had enjoyed having sex with her, but that was before his love had turned to hate. Yet there had never been this gut-wrenching hunger between them, this ache deep inside, an intense pain that promised pleasure. He felt all that and more for Jolie; and it was only a matter of time until she would have to admit she felt the same.

It was highly unlikely they could have a future together. Even if Jolie were to give in to her feelings for him, he doubted she could ever forgive him for being Georgette Devereaux's son. In the end her hatred for his mother might prove to be stronger than her desire for him.

Ironic that of all the women on earth, the one who had made him weak and vulnerable with such desperate longing was Louis Royale's daughter. He had been trying to convince himself that if he made love to her, eased the sexual tension sizzling between them, then what he felt for her would become controllable. But what if after he'd had her, it wasn't enough? What if he only wanted her more?

The telephone on the bedside table rang. Max walked from the balcony into the bedroom and answered on the fourth ring.

"Devereaux."

"Max, I don't know what the hell you're going to do with a million dollars, but everything is set up for the transfer. It will be deposited in your name at the First State Bank in Key West, Florida, at ten-thirty in the morning."

"Thanks, Danny Lee. I appreciate your taking care of this so quickly," Max said. "And I don't guess I have to tell you that this transaction is something I expect to be kept in strictest confidence." Like his father and grandfather before him, Danny Lee Loveless was the president of the First National Bank in Sumarville, as well as a long-time Royale family friend.

"Is there anything going on that I can help you with?" Danny Lee asked. "I've been your financial consultant for years now and if you're going to invest—"

"It's a personal investment," Max said.

"Say no more. Just rest assured that the money will be there when you need it."

"Thanks again." Max ended their conversation, then dialed the manager's office.

"Watson Fritz. How may I help you?"

"Yes, Mr. Fritz, this is Max Devereaux. I'd like you to find a reason to close the pool area for the next two hours, except to Ms. Royale and myself. And please have a pair of swim trunks brought up to my room as soon as possible. Just bill them to my suite."

"Yes, sir, Mr. Devereaux. I believe the pool should be closed immediately for some minor repair work in the area. It will take approximately two hours before the pool can be reopened to our guests. And I'll personally choose the swim trunks for you and have them sent up immediately."

"One other thing."

"Yes?"

"I'd like dinner served here in my suite, at around seven-thirty. I'll leave the selections up to you."

"Certainly, sir."

Max hung up the phone, then went back onto the balcony to watch Jolie. She lifted herself out of the pool, squeezed the water from her hair, and dried off with a white hotel towel. With the pool secluded by a U-shaped hedge and with no chance of anyone interrupting them, what better time than the present to manipulate the situation to his advantage, to lay the groundwork for his seduction. He intended to have Jolie Royale. In his bed. Tonight.

Nowell Landers held Clarice in his arms, soothing her with soft tender words and gentle caresses. She kept mumbling incoherently and shaking her head.

"Theron, how could you have upset her this way?" Yvonne demanded as she stood over him, a reproachful expression on her face. "You know how emotionally fragile she is."

"I'm sorry that Clarice . . . *Aunt* Clarice is so upset and confused. I swear that I had no idea she'd go all weird like that." Theron tried to defend himself, but he could tell by his mother's tight mouth and narrowed gaze that he wasn't going to be able to easily redeem himself. Often the best defense was offense. "But if you'd answered my questions about Roscoe Wells, then I wouldn't have been forced to ask Aunt Clarice about the big secret you two share."

"What did she tell you before she got so upset?"

"Nothing really."

"But you kept pressing her to remember things, to tell you things, and she lost control and went off into her own little world." Yvonne glanced at Clarice. "She is so fragile that it doesn't take much to upset her, and bringing up the topic of Roscoe Wells and what happened that day over forty years ago sent her off the deep end."

"Should you call a doctor for her?" Theron asked. Hell, he hadn't meant any harm to Clarice. He'd known she was a little off and had been since the Belle Rose massacre, but he'd had no idea how mentally unstable she really was.

"All the doctors in the world can't help her," Yvonne said. "I'm just glad you called when you did. Thank goodness Nowell had just arrived at Belle Rose and came straight over here with me. He seems to be able to do more with her than anyone else."

Nowell held Clarice in his arms and spoke to her quietly. "Do you want to go home, honey? I can fix you a nice cup of tea and we can sit in the gazebo and relax?"

"Yes, Jonathan, that would be so nice," Clarice replied. "I want you to meet my sisters, Audrey and Lisette . . . and Yvonne. They'll be my bridesmaids at our wedding." Clarice giggled. "People will be so shocked when they realize Yvonne is part of the wedding party. But I don't care. She's my sister, you know . . . and my very best friend."

Nowell's gaze met Yvonne's and they exchanged sympathetic looks. Theron hung his head.

"We'll go on up to Belle Rose now." Nowell led Clarice off the cottage porch, then glanced over his shoulder. "I'll call later and let you know how she is."

"Yes, thank you." Yvonne watched Clarice and Nowell as they headed up the road. As soon as they were out of earshot, she turned on Theron. "The secret that Clarice and I share is nobody's business but ours. Do you hear me, son? And if we choose to use that secret to protect you, then that, too, is our business. I don't want you to ever question Clarice about it again."

"What if I ask Roscoe Wells about it?"

Yvonne's eyes widened in horror. "Don't you go near that man!"

"Will you tell me one thing, something that is my business?"

His mother stared at him.

"Is Roscoe Wells my father?"

Yvonne gasped; a fine mist of tears glazed her eyes. "No, he's not, thank God. And if you want me to, I can swear to that on a mile-high stack of Bibles."

Chapter 24

In less than twenty-four hours, they would have the Belle Rose massacre files. The truth about the murders had to be there in the files, somewhere. Otherwise, why would they be worth a million dollars? As much as she wanted to get a look at those files, Jolie dreaded the thought of what she would find. Crime scene photographs. Shots of her mother, her aunt, and Lemar. A forensic report, a ballistics report, a preliminary report by the deputies first on the scene and the medical examiner's report. And God only knew what else. Clues that might lead them to the real killer or hard evidence in black and white?

Jolie lathered her arms and legs with sunscreen, then stretched out on the chaise longue by the pool. Waiting until eleven tomorrow wouldn't be easy; already the two hours since Max and she had met with Aaron Bendall seemed more like two days. She lifted her sunglasses off the dry towel beside the chaise, put them on, and closed her eyes.

Relax, Jolie, she told herself. *Worrying about tomorrow won't make the time pass any faster. And escaping from Max for a few hours will not save you from him, either. Face it, you've simply given yourself a brief reprieve.* She had come to realize that Max Devereaux was a force to be reckoned with when he wanted something. And it was obvious that he wanted her.

"Ladies and gentlemen, I'm afraid I must ask you to vacate the pool area," Mr. Fritz said. "There is some minor repair work that we need to do. I apologize for any inconvenience and appreciate your cooperation. The pool should reopen in a couple of hours."

Jolie sighed. Just when she'd settled in, was halfway relaxed and knew she was temporarily safe from Max's presence, the hotel manager decides to close the pool. Great. Just great. She rose from the chaise, picked up her towels and bottle of sunscreen, then started to follow the other hotel guests.

Mr. Fritz approached her. "Ms. Royale, please don't leave. The pool area is not closed to you."

"I don't understand. I—"

"Thank you, Mr. Fritz." Max appeared at the open gate, which was the entrance from the narrow, greenery shrouded, brick walkway that led from the hotel to the secluded pool area.

"Oh." Jolie understood immediately. Max Devereaux wanted complete privacy at the pool, so he'd snapped his fingers and the hotel manager had closed the area to the rest of the guests.

Mr. Fritz disappeared hurriedly, latching the decorative wooden gate behind him. With two tall glasses in each hand, Max walked toward her. *Be still my heart,* she thought, then mentally laughed at her own silliness. *Be still my heart, indeed.* No big deal that Max resembled a half-naked Greek god in his royal blue swim trunks. So the man was drop-dead gorgeous. It didn't matter that her body was already gearing up for some hanky-panky, her nipples peaked and her femininity moistening with each throb; nothing was going to happen between Max and her. She'd be a fool to fall into his arms. There was no way they could have a meaningless affair and then walk away from each other when this was all over.

Max held out one of the drinks to her. She dropped her towels and sunscreen to the patio floor, then reached over and took the glass, careful to avoid touching Max's hand. He sat in the chaise next to the one she'd just vacated and spread out his long lean body. He took a sip of the slushy orange-pink drink.

"Mmmm." Max placed the glass beside his chaise on the patio. "The bartender told me that this drink is called a Coral Blizzard."

Standing over Max, Jolie glared at him. "Did it ever occur to you that I came down here to get away from you?"

"Never entered my mind." He stretched his arms, twined his fingers together and placed his open palms behind his head. "Mind putting some sunscreen on me?"

Jolie slumped down onto the edge of her chaise, glared at her drink, then sipped the concoction through the straw. Fruity, sweet, and pleasantly refreshing. She took several more sips, then set the glass down and glowered at Max. "If you think I'm going to touch you, you're out of your mind."

Max chuckled softly. "What are you so afraid of, *chère?*"

"Dammit, Max, why do you call me *chère?* It's unnerving to hear that sort of endearment coming from you. You probably call every woman who appeals to you *chère,* don't you? Do you honestly believe women find it irresistibly romantic?"

Max eased away his sunglasses, held them in his hand, and looked directly at her. "I've never called anyone else *chère.* Not ever."

This was not the confession she wanted to hear. She didn't want to be special to Max in any way. It would be so much easier to reject him if she believed she was only one in a long line of lovesick fools who'd succumbed to his dangerous earthy charm.

"Then why me?" she asked.

"Because it suits you. And it suits the way I feel about you."

Don't let him sweet-talk his way into your heart—and into your bed. What makes you think Max is any different from his mother? For all you know, he could be a user, a taker, a manipulator, just like Georgette. Ah, but are you still so sure about Georgette? Aren't you beginning to believe that she truly loved your father?

"Did you hear some guy using the endearment when you were in New Orleans? Or since he's originally from New Orleans, maybe your uncle Parry says it to all his lady friends."

"You seem very concerned about a simple little word."

Jolie scooted back in the chaise and crossed her arms over her chest. "You're the one making a big deal out of it."

"Would you really like to know who used that word for the special woman in his life?"

Jolie shook her head. "No, I'm not sure I want to know." A sudden sinking feeling hit her square in the gut and a niggling suspicion formed in her mind.

"I imagine you've already guessed, haven't you?" Max reached over the six inches separating their chaises and ran the tips of his fingers over her arm, from shoulder to wrist. "Louis called my mother *chère*. Somehow that one word said so much about how he felt, about the depth of his emotions."

"Damn, I should have known."

When Jolie started to get up, Max manacled her wrist. She rose from the chair and struggled to free herself. But he held tight, then jerked unexpectedly and toppled her off her feet and into his lap. She sat perfectly still, her breath caught in her throat.

"Please, Max, let me go."

"I can't do that."

When he circled her waist and manipulated her body until she lay stretched out on top of him, she didn't protest. They were eye-to-eye, her face only inches above his. Max reached up and removed her sunglasses. His hand at the base of her spine moved lower to cup one buttock. Jolie sucked in a deep breath.

"I don't want this," she told him.

"Yes, you do."

"No, I don't. This thing between us, whatever the hell it is, can only cause us pain. Look what reckless passion did to my father and your mother? They harmed so many people with their affair. And undoubtedly your uncle Parry has never gotten over Aunt Lisette. He's never married, has he? And just think what loving someone did to Aunt Clarice. She's still in love with her Jonathan."

"She seems to have fallen in love with Nowell Landers, so perhaps it's possible to fall passionately in love more than once."

"Not in that same mindless, all-consuming way," Jolie said, wishing Max would stop caressing her butt, stop staring at her as if he wanted to take her here and now. "Besides, half the time Aunt Clarice thinks Nowell is Jonathan."

"Nowell Landers is a fraud," Max said, his breath fanning Jolie's neck as he nuzzled her earlobe. "I know you disagree, but—"

"Oh, I agree with you. I think Nowell is most definitely a fraud." Melting into Max's body, her breasts pressed against his chest. And his erection throbbed against her mound.

Clutching the back of her head, Max forked his fingers through her damp hair. She gasped as wild fluttering currents zinged through her body. She couldn't let him kiss her. If he kissed her, she'd be lost. Not only now, but forever.

She lifted her hand and pushed on his shoulder. "Max, do you still have that private detective on retainer?"

"What?" He stared at her, his eyes glazed with passion.

"Would do you me a favor?"

"I'll do anything for you, Jolie, if you'll shut up and let me kiss you."

"Oh." She should get the hell off him as fast as possible. He was primed and ready, and she was fast losing control of the situation. "Would you . . . would you call that detective and ask him to run a check on Jonathan Lenz?"

"Why? The man's been dead for over thirty-five years."

"Just call it a hunch. Please, do this for me."

"I'll call Hugh later this evening. Now, is that all?"

"That's all."

Max forced her head down to his. *Don't let this happen,* she warned herself. Max's lips touched hers. Softly. A faint brush of flesh against flesh. Then a delicate nibbling, followed by his caressing tongue outlining her lips. She could feel herself dissolving into him, deeper and deeper with each passing second, as she fell more and more under his spell. Nothing in her life had ever felt this right, as if she had been waiting thirty-four years for this moment, for this one particular man.

"Please, Max, I can't," she whispered against his lips.

He closed his eyes. Every muscle in his body tensed. He tightened his hold on the back of her head and for a split second she thought he was going to force her into a more intimate kiss. But suddenly he withdrew, his movements stiff, as it took a great deal of strength to force himself to release her.

"Get up. Now." The words grated from between his clenched teeth.

"Max, I'm sorry. I just can't handle this. I'm afraid of—"

He shoved her up and off him. She bolted upright, shaky on her feet and breathing roughly. She stood there, shivering, her arms crisscrossing as she hugged herself. He shot up from the chaise, grabbed her chin and forced her head to lift and meet his gaze.

"You can postpone the inevitable, but you can't escape it." Releasing her, he turned and walked away.

Jolie released a pent-up breath. *This isn't love,* she told herself. *This is some sort of sickness. A passion that overrules common sense, that erases the past and the present, that seduces more surely than any narcotic.*

And if Max was right, she was powerless against her own desire.

Roscoe closed and locked the door to his study. Mattie was still in the house somewhere and Garland could come home at any time. This phone call needed to be completely private.

After unlocking the bottom left drawer of his desk, he removed a small brown leather book, then flipped through the pages until he found what he needed. A phone number he hadn't used in years. Another old friend who had been useful in the past. Roscoe silently repeated the numbers several times until he'd memorized them, then replaced the book in its safe hiding place and locked the drawer. He returned his key chain to his pants pocket, picked up the phone, and dialed. As the phone rang, he thought about what should be done first. He needed to deal with Max and Jolie. Then Yvonne was next. She and Clarice had kept quiet for forty-two years. He'd felt safe, even smug, knowing that they'd never tell anyone about what had happened. They'd been young and stupid and afraid of him. And they'd believed what he told them. Thank God for that, because if Mr. Sam had ever found out about what he'd done, the old man would have killed Roscoe with his bare hands.

Yvonne needed to be eliminated because she had threatened him, but who posed the most immediate danger? Yvonne or Max and Jolie?

Parry Clifton sat alone in his room. The cicadas hummed outside as evening turned to night. He should have gone into town, paid for a woman, and gotten rip-roaring drunk. These days about the only time he got any peace was when he was so drunk he couldn't remember anything. Not his childhood, when he and Georgie had been slapped around by their abusive father. Not his teen years when Jules Trouissant had sold the use of his body to rich old men with a penchant for boys and had turned Georgie from a thirteen-year-old virgin into a seasoned whore. And not those dreadful years when Georgie had been married to Philip Devereaux and both she and he had tried so desperately to fit in with the damn blue bloods in Sumarville. And not those wild, reckless, and fun days when he'd fallen in love with Lisette Desmond. Just thinking about her hurt him deep inside, an unbearable pain that ripped at his guts. She'd been so beautiful, so exciting. And she'd been his. But damn her unfaithful little soul, she had betrayed him. And with that sniveling boy. He could have forgiven her for having an affair with Garland Wells, but he couldn't forgive her lies.

Tears streamed down Parry's face. *Lisette. Lisette. Have you come back to haunt me? Do you want my forgiveness? Is that it? What if I say I forgive you? Would you forgive me?*

Chapter 25

Jolie had nixed Max's plans for them to share an intimate dinner in their suite. In retrospect he realized that this afternoon by the pool, he had pushed her a little too far, a little too fast. The more persistent he was in pointing out to her that the strong feelings between them wouldn't go away simply because she wanted them to, the more she dug in her heels, determined to prove him wrong. Jolie Royale was a stubborn woman. And she was running scared. She had returned to Sumarville after a twenty-year absence, buried a father she believed had betrayed her, discovered there had been a cover-up in the double murder case involving her mother's and aunt's deaths, and had barely escaped being killed by a hired gunman. And in the midst of all this trauma, an unsettling desire for a man she thought she despised had stirred to life within her. He understood her confusion; he, too, realized the irony in Louis's daughter and Georgette's son being cursed with what seemed to be an inherited passion. He had never counted on falling for Jolie—falling so damn hard that he was totally stunned by his reaction to her.

"We're stuck in Key West until tomorrow," she said. "But that doesn't mean I'm trapped here at the hotel with you. I plan to go out and soak up some of the local nightlife."

"I'm game if you are. What do you want to do? Where do you want to go?" he asked.

"Anywhere you're not!"

Jolie didn't bother saying good-bye when she left; she just walked away from him, exited their suite, and slammed the door, practically in his face. Apparently she didn't understand that although she might run away from him, she couldn't run away from herself. The yearning inside her wasn't going away; if anything, the more she denied it, the stronger it would grow.

Max waited a few minutes, then followed her, doing his best to keep a discreet distance behind her. Didn't she realize that he was not going to allow her to run around Key West alone? Any woman might be at risk, even in a semitropical paradise, but a woman as beautiful as Jolie would draw men to her like moths to a flame. And because she was so desperately afraid of her feelings for him, she might do something stupid just to prove to him and to herself that there was nothing special between them. The possessive protectiveness he felt where Jolie was concerned was unlike anything he'd ever experienced. It was utterly old-fashioned and perhaps a bit primitive, and God knew he hated himself for being unable to give her a wide berth, for hiding in the shadows like a conspicuous bodyguard or a scorned lover.

Max followed her north on Duval Street, where a gathering of tourists watched the incredible sunset and were entertained by musicians and carnival acts. When Jolie caught a glimpse of him half a block away, she tried her best to blend in with the crowd.

Keep on running, chère. Try your best to escape me. But no matter where you go, I will find you.

As the last rays of sunlight melted into a swath of glorious colors across the western horizon, a piper played the hauntingly bittersweet "Amazing Grace." Slowly but surely making his way toward Jolie, Max maneuvered around the people who were savoring the beauty of the day's end. When he came up behind Jolie and put his arms around her, she gasped and glanced over her shoulder.

"Enjoying yourself?" he asked.

Tension tightened her muscles; anger flashed in her blue eyes. "Stop following me."

"Why not ask me to do something easier . . . ask me to stop breathing."

A barely discernible shudder rippled through her. "Don't. Please, don't." She wriggled in his arms, trying to free herself.

"Don't what?" he whispered, his breath warm against her ear. "Don't want you to the point of madness? Don't think about holding you and kissing you and making love to you . . . all night long."

She jerked away from him and ran up the street. Several people noticed her hurrying away, but when Max didn't pursue her immediately, no one said anything to him.

Giving her a chance to put a little distance between them, Max strolled in the direction she'd fled and soon caught sight of her simple red sundress as she darted into the Margaritaville Café. Standing outside on the street, he listened to the boisterous music blaring from the live band. After allowing her enough time to settle in and feel relatively safe from him, Max entered the café, a casual Key West joint, decorated with lime green walls and an assortment of Jimmy Buffet, sailing, and tropical paraphernalia. He stayed at the bar and waited for her to order dinner; then when her meal arrived, he carried his drink to her table and joined her.

She glared at him when he sat down. "Go away, Max."

He shrugged. "Do you think if you say it often enough, it'll happen?"

"One lives in hope."

He set his half-full glass aside, crossed his arms and rested them on the table, then smiled. "Yes, one does live in hope, doesn't one?"

"Can't you at least let me eat dinner in peace?" She glanced down at her food and then up at him.

"If you're thinking of dumping that in my lap, don't."

"The thought never crossed my mind." A mischievous grin played at the corners of her mouth.

"I'll just bet it didn't."

"If you're staying, I'm leaving."

Max shrugged.

Jolie removed her wallet from her small shoulder bag, took out a couple of bills, and tossed them on the table. "It's paid for. Why don't you stay and enjoy it?" She got up and walked off.

Max grunted. A waiter rushed over, looked at Jolie's untouched plate of food and then at Max.

"She changed her mind," Max said. "You know how women are."

Max got up and rushed out into the street, then grinned when he saw Jolie a block away. Not running. Not even walking fast. Didn't she realize that he was aware of the fact that she wasn't trying very hard to lose him? He followed her from the five hundred block of Duval Street to the two hundred block, knowing that she knew he was never more than half a block behind her.

The bright lights and loud music coming from Sloppy Joe's invited guests to come inside and sample the legendary good times to be found within. A country and western band provided tonight's entertainment, and when Max followed Jolie inside, he noted that the dance floor was full. He caught sight of Jolie at the bar. Nonchalantly, she glanced around the room. Their gazes collided and locked instantly. While he made his way toward her, she didn't move and didn't look away. She was waiting for him. But he didn't kid himself that this meant she had given up the fight. Oh, no. He figured she'd merely changed tactics.

When he reached the bar area, he held out his hand to her and without either of them speaking, both understood the invitation. After only a moment's hesitation, she took his hand and let him lead her into the center of the other couples on the dance floor. She went into his arms as if she longed to be there, and Max felt no reluctance in her body as he pulled her close. After resting her head on his shoulder, she closed her eyes, and when she sighed, every soft, pliant inch of her leaned into him. All he could think about was that Jolie Royale was heaven to touch, and if just holding her in his arms gave him this much pleasure, then what would it feel like when they made love?

Jolie had been fighting a losing battle, but it wasn't in her to give up without one last hurrah. Max was like a fire-breathing dragon, stomping through villages and destroying everything in his path as he hunted for his mate. If she were fighting only Max, then she might succeed, but she was also fighting her own needs, her own desires. If she gave him a little of what he wanted— of what they both wanted—would it be enough? She couldn't understand why this had happened to her. Why had she fallen so hard and so fast for Max Devereaux? This was one complication she didn't need in her life and knew he probably felt the same. But the crazy thing was she felt certain that he was as powerless as she was against the overwhelming passion that sizzled between them.

As they danced, his legs shifted against hers, his thighs solid muscle. And her tight nipples brushed lightly against his hard chest, the friction sending electrical currents from her breasts to her feminine core. Her heartbeat slowed; she relaxed. Max lifted one hand up and under her hair to gently grasp her neck. His other hand drifted down her back, across her waist and splayed across her bottom.

Lost in the crowd, Jolie felt safe. Things could only progress so far in public. A joyous sense of freedom claimed her. She could steal these moments from reality without regrets, with no harm done. For as long as the dance lasted, she could pretend that the here-and-now was all that existed. No tomorrow, when they would meet with Aaron Bendall and exchange a million dollars for the stolen Belle Rose massacre files. No yesterday, when death and betrayal had wedged an insurmountable obstacle between them.

But the music ended all too quickly, returning her to reality. She couldn't bring herself to step out of his arms and walk away. Not yet. Every fiber of her being told her that this was where she belonged. Then, just as she forced herself to lift her head from his shoulder, the band started another melody, softer and slower than the previous one. Max tightened his hold on her neck.

"Don't go," he murmured. "Not yet."

She returned her head to his shoulder and draped her arms around him. They danced one dance after another and time ceased to exist. As long as they stayed here, the fantasy didn't have to end.

Max's erection pressed against her, and her body responded. They were making love to each other, with every touch, every sigh and groan, every slow sweet movement of their bodies. But it wasn't enough. She wanted more, needed more.

Suddenly the music changed from slow to fast. A foot-stomping, hand-clapping song that had the customers hooting and hollering. Jolie eased away from Max, but before she could leave him, he grabbed her hand and led her straight for the exit. Once outside, the tropical breeze caressed their perspiring bodies. When Max headed them back toward their hotel, Jolie balked.

"Let's go for a walk," she said, using any excuse to delay the inevitable.

"You've got to be kidding."

"Just a short walk on the beach to cool us off. Please."

"I don't want to cool off," he told her. "I want to heat things up even more." He all but dragged her along the sidewalk.

She skidded to an abrupt halt. "Max, I can't do this. I won't."

He grabbed her shoulders and glared at her. "We're going back to the hotel. Now. When we get there, you can go to bed alone . . . or you can spend the night in my arms. Your choice."

"I seem to have lost my ability to make logical choices," she admitted. "If we go back to the hotel right now, I'm not sure I'll have the strength to resist."

He ran his hands up and down her arms, then stepped away from her and cursed under his breath. "Damn, what a thing to say to a man who's walking around with the hard-on from hell."

"Don't you think I'm hurting the same way, that I want you so badly that I'm aching? But if we do this, we'll regret it. You know we will."

Like a flash of summer heat lightning, quick and violent, Max swooped her off her feet and up into his arms. "We'll regret it if we don't." He marched up the sidewalk, heading for their hotel, which was only a block away.

"Max, what are you doing?" She flung her arm around his neck to balance herself.

"What I should have done to start with—taking what I want."

"You're crazy." She wriggled, but when he threatened to drop her, she stilled instantly. "If you think this caveman tactic is going to work with me, then buster, you'd better think again."

"Well, it works for me, and right now, my satisfaction is all I'm thinking about."

Max carried her through the empty lobby and into the cagelike elevator that took them up to their suite. Somehow he managed to unlock the door and get inside without much effort. The sitting room between their bedrooms lay in semidarkness, only the golden glow from a small lamp illuminated the room.

"Put me down," she demanded. "You're not going to force me to do anything I don't want to do."

Disregarding her command, he shoved open the partially closed door to his bedroom. Soft moonlight glimmering through the French doors saved the room from total darkness. He carried her across the room and dumped her in the middle of his bed. *My God, he isn't going to stop!* Jolie scurried to the side of the bed and jumped up. Before she could take a step, Max was in her face. She gasped.

He grabbed her hips and hauled her up against him, then rubbed his stiff sex back and forth across her mound. Of its own accord her body undulated against him, seeking a closer union. He thrust his hands up under her sundress, grasped the edge of her panties, and dragged them down her hips, letting them fall to her ankles.

"You won't need these," he told her.

She swallowed hard. Every feminine instinct urged her not to resist. She longed to give of herself and take all that she needed from him in return.

Jolie lifted one foot, then the other, stepping out of her panties. "Max, I'm not sure. I'm afraid—"

With a ruthless surge, he yanked her to him, both hands under her dress, cupping her bare buttocks as his head lowered and his lips claimed hers. His mouth consumed; his tongue mated with hers. Jolie's bones dissolved.

Max's kisses were lethal.

After he had kissed her until they were both breathless, he nuzzled her neck and groaned a reluctant admission. "I feel the same way. Wanting someone the way I want you is frightening. I don't think there's anything I wouldn't do in order to have you."

As her mind reeled with his confession, Max shoved her gently onto the bed and came down over her, his breathing fast and powerful. He shoved her dress up to her waist, unzipped his slacks, and eased his penis from his briefs. Her eyes widened in surprise when, without any preliminary coaxing, he parted her thighs and rammed into her, taking her swiftly and completely. He filled her mind and her heart as well as her body. The realization that she had never wanted a man the way she wanted Max coaxed her body into compliance, uncaring that his actions bordered on ruthlessness.

His big hands clasped her hips and set a steady thrusting rhythm. As his penis rooted deeply and withdrew, then repeated the process, she writhed beneath him, seeking the perfect position to absorb the friction of every thrust against her clitoris. He was large and hard and hot. He grunted. He groaned. He murmured earthy words of intent and appreciation. As the tension built inside her, threatening her with the pain of unfulfilled need and promising the possibility of an earth-shattering release, she rocked against him faster, urging him to intensify his lunges.

"Oh, God, Max . . . please . . . please . . ."

He jackhammered into her with frenetic energy. She responded wildly as she began climaxing, the sensation intensifying until it exploded inside her and sent shock waves through her body. Within moments after she cried out her completion, he shivered and shook as he came, his orgasm demolishing every ounce of his self-control. He groaned and growled and then collapsed heavily on top of her. It was a weight she bore gladly.

Jolie wrapped her arms around Max and buried her

face against his neck, knowing that nothing would ever be the same again. And she didn't care. The only thing that mattered was this moment, this night—and never letting go of the man she loved, who was also the man she hated.

Chapter 26

Jolie lay in the bed beside Max, her breathing slow and even, her eyes open and staring up at the dark ceiling. She'd never had sex like that before, so raw and primitive, so all-consuming. The very intensity of her need for Max frightened her. How was it possible to want someone so desperately that all rational thought ceased to exist once you came together? She had considered him her enemy for so long that even now, after having shared with him the most mind-shattering sex of her entire life, she guarded her heart from him. She didn't dare let him know he possessed the power not only to hurt her but to destroy her.

"I hate you," she said softly.

"Yes, I know. I hate you, too, for making me lose control. I pride myself on being able to handle my emotions." He rolled out of bed and stood. "I feel like I've been run over by a steamroller. A part of me likes it, but another part of me despises it."

Suddenly realizing that her sundress was still hiked

up to her waist, Jolie jerked the red cotton material down to cover her nakedness. "Well, now that we've done it . . . now that we've had each other, there's no reason for—"

Max moved with lightning speed, grabbed her, and yanked her out of bed. She stood on wobbly legs, her eyes wide with shock, her mouth gaping open as she stared at him.

"You don't really think once was enough, do you?" His gaze raked over her. "Why don't you take off that damn dress?"

"What?" She gulped. Mercy, she wasn't sure she could survive another round of frenzied lovemaking so soon.

"I'm going to take a shower." He removed his shirt and tossed it on the floor. "Get out of that dress and come with me."

He kicked off his shoes, slipped out of his socks, and then undid his belt. Her gaze traveled south, as he unzipped his slacks, and she watched in utter fascination as he shucked off his pants and briefs. Maximillian Devereaux was a magnificent man, muscular yet lean, with a light dusting of black hair on his arms, legs, and chest. And a very impressive penis nestled in a thatch of dark hair between his powerful thighs. Remembering what it felt like to have him buried deep inside her excited Jolie anew. How was it possible to want him again almost immediately after being thoroughly satisfied?

Not giving the consequences a thought, she unzipped the side closing of her sundress and lifted it up and over her head. She stood before him, naked and totally unashamed. Max's hot glare swept over her, so intense she could feel its warmth as it skimmed along her neck, over her breasts, down her belly, and to her mound. She quivered, every nerve attuned to his inspection, her flesh responsive, her entire body totally aware. His big hand lifted, touched her face, glided down her neck, over one breast, and leisurely clasped her waist. Without a word, he guided her from the bedroom into the bath, where he turned on the shower and led her inside the tile-and-glass cubicle. Within the steamy confinement, Max became her adoring servant, lathering her body, scrubbing gently, giving special attention to her breasts and buttocks. She ached unbearably, her core throbbing with need. But he didn't touch her there, as if he knew how desperately she wanted him to and was making her wait, prolonging her torment.

When he handed her the soap, she was breathless with anticipation, her hands yearning to touch him as he had touched her. As she washed his chest, his nipples peaked, prompting her to rinse them and then lick them. Max growled. She turned him around and scrubbed his broad muscular back. Her mouth followed the water's trail, downward over his back, his waist, and his taut buttocks. Then she eased him around again, carefully avoided his genital area, and washed his long hairy legs. As she moved back up his body, his jutting penis confronted her, practically demanding attention. She allowed it only the briefest flick, her fingertips skimming over the tip and moving away quickly. Max groaned, then shut off the water and pulled her out of the shower. He grabbed a small towel and draped it around her head, then took a huge towel and dried her quickly. Still wet himself, he lifted her up and onto the vanity, spread her legs, and eased between them.

As he splayed one big hand across her back, he lowered his head and took her mouth. She responded by opening herself to him, her mouth, her femininity, and her heart. When she felt his fingers exploring her soft dampness, she sighed and lifted her hips up and down, riding the strumming motion of his fingertips. He deepened the kiss and the intimate caresses until Jolie whimpered and writhed. Close, so close. Now . . . now . . . now! The orgasm hit her like a tidal wave, washing over her with surge after surge of sensation.

Crying out, she slumped against him. He held her as the aftershocks rippled through her body. Then when she rested in his arms, momentarily sated and relaxed, he lifted her and carried her into the bedroom. He laid her on the bed. Standing over her in the shadowy moonlight, he appeared huge and dark and dangerous. She could feel his gaze on her, caressing her. Why was he standing there? What was he waiting for?

His chest rose and fell with each deep, hard breath. Jolie rose into a sitting position, slid to the edge of the bed, and lifted herself onto her knees.

"Max?"

"Hmmm?" His voice sounded tortured.

"What's wrong?"

She looked up at him; he closed his eyes and gripped his hands into fists. Her heartbeat accelerated alarmingly.

"Max, you're frightening me." She reached up and placed her open palm in the center of his chest, then shuddered when she felt the powerful thumping of his heart.

He grabbed her wrist, shoved her flat onto her back, crossways in the bed, and came down over her, straddling her. She gazed up into his face and gasped. The strain showed plainly in his expression, tension etched on his features.

"I don't want to frighten you," he told her, his voice deep and gravelly. "But the way I feel about you . . . the way I want you . . . the things I want to do to you scare the hell out of me."

"Oh, Max." She reached out to him with her free hand.

He grasped that hand, too, and flung both of her arms over her head, pinning them there, trapping her beneath him. Panting as uncertainty combined with heady desire, Jolie waited, anticipation preparing her body for his domination. He ravaged her mouth, kissing, plunging, sucking, nibbling. And when he had it conquered, he moved on to new territory. Her neck, her shoulders, her breasts. He lingered over her breasts, laving each nipple, sucking greedily, and then pulling gently with his teeth until she squirmed and whined and pleaded.

"Max?" She ached with need.

"Shh." He soothed her with kisses across her rib cage, then he eased his hold on her hands, as he moved down over her belly, sampling her navel on his trip to exotic southern regions.

He parted her legs and placed his head between her thighs. She lifted her hips and caught either side of his head with her open palms. He glanced at her, his gaze blazing with salacious intention, and then he opened his mouth and delved his tongue into her moist depths. She bucked, lifting herself up to him. He grabbed her hips and held her in place for his marauding mouth. His tongue flicked over her clitoris, then laved with deep powerful strokes. And when she mewed loudly as she clutched his shoulders, he increased the pressure and the pace until she went wild. While she climaxed, he rose up and over her, then thrust into her, again and again and again, battering her body with the force of his need.

When he came, trembling and grunting with the strength of his release, she cried out, shocked that she had come again so quickly.

Max rolled over and off her, taking her with him, pulling her on top of him. She clung to him, savoring the sweet ecstasy of having him still inside her. He wrapped his arms around her and kissed her temple. Within minutes, they fell asleep.

In the predawn hours, he woke her and made love to her again. Slower, longer, and yet no less savage. And as she drifted off to sleep, a tantalizing yet unnerving thought drifted through her mind. No matter how many times they made love, it would never be enough. She would want him again . . . and again . . . and again. She would need him more and more, and love him until the day came when he would be as essential to her as the very air she breathed—just as Georgette had become to her father.

Jolie woke suddenly, then realized that bright sunlight poured into the bedroom through the balcony doors. As she opened her eyelids, her eyes slightly unfocused, she saw a large shadow hovering over her. After blinking a couple of times, her vision cleared and the shadow turned into Max Devereaux, fully dressed, standing by the bed.

She shot straight up. "Oh, God, what time is it?"

He offered her the cup of coffee he held in one hand and the large muffin perched in the center of a small plate that he held in his other hand. As she reached for the coffee, she realized she was naked. She dropped her hand, grabbed the hem of the sheet, and lifted it over her breasts.

Max sat on the edge of the bed, jerked the sheet down to her waist, grabbed her wrist and placed the coffee in her hand. "I've already seen it, *chère*. Every luscious inch."

He was right; what was the point of modesty now? He *had* seen every inch. Hell, not only had he seen every inch, he'd touched, kissed, tasted, and explored every inch.

"What time is it?" she repeated.

"Eight-thirty," he replied as he rose to his feet.

She lifted the cup to her lips and took a sip of the delicious coffee. Strong but diluted with just the right amount of cream. She sighed, then looked at him. "How long have you been up?"

"Long enough to shower, shave, and order breakfast."

Jolie drank the coffee slowly, savoring each sip. "Should we talk about—"

"No."

"But don't you think—"

"No." He stood at the French doors, his back to her. "We should concentrate on meeting with Bendall and making the exchange. Once we have the files, we'll fly back to Sumarville. After we find out exactly what secrets those files contain and learn what our options are, then there will be time enough to sort through our personal feelings and—"

"My goodness, Mr. Devereaux, aren't we all business this morning."

Jolie tossed back the sheet and got up, her empty cup in her hand. Before she reached the bedroom door, Max shot toward her, grabbed her around the waist and hauled her up against him. His piercing blue-gray eyes bored into her, his gaze suddenly heavy and sultry.

"It is taking a great deal of effort on my part not to make love to you again." He rubbed his cheek against hers. "And unless you want us to be late for our appointment with Bendall, then I suggest you get on some clothes as fast as you can."

A giddy feeling of euphoria bubbled up inside her. Knowing that Max wanted her now just as much as he'd wanted her all during the night imbued her with an incredible sense of power.

"Then you'd better let go of me." She wriggled.

When he released her, she ran from his room, through the sitting area and into her bedroom. After laying out a pair of linen slacks and a short-sleeved, cotton-knit top, Jolie hurried into the bathroom. All the while, she made a mental list of everything she needed to do in preparation for what could prove to be one of the most important meetings of her life and tried to convince her body that it could do without Max's touch for a few hours.

Jolie checked her watch for the dozenth time. Max glanced at the clock on the wall inside the First State Bank on Whitehead Street. Twelve-thirteen. By now it was apparent that for whatever reason, Aaron Bendall was not going to meet them. Max was angry and frustrated. Jolie was nervous and fidgety.

"He isn't coming, is he?" Jolie asked.

"I'd say that's a pretty reasonable assumption."

"What could have happened? Why would he give up a million dollars?"

"He wouldn't," Max told her. "Not unless someone offered him more."

"Roscoe?"

"Probably." Max grabbed her arm. "Let's check out the marina and see if Bendall's cruiser is gone."

"And if it is? What do we do then?"

"We go home. And my detective starts searching for Bendall all over again. But if he's gotten his hands on a million-plus, then I doubt we'll ever find him."

"Him or the Belle Rose massacre files."

Twenty minutes later, after having questioned the marina's manager, they walked down the pier, past the docked boats and toward the parking area. The manager had told them that Bendall had sailed out of port at ten-forty this morning, leaving no forwarding address and his rent paid up for the next three months. The guy was long gone and Max doubted anyone would ever hear from the former sheriff again. If he had simply disappeared and his cruiser had still been docked, then Max would have suspected foul play, but since Bendall had sailed off hail and hearty, then someone had topped Max's million-dollar offer.

Deep in thought, Max followed Jolie to the rental car. Just as he reached around her and unlocked the passenger door, the *rat-a-tat-tat* of gunshots came from out of nowhere. A wave of bullets sailed around them. Max knocked Jolie to the pavement and covered her body with his.

Chapter 27

"Telephone for you, Mallory." Yvonne knocked softly on the closed bedroom door. "Mallory, did you hear me? There's a call for you."

Mallory flopped over in bed, grumbled sleepily and forced her eyes open. "Who is it?"

"I don't know. He didn't say."

"He?" Mallory's heart fluttered. *It must be R. J.* She sprang into a sitting position, grabbed the receiver off the telephone base and called out to Yvonne. "I've got it. Thank you."

"Hello."

"Hi, Mal."

It *was* R. J. They hadn't said good-bye until shortly after three this morning. With Max out of town, it was a whole lot easier sneaking in past her curfew. No one else in the house kept close tabs on her, not even her mother, who seemed lost in her own little world of grief these days.

"Do you miss me already?" Mallory asked, her body

softening and tingling just thinking about R. J. He had made her a woman . . . and she loved him wildly, passionately, completely. "I miss you."

"Mal, babe, listen up, will you?"

"Sure. What is it?"

"Well, it's like this—I'm fixing to head out to Texas. A buddy of mine called awhile ago and said he's got this really fantastic job out there just waiting for me."

Mallory felt as if all the wind had been knocked out of her. "You're leaving Sumarville?"

"Yeah, I gotta go. This job is just too good to turn down."

"When—when will you come back?" *For me,* she added silently.

"Well . . . that's just it. You see, I probably won't be back."

"Not ever?" *Please, God, please let him ask me to go with him.*

"Hey, sugar, we've had a great time, haven't we? Lots of fun in the sack. We're lucky we're ending it before we got bored with each other. Right?"

Emotion lodged in her throat, threatening to choke her. Somehow she forced the words of a reply past the restriction. "Right."

"If I'm ever back this way, I'll look you up," R. J. said. "But by then you'll probably be married or something."

"Yeah, I probably will be . . . married or something."

"You're one fantastic lady, Mal. I'll never forget you."

"I—I'll never forget you, either."

"Good-bye, babe."

The dial tone hummed in Mallory's ear. "Good-bye." The telephone dropped from her hand as she slid off the side of the bed and onto the floor. She sat there, staring off into space, the singsong, off-the-hook-warning blaring from the receiver.

* * *

Another barrage of bullets ripped through the car door and shattered the back windshield. As the gunfire peppered the asphalt beneath the trunk, Jolie prayed harder than she'd ever prayed in her life. Max lay on top of her, large and heavy, his big body shielding her from the attack. Suddenly she heard screeching tires mingling with hysterical screams. Then Max rolled off her. She opened her eyes and looked at him. They lay side-by-side, on the ground by the rental car, her shoulder brushing the front right tire.

"Are you all right?" he asked.

"Yes." Her trembling hand reached out to touch his face. "Are you?"

"Yeah, I'm fine. Whoever was shooting at us wasn't much of a shot or we'd both be dead."

"Another hired gunman?"

Max stood and assisted her to her feet. "My guess is that he was just some goon who got sent out on the spur of the moment. Probably hired through several people passing along the assignment."

"He could have killed us."

"Yeah, he had enough firepower to have mowed down a dozen people," Max said. "I'd say his orders were to scare the shit out of us, not kill us."

"A warning?"

"Oh, yeah. A major warning."

A crowd of curious excited bystanders hovered nearby. One tall slender gray-haired man, dressed in casual white slacks and a striped cotton shirt, came forward and said, "We've called the police. Are either of you hurt?"

Max wrapped his arm around Jolie's waist and held her close. "We're okay. Just a little shaken. Did anybody get a good look at the car or the shooter?"

"It all happened so fast," the man said. "I don't believe anyone got a good look at the man, but he was driving a late model, red Ford truck."

Max inspected Jolie, apparently wanting to make sure

she was truly all right. He frowned when he saw the
tears in her linen slacks and the blood seeping through
from the scratches on her knees. He grabbed her hands
and turned them palms up.

"Damn." He removed a handkerchief from his
pocket and tenderly smoothed the blood off her raw
palms, then he lifted first one hand and then the other
to his lips.

Adrenaline pumped through her at a high velocity.
She laid her head on his chest and slipped her arms
around him, her heart hammering madly and her body
shivering with the aftershocks of fear.

After spending several hours at the police station in
Key West, Jolie and Max went on a quick shopping
spree. They bought new clothes, since when they were
attacked, they'd been wearing the only change of clothes
they had taken with them on their trip. On the plane
ride home, they discussed their options concerning the
Belle Rose massacre case. They both knew chances were
slim that they'd ever get their hands on the stolen files.

"Bendall did give us a clue," Max said. "It's not much,
but it's all we've got."

*"Lisette Desmond was pregnant and you'll never guess who
the daddy was."* Jolie quoted Bendall's exact words.

"Was Lisette pregnant when she died? And if she was,
why is the father's identity important?" Max asked.

"If she was pregnant, the father's identity has to be
a clue to who the real killer is. Did the baby's father
have a reason to kill her? Did my mother and Lemar
simply get in the way that afternoon?"

It was late evening by the time Max and Jolie arrived
at Belle Rose. The entire family had congregated in the
front parlor, awaiting their arrival. Georgette perched
on the sofa, a sulking Mallory beside her. A medicated

Aunt Clarice lounged in one of the wing chairs; Nowell Landers hovered directly behind her. A bleary-eyed, slightly tipsy Parry Clifton stood by the fireplace, a bored expression on his face. And Theron sat in his wheelchair, Yvonne at his side.

As they entered the foyer at Belle Rose, Max dumped their bags on the marble floor; then cupping Jolie's elbow, he led her into the front parlor. She couldn't help thinking about how easily she accepted Max's touch, how a man who had been little more than a stranger to her several weeks ago was now the most important person in her life.

When they entered the parlor, all eyes focused on them. Parry lifted his whiskey glass in a salute. "Hail, hail the conquering hero."

"Oh, shut up, Uncle Parry," Mallory said. "You're drunk!"

"Please, Mallory . . . dear . . ." Georgette spoke to her daughter, but her gaze never left Max and Jolie.

"Where the hell did you two go?" Parry asked. "Slip off somewhere for a night of debauchery? A little private slap and tickle away from prying eyes?"

"Parry!" Georgette scowled at her brother.

"Did you get them?" Theron asked, completely ignoring the others.

"Get what?" Trying to focus, Clarice blinked as if awakening from sleep. "Jolie, dear girl, you left in such a hurry. You didn't even say good-bye."

Max looked directly at Theron. "We came close. I bid a sizable amount of money for them and struck a deal, but it seems someone else upped my offer, and we weren't given a chance to make a counteroffer."

"So, you don't have them?" Grimacing, Theron tightened his hands into fists and then loosened them over his knees.

"Don't have what?" Georgette asked. "Where did you and Jolie go and what did you make a bid on?"

Jolie walked over to Clarice, leaned down, kissed her

cheek, and said, "I'm sorry I didn't say good-bye before we left, but we had to fly to Key West immediately."

"Nice vacation spot," Parry said. "Very romantic. Surf and sand and brilliant sunsets."

"Dammit, Uncle Parry, shut the hell up!" Mallory marched over to her uncle, planted her hands on her hips and glowered at him. "You don't honestly think Max would take *her* away on some romantic holiday, do you?"

Max cleared his throat. "Jolie and I flew to Key West to speak to Sumarville's former sheriff, Aaron Bendall. It seems that when he left office fifteen years ago, he took the Belle Rose massacre files along with him."

Gasping, Georgette's gaze met Parry's. "Why—why would he take those files with him?"

"So he could blackmail someone with them," Jolie said. "Someone who didn't want the truth to come out. Someone who knew that there was evidence in those files that probably proved Lemar Fuqua didn't kill my mother and aunt."

"That's the most ridiculous thing I've ever heard." Parry attempted to set his glass on the mantel, but missed by a fraction of an inch, sending the tumbler crashing to the marble hearth.

Clarice jerked and cried out. Georgette jumped.

"Someone has been paying Bendall hush money all these years," Max said. "And that same someone offered Bendall more than a million dollars to disappear and take the files with him."

"A million dollars?" Mallory's eyes rounded. "You offered the man a million dollars? Why? What difference does it make who killed those women? What's it to you, Max?" Narrowing her gaze, Mallory glared at Jolie.

"Mallory, please be quiet," Georgette said. "You're being terribly insensitive. Those women were Jolie's mother and aunt, as well as Clarice's sisters."

Mallory shrugged.

"The bottom line is that you didn't get the files,"

Theron said. "So we don't have the evidence we need to reopen the case. Not even one more clue that might lead us to the real killer."

Jolie looked at Max, silently asking for his agreement before she revealed their one small tidbit of information. Max nodded. "Bendall gave us what he referred to as a 'freebie.' So we do have a clue, but unless we can exhume Aunt Lisette's body, the clue is useless."

"Exhume Lisette's body?" Georgette rose from her chair.

"You're crazy!" Staggering toward Jolie, Parry wagged his index finger at her. "I'll not stand for it! Do you hear me? You will not disturb my poor Lisette."

Clarice grabbed Jolie's hand. "Why do you want to do this terrible thing?"

Jolie knelt beside her aunt's chair. "Because we need to have another autopsy performed."

"But why?" Clarice gazed at Jolie with utter confusion in her hazel eyes.

"Aunt Clarice, was Aunt Lisette pregnant when she died?"

Clarice gasped. "Pregnant? Oh, dear. Oh dear. No one was supposed to know. Not until after the wedding She didn't tell a soul except Audrey and me and she swore us to secrecy."

Jolie let out the breath she'd been holding. "Do you know who the father was?"

"The father?" Clarice glanced at Parry. "I assumed the child was Parry's. After all, they were engaged to be married."

Just as Parry reached down for Jolie, rage contorting his features, Max crossed the room and grabbed his uncle's arm. He whirled Parry around to face him. "Was the baby yours?"

Parry swayed back and forth. Max gripped his shoulder to steady him. "Yes, of course, the baby was mine. And if you'd gotten your hands on those files, you would have read where I was questioned about Lisette's pregnancy and I told the sheriff that the baby was mine."

"Poor, poor Parry," Clarice said. "Losing not only Lisette, but his child, too."

Jolie stood and moved to Max's side. "I don't understand, then. If the baby was Parry's, why would Bendall think the father's identity would be a clue to the killer's identity?"

"Unless the man was implying that Parry was the killer," Nowell Landers said.

"What?" Clarice shook her head. "No, no, that's not right. Parry and Lisette were engaged. They loved each other."

"For once, Miss Loony Tunes is right," Parry said. "Why would I have killed the woman I loved? Bendall gave y'all a false clue. Hell, this is ridiculous." Parry glared at Yvonne and then at Theron. "Lemar Fuqua killed Lisette because he was crazy in love with her and couldn't have her. And he killed Audrey because she knew what he'd done."

"That's a damn lie!" Theron shouted.

"Then prove it, boy. By God, prove it!" Parry stormed out of the parlor.

"I'm sorry." Georgette looked pleadingly at Yvonne. "I apologize for the way Parry acted, for what he said."

"Lemar cared for Lisette, as he did Clarice," Yvonne said. "It was a brotherly affection. Nothing more."

"Then it's not possible that Lemar was the father of Lisette's baby?" Jolie asked.

"No, it's not possible," Yvonne replied.

"There's only one way to prove it," Theron said. "If we can exhume her body and test the baby's DNA."

"We can't do that, without permission," Max said. "The next of kin would have to—"

"Do it," Clarice said as she tightened her hold on Nowell's hand. "I'm Lisette's closest living relative. I'll sign whatever papers are necessary."

"But why put yourself through the torment?" Georgette asked. "Parry has already admitted that he was the baby's father."

"Because Lisette Desmond had numerous lovers," Jolie said. "My aunt could have told Parry he was the father, when in truth, the baby could have belonged to another man."

"And this other man might have killed her," Yvonne said.

"Aunt Clarice, if you truly are willing to give us permission to—"

"I am," Clarice declared.

"Then tomorrow morning, we'll contact Ike Denton and find out just what we have to do to have Lisette's body exhumed," Max said.

Jolie lay in Max's arms, in the four-poster in her childhood bedroom. It was a young girl's room with white eyelet lace curtains and bedspread edged in tiny pink satin roses, pale pink-and-white striped wallpaper, and a huge antique bookcase filled with expensive collectable dolls that had belonged to Audrey, Lisette, and Clarice Desmond when they were children. Max had come to her room long after everyone had gone to bed, when the house was quiet and dark. She had welcomed him into her arms and into her bed, and never for a moment considered turning him away. They had made love with a passion as hot and demanding as it had been the first time, then they'd slept for a couple of hours.

He nuzzled her neck. "I should go back to my room soon."

She turned over and cuddled against him. "Stay awhile longer."

"I could be persuaded to stay."

She breathed in the scent that was Max Devereaux's alone. Her lips painted wet kisses from his chest to his chin; then she rose up and over him, straddling him. She swooped down to lunge her tongue inside his

mouth. Her movements brushed aside the sheet and
light quilt, leaving her naked body exposed to the
golden moonlight coming in through the windows . . .
and to Max's hungry gaze.

"Still want to leave me?" she asked.

"I never want to leave you." Max lifted his hips, bringing his sex in direct contact with hers. "But what I want
and what must be . . ."

Jolie positioned herself, circled his penis with her
hand, and guided him into her. When she impaled
herself on its hard length, he grasped her hips and
together they set a steady rhythm. She rode him, placing
pressure on the precise points of pleasure, while he
catered to her needs with caresses and kisses. They climaxed simultaneously, falling apart with groans and
moans and whispered words that were said in the heat
of passion, meant to be forgotten in the cold light of
day.

Yvonne woke with a start. She lay in bed and listened.
Silence. What had awakened her? A noise? Theron?
No, she'd heard nothing. She'd been restless for hours,
tossing and turning, until finally exhaustion had
claimed her. It was the smell that had roused her from
a light sleep.

She sniffed. Smoke?

Yvonne kicked back the covers and jumped out of
bed. She sniffed again. Definitely smoke. She ran to the
door, and when she flung it open, billows of dark smoke
attacked her.

Dear God, the house was on fire!

Theron!

Chapter 28

The household at Belle Rose had been awakened by the whine of sirens. Within minutes Georgette and Clarice were shrieking as they came running from their rooms. No one except Mallory, who gave them a hateful glare, seemed to notice that Max and Jolie emerged together from Jolie's bedroom.

"It's Yvonne's house. It's on fire," Clarice said. "I could see from my bedroom window that the sky is lit up very brightly in that direction. I'm going to call Nowell and tell him to meet us at Yvonne's." As she returned to her room, she mumbled to herself. "Please, God, please let Yvonne and Theron be all right."

Max took charge, issuing orders as he rushed to his room to dress. Jolie hurried back to her room, flung off her robe, and put on a pair of jeans and a T-shirt, then slipped on a pair of sandals. By the time she went back into the hall, she saw Max, fully clothed, heading down the stairs.

"Wait," she called.

He paused, then motioned for her. Aunt Clarice followed them within minutes, as did Mallory.

Parry flung open his bedroom door. "What the hell's going on? Are we being invaded by Mars?"

"Yvonne's house is on fire," Georgette told him as she ran out of her room. "We're going over there to see if Yvonne and Theron got out all right and to bring them back here with us."

Five minutes later, Jolie pulled her Escalade up to the side of one of the fire engines, and she, Max, Aunt Clarice, and Mallory jumped out. Georgette had stayed to wait on Parry, telling the others that they would follow shortly. The cottage that had stood on Belle Rose property for well over a hundred years burned a glowing golden red, like campfire logs, shooting sparks into the sky. Smoke broiled from the crumbling structure, its swirls curling into the air like fat dark snakes.

Max and Jolie charged into the fray.

One of the firefighters blocked their path. "Please stay back!"

"Yvonne Carter and her son were inside," Jolie said.

"Yes, ma'am. Mr. Carter called us on his cell phone." He nodded toward the ambulance parked on the far side of the burning house. "His mother got them out of the house. They're both all right. They're being treated for smoke inhalation."

With Mallory supporting her, Clarice came toward them. "Where is Yvonne? Are she and Theron—?"

"They're fine," Max replied.

"Where are they?" Clarice asked. "I want to see them. We must take them home to Belle Rose with us."

By the time they made their way around the fire trucks and over to the ambulance, Georgette and Parry arrived. Max waved to them.

Theron sat in the ambulance's open back doorway, an oxygen mask on his face. Soot stained his face, naked chest, and pajama bottoms, and when Jolie drew closer, she saw that his eyes were bloodshot and watery. As the

Belle Rose mob descended on him, he jerked off the oxygen mask. Jolie and Clarice hugged him and asked him repeatedly if he was all right.

After assuring them that he was okay, he looked from one to the other and said, "Go find Mama, will you?"

"Where is she?" Jolie asked. "I thought she'd be with you."

"She disappeared a few minutes ago," Theron said. "I saw her head out on foot, going toward Pleasant Hill. Some of the firemen told us that it was pretty obvious that someone had set the fire. They'd poured kerosene across the front porch and probably struck a match. Once Mama heard that, she said, 'I warned him. He should have listened to me.' I've never seen her so upset."

Clarice gasped. "Roscoe Wells. She thinks he's responsible for the fire, doesn't she?"

Theron nodded. "Please, go find her. Stop her before she . . . Damn, just make sure she's safe."

Max laid his hand on Theron's shoulder. "Mallory and Aunt Clarice will stay here with you and when you're ready, they'll take you to Belle Rose. In the meantime, we'll find Yvonne."

Theron grabbed Max's arm. "Mama might have taken the Beretta I keep in my car. I saw her inside the car, but I couldn't get these medics to help me get to her in time to stop her."

"You think she's going to shoot Roscoe?" Max asked.

Theron's gaze locked with Clarice's. "What do you think? Will she try to kill Roscoe?"

Shivering as if she were suddenly cold on this hot humid July night, Clarice nodded.

"We'd better hurry," Jolie said. "We should be able to catch up with her before she makes it to Pleasant Hill on foot."

"I'm coming, too," Clarice said.

"No, please, stay here." Jolie grabbed her aunt's hands. "I don't want to have to worry about you, too."

Nowell Landers parked his Harley behind the growing number of vehicles spread out across the lawn and marched straight to Clarice. Georgette and Parry followed closely behind him. The moment Clarice saw Nowell, she flew into his arms.

"He'll look after her," Jolie said. "Let's go."

Within minutes, Max and she headed her SUV out onto the weed-infested gravel road that stretched between Belle Rose and Pleasant Hill. They didn't see Yvonne on the road, but when they parked in front of Roscoe's mansion, they noted that several downstairs lights were on. At two-thirty in the morning. Just as they got out of the Escalade, a single gunshot shattered the predawn solitude.

"Oh, my God!" Jolie gasped, then broke into a run.

Max raced behind her. The double front doors stood wide open. Max grabbed Jolie's arm, halting her outside the doorway. The sound of voices reverberated through the huge foyer.

"Hell, woman, you're supposed to be dead," Roscoe Wells said. "You and that son of yours should be toast by now."

Jolie's eyes widened; she looked at Max, who placed his index finger over his lips, a sign for her to keep quiet. He motioned her to come with him, and together they eased quietly along the side of the wall, slowly but surely making their way toward the sound of Roscoe's voice, which had come from his study.

"You're an evil man, Roscoe Wells. Clarice and I should have told Mr. Sam what you did. He would have killed you, and then you couldn't have hurt anybody else ever again."

"So you thought you'd come here and shoot me? Well, firing that damn pistol over my head ain't going to get the job done."

Hovering outside the door, Max and Jolie could see into the study. Yvonne's back was to them, and from where he stood behind his desk, Roscoe couldn't see them either. Suddenly footsteps thundered down the spiral staircase behind them. Garland Wells, a Colt revolver in hand, raced down the stairs and across the marble foyer.

"What the hell's going on? I heard a gunshot." He glanced from Jolie to Max; neither made a sound or moved an inch.

"Garland, is that you, son?" Roscoe bellowed. "Come on in here. We got us a situation that needs to be taken care of. You got a gun with you, haven't you, boy?"

Max motioned for Gar to go into the study. Clutching Max's arm, Jolie glared at him. Did they dare trust Gar? Max shook his head, warning her to do nothing.

Garland walked into the study, the gun in his hand pointing straight ahead, then he paused when he saw Yvonne.

"What's going on?" Gar asked.

Yvonne whirled around, aimed the gun directly at Gar, and then backed up just enough so that she could keep both father and son in her line of vision. "Come on in, Gar," Yvonne said, her voice deceptively calm.

"Yvonne, what are you doing here? Why do you have a gun?" Gar eased his hand holding the revolver down to his side.

"Shoot her, son. Shoot her now before she gets off another shot." Roscoe's eyes brightened as he motioned to Gar. "She just tried to kill me."

"I don't understand. Why would Yvonne want to kill you?"

"Damn it, boy, shoot her. We gotta kill her. If we don't, she'll destroy us. She'll put an end to your political career before we can get it off the ground."

Roscoe rounded his desk and took a couple of tentative steps toward Gar. Yvonne aimed and shot again; this time the bullet hit only inches from Roscoe's feet.

"Goddammit, woman!" Looking straight at his son, Roscoe said, "See, she's trying to kill me."

"I should have killed you forty-two years ago," Yvonne

said. "Killing you now won't change a thing, but it'll rid this world of a monster. Clarice and I have lived all these years with what you did to us, but that was only one of your many sins, wasn't it? You tried to have my son, Theron, killed. And you sent somebody to kill Jolie, too, because they wanted to find out the truth about the Belle Rose massacre. And tonight you had my house torched, hoping Theron and I would burn to death inside."

"What's she talking about?" Gar asked. "What have you done?"

"Everything I've done, I've done to protect you." Roscoe inched a little closer to Garland. "I want you to listen to me very carefully. Shoot Yvonne and we'll tell the sheriff that she came here ranting and raving and tried to kill me. We'll say you shot her in order to save me. That'll be the truth."

"What do you mean that everything you did was to protect me? Protect me from what?"

"Son, I know what you did." Roscoe reached out for Gar but halted when Yvonne shook the Beretta at him. "But I made sure nobody ever suspected you. I called in a heap of favors and I paid off a lot of people. I made sure it looked like Lemar Fuqua killed Lisette and Audrey. There is no reason for anybody to ever know any different." Roscoe glared at Yvonne. "If that damn boy of yours hadn't started snooping around, and if Jolie hadn't come back to town and joined forces with him, none of this would have happened."

"Daddy, are you saying that you think I had something to do with Lisette's death?"

"I know it wasn't your fault. That Lisette was a vixen. The type of woman who could drive a man mad."

"You think I killed her?"

"It's all right." Roscoe grabbed Garland's shoulder and squeezed. "I understand. I know you went over there that morning. I suspected what was going on between you two. I don't know what happened or why you had to kill her, but—"

"I didn't kill anybody!" Gar shouted.

"Son, I saw you when you came home from Belle Rose that afternoon. You had blood on your shirt. And you were crying." Roscoe ran his hand down Gar's arm, patting him affectionately. "When I heard about the killings at Belle Rose, I knew then what had happened. I got rid of your shirt. Got it out of the garbage and burned it. And I started working behind the scenes to manipulate things, to make sure no suspicion ever fell on you. And lucky for us that prick, Parry Clifton, thought Lisette's baby was his."

"You killed Lisette and Audrey and my brother?" Yvonne focused on Gar. "You?"

"No, I swear, I didn't—"

Roscoe grabbed the revolver out of Gar's hand, aimed it at Yvonne and smiled. Max shoved Jolie aside, but before he could get to Roscoe, a gun fired. The sound echoed in Jolie's head. *Yvonne!* she screamed silently. *Oh, God! Oh, God!*

But then Jolie saw that Yvonne still stood, her pistol in her hand. And Roscoe Wells slumped to the floor. What happened? Had Yvonne shot Roscoe? Then when Roscoe hit the floor, exposing the back side of his head, Jolie screamed. The bullet had hit Roscoe directly between the eyes and took off the back half of his head.

Gar rushed to his father and dropped on his knees, crying and trembling. Yvonne's death grip on her weapon eased and the pistol slipped from her fingers.

"I—I didn't shoot him," Yvonne said.

"No, she didn't. I did." Nowell Landers, rifle in hand, stood in the foyer, Aunt Clarice several feet behind him.

Chapter 29

Max helped Gar to his feet, led him to the nearest chair, and then telephoned Ike Denton. Jolie grasped Yvonne's arm and led her out of the room and into the foyer. Yvonne trembled uncontrollably.

"It's over," Jolie said. "You're safe. Everything is going to be all right."

Yvonne nodded, but didn't speak.

Nowell Landers escorted Clarice outside, where Jolie and Yvonne soon joined them on the front porch. Complete and utter silence descended on Pleasant Hill.

"Come on, Gar," Max said. "You don't need to stay in here. Let's go outside with the others."

"I don't understand how he could have believed for all these years that I killed Lisette." Gar kept shaking his head, a glazed sheen misting his eyes.

Max helped Gar to his feet, then led him through the foyer and outside. Everyone turned and stared at him. He looked from one person to the next, shaking his head and moaning; then he crumpled into a heap, weeping as he fell to his knees.

Damn! Max didn't know what to do, didn't know what to believe. Was it possible that Garland Wells, his friend and attorney, was a cold-blooded killer? He could have believed it of Roscoe, but not of Gar. The man was no saint, but he had a gentle easy-going nature.

Max leaned down, put his arm around Gar's shoulders and lifted him to his feet. "Come on, Gar, don't do this. It won't help."

Gar shook his head, then wiped his face with his hand, and sniffed back tears. "I didn't kill anybody. I swear I didn't. Yes, I saw Lisette that day. She told me she was pregnant and the child was mine, but she was going to marry Parry and pass the baby off as his. She told me I was just a kid, not ready for the responsibility of a child, and that I'd forget all about her when I found someone else." Gar staggered across the veranda and leaned against one of the portico's white columns. "She was wrong. I've never forgotten her. And I've never loved anyone else the way I loved her."

"Was Aunt Lisette alive when you left Belle Rose?" Jolie asked.

"Yes, she was alive. And so was Miss Audrey." Closing his eyes, Gar pressed his cheek against the pillar's cool surface.

"What about Lemar?" Yvonne asked.

"Lemar wasn't there," Gar replied. "I met him on the road coming in as I was leaving."

Max went over to Jolie and eased his arm around her shoulders. What must she be feeling right now? Did she believe that Gar might have been the one who tried to kill her that day? Jolie leaned into Max; he rubbed his cheek against her temple in a comforting gesture.

"Roscoe said you came home that day with blood all over your shirt." Jolie's arm slipped around Max's waist as she questioned Gar. "Is that true?"

"Yes, it's true." Gar kept his back to them as he

replied. "I was so upset when I left Belle Rose that I didn't see this dog run out in front of my car. I hit the poor animal, so I got out and picked him up and put him in my car. I drove into town to Doc Hillard's and left the dog with him. The blood on my shirt was the dog's blood."

"Why didn't you explain to your father what happened and why you had blood on your shirt?" Jolie asked.

"I didn't even know he saw me come in that afternoon. I had no idea that, after he heard about the Belle Rose massacre, he assumed I was the killer. I didn't realize he knew about my affair with Lisette. My God! If only he had come to me and asked me."

"If we were to check with Doc Hillard, do you think he'd be able to collaborate your story?" Max asked.

"I don't know. Doc Hillard's nearly eighty now and partially deaf and nearly blind," Gar said. "But maybe he'd remember. Or it could be that the information is in his old files." Gar bumped his forehead against the column several times in frustration, then groaned. "I cannot believe any of this. Daddy thinking I was a murderer, tampering with evidence, paying off people to make sure Lemar Fuqua was blamed for the crime. Trying to kill Yvonne tonight. Nowell Landers shooting Daddy. God, help me! Am I losing my mind?"

No one had an answer for Garland Wells. But everyone had unanswered questions. About tonight. And about the past.

Max whispered to Jolie, "Are you all right, *chère?*"

"I don't know. I'm just sort of numb, I think."

Clarice and Yvonne sat together on the veranda steps, holding hands, clinging to each other as if there were no one else in the world except the two of them. Max didn't think the women were aware of what was going on around them or of anything being said. Nowell Landers' rifle leaned against the brick wall beside him as he watched Clarice, his gaze focused directly on her.

"Where did you learn to shoot like that, Landers?"
Max looked point-blank at the older man.

"I was a sniper in Vietnam," Nowell replied.

"Do you carry around a rifle with you all the time?"
Max asked.

"Nope. I don't even own a gun."

"Then whose rifle is that?" Jolie asked.

"It belonged to Mr. Sam Desmond." Nowell looked
directly at Jolie. "Clarice insisted that we go to Belle
Rose and get her daddy's Winchester before we came
on over here to Pleasant Hill."

"Aunt Clarice suggested you bring Granddaddy Desmond's rifle with you? But why?" Jolie stared at Nowell,
her puzzled gaze questioning him.

"I think Clarice had made up her mind to kill Roscoe
Wells when we got here, if Yvonne hadn't already done
it." Nowell glanced at the half sisters, still sitting snuggled closely together.

"You're saying that she wanted to kill Roscoe because
she believed he'd hired someone to set Yvonne's house
on fire," Max said. "I can't believe that Aunt Clarice
would—"

"Forty-two years ago when Clarice was eighteen and
Yvonne was sixteen, the girls went blackberry picking,"
Nowell said.

Max and Jolie exchanged bewildered looks. What the
hell did blackberry picking have to do with killing
Roscoe?

"Roscoe Wells had been out running his dogs, doing
a little rabbit hunting and a lot of heavy drinking,"
Nowell continued. "The girls met up with him and . . ."
Nowell cleared his throat, then glanced at Clarice. "He
made some unwanted advances to Yvonne. He told Clarice to get on home, and he'd send Yvonne along when
he was finished with her."

"Oh, no." Jolie bit down on her bottom lip.

Knowing that Jolie suspected the outcome of Nowell's

story, Max hugged her to him, bracing her and himself for the ugly truth.

Nowell's low deep voice seemed amplified in the hush of predawn. "Roscoe threw Yvonne down on the ground and—"

"And he started tearing off my clothes." With her back to them, her fingers still entwined with Clarice's, Yvonne recalled the events of that day. "His hands were everywhere and his sour breath was all over my face. When he unzipped his pants, I screamed . . . and screamed. And kept on screaming."

"That's when I hit him over the head with a rock," Clarice said. Her slender shoulders rose and fell as she breathed deeply. "But it didn't knock him out, it only stunned him for a minute. Long enough for me to grab Yvonne up off the ground. I told her to run."

"She told me to run, to get away," Yvonne said. "So I ran and ran and ran. I thought she was behind me. I didn't realize . . . not until I was nearly home, that she wasn't following right behind me."

"Roscoe caught me . . . and . . . raped me," Clarice said. A matter-of-fact statement, calm, unemotional. "And when he finished, he got up off me, zipped up his pants and said it was my own damn fault, that he'd wanted . . . wanted some chocolate pussy, that I should have let him have Yvonne. . . . Then he said that if I told anybody, it would be my word against his, that he'd tell people it hadn't been the first time we'd met out in the woods."

"When I realized that Clarice wasn't behind me, I didn't know what to do." Yvonne's voice trembled ever so slightly. "I was scared. Awfully scared. I just sat down on the ground and cried. I don't know how long I sat there before Clarice found me."

"We swore we'd never tell a soul what happened that day. We knew that if Daddy ever found out, he'd kill Roscoe, and then Daddy would wind up spending the rest of his life in prison." Clarice released her hold on

Yvonne's hand and rose to her feet. She turned and faced Nowell. "I never told anyone, except Jonathan. I wanted him to know the reason I didn't come to him a virgin."

"Our lives went on after that day," Yvonne said. "We didn't talk about it again. Not until Clarice realized she was pregnant."

"Oh, God, Aunt Clarice!" Jolie rushed to her aunt and wrapped her arms around her.

Clarice patted Jolie's back. "It's all right, dear girl."

"Clarice devised a plan," Yvonne said. "She talked Mr. Sam into letting her go to New Orleans on a shopping trip, with me along as her companion."

"I had an abortion." Clarice caressed Jolie's face. "One of those back alley affairs. I nearly bled to death. Yvonne took care of me, but it messed me up pretty bad. I wound up having to have a hysterectomy when I moved to Memphis. I was twenty-two then."

Jolie hugged her aunt, who remained dry-eyed, while Jolie wept. Strange, how Clarice seemed so sane and calm, as if she were recounting events that had happened to someone else.

The wail of sirens screamed in the distance. Within minutes, Ike Denton arrived, along with a couple of deputies. He'd no sooner got out of his car than the ambulance drove in behind him.

"Where is he?" Ike asked.

"Daddy's in his study," Gar replied.

Ike motioned to the medics, who rushed inside, followed by the two deputies.

Ike turned to Max. "Want to tell me what happened?"

"The short version is that Roscoe tried to kill Yvonne, but Nowell Landers shot Roscoe first ... and saved Yvonne's life."

Ike rubbed his jaw. "And Wells is dead?"

"Yeah, he's dead," Max replied.

"I'll need statements from everybody." Ike glanced around at the others. "Mr. Landers, I'll have to ask you to come into town with me. The rest of you can come on in—"

"Sheriff, would it be all right if the ladies go on home now and then make their statements tomorrow? Nowell and Gar and I can tell you everything that happened." Max glanced past Ike, his gaze meeting Nowell's in a unspoken understanding that Clarice and Yvonne's tragedy would remain a secret.

Ike studied Clarice and Yvonne, then turned to Jolie. "Why don't you take your aunt and Mrs. Carter on home."

"Thank you." Jolie looked from Ike to Max.

"Go on," Max said. "Explain everything to Theron, but just tell the others what's absolutely necessary. I'll be home as soon as I can."

Jolie sat on the balcony and watched the dawn break across the eastern horizon. It had taken quite some time to explain to Mallory, Georgette, and Parry what had happened. She'd had her hands full with Aunt Clarice and Yvonne, who both seemed to be in a state of mild shock but refused to see a doctor. Georgette was useless in an emergency, and Parry wasn't sober enough to be of any assistance. Thankfully, Mallory had taken charge of her uncle and mother, thus freeing Jolie to get the others settled. Clarice had insisted that Yvonne share her room; and after a long talk with Theron, Jolie had shown him to one of the empty guest bedrooms.

How long would Max have to stay at the sheriff's office? Would they be able to make Ike understand that Nowell Landers had killed Roscoe to save Yvonne's life? And what about Gar? Was there any chance that Ike might arrest him? God, she hoped Max would come home soon. In all the craziness that had gone on around her, one sane thought registered in her mind. She loved Maximillian Devereaux. It didn't matter who his mother was.

And one question haunted her. If neither Garland Wells nor Lemar Fuqua had killed her mother and aunt, then who had? And she knew, without any proof other than his sworn denial, that Gar was not a killer. Why had it been so easy for Roscoe to believe his son capable of such a heinous crime? Was it because Roscoe had been capable of doing just about anything and thought his son was just like him?

Jolie knew that there was something missing from the scenario, some small bit of information pointing to the truth. But what was it? What were they overlooking?

Gar had been here at Belle Rose that day; he'd seen her mother and aunt alive. And he'd met Lemar coming to the house as he was leaving. Someone else had come to Belle Rose, after Gar left and after Lemar arrived. But who? And why? *Think, Jolie, think. Go over everything that Gar said. Maybe he knows more than he realizes.*

"May I join you?" a feminine voice asked.

Jolie nearly jumped out of her skin. She shot up from the wicker chair, turned quickly and faced Georgette Royale, who stood by the open French doors that led out onto the balcony.

"I'm sorry," Georgette said. "I didn't mean to startle you."

"I thought everyone had gone to bed. After what happened at Pleasant Hill, I'm nervous and jittery. It's not every day that I see a man get his head blown off."

Georgette cringed. "I want to thank you. With Max not being here to handle things, I don't know what we would have done if you hadn't taken charge and gotten everyone settled. I'm afraid I'm not very much help in a crisis."

Jolie looked at her stepmother, truly looked at her, and for the first time in her life, she saw the real woman. Sad. Fragile. And incredibly beautiful, even in her late fifties. Not a monster. Not a vile, wicked bitch.

"Mallory was a great deal of help," Jolie said. "I think

she and I both inherited Daddy's bossy, take-charge genes.''

"Louis loved you very much."

Don't you dare cry! "I could never forget seeing the two of you—the very day my mother was murdered—making love in the old shack in the woods.

"Yes, I know. And your father understood how you felt. He regretted . . . we both regretted so many things."

Jolie turned and went back out to the balcony. Georgette followed her. The two women stood side-by-side.

"Belle Rose is a beautiful place and I've loved living here," Georgette said. "But I would have loved living anywhere with Louis."

"You really did love him, didn't you?" *Sometimes the truth hurt.*

"I wanted you to know that I'm going to tell Max that we should leave Belle Rose. Mallory will go away to college in the fall and Clarice will probably marry Nowell Landers. I'm sure Max will stay on here in Sumarville, but I think Parry and I should move away, maybe go back to New Orleans."

Jolie stared at Georgette. It was there in her eyes, in the odd expression on her face—she was hiding something. But what?

"Do you know who killed my mother and aunt?"

Silence.

"Lemar Fuqua didn't shoot them," Jolie said. "Whoever murdered them killed Lemar, too."

Georgette nodded.

"And Gar Wells didn't kill them, did he?"

"No."

"Then who did?"

No response.

"Either tell me now, or tell Max and me later," Jolie warned.

Georgette wilted like a hothouse flower exposed to the elements. She seemed to realize that she could no longer keep her secrets buried. "At first, I—I believed, as most people did, that Lemar killed Audrey and Lisette."

"When did you first realize that he wasn't the murderer?"

"I'm not sure. It wasn't a conscious realization. Not at first. I didn't want to believe what I suspected."

Jolie closed her eyes, praying for the strength to endure, to hear the truth and find a way to live with it, whatever it was. Her muscles tensed.

"I didn't actually allow myself to consider the possibility until recently." Georgette's voice was little more than a whisper, as if somehow saying it softly and quietly might make what she was saying less true. "Not until you and Theron decided to try to have the case reopened. With you back at Belle Rose and looking so much like Lisette . . ."

Parry called out from Jolie's open bedroom door, "There you are, Georgie. I wondered where you'd gotten off to."

Georgette gasped as she lifted her fluttering hand to her throat. "I'll leave you now and see if I can't get Parry back to his room. He's never very nice when he's been drinking."

Jolie reached out and grabbed Georgette's wrist. "Wait."

"Not now." Her voice changed to a harsh plea. "Later." Georgette dashed to her brother, put her arm around his waist, and tried to turn him around and head him out of the room.

"What were you telling her?" Parry asked. "You two looked awfully chummy."

"I was thanking Jolie for taking charge of things and getting everyone settled," Georgette said. "Come on, Parry, let me walk you back to your room. You need to get some sleep. You'll feel better if you—"

Parry broke free, shoved his sister aside, and stomped across the room toward Jolie, who watched from outside on the balcony. After catching the door facing to steady herself, Georgette reached out to grab Parry but caught thin air instead.

"Parry!"

Georgette rushed after him, but before she could reach him, he charged at Jolie with remarkable speed for a drunk. He grabbed her hands, whirled her around, clutched her hands behind her back and slung his arm across her neck.

"Did you really think I'd let you get away with it, Lisette?"

Georgette cried, "Parry, don't . . ."

"Go on to your room, Georgie," Parry said. "I'll handle our little problem. I always take care of things for us, don't I? Didn't I make Jules Trouissant's death look like a suicide, after you smothered him? Didn't I take care of Philip for you?"

Georgette gasped. "Oh, dear Lord, you didn't. Not Philip."

"Of course, Philip. He had disappointed you. Let us both down when we were depending on him. He embezzled all that money and would have taken us down with him if he'd gone to prison. I simply helped him do the honorable thing."

Jolie's mind worked at lightning speed, trying to process all the jumbled information. "You killed Philip Devereaux? I thought he committed suicide." *And everyone believed Lemar Fuqua committed suicide, too! Oh, God! Oh, God!*

Parry tightened his arm at her throat. For a split second, Jolie couldn't breathe. Gasping for air, she squirmed to free herself.

"Loosen your grip on Jolie," Georgette said. "You're hurting her."

"Why do you want to help her?" Parry asked. "Why were you going to tell her that I was the one who killed Audrey and Lemar? We've never betrayed each other. Not when I hung Jules from the chandelier in his office to make his death look like a suicide. And when I shot

Philip in the head, you didn't tell anyone. And when I killed Lisette and Audrey and Lemar, you never told a soul."

Jolie prayed more fervently than she'd ever prayed in her life. "Why—why did you kill them?"

"Who?" Parry asked, dragging Jolie farther out onto the balcony.

"My mother and Aunt Lisette and Lemar?"

Georgette rushed to the open French doors. "Parry, please come back inside."

"I will, Georgie. Just as soon as I get rid of Lisette."

"Lisette is dead," Georgette reminded him. "This is Jolie, not Lisette."

"I thought so, too . . . at first." Parry flipped Jolie in front of him so her body pressed against the wrought-iron railing around the balcony. "But she is Lisette. She's come back to haunt me. She wants to punish me for what I did. But I can kill her again. And this time, she'll never come back."

"Please, Parry, don't do this . . . don't . . ." Tears trickled down Georgette's face. "I don't want you to hurt her. Please, please don't hurt her."

"Sweet Georgie. So tenderhearted. I killed Audrey for you, you know. I could have gotten out of the house without her seeing me. She was outside talking to Lemar when I shot Lisette. They didn't hear the shot because Lisette had the stereo in her room blaring so damn loud. I could hear them talking when I came downstairs. I watched while Lemar went around the house to get started on the yard work, and I thought to myself, 'Why not get rid of Audrey for Georgie?'

"I sneaked up on her in the backyard, put my hand over her mouth, and shot her in the head, just like I shot Lisette. Then Lemar came around the side of the house asking her about the noise that sounded like a gunshot. That's when my brilliant idea hit me. I made Lemar carry Audrey into the kitchen so he'd have her blood all over him. Then I made him go upstairs. When

he saw Lisette, he went all to pieces, so while he was
down on his knees, I knocked him out with the butt of
the gun, then put the gun in his hand and . . . violà—
suicide!"

Help us, God! Please help us! Parry Clifton was insane.
He was a homicidal maniac.

When Parry lifted Jolie off her feet, she kicked at him,
but he seemed oblivious to the strikes against his legs.
He's going to toss me over the railing, Jolie realized. *He's
going to kill me.*

"Who was Jules Trouissant?" Jolie asked, trying to
think of something—anything—that might buy her
some time.

"Jules was Max's father," Parry said.

"No, no." Georgette whimpered. "You believed he
was Max's father, but we don't know that for sure. I told
you then that it could have been any one of a dozen
different men."

"Jules sired your son. I've never doubted it," Parry
told her. "Our demon pimp. Our tormentor. The man
who sold our bodies for his own profit. He deserved to
die. You had every right to kill him."

"You told me that I killed him, but I don't remember
doing it." Georgette dropped to her knees. "Parry,
you're my brother and I love you. I've always loved you.
I know everything you've done, you've done for me.
Please, do one more thing for me. Let Jolie go."

"I can't do that."

Max and Nowell barged into the room. "Uncle Parry,
what are you doing?" Max eased farther into the room,
bent down, and lifted his mother to her feet. "What
the hell's going on?" he asked her quietly.

"Max!" Jolie cried.

"He thinks she's Lisette," Georgette whispered to
Max. "He—he's the one who killed Lisette, and he
thinks she's come back to haunt him. Max, he's drunk
and . . ."

"And crazy." Max released his mother and moved

straight toward the French doors. Parry lifted Jolie higher; her feet dangled over the edge of the railing.

"She isn't Lisette," Max cried. "She's Jolie Royale. Louis's daughter. You don't want to hurt her."

"Lisette. Jolie. What difference does it make? She's a woman and they're nothing but trouble for us. I loved Lisette and I thought she loved me. I didn't mind her sleeping with other men. I had my own little indiscretions. But when I heard her telling that damned Wells boy that the baby she was carrying was his, but that she was going to pass it off as mine, I knew she didn't love me. She was going to lie to me. She was going to pass off her bastard as mine. Your mama might have been able to trick Philip Devereaux, but no woman was going to make a fool of me."

"All women aren't alike," Max said. "Jolie is nothing like Lisette."

"Felicia was. She liked it rough," Parry said. "Did you know that? She enjoyed drinking and partying and experimenting the same as I did. Felicia and I were well suited, even more so than Lisette and I had been. And I didn't love Felicia, so she couldn't hurt me, couldn't disappoint me. But the damn bitch was too good at listening to my drunken babbling, too good at remembering things she should have forgotten."

"What did Felicia hear?" Max asked. "Did you tell her how you murdered Lisette?"

"She threatened me, the stupid cunt. I knew that sooner or later she'd destroy me, destroy everything Georgie and I had."

"You killed Felicia?" Jolie knew she was going to die. Parry Clifton had murdered six people, what was one more?

"She didn't leave me any other choice." Parry's gaze met Max's. "Hell, boy, you were better off without her. You should thank me for getting rid of her."

"Damn!" Max cursed loudly. "It's all in the past. Nothing can be changed. But this time you can do what's right. The woman you're holding is not Lisette," Max said. "She's Jolie. And it does make a difference who she is. Do you hear me, Uncle Parry?"

"Why do you care? She's nothing to you."

"That's not true," Max said. "I love Jolie."

"Then you're as big a fool as I was. She's not really Lisette or Jolie—she's both of them. One and the same. She's a damn witch who seduces men with her beauty and lures them to their deaths with her body."

"If you hurt Jolie, then you hurt me," Max said. "If you kill Jolie, you kill me. If she dies, I die."

Jolie felt Parry's arms around her loosen. *Oh, God, he's going to drop me!*

"Parry, if you love me, let her go," Georgette pleaded. "Do this one last thing for me . . . please."

Parry stared at his sister for a moment that seemed endless to Jolie as she hung between life and death. "I do love you, Georgie."

"And I love you, Parry."

"I know. You're the only one who's ever really loved me."

Jolie suddenly realized that Parry was easing her down onto her feet. She held her breath, hoping beyond hope that Georgette had gotten through to him. In a flash, Parry released her; but before she could take even one step away from him, he leaned over the balcony railing, staring down at the ground below him.

"Take care of her, Max. Promise me to always take care of little Georgie." Parry gripped the railing, lifted himself up and over the edge before anyone realized what he was going to do. Instinctively Jolie reached for him. Georgette screamed. Max rushed onto the balcony, half a minute too late to catch his uncle before he fell to his death. Max turned, jerked Jolie into his arms, and crushed her to his body. Trembling from head to toe, she wrapped her arms around Max and buried her face against his chest.

Chapter 30

Jolie neatly folded the last garment, then placed it in her suitcase. She had a late-afternoon flight to catch, back to Atlanta. She had stayed on for Parry's funeral, a private affair for family only. She had thought Max would ask her to stay at Belle Rose. But he didn't. After that traumatic morning five days ago, he had taken charge, as he usually did, making arrangements, caring for everyone's needs, neglecting himself. And he had said very little to her, speaking to her only when absolutely necessary. She had tried to figure out what was wrong, why he was treating her as if they were little more than strangers. Hadn't he confessed his love for her? Hadn't he told his uncle that if she died, he would die, too? Had it all been a ruse, a trick to persuade Parry not to kill her?

Jolie zipped her suitcase, lifted it off the bed, and placed it on the floor. Now was the time to say her good-byes. Had it been only a month ago that she had returned to Sumarville? Odd that her life could change so much in such a short time. She had come home seeking revenge and instead she had discovered the truth . . . and had fallen in love.

As she passed by Mallory's room on her way to the stairs, she heard an odd noise. She paused, listened, and realized someone was throwing a temper tantrum. Mallory? Who else? Her half sister had been unusually subdued since Parry's death. Max had been too busy propping up Georgette and persuading her not to confess to Jules Trouissant's murder to notice how lost and lonely Mallory was. Jolie peered inside Mallory's room. A china figurine sailed past Jolie's head and hit the wall behind her.

Mallory gasped when she saw Jolie. "Damn! I didn't see you. I wasn't throwing it at you, honest I wasn't."

"Are you all right?"

"What do you care? What does anybody care?"

Jolie walked into the bedroom and over to where Mallory sat on the edge of the bed. She held something in her hand. A narrow plastic stick of some kind. Jolie sat beside her, reached out and pulled the pregnancy tester out of Mallory's hand. She looked at the indicator. Blue.

Mallory shrugged. "Yeah, I'm pregnant. Just what this family needs right now. Max is going to go ape-shit and Mother will probably have a heart attack."

"What about the baby's father?"

"He's long gone. Drove off to Texas without a backward glance. Told me it was best to end it before we got bored with each other."

"I see. A very immature attitude."

"God, what am I going to do? I lied to him about being on the pill. But I—I had to have gotten pregnant the second time we did it, when he didn't use a rubber." Mallory covered her face with her hands and groaned. "I'm such an idiot. I thought if I got pregnant, he'd . . . I wanted . . . I needed . . ."

Mallory burst into tears. When Jolie draped her arm

around her sister, Mallory turned and pressed her face against Jolie's shoulder.

"What do you want to do?" Jolie asked. "I can help you, however you decide to handle the situation. If you want an abortion, I'll make the arrangements and go with you. If you want to have the baby, you can come to Atlanta and stay with me. It would give us a chance to get to know each other."

Mallory lifted her head and gazed at Jolie. "I can go to Atlanta with you?"

Jolie nodded. "You can leave with me this afternoon, if you'd like."

"Mother and Max wouldn't have to know that I'm pregnant?"

"Not yet. But if you decide to keep the baby, you'd have to tell them sometime soon."

A soft knock on the door frame gained their immediate attention. Jolie and Mallory jumped, gasped, and turned around simultaneously.

"I'm sorry to bother y'all," Yvonne said. "But everyone else is in the dining room and we're waiting on you two."

Max met Jolie and Mallory at the foot of the stairs. Jolie's heart leaped with hope, but that hope was dashed when she saw the dark scowl on Max's face.

"Go on in to lunch," Max told Mallory. "I need to speak with Jolie for a moment."

"After y'all have your little talk, then I need to tell you something that Jolie and I have planned," Mallory said.

"Fine. Whatever it is, we'll discuss it later." Max indicated for Jolie to follow him.

He led her to the study, but left the door open after they entered. She looked directly at him, but he glanced away quickly.

"I thought you'd like to know that Hugh Pearce, my

private investigator, ran a check on Jonathan Lenz, as you requested. He called this morning with a report. And he faxed me a couple of pictures."

"And?"

"Jonathan Lenz didn't die in Vietnam. He was listed as missing in action. He spent five years as a POW. When he returned to the U.S., he became a drug addict. He pretty much dropped out of sight until about eighteen months ago." Max lifted the faxed photos off the desk and handed them to Jolie.

"Let me guess," Jolie said. "These pictures are of Nowell Landers, aka Jonathan Lenz."

"You suspected the truth all along, didn't you?"

She nodded. "Have you told them?"

"I thought perhaps you'd want to."

"She already knows." Jolie laid her hand over her heart. "In here. Aunt Clarice knows he's Jonathan."

After lunch, when Georgette was once again conspicuously absent, Jolie told Mallory to pack and then they would speak to Max before they left.

"He's going to wonder why I'm going off with you," Mallory said. "He knows that you're not . . . well, that you haven't exactly been my favorite person."

"We'll tell him a half-truth," Jolie suggested. "We'll say that we want a chance to get to know each other and you need to get away from Belle Rose for a while."

"I wouldn't mind getting to know you. Maybe you're not as bad as I thought you were."

Jolie smiled. "I have a feeling we'll find out that we have a great deal in common."

When Mallory whirled around and ran up the stairs, Jolie went in search of Aunt Clarice. She found her with Nowell, outside in the gazebo, holding hands as they talked to each other.

Jolie waved and Clarice motioned for her to come to them. She paused just outside the gazebo.

"I'm leaving this afternoon. I want you two to come to Atlanta and visit me. Often."

"We will," Clarice said. "Perhaps on our honeymoon. We've decided not to wait to get married. We're not going to have a wedding. It would be inappropriate. But we've decided on next weekend. Just a simple ceremony, here at Belle Rose. No one but family. I wish you would stay."

"Oh, Aunt Clarice, I—I . . . I'll fly in for the day. How's that?"

"I've waited thirty-six years to become Mrs. Jonathan Lenz," Clarice said. "I'd be a fool to wait any longer."

Jolie looked at Nowell Landers. "I think you should know that I asked Max's private detective to run a check on Jonathan Lenz."

"And he found out that Jonathan didn't die in Vietnam," Clarice said. "Jonathan's mother told me that he was killed in action instead of the truth, that he was missing in action. But in my heart, I never accepted that my Jonathan was dead."

"Did you tell Aunt Clarice the truth?" Jolie asked Nowell. "Has she known all along?"

"No, I didn't tell her. Not at first," Nowell said. "But she guessed the truth and I finally told her, the night after I shot Roscoe Wells.

"When I returned from Nam, I was all messed up. I got on drugs, became an alcoholic, lived in the gutter, did time in the pen. I was glad my mother had told Clarice I was dead. I wasted most of my life. But eighteen months ago, I underwent rehab. And I promised myself that if I could stay clean and sober for a year, I'd look up Clarice. I figured she'd be married to somebody else. When I found out she was unattached, I chickened out telling her who I was. I made up a phony name and pretended that I'd been Jonathan's friend."

"How could I have ever married anyone else when I never stopped loving you?" Clarice stared adoringly at the only man she had ever loved.

Jolie hugged Clarice and Nowell—Jonathan—then hurried inside to see if Mallory was ready to face her brother with the news that she was going to Atlanta with Jolie. As she rushed down the hall, Georgette opened her bedroom door.

"Would you come in and talk to me for a moment?" Georgette asked.

Jolie hesitated. What could they possibly have to discuss? "All right. But only for a minute. I'm leaving this afternoon and I still have several things to do."

"This won't take long. Please, come in."

Jolie followed Georgette inside and left the door open. "You know, I used to wonder if you and Daddy sleep together in my mother's room . . . in her bed."

"Neither of us could have done that. Louis had this room completely renovated before we married. The room your father shared with your mother has been one of the guest rooms for years now."

"I couldn't understand how the two of you could have . . . I had no idea that people could love so passionately that nothing mattered except their being together."

"But you understand now, don't you." Georgette grasped Jolie's hand. Their gazes met and locked. "You love Max the way I loved Louis."

Jolie jerked her hand away.

"Don't leave him, Jolie. If you leave him, he will die. Oh, not physically, but emotionally."

"Max doesn't want me here. He doesn't love me. He—"

Georgette grabbed Jolie by the shoulders. "He thinks you couldn't possibly want him. Not now. Now that you know his uncle murdered your mother and aunt."

"But it's not Max's fault that—"

Georgette shook Jolie gently. "You must tell him that you love him, that learning the truth about his uncle Parry's insanity, about his horrible deeds, and about me—that I killed Jules Trouissant—doesn't change the way you feel about him."

"Is this the reason he's acted so strangely toward me? The reason he won't even look at me? He believes I can't love him because of Parry? Because of your past?"

"Yes. Yes. Please, go to him. Don't leave Belle Rose. My son loves you . . . and he needs you."

Tears collected in Jolie's eyes and a few drops spilled over onto her cheeks. "Thank you for explaining. I—I'll go find Max. And while I talk to him, you should talk to Mallory. She needs her mother very badly right now."

Jolie rushed out of Georgette's room, up the hall and down the stairs. Thinking she might find him still in the study, she went there first. Empty. She began searching the first floor rooms and came upon Theron in the library.

"Have you seen Max?"

"He just left." Theron nodded the direction. "He said he needed to go to the office in town and catch up on some work."

"I have to stop him."

Jolie ran through the foyer and out the front door, then down the steps. She saw Max inside his Porsche, then heard the motor start.

"Max!" she screamed his name. "Max! Wait!"

At first she thought he hadn't heard her, so she darted out into the circular drive, directly in front of the Porsche. Max killed the engine, opened the door, and got out of the car.

"What's wrong?" He walked toward her.

Jolie threw her arms around his neck. Max stiffened.

"I love you, Max Devereaux. I love you more than life itself. And if you think for one minute that I'm going to let you go—now or ever—then you're out of your mind."

"Jolie, don't do this." He stood rigid as a statue.

She kissed him. He didn't respond. She kissed him

again. He grabbed her shoulders and shoved her away from him.

"Tell me that you don't love me," she said. "Tell me that you don't want me so badly you ache with the need to hold me and kiss me and make love to me. Tell me that what we had—what we have—isn't more important to you than anything in the whole wide world."

"You know I can't tell you that I don't love you. But love isn't enough. All the love in the world won't change who I am."

"And who are you, Max?"

"I'm the bastard son of a New Orleans whore, who can't even tell me who my biological father is because she doesn't know for sure. It's possible that she killed a man who could have been my father. A sleazy pimp. And I'm the nephew of a man who murdered six people, including my wife and your mother. God only knows what kind of blood runs through my veins. How could you ever look at me, ever hold me in your arms, ever . . . without wondering."

"You're a good man, Max. It doesn't matter who your father was or that Georgette was once a prostitute or that she might have killed an evil wicked man. And as for Parry . . . you're nothing like him. You're strong and brave and caring and everything a man should be. You're everything I want."

"Are you saying that you'll stay in Sumarville, that you'll marry me, that you'll . . ."

"Yes, yes, yes. I'll stay. I'll be with you wherever you are. And I'll marry you today, if that's what it takes to convince you. And I want your babies. Our babies."

Tears glistened in Max's eyes. He reached out and grabbed Jolie, then held her so fiercely that she could barely breathe. He released her abruptly, grabbed her shoulders and held her away from him. "This is your last chance to change your mind," he told her. "If you stay, I'll never let you go."

"I'm staying," she told him. "I'm staying with you for the rest of my life."

He clasped her face with his hands, lowered his head, and kissed her. And Jolie knew that she was truly home. Home to stay.

Epilogue

The day that Mallory Royale went into labor would forever after be considered a red-letter day for the family. At precisely twelve noon, Mallory's first contraction hit her. At one-twenty, Jolie's obstetrician informed her that she was pregnant. At two o'clock, on a late lunch break, Theron proposed to Amy. And at three o'clock, R. J. Sutton rang the doorbell at Belle Rose.

By five-thirty, the entire extended Desmond-Royale-Devereaux family had congregated in the maternity waiting area of Desmond County General. Max and Jolie. Georgette, Yvonne, Clarice, and her Jonathan. Theron and Amy. And at eight that evening R. J. Sutton cut his daughter's umbilical cord and vowed to his little girl and her mother that they could count on him to take care of them.

At ten-forty-five, Jolie lay naked in Max's arms, the tingling aftershocks of her orgasm radiating through her body. She rose up, lifted her head, and stared at the husband she adored.

"Aunt Clarice is very excited about there being a baby at Belle Rose again, after all these years," Jolie said. "I can't imagine how thrilled she'll be in another seven months when there are two babies at Belle Rose."

"Two babies?" Narrowing his gaze, Max stared at her.

"Since Mallory had a little girl, I think I might like our first child to be a boy." Jolie rolled over on top of Max. "What do you think, Max? Would you like for our baby to be a boy? Do you want a son?"

"Our baby." Max threaded his fingers through Jolie's hair, clutched the back of her head and forced her down until they were eye-to-eye. "Mrs. Devereaux, is this your subtle way of telling me that you're pregnant? That we're going to become parents?"

"Yes, Mr. Devereaux, it is. And I am. And we are."

BOOK YOUR PLACE ON OUR WEBSITE AND MAKE THE READING CONNECTION!

We've created a customized website just for our very special readers, where you can get the inside scoop on everything that's going on with Zebra, Pinnacle and Kensington books.

When you come online, you'll have the exciting opportunity to:

- View covers of upcoming books
- Read sample chapters
- Learn about our future publishing schedule (listed by publication month *and author*)
- Find out when your favorite authors will be visiting a city near you
- Search for and order backlist books from our online catalog
- Check out author bios and background information
- Send e-mail to your favorite authors
- Meet the Kensington staff online
- Join us in weekly chats with authors, readers and other guests
- Get writing guidelines
- AND MUCH MORE!

**Visit our website at
http://www.kensingtonbooks.com**